Involuntary

DARIE MCCOY

For the lost ones, you deserve to have someone looking for you.

"I have spread my dreams beneath your feet; tread softly because you tread on my dreams."

— WILLIAM BUTLER YEATS

Acknowledgments

My sincere thanks to everyone who had a hand in turning a heart thumping dream into a novel that I'm very proud to have written. To my writing partners, Brianna and Niccoyan, who always give me the raw truth while constantly encouraging me to let my characters be great, my heartfelt thanks. You see my words long before they're ready for an editor. I couldn't ask for a better Alpha readers. Michel and Dahlia, I can't express how valuable your friendship, feedback, guidance and support have been to me. Shara Azod... You know this is all your fault right? I was going to happily enjoy life as a reader until you intervened. Thank you. Unfortunately, I can't mention everyone by name. It doesn't mean your contributions aren't equally as important. I'm sincerely thankful to everyone who lends even the slightest encouragement for my continued growth as an author

Author's Note

First, thank you for reading. I sincerely appreciate you. In the interest of providing the best reading experience possible, there are a few things you should know about **Involuntary**. This story came to me in a dream. I awakened with my heart pounding as I felt Stephanie's emotions. A large part of the first chapter is the product of the dream that sparked the novel.

If you read the excerpt in **Sano's Queen**, you already know what happened. If not, you'll read it here for the first time. The story evokes strong emotion due to the sensitive subject matter portrayed. It contains adult themes which include rough language, sexual content, violence, death, child abandonment, drug use and references to human trafficking.

Nothing was written for shock value. I simply told the story as the characters presented it to me. I hope you enjoy Jian and Stephanie's journey to their Happily Ever After.

Chapter One

STEPHANIE

Please God. Please let my baby be okay. Rushing through the security checkpoint at the ER entrance, my hands shook so badly I could hardly empty my pockets at the guard's request. The thundering beat of my heart was so loud in my ears, I could barely hear him speaking. Finally, I made it through the security check. My cousin Gene wasn't far behind, taking his turn at the access control point. Thank God he was at the salon when I got the call. The way I felt, I would've ended up in an accident trying to make it to the hospital.

There's a lone woman sitting at a desk behind the glass separator as I entered the reception area. Reading the Registrar nameplate, I hurriedly approached the glass. I glimpsed the badge pinned to the collar of her scrubs–*Charlotte Wright*. The ER was crowded. I said a prayer of thanks there wasn't a line at the Registrar's desk.

All the nerves in my body screamed for me to get to Saffi. I knew the woman heard me approach the desk. She looked up at me then back at her computer screen. I mustered every ounce of self-control I had and stood quietly at the desk. Waiting. And waiting.

Charlotte typed away on the computer as though I wasn't standing less than five feet in front of her, separated only by the desk and protective glass. It was likely that only a couple of minutes passed, but it felt like hours. *This is some bullshit.* Attempting to get her attention, I rapped my knuckles against the counter.

"Excuse me, ma'am. Can you help me? I got a call that my daughter was here."

I promise. I tried to sound as nice as my frayed nerves allowed. Giving me a sour expression as if I inconvenienced her by expecting her to actually do her job, Charlotte stopped typing. I didn't have time for her bullshit. I pinned her with my, *get off your ass and do your job,* look.

"If you'll give me a minute, I'll be right with you." Her words weren't rude. In contrast, her tone and countenance said things her words had not. *This chick is testing me.* Internally, my anxiety screamed. I struggled against being *that* person. The person who cut up. The one who cursed out people in service jobs. However, it was a damn Emergency Room. She could at least **pretend** she understood her environment.

I opened my mouth, but Gene placed a hand on my shoulder. He shook his head, stopping what was coming next. Gently moving me to the side, he stepped closer to the desk. I didn't play when it came to Saffi and he knew that. If I had to wait on something dealing with me, no problem. Not when it came to her.

"Ma'am, we don't mean to rush you. We're just worried. My little cousin is here. She's only twelve years old. She was attacked. She's probably scared out of her mind right now."

Motioning to me, he pasted on a smile giving her his charming best. "My little cousin's name is Chloe Barker. This is her mother, Stephanie. Can you help us?"

My cousin is a beautiful black man. Tall, with broad shoulders that tapered down at his waist and hips, he constantly drew attention. Thick, sculpted, muscle packed his physique. The dark brown skin wrapping his frame glowed with good health. A well-maintained goatee outlined his full lips. Upon first meeting him, his overall appearance struck the unsuspecting person dumb—regardless of gender.

Apparently, Charlotte was no exception. The fingers tapping away at the keyboard stopped moving. Her pale green eyes unglued themselves from the computer screen to view the source of the deep, raspy voice with a touch of country boy thrown in. Hungry eyes raked over the parts of Gene not obscured by the half-wall, and her cheeks flushed pink.

"Of course, I can! Let me just check the admissions log," She showed damn near all thirty-two of her teeth when she smiled at him. "You say her name is Chloe Barker?"

Only concentrating really hard on my baby kept me from telling her about her fake, horny ass. *I'm not like this... I swear I'm not.* I've been told I was too nice. They said I gave people too many chances, but this trick was begging to meet my dark side.

"Shh, cuz. I gotchu," Gene whispered, patting me on the back. I needed to give him a raise. He possibly saved me from jail, because I could **NOT** with Charlotte. As a business owner, service was my life's blood. People in service jobs, who were crappy at it and obviously didn't want to do it, triggered me. Taking a deep breath, I focused on staying calm. *Focus on Saffi. You can't help her from the back of a squad car.*

Charlotte was super helpful—when Gene asked. I didn't miss the way she sat up taller in her chair, flipping her blonde hair. She tugged on her scrub top making it stretch tighter across the nubs passing for breasts on her chest. *I knew the thought was petty, but I couldn't help it.* Anything she did aside from getting me to my baby annoyed the shit out of me.

"Oh!" Lifting wide eyes from the computer screen, she looked from Gene's face to mine. "It says here that her mother, Danielle, arrived with her."

Her face pinched in irritation. I guess she thought Gene was lying to her. He wasn't lying. Legally, Saffi was **my** daughter—even if Dani gave birth to her.

She'd never taken care of Saffi, leaving her first with our grandmother, then with me. Before she passed away, Grandma Viola helped me adopt Saffi officially. So, no matter what Dani said, Saffi was my child.

"I'm afraid I can't let you go back. There's only one visitor allowed, and her mother is already with her."

The gleeful twinkle in her eyes said she wasn't sorry at all to deny me access.

"Ma'am, I don't care what that woman said. *I* am Chloe Sofia Barker's mother. **Not** her." Pissed beyond belief, I was prepared to burst through those doors searching every room individually.

Shaking off Gene's hand of caution, I continued, "Saffi has been to this hospital before, when she had appendicitis. If you will check your records, you will see the name of her parent is listed as Stephanie Barker. *Me*. *Not* Danielle Barker."

Even though I was adamant, I didn't raise my voice. Maintaining my composure was a struggle, because all I could think about was how frightened Saffi must be. By now, a line had formed behind us. Pinging her eyes between us, Charlotte noticed the growing queue.

"Look, I don't know what else to tell you. From this entry, her mother is already with her. There can only be one person at a time in the treatment area, so you'll have to wait or call Ms Barker and ask her to come out so you can go in. Now, if you'll step aside, I need to help the person behind you," she snipped.

Aw hell naw!

"No Charlotte. I will not step aside," raising my voice, I shrugged off Gene's attempts to calm me.

"Listen, I've had enough. I'm not sure what is going on to make you first ignore me, then not even have the courtesy of looking to verify the accuracy of the information I'm giving you. I want to see my child, and I want to see her RIGHT NOW!"

If I had the type of skin that more easily showed my moods, my face would've shone beet red. It felt like a boiler was heating me from the inside out and steam poured out of my ears.

Charlotte's entire face closed up; her lips pinched so tightly together her mouth bore a disturbing resemblance to a sphincter. "Listen you–"

"Is there a problem here?" A voice cut across the comeback Charlotte was set to deliver. We all looked to the petite brunette approaching the registrar's desk.

"No!"

"Yes!"

Charlotte and I answered simultaneously. I'd hazard a guess that the woman was important, because Charlotte attempted to fix her face. If the woman was important, I considered that maybe she could get our unfriendly registrar to do her job.

"I'm Princess Wells, the Administrator on this shift. What seems to be the problem?" Turning to my current nemesis first, she prompted, "Charlotte, please explain."

Aw, here we go. When she allowed pinched-face to speak first, I knew my chances of seeing Saffi anytime soon were circling the drain. Fists clenched at my sides, I waited to hear which lie fell from Charlotte's lips first.

"Well... I was just informing *these people* that only one person was allowed back in the treatment room. Since the patient they asked about already has someone in the room, they can't go back. Then, she started yelling at me. I have no idea why. I didn't make the rule," she whined.

Her cheeks pinkened and her eyes welled with tears. Fake ass tears, because I hadn't done anything for her to cry about. Not yet. If she really wanted a reason to leak like a faucet, I could make that happen in two ticks or less.

Looking at Ms Wells, who wore office attire instead of scrubs, I couldn't read her expression. She directed dark grey eyes to my face expectantly. I had no problem obliging the unspoken request. I very bluntly, and much more honestly, related the situation and its urgency.

Once I was done, her façade and voice tightened. I just knew she was going to ask for security to remove me when she rotated towards Charlotte. Instead, she picked up the phone to call someone from the back to open the second desk to assist the people in line behind me. Then, she instructed Charlotte to move away from the computer and she sat in front of the monitor.

Relief flooded my body as she began actually doing what I'd been asking Charlotte to do all along. It's a hospital, there are laws. So, the information I gave had to be verified before she could give me access. Fine with me. I didn't flinch when she asked for ID to confirm my identity.

When we'd taken care of that task, she pressed the button, buzzing me through the doors. Gene was going to stay behind, but she waved him in as well. She told Charlotte she would be back to speak with her after she walked me to Saffi's room. From the way Charlotte shrank in her seat, the conversation wasn't going to be pleasant. *Good.*

"Mrs. Barker –"

"Miss."

"Miss Barker, if the woman in the room with Chloe isn't her mother, who is she?"

It was a legitimate question. As Administrator she should be informed of possible issues with patients. For all she knew, Dani was a security risk.

"She's my sister Danielle. She's Chloe's birth mother. I adopted Chloe when she was five. So, legally, I'm her mother," I explained.

I never wanted to deny Saffi access to Danielle. However, if I found out Dani played a part in what happened to my baby, she would get cut off completely. She was more than welcome to fuck up her own life. I wouldn't let her put Saffi in danger.

We reached a door and Ms. Wells knocked before pushing it open. Under the glaring lights, I spied my little girl on a gurney in the center of the small room. A woman and man dressed in scrubs were standing to either side of the bed. Some kind of gauze like paper was laid across her forehead and nose, covering part of her face and hair.

My heart seized in my chest. My breath caught in my throat when I noticed the three long slashes on her cheek and jaw. Two of the slashes were horizontal and one was vertical. All of them looked deep.

Her formerly neat clothing was in tatters. One sleeve of the short-sleeved top was barely hanging on. Blood was splattered all over the front—the majority of which was on her left side. Even more blood streaked her jean shorts.

The sneakers, which were white when she left home this morning, were now splashed with red dots. Anxiously cataloguing her condition, my heart thudded loudly in my ears. Remaining focused was difficult, but not having a clear head wasn't an option.

I placed my attention on the man to Saffi's left. Strands of ginger hair peeked from beneath the *Star Wars* themed scrub cap he wore. He appeared to have just finished cleaning her wounds and was reaching to a tray. I didn't know if this guy was a resident, a regular ER doctor or what. He looked really young.

Turning to Ms Wells, I made a request before the young physician could do anything more.

"Please ask him to stop what he's doing. I have questions and concerns."

Without asking for an explanation, she honored my request. A rush of appreciation flooded my senses. My emotions were all over the place. I was on the verge of a complete come apart. I couldn't predict how I'd respond to being ignored again.

"Dr. Pearson, please stop what you're doing." Ms Wells held out a hand to the physician.

"This is Chloe Barker's mother Stephanie Barker. She has questions about her condition." Stepping to the side, she moved farther into the room to give us space.

From the corner of my eye, I glimpsed Danielle sitting in the room's lone chair. While I detected the guilt contorting her posture, I didn't acknowledge her. She wasn't my main priority. I'd definitely get to her once I made sure Saffi was getting the best care possible.

I desperately wanted answers as to what happened and how it happened, but I'd have to wait for those too. *One thing at a time, Step. Take care of Saffi first. Beat Dani's ass second.*

The antiseptic smells of the hospital room assailed my senses as I approached the end of the bed. Touching Saffi's leg, I rubbed it gently. "Dr. Pearson, are you a general physician or a specialist?"

I'd read somewhere a patient could request a plastic surgeon for times like this. If he wasn't a plastic surgeon, I wanted one.

"I'm the Chief ER resident on this shift, ma'am. I'm more of a general physician."

Dr. Pearson didn't appear insulted by my question. Good, because things could get sticky when I requested a plastic surgeon.

"Could you quickly explain to me your treatment plan? How were you planning to close the cuts on her face? Stitches? Glue?" My gaze locked on his. From the corner of my eye, I caught Dani's nervous shifting.

No one asked her for her two cents, yet she gave it anyway. "I told them to use glue or stitches. Whatever, just stop the bleeding."

This bitch... She's my sister, but sometimes... Ugh! I really wished she'd just kept her mouth shut.

"Dani, I wasn't talking to you. I was talking to Dr. Pearson. Besides, it wasn't your decision to make." I turned back to Dr. Pearson, but my sister decided she wasn't done chipping in her two cents.

"Whatchu mean it's not my decision? I don't remember you laying up in the hospital for ten hours giving birth to her." Her eyes shined with malice and a hint of smugness, knowing I couldn't refute the fact she'd given birth to Saffi.

I'd promised myself I wouldn't argue with Dani in front of Saffi. My sibling was making it really difficult to keep that promise. No. I didn't lay in a hospital for ten hours giving birth to Saffi. What I did was get up every two hours to feed her once she came home from the hospital. I was still in college, so I rearranged my class and work schedules to be available to help look after my niece.

Not one day of Saffi's life had Danielle ever actually been a mother to the child she brought into the world. A week after giving birth, Dani left. She didn't say a word to anyone. She simply left. After six months with no word from her, my grandmother went to a social worker who helped her become a foster parent in order to have legal guardianship over Saffi. My grandpa had passed away years earlier, so it was just the two of us left to care for Saffi. Between us, all of her needs were met.

When Grandma Viola got sick, with her blessing, I went back to social services and petitioned for custody of Saffi. She was only two years old. I took all the classes. I did everything required to make myself a desirable candidate. From the day she was born, I made sure Saffi knew she was loved. I never wanted her to feel anything other than affection for her birth mother.

No matter how much my stomach knotted up whenever she asked to see Dani, I didn't bad-mouth my sister. *Yep.* Saffi asked for Dani. I could count on **one** hand the amount of times Dani had actually called asking for Saffi. Today was one of those days and look what happened.

Saffi landed in the hospital with her face cut up while Dani couldn't care less if she ended up with permanent physical scars to go along with the emotional scars she was bound to have from the experience.

My body was taut with tension like a bow string pulled back with an arrow notched ready to launch. I knew where the arrow would land and how much damage it would do, so I looked at Gene, "Will you take her out of here? I can't do this with her right now."

Gene upped his cred as my favorite cousin and trusted friend. He hustled Dani out of my sight as soon as the words left my mouth. Everyone ignored the parting remarks she spat out, while he bodily moved her through the door and out into the lobby. Ms Wells followed quietly behind them.

Reverting my focus back to Dr. Pearson, I resumed my questions. "You were saying?"

My opinion of Dr. Pearson increased when he explained his treatment plan for dealing with the slashes on Saffi's face, then followed it up with an offer to contact the plastic surgeon on call.

I jumped on the suggestion. I didn't care about the cost. I didn't want Saffi to look in the mirror on a daily basis and see a visible reminder of this horrific ordeal.

Dr. Pearson also informed me that they'd given her something for the pain once they confirmed she didn't have any medication related allergies. From the way she was laid out, they'd done more than given her something for the pain, she appeared to be sleeping, so I asked, "Did you sedate her?"

"Yes ma'am. We had to. She was still very agitated when the paramedics brought her in. She wouldn't let us get close enough to assess her injuries. She kept calling out for Aunt Cee-Cee. I'm guessing you're Aunt Cee-Cee." He stared at me with kind, cinnamon-colored eyes.

Thinking of Saffi crying out for me, and me not being there for her, brought tears to my eyes. Clearing my throat. I swiped at the tears before they could fall, my gaze roamed over my baby's motionless body taking in every detail. That's when I noticed the way her fists clenched and the grimace on the side of her face not covered by the draped cloth.

"Are the slashes on her face her only injuries? She still looks like she's in pain." My brow crinkled in concern. *What happened to my baby girl?*

"She has some bruising on her abdomen and back. The cuts on her face seemed to be the primary damage." Dr. Pearson was efficient, but I had a nagging feeling they missed something.

"The medicine you gave her was also for pain, right?"

My eyes bounced between the doctor and the nurse still standing beside the bed. The nurse checked the tablet attached to the rolling stand, confirming the doctor's statement.

"So, should she still be grimacing? Look at her hands, the way her fists are clenched. When she had appendicitis, once they sedated her, she didn't move at all. I think there's something else wrong."

So far, Dr. Pearson had been helpful, I prayed this wouldn't be one of those times a physician failed to listen to the concerns of an African-American patient. It happened far too often. I wouldn't allow Saffi to become a statistic. Not if I could help it.

Because of her age and current state of unconsciousness, she couldn't tell them what was going on, but my instincts wouldn't allow me to let it go. *Something wasn't right.*

Dr. Pearson looked down at Saffi, checking for the signals I'd described. It only took a few moments of him visually inspecting her, for him to start issuing instructions to the nurse at his side.

I didn't realize I was holding my breath until I released it, along with some of the tension in my shoulders. I kept reminding myself this was a good hospital, which was why I'd brought Saffi here when she'd required serious medical attention in the past.

Hyperaware of everything, I immediately picked up on the change in Dr. Pearson's demeanor. He'd been gingerly pressing along Saffi's torso when he suddenly snatched the stethoscope from around his neck, putting the earpieces in his ears.

His facial expression was intense as he placed the head of the scope in different places on her chest. Delivering short taps to her chest, he continued to listen through the device. Cursing under his breath, he snatched the buds from his ears.

"Nurse Stevenson, page Dr. Anderson, we might need him. Page Dr. Maxwell too," Dr. Pearson directly tersely.

Whatever he heard through the stethoscope sparked an urgency in him, and I couldn't prevent the words tumbling from my mouth even if I'd wanted to stop them.

"What is it? What's wrong?" The pleading note in my voice was foreign to my ears as I anxiously awaited an explanation.

With his hands efficiently placing a large gauze bandage over the injured side of Saffi's face, Dr. Pearson gave me a quick assessment.

"If what I felt and heard is correct, she has a couple of cracked ribs. She's struggling a bit to breathe, so I'm concerned she may have a pneumothorax. I'm going to get her upstairs for chest X-rays. I've asked for the cardiothoracic surgeon on shift to be called to consult. We'll have to operate if he determines it's necessary."

"Wait! A Surgeon! Operate! What's a pneumothorax?" Frantic didn't accurately describe my feelings. I was perilously close to coming completely unglued.

Shifting about the small room, prepping Saffi, he answered my question, "In laymen's terms, a pneumothorax is a collapsed lung. Depending on how badly her ribs are injured, they could have punctured her lung, allowing air to fill the area between the chest cavity and the lung itself."

In quick strides, Nurse Stevenson bustled through the door, propping it open, just as Dr. Pearson finished readying Saffi for transport. Dismissing me to focus on their patient, they rolled her out of the room and down the corridor.

"Oh my God... Oh my God!" I failed miserably at remaining calm. *Broken ribs! A punctured lung! What the FUCK happened to my child?* Moving my legs as fast as I could, I hustled to keep up with the medical team zipping through the ER maze to the elevators. There was no way they were leaving me behind.

Chapter Two

JIAN

I heard my name being called by the nurse at the nurse's station nearby as I walked out of a patient's room. I'd just performed a routine post op check-in. Normally, I didn't do post-op checks at night, but I figured if I had to be at the hospital on night shift, I might as well check in on my patients.

Paige Carmichael, the charge nurse, summoned me as I approached the station. "Dr. Anderson, I just got a call from the ER. They have an adolescent patient with a possible pneumothorax. They've asked for a consult. Dr. Pearson has taken the patient for X-rays to confirm. Radiology room twelve."

Not slowing down, I flashed her a smile as I walked past her, making my way to the elevator. "Thank you, Nurse Carmichael. Please let him know I'm on my way down."

I ignored the way her cheeks flushed, and I pretended not to notice her staring at my ass as I walked away. When I was younger, I was flattered by the way women responded to me. I'm no saint. I'd partaken in the offerings from women frequently over the years.

Closing in on forty, being looked at like a piece of man-meat had gotten old. Not that the attention wasn't appreciated. I'm a heterosexual man. By strict DNA coding, we enjoyed knowing women find us attractive.

The sly looks, blushes and comments increased in frequency once the *Netflix* series *Wu Assassins* became popular. The female staff spent far too much time discussing how uncanny the resemblance was between me and the actor Byron Mann, who played the character *Uncle Six* in the series. I'm slightly taller, a little heavier. Even with those differences, I had to admit the similarity was there. Similar. Nowhere close to identical. Not in my opinion.

When I first joined the staff at Talbot Memorial, it seemed every unmarried woman in the place was looking to add me as their plus one. Either as a conquest for bragging rights, or in the hopes of becoming a surgeon's housewife.

I have a firm policy against dating or fooling around with my colleagues. Besides the no co-workers policy, I never understood why any person would spend years obtaining education only to give up their career. The invitations had come from women who'd spent years in school, then additional time building their professional reputations.

I'd asked my mother once if she regretted giving up her career to essentially become a stay-at-home mom. Offering me an indulgent smile, she assured me she had no regrets. She said being my mother was the most important work she'd ever done. So, she was honored to be able to be there for me in that way. I accepted her words, but I didn't understand her perspective.

She'd worked hard to obtain her doctorate and was on a tenure track at her Alma Mater. Everything changed following my arrival. She drastically reduced her schedule to be there for me on a daily basis. While I'm thankful for her, for both my parents, I couldn't fathom the sacrifices she made for me. Sacrifices she's told me repeatedly were her honor to make.

The elevator doors opened and I stepped out onto the Radiology floor. Approaching room twelve, I spied a woman pacing at the end of the hall with a cellphone pressed to her ear. I couldn't distinguish much of her face because of the way she was turned. I could only see her in profile. The phone covered most of the side facing me.

She spoke in hushed tones. Her free arm wrapped under her generous bosom lifting them slightly, while her hand tightly gripped the side of her shirt. Her entire demeanor was the definition of concerned family member. Instinctively, I redirected my steps toward her instead of the radiology room. Before I could speak to her, the door to room twelve opened capturing both of our attention.

The ER resident, Pearson, was framed in the doorway with the radiologist and a nurse standing inside the room.

"Great! You're here. We have the x-rays for our patient Chloe Barker."

He waved me into the room. The radiologist inside immediately went over his interpretation of the x-rays with us. As we spoke, my eyes drifted to the unconscious pre-teen lying on the gurney. I wasn't sure what her complexion normally looked like. Currently, her deeply tanned skin held a pallor under the bandage covering half of her face. I'd heard and seen enough.

"Nurse Stevenson, please book an OR equipped for the possibility of having to open the chest cavity. Hopefully, it won't come to that."

Pearson added on, "Could you also make sure Dr. Maxwell has what she needs in there?"

Dr. Georgina Maxwell was the best plastic surgeon on staff, possibly the best on the East Coast. *Why would she join me in the ER?*

"Dr. Pearson, why do we need Dr. Maxwell for a pneumothorax? She's plastics."

Motioning to the left side of his face, he gave me a quick rundown about the cuts the child had sustained in addition to her other injuries. I'd noticed the bandage, but I was more focused on the issues with her lungs. I thought my years of practicing medicine, along with my own tour of the ER as a resident, had hardened me to the things people did to one another. I was wrong.

I listened as Pearson detailed the patient's injuries. When he described how her state of trauma was so severe she had to be sedated, my blood boiled. Who would do such things to an innocent child? Gritting my teeth, I worked to keep my anger in check.

"Her mother, the woman in the hallway, asked for a plastic surgeon to treat the child in the hopes the wounds would heal with minimal scarring. I can't say I blame her. I do damn good sutures, but they don't compare to Dr. Maxwell's level of precision. She does amazing work."

He was right. Georgina was a miracle worker. She was hands down one of the most gifted plastic surgeons I'd ever encountered. Waving for him to follow me, we stepped into the hallway to speak with Chloe's mother. We had to make it quick; I didn't like the sounds of the child's breathing.

I allowed Dr. Pearson to take the lead since he had a rapport from meeting her in the ER. "Miss Barker, this is Dr. Jian Anderson. He's a cardiothoracic surgeon."

She was no longer on the phone, so I could see her entire face. Even with the puffiness around her startling black eyes from a recent crying jag, and her face devoid of make-up, she was breathtaking. *Like seriously, I quit breathing*. Her skin was a flawless canvas painted the shade of rich mahogany.

Full lips, pursed in a concerned pout, sat below a button nose. She was too beautiful to be real. Against my will and good decorum, my eyes drifted from her face to sweep her frame. They raked over her compact body. Generous curves made up for what she lacked in height. Clearing his throat, Pearson brought me back to the current situation.

Thankful for the nudge back into reality, I extended a hand to shake hers as I shifted into surgical mode. With as much clarity as possible, I explained to her what was needed. Her consent was required to perform more invasive surgery if initial treatment options weren't successful. Once she signed the consent paperwork for the surgery, anesthesia and blood, we were set to get moving to the OR.

Two surgical aids rolled Chloe from the room to prep her for surgery. Visually following the progress of the gurney down the hall, Miss Barker's eyes filled with tears which refused to fall. An invisible fist gripped my heart, squeezing. Unconsciously, I rubbed my chest above the malfunctioning muscle. Her obvious emotional pain caused me physical pain. However, I had neither the time nor willingness to delve into the reasons why.

Clasping her free hand between both of mine, I ignored how good her silky skin felt against my palms. Capturing her gaze, I spoke to her softly.

"Hey... I know it's a bit scary. Try to keep a positive outlook. Your daughter is in very good hands. We will do our best to take care of her."

I held on to her gaze, gently squeezing her hand until I received a nod of agreement from her. Sticking my head into the now almost vacant room, I asked the radiologist to show Miss Barker to the surgical waiting room.

Deciding Pearson's quick thinking and thoroughness deserved a reward, I tossed him a glance. "Do you want to scrub in with me?"

I saw the answer written across his face before he opened his mouth to accept. Pearson was a good kid. Although he worked mostly in the ER, he was still entertaining a specialty. I wanted to see where his head was regarding cardio. Talbot was a teaching hospital, but I was extremely selective about whom I invited into my OR. Pearson recognized the boon for the rare opportunity that it was. He quickly accepted my invitation.

Things in an operating room are unpredictable, so I always function under the motto *'expect the unexpected'*. Tonight, the *unexpected* occurrence was everything going smoothly. Although the patient's broken ribs had punctured her lung, allowing air into the chest cavity, it wasn't so severe it required invasive surgery.

It had been caught early enough for us to use needles to relieve the pressure. If the child hadn't been covered in bruises with lacerations on her face, I would've said she had a guardian angel watching over her protectively, making her life a charmed one.

As if she had her ear to the door, Dr. Maxwell arrived with her resident in tow while we were placing bandages around the relief port I'd leave in for a short time, to mitigate another lung collapse. After a quick assessment of the patient's facial injuries, she got right down to business. I didn't have to, but I stayed to watch her work, while monitoring Chloe's vitals. I'm normally thorough, so I didn't want to think too much about why I stayed.

Usually, in situations where my patient required more than just my expertise, I would step out to update the family after I was done with my portion. The only times I didn't do so was when the patient's condition was still too critical to call, without waiting for the other surgeons to complete their part of the procedure. With Chloe, everything was going extremely well, which put me slightly on edge.

Every physician dreaded delivering unfavorable outcomes to their charge's families. However, the angst I felt at the possibility of giving Stephanie Barker bad news about her child wasn't my version of normal. While my eyes alternated between the vital sign readouts and the monitors displaying Dr. Maxwell's progress restoring Chloe's still child-like face to its formerly unblemished state, my thoughts drifted back to the woman who'd stolen my breath with a mere glance.

Pearson and I worked together to reestablish function to Chloe's lungs. Once I was sure she was out of danger, I pumped him for information on the stunning Stephanie Barker. All under the guise of gaining a clear picture of the patient and any potential dangers.

Pearson seemed none the wiser. As medical professionals, we were required to report any suspected child abuse to the authorities. I didn't for a second think Stephanie would hurt the angelic looking pre-teen, but I needed a plausible reason to ask questions.

Turned out Pearson didn't know much other than Stephanie was Chloe's aunt by familial ties. Legally, she was her adoptive mother. The child had been brought to the hospital in an ambulance, accompanied by a woman who claimed to be her mother. Pearson relayed the tense interaction between the two women and a large man whose name he didn't know. As much as I wanted to know about the unknown man, I didn't press.

"Ok Sweet Pea, we're all done now. Scar or no scar, you're beautiful. However, I think I made sure you won't have to re-live this day every time you look in the mirror."

Dr. Maxwell's soft voice pulled me from my thoughts to refocus on what was taking place in the operating room. No one commented on the doctor speaking to the patient as if she was fully conscious and could hear. It was Georgina's thing.

Giving instructions to the techs, Georgina and I removed our protective gear as we exited the OR. We left Pearson and Georgina's resident behind to make sure our orders were carried out as instructed. In silent consensus we turned towards the elevators to make our way to the family waiting area.

"Not complaining about the additional company, but you want to fill me in on why you hung around the OR an extra hour and a half watching me work?"

I should've known she would call me out. Georgina and I were among the handful of Asians on the surgical staff at Talbot, so we'd become friendly over the years. Nothing romantic, I wasn't her type. We were colleagues, so I wouldn't cross that line even if I was her type. Besides, she was married.

Me being Chinese-American and her being Filipino-American gave us a sort of kinship in an environment where we rarely saw peers who looked like us. There were more than a few Asian doctors and nurses, but not in the surgical group.

The surgical group was predominantly white and male. Talbot Memorial had a very ethnically diverse staff. Still, the number of white males in the higher-end fields eclipsed the minority groups.

Brushing off Georgina's comment about the extra attention I gave the patient, I answered, "I just thought it would be better if we spoke to the family together. I've only met the mother, Stephanie Barker. She was pretty shaken up. From what I heard, Chloe was the victim of a vicious attack. I had a feeling if I went in to update her and couldn't give her the whole story, it wouldn't go over well."

Try as I might to project a professional tone and demeanor, I wasn't sure it worked. She knew me too well. We'd even double dated a couple of times when I'd actually had a significant other.

"Uh-huh. That's what you're going with?" She regarded me shrewdly. "Ok. I'll allow it. *For now*," she conceded as we exited the elevator and walked toward the double doors leading away from the surgical suites.

As we drew nearer to the waiting area, I heard raised voices. Shooting a quick glance at Georgina, I picked up my pace. It's normal for tensions to run high when a loved one had to undergo surgery. Instinct told me our patient's family was the source of the noise. The possibility of Stephanie being subjected to any more distress didn't sit well with me. Not in the least.

Rounding the corner into the waiting area, I surveyed the room in one sweeping glance. Four people were in the space. Stephanie was the only person I recognized. Standing with her were a pretty African-American woman and a tall, muscular African-American man.

Sitting a short distance away, separated from the others by body language and the low padded benches, was another very pretty African-American woman. There was a slight resemblance between the woman seated and Stephanie. A relative? I didn't know and wouldn't ask.

The woman had her arms folded across her chest. Her face set in a stubborn expression. When we'd entered the space, there was dead silence—a complete contrast to what we'd heard as we walked toward the waiting room.

"Don't you dare sit there looking at me like I'm stupid. I know you know who it was!" Stephanie's voice barked out into the silence, directed at the seated woman.

Turning her face to the television mounted on the wall, the woman snapped back, "I already told you I don't know nothin'."

Everything after her declaration happened at lightning speed. Stephanie took two steps and launched herself over the low bench, landing on her feet directly in front of the seated woman. I didn't think as I hurried over to diffuse the situation.

I wasn't quick enough to stop her from connecting with a back-handed blow to the woman's face knocking her head into the wall behind her. *Shit!* The blow looked like it hurt like hell. The woman cried out grabbing her cheek with one hand and the back of her head with the other.

Wrapping my arms around Stephanie, trapping her arms to her sides, I moved her away from the woman, while she kicked out making threats. If the other woman attempted to fight back, I didn't notice.

"Let me go, Gene! I'm going to stomp a mudhole in that stupid, selfish, bitch's ass!" She ground out.

Placing my face next to hers, I spoke lowly, directly into her ear, "It's not Gene. I'm Jian. I need you to stop struggling, Sweetheart."

Her body completely stilled. Relieved, I exhaled deeply. For a moment, I was concerned her anger wouldn't allow her to hear anyone else.

Continuing in a low, hopefully calming, voice, I encouraged her. "That's it."

My chest was pressed into her back; I felt her heart still thumping rapidly. Keeping her snuggled against me, her feet barely touching the floor, I worked to soothe her.

"Breathe... In... Out... Nice and easy...It's not going to help your little girl if security has to escort you out of the hospital."

The breathing exercise helped. It was my last statement which seemed to really do the trick to get her body to completely relax. Her heart rate remained quick, but I felt the beats slowing. Either my mind was playing tricks on me, or the pulsations slowed until they matched my own.

Pushing the thought away, I gently placed her on her feet. Reluctantly, I released her from my arms. Raising to my full height, I stood in front of her, obscuring her view of the woman silently seething in the chair.

Ignoring the other people in the room, I captured her hands with mine, probing her dark eyes with my own. Silently, we assessed one another. I couldn't say what conclusion she reached, but her face softened before she tugged lightly, trying to remove her hands from mine. Grudgingly, I allowed it.

"Thank you," she said softly, her eyes drifting away from mine to notice Georgina's presence in the room. I quickly made introductions. In turn, she introduced us to the man and the other woman in the room. She blatantly refused to acknowledge the seated woman. As she introduced them, she explained the man was her cousin, Gene. The other woman was her friend, Joy.

My relief in hearing the man was a relative was enough to make me want to break out in my happy dance. That wasn't an option; so, I danced on the inside. *Why?* The reason's not important.

Georgina and I ushered them over to another group of chairs to relay the outcome of the procedures. I managed to stop myself from gathering Stephanie back into my arms when she teared up upon hearing Chloe would most likely make a full recovery with minimal, if any, scarring to her face.

Unable to resist, I placed a hand atop the one she rested on her own thigh, "Chloe will be in recovery for another hour or so, then we'll move her to a room. She'll need to stay here for another couple of days for us to monitor the situation with her lungs to be certain she won't require further intervention. As soon as she's assigned a room, someone will let you know."

"Thank you, Dr. Anderson. Thank you too, Dr. Maxwell," her honeyed voice was tinged with the scratchy remnants of closely held emotions.

"You're welcome. We're happy to do what we can to help," Georgina responded, getting to her feet. I felt her eyes boring into the side of my head. Reluctantly, I released Stephanie's hand and stood alongside Georgina.

As we prepared to make our exit, two uniformed police officers entered the waiting room, visually scanning everyone present. The older of the two spoke for the duo. "Excuse us, we're looking for the parents or guardians of a Chloe Barker."

My eyes shot to Stephanie's face; my body went rigid. Georgina tugged at my sleeve to get my attention. She whispered, "I think we should go now."

I was reluctant to leave. I knew I had no real reason to remain behind. Aside from performing the procedure to repair Chloe's lung, I had no ties to her nor Stephanie. *So why can't I walk away?*

Slowly, I turned and followed Georgina from the room. As we left, I took mental note of the officer's names. Memorizing them, I flicked one more reassuring glance in Stephanie's direction. Instead of catching her eyes, I caught the expression on her cousin's face. His facial countenance was neutral, but his eyes probed mine.

For a short moment, we stood this way, speaking without words. Finally, he dipped his head in an almost imperceptible nod before turning his attention to the officers speaking to Stephanie. Nothing left to say or do, I left the room, trailing behind my colleague.

After we made it to the elevator, Georgina spoke again, "You know you're eventually going to have to tell me what's up right?" Not hearing nor waiting for a response, she continued into the elevator and pressed the button for her floor.

I wasn't ready to talk to anyone about my actions because I needed time to figure out what was going on myself. I'm not a eunuch. However, I've never had my attraction to anyone be so instant. Not ever had it been so all-consuming that it took a concerted effort for me to remain detached and professional. If I were being completely truthful with myself, I didn't succeed at remaining detached. I failed at that one. *Big time.*

Chapter Three

STEPHANIE

I was actually surprised to see the cops. Saffi was attacked a little ways down the block from Grandma Vi's old house. The house wasn't in a bad neighborhood, but crime had picked up over the last year. As it happened so often, when the police came around, everyone went deaf and blind. Which meant, the police soon stopped expecting cooperation. They stopped putting in the effort necessary to actually find the suspects and make arrests. That's why I didn't expect to see them in the waiting room.

When Grandma passed, she left me the house. It pissed Dani off. I really didn't know why she expected anything different. Why should she have been left even a portion of the home she couldn't wait to get out of? She was so anxious to leave and shirk responsibility, she left her newborn. She didn't even put up a fight when her parental rights were stripped away.

Against my better judgement, and advice from Gene, I allowed Dani to live in the house. I could've rented it out, but my sister was essentially homeless at the time.

Before I opened my second salon location, I'd already purchased a larger home in the suburbs, farther out from the city. I moved us to the burbs to get Saffi into a better school district. This was before I pulled her out of public school placing her in a private academy. Even in a better school district, she wasn't being challenged enough. So, I sucked it up and paid the insane tuition to give her access to the education I felt she deserved.

Tearing my gaze away from Dr. Anderson's retreating back, I trained my eyes on the officers. "I'm Stephanie Barker. I'm Chloe's mother."

I ignored the scoffing noise coming from the corner of the room. Now was absolutely the wrong time for me to go back to beating Dani's ass. *Orange is **not** the new black*. I can't help Saffi if I'm locked up.

I didn't even look in Dani's direction. There was no need to call the cops attention to her quickly swelling, reddened face. Danielle's pale complexion meant every little mark or blemish showed up easily. So, the spot on her face, where I clocked her, was standing out loud and proud. Surreptitiously, Gene slid into the space next to me, blocking the officer's view of Dani with his big body.

Extending his hand, the first officer made the introductions.

"Hello ma'am. I'm Officer Gregory, this is Officer Daniels."

Giving him a firm handshake, I performed the same routine with the second officer. In turn, I introduced Gene and Joy.

Officer Gregory was a clean cut African-American man with kind dark brown eyes. He appeared to have seniority as he did most of the talking, while Officer Daniels scribbled into a small notepad. Following the introductions, Officer Gregory explained why they were at the hospital.

"We were first on the scene. We interviewed a few people, but don't have any solid information at this time. We're hoping you might be able to shed some light on what occurred."

With a shake of my head, I relayed to him what I knew. "I wish I could tell you what happened. I'm still hoping to learn myself. When I got here, Chloe was sedated, then rushed to surgery. I haven't been able to speak to her to find out who did this, since I wasn't there.

All I know is she'd called me to pick her up, because she was ready to go home. I was on the other side of the city, so I told her I would be there in about an hour. The next thing I know, I'm receiving a call from an old neighbor telling me Chloe's being brought here."

Pouncing on that bit of information, Officer Gregory asked, "Could you give me the name and contact information for the person who called you?"

"Myrtle Simmons," I supplied without hesitation.

Miss Myrtle was good people. She used to babysit Dani and I when we were young. Until I moved away, she was my go-to sitter for Saffi. I couldn't see her refusing to help. She doted on Saffi like my little girl was one of her own grandchildren.

Turning to his partner, Officer Gregory asked, "Daniels, didn't we speak to a Mrs. Simmons earlier?"

Flipping back a few pages in his little notepad, Officer Daniels responded, "Yes. She gave a statement. Unfortunately, she didn't see the attack. However, she gave us information on a possible vehicle used to flee the scene. I sent it over to dispatch. Nothing back so far."

My heart picked up in hope at hearing Miss Myrtle had information, then sank just as quickly when the officer said she didn't actually see the attack.

I knew who had more information. Dani. For whatever reason, she was reluctant to share the details with me or anyone else. Her reluctance alone made me suspicious.

As much as I'd like to think she didn't have a part in what went down, her silence and staunch refusal to cooperate could only mean she was hiding something. The something she was hiding had to implicate her in some way.

Knowing Dani wouldn't cooperate, I was anxious for the cops to leave. I clasped my hands together in front of me to keep from clenching and unclenching my fists in anticipation of planting them in my sibling's *'I don't know nothin'* face.

Seeing the fruitlessness of continuing, Officer Gregory took down my information. He also gave me his card in case I came across anything new. Promising to pass my information on to the detective assigned to the case, he assured me they would be in touch to follow up. Then, he and his partner made their exit.

Waiting until I heard the ding of the elevator signaling the complete exit of the police officers, I rounded on Dani in the corner. Smoothly intercepting, Gene slid in front of me.

"Step, come on. Not here." Holding his hands up in front of him, he prevented me from moving any closer.

Flicking my eyes to his, I assured him. "I'm cool. I just want Saffi's stuff."

Saffi was never without her e-reader and cellphone. The e-reader was a beloved gift from Alanna Gibson, her mentor. A voracious reader, Saffi took the e-reader everywhere. The cellphone was also a prized possession, because she'd saved her allowance and odd job money for a year to match the half I said I'd give her to purchase it.

Just because I had the money to buy her everything she asked for, didn't mean I gave her everything she desired. I wanted her to learn the value of earning the things she wanted in life.

Along with her coveted e-reader and smartphone, she also had a small designer crossbody Gene gave her. She loved that little purse. She would never willingly part with any of those things. Nor would she leave them lying around. Holding out my hand in Dani's direction, I was almost nice when I spoke to her.

"Dani, where's Saffi's stuff? Her tablet? Her phone? Her purse?"

Shrugging, Dani muttered avoiding making eye contact. "I already told you I don't know nothin. I don't have her stuff. She didn't give me anything to hold for her."

Once again, my sister proved she could incite my anger faster than any other human on earth. If she'd told me she was focused on getting Saffi to the hospital and it slipped her mind to grab her belongings, I could've taken that.

Even if she'd said she was so upset it didn't occur to her to pick up Saffi's things, I would have accepted it. But this blatant disregard and blasé attitude? Nah. It didn't fly with me.

"What the hell do you mean, she didn't give it to you to hold for her?" Cocking my head to the side, I glared at her in disbelief. "How the fuck would she have the presence of mind to ask you to hold something for her after she's been beaten and cut up? You're the damn adult, you're supposed to take care of her, not the other way around."

"Why are you always acting like I'm stupid? I know I'm the damn adult. Shit. Chloe's old enough to keep up with her own stuff. I shouldn't have to run behind her like she's five."

Dani's eyes blazed with anger. Then, she had the sheer audacity to turn her face away from me, dismissing me as if I was the one being unreasonable.

Before I thought about it, my body was in motion. Abruptly, I was snatched back, Gene's arms banded around me like a vice. Joy planted herself in between me and the demon posing as my sibling.

How could Dani be so cold? Even if she hadn't really been a parent to Saffi, she was still blood. I don't think I'd ever understand how she could carry a child for nine months and not show an ounce of compassion for the life she brought into the world.

Putting her hands palms up facing me, Joy tried to dissuade me from putting my foot in my so-called sister's ass.

"Come on Step. You know we can't let you do what you wanna do right now. It's just stuff. It can be replaced."

Leveling me with her best, *please see reason* expression, one of my best friends held her ground.

"Stop looking at me like that. I don't want to be reasonable. I want to stomp a mudhole in her selfish ass."

Even though my body shook with rage, I didn't struggle against Gene's hold.

"First, she's not paying attention to what's going on. So, my baby gets attacked by God knows who, IN FRONT OF HER FUCKING FACE! Then she was going to let those doctors leave Saffi with permanent scars because she didn't care enough to make sure she was getting good medical care.

Now, she can't be bothered to speculate as to what happened to my baby's possessions. Here's a thought. Maybe whoever attacked her **stole** them!"

I shot my words in Dani's direction. I knew she heard me despite me being unable to see her.

The more I thought of the possibility, the more the idea seemed viable. Taking deep breaths, I worked to bring my emotions under control. I wasn't this person. I didn't fly off the handle. I didn't settle things with my fists—usually. Hurt my child, all bets are off. Everyone who knew me understood and respected how protective I was over Saffi.

Giving myself a moment, I was able to think more clearly. I'd been gone from the neighborhood for a while, but people there still knew me. I'd spent most of my younger life there, so anyone from those few blocks knew better than to mess with any child of mine. Which meant whoever jumped Saffi wasn't from there or was a recent transplant.

I had some thoughts about what to do next. It wasn't about the stuff. I could replace all of the *stuff* without putting a dent in my shopping fund. It was about the attack on my child. *My Child!* That shit couldn't stand.

Tugging at Gene's hands, I tried to convince him I was calm enough to be trusted not to slap a Ho. My quest for freedom was aided by the nurse who came to tell us Saffi was in a room and could have visitors. She informed us Saffi was still sleeping off the meds. Then, she gave us directions to get to the room, which was located on a different floor.

Grabbing my bag from my long-vacated seat, I asked Gene for another favor. "Can you get her out of here? Drop her at home, or wherever. I don't care. I just don't want her near Saffi. Especially not now."

I saw Dani's posture stiffen. Her nose tipped into the air. I didn't care. She'd lost her rights to Saffi and her presence kept my anger at a boiling point. Having her here put me in a bad headspace. Being an angry hothead wasn't the image I wanted to project. This wasn't the time and it was far from being the place.

She might play dumb, but Dani wasn't stupid. While Joy and I turned one way, she went ahead of Gene in the opposite direction. Walking backwards, Gene called out, "Tell my Lady Bug I love her and I'll be by to see her in the morning."

Nodding in agreement, I continued with Joy, meandering through the hallways. I had no doubt he would keep his word. He projected a tough-as-nails image. It was an act. He was a pushover for kids. Me, Gene and my sister-circle did what we could to make up for what Saffi lacked not having her biological parents in her life. We did everything in our power to assure she always felt loved.

Finally, we reached the door of the room. Looking at the number painted beside the door, I double-checked to be certain we were in the right place. Releasing a pent-up breath, I pushed the door open. Barely contained anxiety had my eyes pinging around the room before landing on Saffi, partially reclined, looking tiny and vulnerable in the hospital bed.

She was twelve and tall for her age. She towered over my five-foot two-inch frame by a good four inches, but the bed seemed to swallow her form. Maybe it was just me. Maybe my inability to see her as anything other than my baby made her appear small.

Moving farther into the room, I rounded the bed. My gaze raked over her motionless form, cataloguing every detail. Of their own volition, my fingers moved to her hair trying to bring it into some semblance of order. When she'd left home earlier, her hair was smoothed high on her head in a natural kinky, coily, puff.

The elastic band holding it in place was long gone. Her once neat hair stuck out from her head in odd directions. Closer inspection of the thick mass led my eyes to yet another thing to set my blood on fire. There were obvious places where her hair had been torn from her head, all the way from the root.

"I need some stuff from the salon to try to do something with her hair." I said aloud, mostly to myself. Joy responded anyway.

"Tell me what you need. I'll get it. I'll also go by your place and get a bag together for the two of you."

Continuing to lightly smooth Saffi's hair, I didn't respond to her. Moving to stand beside me, she nudged my shoulder.

"Heeeey, Step. Look at me," she said lowly.

After a few moments of feeling her gaze burning into the side of my head, I turned to face her. I knew she read my face perfectly, because I saw my pain reflected in her eyes.

I felt like I failed Saffi. Logically, I knew I couldn't be everywhere at once. It didn't stop me from feeling responsible for her going through something so horrible. Keeping her voice low to avoid waking Saffi, Joy tried her best to head off my self-blaming thoughts.

"This is not your fault. There was no way you could have known something like this would happen. Chloe has played on that block for years without anything happening. As much as you like to think you can, you can't plan for every eventuality. It sucks monkey balls, but it's true... Please don't beat yourself up."

The monkey balls comment dragged a small smirk to my face. She probably planned for my reaction to her comment. My over analytical friend knew me too damn well...

When it came to Joy, *resistance was futile* once she'd made up her mind. I could tell by the set of her jaw she wouldn't accept anything less than agreement. Giving up the fight, I reached into my bag fishing out my house keys.

"I'll text you the codes and a list of what I need. Thank you for this. And for being here."

Bumping her hip against mine she brushed off my gratitude.

"It's what we do. You know this."

Stretching around me, she gave a few light pats to Saffi's limp hand before leaving the room.

Pulling the nearest chair closer to the bed, I dug inside my oversized purse for my cell phone. I needed to keep my brain moving, focusing on anything other than the silence of the room punctuated only by the hum of the equipment. Occasionally, hospital noises drifted in from the hallway.

It didn't take long for me to tap out a list of items as well as instructions on where to find them. Using the shorthand from our college days, I sent the code information to deactivate the alarm at my home. I actually had everything I'd need at the house, so there wasn't a need for Joy to go to the salon.

As I placed the phone back into my tote, it buzzed. Swiping the screen, I opened the text message from my life-long friend, Nikki.

I steeled myself for the possible backlash of not reaching out. Nikki was arguably my best friend. A wave of guilt hit me thinking of how I hadn't called or at least texted her to tell her what happened to Saffi.

She loved my baby almost as much as I did. I could only blame my singular focus on the misstep. I hadn't even called Joy. She went by the salon looking for me. That's how she found out.

Nikki was my girl from way back, as in we grew up together. The bond was different than the one I shared with Joy; however, it was no less enduring.

Nikki: Stephanie. Cecile. Barker. WTF! Why didn't you tell me somebody put hands on Baby Girl?

Me: Hey Nik. My bad... I'm struggling trying to keep my head on straight. I was gonna call you, but I want to talk to Saffi first.

Nikki: You better be glad I know your ass is probably losing your shit, or I'd really go in. How's my Peanut?

Me: She's okay now. I don't know exactly what happened to her yet. She's still sleeping off the meds and I don't want to leave her alone. I promise I'll call you later.

Nikki: Alright. Bet. Your ass betta call me too! Don't make me jack your short ass up about my Peanut!

Me: I promise. I'll call. WNTFSSU. Check with Pootie about Safari.

Nikki: Word. I gotchu.

I pressed the button to lock the screen and slid the phone back into my purse. I didn't have to explain to Nikki what I meant. She knew I wouldn't go into details over text. Details were done face to face.

Although I didn't use it often, *WNTFSSU* was our shorthand long before social media made it popular to use letters in internet slang. *We Need To Fuck Some Shit Up,* was Nikki's favorite.

I hadn't used it in years. There hadn't been a need. But, if my hunch about Saffi's attack was a good one, I foresaw us doing some damage in the near future.

Pootie was Nikki's cousin on her dad's side. He was in love with all things 90's. So in love he still drove a 1996 Chevy Impala, he'd lovingly named *Safari.* The car only seated two people, because he'd pulled the back seats out to install his monstrosity of a sound system.

He'd let Nikki borrow it, no questions asked, because he knew she was the only reason I took him on as a client. After almost two decades doing hair, I saw very few personal clients. The stylists I employed actually worked more with hair than I did these days. Pootie, whose real name was Bernard, had a standing bi-weekly appointment for me to maintain his waist-length loc'd hair.

I sat near Saffi's bedside with nothing further to occupy my hands or my mind. The absence of a distraction allowed the gripping sorrow, I'd been holding at bay, to push through to the forefront. First, my face heated. Then my vision blurred as the tears I'd refused for hours made their appearance.

Wrapped in my feelings, I didn't hear the door open. When I felt the warmth of a hand on my back, I was unprepared. Gasping, my gaze flew upward, eyes wide with surprise. Standing beside me was Dr. Anderson, watching me, with concern creasing his smooth brow.

He offered no words as he pulled me up from the chair, into his embrace. It wasn't normal. It probably was against some kind of rule. I didn't care. He was giving me exactly what I needed in the moment—silent support. Somehow, he maneuvered us into the small lavatory and shut the door without me being aware I was being guided.

The light snick of the door closing was like a starting gun to my pent-up emotions. The silent tears gave way to body-wracking sobs. Holding me tightly to his chest, this man, who I didn't really know, gave me everything I needed and would've never asked anyone to provide. Without conscious thought, my hands slid under his white coat. My fingers curled into his sides, gripping at his shirt.

If asked, I wouldn't be able to give an honest answer for how long we remained in the cramped space. Eventually, my tear ducts dried and all I had left in me were light sniffles. Still, Dr. Anderson held me rubbing soothing circles on my back.

Though I was reluctant to leave the warmth of his embrace, I knew I couldn't stay there forever. Lifting my face, my eyes were immediately captured by his piercing cognac-colored orbs. Uncomfortable with the proximity, I attempted to look away, only to have one side of my face captured by his hand with his thumb tipping my chin, forcing me to meet his penetrating stare.

He searched my eyes like he was trying to uncover my every secret thought. Blinking, trying to break the spell, I snaked my hands between us. I pressed lightly on his chest. His well-developed pectoral muscles jumped under my touch. Ignoring the way his hard body felt under my hands, I continued to put physical distance between us.

Clearing my throat, I attempted to infuse a little cheer into my voice, "Thank you. I guess I needed a good cry."

When he remained silent, I thought maybe my stab at levity had fallen flat. The silence seemed to drag on forever before he apparently found what he was looking for in my eyes.

"You're okay now."

It wasn't a question. Somehow, he'd been able to see I really was in a better head space and no longer required his broad shoulders to cry on. Don't ask me why I wasn't afraid of being enclosed in a small space with a man I didn't even know.

I had no answer to that question. I wasn't afraid, but the stirrings of other feelings have me reaching for the door. The warm feeling in my center had been missing so long, it was almost foreign. There was no time. Also, I had no energy to delve into my unexpected reaction to being in close proximity to the Good Doctor Anderson.

Without comment, he guided me away from the door and opened it. A quick glance at the bed confirmed Saffi was still sleeping soundly.

"Is it normal for her to still be asleep?" I asked, worrying my bottom lip with my teeth.

Walking with me, he passed the bed picking up the tablet he must have placed on the mobile cart on the other side. After a few swipes at the screen, he spoke.

"People respond to anesthesia differently. Between the medications used to keep her sedated and the ones she's receiving through the IV for pain, she'll most likely be asleep until sometime later in the morning.

With pediatric patients, it's not always easy to tell. Experience along with the information I see in her chart, tells me she's sleeping off the effects of the anesthesia."

Walking back toward the bed, he continued to glide his finger over the screen, scrolling through the information.

"The recovery notes look good. I didn't anticipate any issues. Since my shift is almost over, I wanted to check on her before I left."

At his mention of leaving, I noticed the time. Five a.m. Wow. I'd been awake a solid twenty-four hours. However, sleep was only a vague possibility until I could talk to Saffi and hear her sweet voice.

Just as Dr. Anderson opened his mouth to speak again, Joy swept back though the door walking backwards.

"Alright Chica, I have bags filled with everything you asked me to pack for both you and Baby Girl. I also stopped and grabbed you some breakfast, because I know you haven't left this room. You need to eat something."

Depositing the bags on the closest chair, she turned around. The rest of her words dried up when she saw Dr. Anderson standing closely beside me.

Chapter Four

JIAN

It was probably a good thing her friend showed up when she did. I couldn't say I wouldn't have looked for another excuse to hang around.

The woman drew me to her like a high-strength magnet. It wasn't purposeful on her part—it was me. I couldn't stop myself from gravitating closer to her. And when I was near her, it was a struggle not to touch her.

Taking the opportunity to exit and get myself together, I quickly said my goodbyes. Unable to deny myself a touch, I gently rubbed her arm. I promised to stop by during my next shift.

Chloe had come through the procedures well. So, I anticipated being able to release her from the hospital by the start of my Sunday night shift, or Monday morning before I left my quarterly rotation on weekend night shift.

Walking through the corridors, I stopped at the nurse's station to check on my other patients once more before heading to my office to write up my notes. I'd already made notations in the patient charts, but I liked to keep my own, separate notes.

As I typed, my mind wandered back to the Barker family, Stephanie

Barker in particular. What was her story? How did she come to be the adoptive mother of her niece? She didn't look a day over thirty. Chloe was on the verge of being a teenager. Stephanie had to be a baby herself when Chloe was born.

Her sister seemed healthy and of sound mind, so why wouldn't she have custody of her own child? Why was Stephanie's relationship with her sister so contentious, or was it just the stress of the moment making it look like they were constantly at odds? The questions swirled in my head. Occupied with the conundrum, I knew I wasn't going to be productive. So, I saved the file. I shutdown my laptop before unplugging it and sliding it into my messenger bag.

Checking my watch, I noticed my shift was technically over, relieving me of any feelings of guilt for not finishing the extra set of notes. Knowing I was far more invested in Stephanie Barker and her daughter than I should be didn't stop me from firing off a text to my longtime friend, Ash, before walking out of my office.

Asher Peterson was a lead detective on the local police force. He'd have access to information to get answers to some of my questions. He could also make sure someone was actively working on Chloe's case. Whoever attacked her didn't deserve the freedom they enjoyed while that sweet little girl lay in a hospital bed battered and bruised.

Though I liked to shower at home, I opted to shower at the hospital before leaving. Once I changed into my street clothes, I headed straight to the parking structure. I managed to make it to my car without being pulled into any cases or conversations, which was a miracle within itself.

People seemed to get chatty when I was trying to leave, be it early morning or late in the evening. This morning, they were either too wrapped up in what they were doing to bother me, or I was giving off some serious 'Do Not Disturb' vibes. Whatever the reason, I was thankful for the reprieve.

By the time I'd made it to my car, I figured I'd waited long enough for Ash to respond to my text. Uncaring about the early hour, I gave the voice command to call him as soon as my phone connected to the Bluetooth system.

Tapping my fingers on the steering wheel impatiently, I mentally urged Ash to answer the phone. I was fully prepared to hang up and call right back when his groggy sleep-filled voice growled through the speakers.

"Why the fuck are you calling me at seven a.m. on the **one** fucking Saturday I've had off in the past two months?"

"Get dressed and meet me at Aunt Lois's for breakfast."

Ignoring his grumpy question, I tempted him with what I knew he couldn't reject—the delicious food at Aunt Lois's.

Lois's Diner was a local staple. We'd discovered the spot during our junior year in college. We'd been hooked ever since. The diner was owned and operated by a tiny, sassy black woman, with a personality big enough to make you forget she didn't quite reach five feet in height.

Affectionately called *Aunt Lois* by all the regulars, she treated everyone who entered the doors of her restaurant like family. Whenever we ate there, she flirted shamelessly with both of us. Somehow, we always ended up with a little something extra to go with our orders. She pampered us and we loved every minute of it.

Knowing how much he loved it there, I was banking on Ash not being able to turn down the opportunity for some of Aunt Lois's famous, melt in your mouth, buttermilk biscuits with gravy. I heard the rustling of bed covers while he grumbled.

"This better be fucking important. Don't forget your wallet. Your ass is paying and I'm not ordering the special."

I ended the call after a minute or two of listening to him slam around his bedroom hurling curses about inconsiderate, spoiled ass friends. Since I'd established he was meeting me, there was no need for me to stay on the phone while he cursed me out for interrupting the one morning he'd been able to sleep in. We'd been friends long enough for him to know when I called like this, something was eating at me. He knew I wouldn't let up until I had a resolution.

Arriving at the restaurant first, I secured a table then ordered a coffee for Ash and water for myself. With another nightshift ahead of me, I didn't want coffee keeping me from getting to sleep once I made it home. Sipping the water, I looked over the menu while I waited for my cranky friend to show.

I knew the menu like the back of my hand. I looked anyway. Occasionally Aunt Lois would change things up, adding a limited time item to the available choices.

I didn't have a long wait. I'd been looking over the menu less than ten minutes when Ash strolled in looking like he'd pulled a triple shift. His clothes weren't rumpled, but his hair looked like he'd used his fingers to comb it, instead of an actual comb or brush. His normally well-kept facial hair looked a bit overgrown and his eyes were tinged pink.

"Damn man, you look like death warmed over. What the hell have you been doing?"

Normally, I was much more tactful. He looked so different from his usual crisp appearance; the words flew from my mouth before I could call them back.

"Fuck you too."

Ash responded as he dropped his over-sized body into the chair across from me picking up the menu at the same time. He didn't need the menu either. He habitually checked for surprises the same as me.

Sweeping my gaze over his tousled sandy blond hair, from the dark circles around his eyes, to the extra facial scruff, then to the very normal looking t-shirt and jeans he was wearing, I pushed my reasons for meeting aside.

"Seriously Ash, what's up? No offense, but you look like shit."

"Offense taken, asshole," he grunted, then leaned back in the seat. "It's this fucking case man. It's messing with my head."

He scrubbed his fingers through his shaggy mane. Flicking his eyes up from the menu, he sighed, lightly tossing it to the table.

"It's more of a task force than a case. The shit is never-ending. People do unbelievably cruel things to other humans. I need some space from it. I almost wanted to go back to a time when I was clueless to just how many sick, depraved, monsters walk among us."

Before he could continue, our waitress came to take our orders. Accepting the short reprieve, we gave her our choices. True to his promise, Ash didn't order the special. He asked for a double order of biscuits with gravy, country ham, and scrambled eggs with skillet hash browns. I went for lighter fare. I was heading home to bed and I preferred to sleep without nightmares.

While we waited for our food, Ash filled me in on some of the bare bones of the task force to which he was recently assigned. Human Trafficking. I'd taken the required informational training as a medical professional. So, I was aware it had become more prevalent. Atlanta was apparently a hub where trafficked people were recruited, kidnapped, or handed off to be moved to another destination.

Ash's involvement with the task force gave him a perspective I hadn't received in my continuing education course. Even with him skipping most of the gory details, it was still enough to turn my stomach. It was fucked up on so many levels.

Giving us a break in the gruesome conversation, Aunt Lois showed up with our waitress to bring our food. The delicious smells wafted from the plates, making my mouth water and my stomach grumble.

"Well, if it isn't my favorite flavor combination, Butterscotch and Heavy Cream, gracing us with their presence this morning."

She placed two plates in front of me as the server placed a mountain of food before Ash. With one hand on my shoulder, she sent the waitress away with a look and a wave.

"It's been a while. I thought y'all found another spot. I was sure you were cheating on me," she pouted.

I didn't believe for a minute she was hurt. She liked giving us grief when we stayed away too long. In a sense, we'd become family in the ten plus years we'd been coming to the diner. Unless things were really hectic, Ash and I met here twice a month—more if the mood struck us.

Flashing the smile which dazzled far too many women, young and old, Ash clasped her free hand. He used it to draw her closer to him— away from me. Slipping into his deep, South Alabama country boy drawl, he laid it on thick.

"Come on, Auntie. You know we can't stay away. If I can't have your good cooking, I might wither away to nothin'. I'm a growin' boy."

Slapping playfully at the arm he slid around her waist, Aunt Lois scoffed. "Boy quit playin'. Big as you are, it would take years of missed meals for you to wither away."

Clutching his chest above his heart, he feigned hurt.

"You wound me, Auntie. I'll have you know I'm down two whole pounds since the last time I was here."

Interacting with Aunt Lois always brought a smile to my face, so I couldn't resist joining in on the playful exchange.

"I don't know if you'll be able to get those pounds back by eating here, my friend. I think she might be into that low-fat low-cal kind of thing I normally go for." I said, wagging my head. "Besides, you know they say you can't trust the food if the cook is too thin."

Whipping the kitchen towel from its permanent home on her shoulder, she swatted me on the arm. "Oh! So now my food is nasty because somebody is hating on my metabolism keeping me spry and fly?"

Giving an exaggerated dip of her knees, she propped a hand on one slender hip causing both of us to erupt into laughter. Shaking my head, I didn't suppress the smile taking over my face.

"Auntie, no one says fly anymore."

"Yeah... I'm pretty sure spry is old people talk," Ash added.

"So not only can I not cook, now I'm a retirement home candidate? I see how you are. See if I keep feeding you my good food. I'll let you wither away for real." She huffed, folding her arms across her slim frame, shooting Ash a slit-eyed mock glare.

They kidded about his size, but Ash's large body was the result of genetics and a strict exercise routine, not indulgent over-eating. He was solidly built like the offensive lineman he once was, even though he'd retired from professional football in his twenties. When he played, he was actually pretty good. His problem was, he didn't have a passion for it. So, he only played long enough to secure his financial future. Then, he quit to join the police force.

Some people thought it was a publicity stunt like when Shaq said he wanted to be a Highway Patrolman. They eventually figured out Ash was serious when he completed the academy. He quickly moved up the ranks making detective in almost record time. He was constantly recruited for special task forces working with federal agencies.

Raising one eyebrow, Aunt Lois gave him one last swat and moved away. "You don't need me to fatten you back up anyway. If you lost weight, Butterscotch didn't find it. He's just as trim as ever."

She joked, raking her eyes over my lean, muscular frame. Where Ash had a football player's broad body, I had more of a swimmer's physique.

Ash pretended to be hurt, but this was their thing. They bantered, he claimed to be losing weight. Then she gave him extra portions of whatever he ordered. She spoiled us both rotten.

Like today, I'd ordered a spinach egg white omelet with whole wheat toast. What she placed in front of me was the extra-large western omelet overflowing with meat and veggies. A short stack of pancakes was placed in front of me as well. If we ever got exactly what we ordered, there was *always* a little something extra.

Chuckling lightly as Aunt Lois moved away from the table, we each said a quick prayer before digging into our food. We weren't more than a few bites in before Ash lifted his head, pinning me with his sharp gaze.

"So, are you going to tell me what's eating you to have you drag me out of bed bribing me with biscuits?"

I brushed off his latest complaint at being awakened early on a Saturday with a flip of a hand.

"Stop being a baby. At least you were in bed. I'm operating off four hours of sleep in the past twenty-four. I spent more than half of that time on my feet in surgeries. You'll survive having your eight hours of sleep cut to six. As soon as we're done, you can head back home and continue to sleep your day away."

Grunting around the forkful of food he shoved into his mouth, Ash replied, "Now who's whining? Spill. What's got your brain working overtime to the point you couldn't wait for me to respond to your text?"

Over the remainder of our meal, I filled Ash in on the events from the night before. I wasn't concerned about overstepping. I was certain the detective assigned to the case would eventually ask me about the extent of Chloe's injuries. Who knew when they would actually get around to contacting me though?

Some things were given more priority than others. Ash had influence amongst the other detectives. I needed him to make sure whoever got the assignment didn't drop the ball.

If asked, and Ash did ask, I couldn't explain why I was so affected by this particular patient. Well... I knew, but it was hard to verbalize why Stephanie Barker and her niece had quickly become my priority.

I didn't really understand it myself, so hell if I could explain it to him beyond saying it hit me harder than usual. It was true. *Kind of.*

Stacking his empty plates to make it easier for the server to carry away, Ash listened. Afterwards, he agreed to look into Chloe's case.

"I can't make any promises. You know that, right? I'll check the roster to see who caught it, make sure they aren't slacking off," he said, tapping his fingers lightly on the table.

Nodding in understanding, I met his gaze with gratitude.

"That's all I can ask. I appreciate you looking into it. The officers who came to take statements didn't stay long. It makes me think they're going to brush it off as just one of those things. Whoever hurt her should be made to pay for their crime."

No sooner had the words left my mouth, than the waitress came back to leave the bill taking away the empty dishes. Despite my desire to eat light, I'd finished everything I was given—the same as Ash. Dropping the amount of the meal plus a generous tip on the table, we said our goodbyes to Aunt Lois and left the diner.

Chapter Five

STEPHANIE

Joy's eyes bounced between me and the exiting Dr. Anderson. A slow smile spread across her face. I was familiar with the look.

I rushed to head her off before she went on a tangent. "Don't start, Joy. Let it go." I said quietly.

Hunching her shoulders and lifting her hands innocently, she responded. "What? I didn't say anything." Her hazel eyes sparkled mischievously.

"You didn't have to. I know you."

I lifted the duffle from the pile of bags Joy had placed in the chair. Propping one hand on her hip, with the pointer finger on the other hand in the air, she gifted me with one of her signature looks.

"So, you just wanna pretend that fine ass doctor wasn't in here making a visit surgeons rarely make after surgery is complete? Alone? Without another member of the team with him?"

Holding an open palm in my direction, she pierced me with a knowing stare.

"Before you answer, keep in mind my sister is in the medical field. She talks about hospital stuff all the damn time. So, I know surgeons don't check on their patients nearly as much as the medical shows on TV would have you believe."

"I don't know what you're thinking. I have nothing to tell you." I was determined to get her off the subject.

Yes. I found Dr. Anderson extremely handsome, but there wasn't anything going on between us. I wouldn't utter a word to Joy about him holding me while I cried.

Nor would I tell her about the way he cradled me close to his chest with his strong arms wrapped around me, because those things meant nothing. They were acts of kindness. Plain and simple.

"Dr. Anderson came by to check on Saffi. He said he was making his rounds before leaving. I asked him about her still being asleep. That's it."

Unconvinced, Joy shook her head as she sat in the chair I'd vacated. "I know you're lying. I'm gonna let you have this one though. I'll find out eventually. I always do. Trust."

Happy for the break from her scrutiny, I continued my search through the contents of the duffle. I lined up various items on the rolling tray table I'd pushed against the wall.

Just as I rolled the table closer to the bed, Saffi started to stir. I'd planned to let her wake naturally until I noticed the way she thrashed about. I didn't want her to hurt herself or dislodge the IV. So, I took hold of the arm with the IV, rubbing her hair gently while making shushing noises.

"Shhh... It's okay, Baby. I'm here. You're safe. No one's going to hurt you now. Shhh..."

Joy mirrored my actions from the other side of the bed, rubbing Saffi's other arm. Popping her eyes open, Saffi's frantic gaze found me immediately. The tears came soon after.

Mindful of the IV and her injuries, I climbed into the bed beside her, gathered her to me as best as I could. I didn't say anything else, I simply let her cry.

"I was so scared, Aunt Cee-Cee." Sniffling, her voice slightly muffled as she pressed the unbandaged side of her face to my chest.

"I know, Baby. I know." I spoke to her softly, soothing her the only way I knew how. "It's over now. They can't hurt you anymore."

Once her tears stopped and the whimpers tapered off, I eased into the conversation I wanted, no *needed*, to have. I *had* to know who dared attack her and how it happened. She was blessed to not be more seriously injured. I was thankful she would recover fully. But I needed to know what happened.

"Saffi, baby, can you tell me what happened? Who hurt you, Sweetie?"

Don't ask me how I managed to keep the tension from my body and my voice when I asked such a loaded question. I had no idea how I wasn't still shaking with anger.

Using control I didn't know I possessed, I listened quietly as Saffi told me everything. I prompted gently when she stumbled through telling how she wanted to leave Grandma Vi's house, so she called me to come get her.

That part I knew. The next part I didn't know. I didn't know she didn't want to stay there because Dani had her new boyfriend at the house. Saffi didn't want to wait inside with them, so she walked down to Mrs. Simmons' house instead.

On the outside, I appeared calm. The eyes which met Joy's over Saffi's head were blazing with fury. Dani knew how I felt about Saffi being around strange men. With the way men paraded in and out of Dani's life, there was no way of knowing what kind of men they were.

Her man-meter was severely handicapped. The only good man she'd ever chosen was Saffi's biological father, Andres. Even though he didn't marry Dani, as she expected when she told him she was pregnant, he was a genuinely good guy.

Andres knew Dani didn't really want him. Maybe she wanted to recreate the fairy tale she thought our parents lived before our father died in the first Gulf War. Before our mother got hooked on drugs and we were placed into foster care. Our mom eventually overdosed after we'd been in the system for a couple of years.

Andres Colon was also a foster kid. That's how we met him. He lived in our second foster home, before our grandparents rescued us. Andres protected us from our foster parents' creepy biological son.

He was the one who helped me find the contact information for Grandma Viola, which eventually led to our grandparents finding us in the foster care system. He was a few years older and more knowledge-able. Without his help, who knows what would have happened to us.

Grandma and Grandpa were notified of our mom's death, but they had trouble navigating the foster care maze to find where we were placed. Six months after our mother died, our grandparents were awarded custody. They brought us to Atlanta to live with them.

Andres was Dani's one good choice. Every other man in her life since was a variation of the slimy dude at the club. The guy you avoided making eye contact with, hoping he didn't gather the courage to speak to you. Dani not only made eye contact with the slimy dude. She entertained the foolishness and lies far too often for me to be comfortable allowing Saffi to visit her when she had a boyfriend.

Had I known she had started up with someone new, I'd have come up with an activity preventing Saffi from visiting until I could go with her. According to the family grapevine, Dani actually had a job. When she was working, it usually meant she wasn't seeing anyone. She knew the only thing she'd get from me was access to live in our old home. Utilities and anything else she needed to support her lifestyle were on her.

So, when she was between benefactors, she picked up work. Usually, it was something that didn't require a high school diploma. Not because she didn't have one. She did. My sister wasn't interested in an actual career. She preferred jobs with high turnover rates so she could walk away whenever she pleased.

Dani was an exceptionally beautiful woman. Unfortunately, she'd bought into the myth which told her being pretty was all she had to be in life. Whoever she was with supported her financially. It was a requirement. We weren't raised with those beliefs. It's the value system she'd developed for herself somewhere along the way.

The relationships, using the term very loosely, never lasted longer than a year. They frequently ended with her rushing to pawn the jewelry and other trinkets in order to keep the lights on. Usually, she had more than one guy on the hook so she could stay flush in the event one of them dropped her because they'd had enough of feeding her ego with expensive gifts.

Pulling myself away from the anger burning in my eyes, I gently pressed Saffi for more information.

"Is that when someone jumped you—while you were walking to Mrs. Simmons' house?"

Nodding, she inhaled a shuddering breath. "Yes ma'am. Flossie and Nee-Nee." Moisture clung to Saffi's lashes from her crying jag. "They're older. Grown, or almost grown. They were at grandma's house when I first got there, but they left. I thought they were gone until they blocked my way on the sidewalk."

Frowning at this new information, I prompted her. "At grandma's? They're friends with Dani?"

Leaning away from me, settling herself on her pillow, Saffi hunched her shoulders. "I don't know if they're her friends. They didn't seem like they liked her. They mainly talked to each other before her boyfriend said it was time for them to go."

"So, the boyfriend told them to leave?" Him asking them to leave sounded strange to me. Why would he have anything to say to them about staying or going from a house he didn't own?

"Well... He didn't actually tell them to leave. He just reminded them of something they said they had to do. I think he said something about picking up sweets before work. He said they wouldn't want to be late." Saffi replied with frown lines creasing her brow.

Pretending my blood wasn't boiling, I urged her to continue. She was heavy on the details leading up to the attack. I could tell she was trying to avoid the more painful specifics of the actual event. I understood her reluctance, but I needed to know everything—including the painful things.

"Aunt Cee-Cee, I don't know what I did," her voice cracked with confusion. "I didn't even talk to them at grandma's house. Before they hit me, they kept saying I thought that I was too good. Too good for what? Then, they said some stuff about my body—"

Her slender frame trembled and I wrapped her in my arms again. Joy remained silent comfortingly patting Saffi's blanket covered leg.

"Sweetie, you're the nicest person I know. I'm certain you didn't do anything to them. Their problem was all in their mind. You can't blame yourself for things people make up about you in their own heads."

I kept my tone even. Inside, my blood was literally bubbling. "Go on, baby. Tell me the rest."

"I tried to walk around them, but they kept blocking me. Then, one of them grabbed my phone. When I tried to get it back, they started hitting me.

I tried to get away. I tried really hard. I just couldn't get them off me. They took all my stuff. After they started hitting me, I didn't try to stop them from taking the stuff. They kept hitting me even when I let them have everything."

The wailing quality of her voice broke my heart while simultaneously firing my blood.

"I'm not sure who did what after that, other than I know Flossie was the one who cut me. I didn't know she had a knife. She cut me so fast, I didn't know I'd been cut until I saw the blood on my hands. I don't remember much else after seeing the blood. The next thing I remember was being in the ambulance."

Retelling her story brought the tears again, so I shushed her. Gathering her close to me, I held her—rocking her gently. I resolved myself to stay right there, curled beside her in the bed, holding her in my arms as long as she needed in order for her to feel safe again. Her safety and well-being were my priorities.

The morning progressed with the nurse coming in to check Saffi's dressings and valve port site. Afterwards, food service brought in breakfast which actually looked good. For hospital food. I guess it tasted as good as it looked, because Saffi devoured it. After which, she promptly fell asleep.

I spent the first part of Saffi's nap getting her hair back into some semblance of order. Fixing her hair reminded me of when she was a toddler. She couldn't stand for her tresses to be combed. I'd style or braid it while she slept to make the process easier on both of us.

I was flooded with memories of Saffi stretched across my lap as I braided her hair into intricate styles with pretty beads. Styles similar to the way my mom had braided mine and Dani's hair when we were young.

Those days, of her braiding our hair, were way before the drugs took control, turning her into a different person. Since Grandma Vi wasn't one to spend time on cute hairstyles, the bulk of Saffi's grooming fell to me from the moment we brought her home from the hospital.

Joy kept me company for a little while longer, then left to get some rest. She promised to come back later to allow me a chance to get a break from my bedside vigil.

I assured her it wasn't necessary. I knew she wouldn't listen. The bond we'd developed while pledging the same sorority in college was stronger than most. So, I knew she would come back and force me to rest if necessary.

Scant minutes after Joy left, Gene returned bearing gifts for Saffi along with more food for me. It was close to mid-day, but I wasn't hungry. Gene's entrance roused Saffi from her nap. I left the straight-backed chair beside the bed. I sat on the sofa near the window, giving Gene the space closest to his *Lady Bug*.

While he entertained Saffi, I stared out the window—looking, yet not really seeing anything in particular. I halfway listened to their conversation. It mostly served as background noise to my thoughts. I knew he wouldn't ask her about the attack. I'd filled him in through a series of texts after Saffi told us what happened.

My fingers itched to grab my phone and text Nikki. Armed with actual names, I formulated a plan. A few things needed to be set into motion first. Logically, I knew I should contact the police and update the detective. I knew. I simply wasn't ready yet.

A part of me, the part fully controlling my actions, wanted to make sure my baby's attackers felt her pain ten-fold. It wasn't guaranteed the police would even try to find them, let alone arrest them so they'd have to face the punishment for their crimes.

Giving in to the urge, I snatched up my phone quickly tapping out a message to Nikki. I gave her the names of the tricks who thought it was ok to put their hands on my baby. She didn't know anyone named Flossie or Nee-Nee, but she said she'd find out. Nikki had connections. If they could be found, she'd find them.

While I was texting her, a thought dropped into my brain like a two-ton hammer. *Motherfucker!* I mentally kicked myself for not thinking of it sooner. How did I forget I'd put a tracker in the designer bag Saffi had with her yesterday?

I wasn't worried about someone stealing the little purse. It was a thing. Things were replaceable. My concern was finding Saffi in an emergency situation. She loved that little purse, so she was never far from it.

It was a pretty sure bet she'd have it with her at all times. Besides the tracker in the purse, there was also the *Find-My-Device* feature on the tablet and phone. Batteries of electronics weren't dependable. So, I'd slipped the trackers into the protective covers for the tablet and cellphone.

I pulled up the tracking app on my phone. Using the app to locate the two women was a long shot. If they had any sense, they disabled the tracking feature on the electronic devices. But, they wouldn't know to look for a separate tracker. At least, I hoped they still had at least one of Saffi's things with them.

Once again, my conscious nudged me to contact the police. I knew I should bring them into the loop. I squashed the thought immediately. Instead, I focused on editing the app filters to show only the items I wanted to see. One could call me paranoid. I didn't care. I'd placed trackers in quite a few of Saffi's most prized possessions.

It paid to be friends with Nikki. Security specialists could procure just about anything. She'd supplied me with stuff not currently available to the general public. Her protectiveness toward Saffi rivaled my own.

I didn't put the trackers in Saffi's things because I didn't trust her. Not at all. Little black girls were going missing at alarming rates. I wanted every tool available to me if my child ever became one of those missing children.

Quickly, I silenced the notifications on my phone to not draw attention to myself with the dings and beeps. If either Saffi or Gene bothered to look my way, my posture alone would've given me away. I'd gone from looking out of the window semi-reclined on the love seat, to sitting straight up intently focused on the device in my hands.

The appearance of three little red dots on the cellphone screen sent adrenaline rushing through my body and my pulse pounding in my ears. Swiping my fingers across the screen, I zoomed in closer to see the location of the dots.

I saw two of the dots overlapped. So, those items were in the same place, while one was a distance away. Double tapping on the lone dot, I pulled up the tracking information. It was the tablet. It looked to be about a mile away from the old neighborhood.

Swinging my legs off the small sofa, I slipped my feet into my shoes. Modifying my original plan on the fly, I decided to check out the location of the tablet. I was almost certain Flossie and Nee-Nee hadn't kept it. I'd bet money they didn't think an e-reader was worth their time, so they tossed it. They probably still had the purse and phone though. They were high dollar items.

Yet another clue to their ignorance. If they had half a brain, they would have at least tried to pawn it. Saffi's e-reader wasn't a run of the mill, off the shelf gadget. Before Alanna gave it to her, she configured it with a crap ton of memory. The battery she installed kept the device powered for weeks at a time from one charging session.

I'm no hacker, so I wouldn't begin to know how to search for devices that were powered off. But, I was confident I could use the pings from the *Find-My-Device* feature when I got closer, to narrow down the search area. Silently thanking Alanna's genius, I stood up.

"Gene?" I pulled my cousin's attention away from entertaining his favorite little human.

"Yeah?" He looked at me with questioning eyes.

"Do you think you could stay with Saffi for a little while? I need to go home for a bit."

I didn't know how, but I managed to keep the anxiousness from my voice and a calm expression on my face.

"Yeah..."

There was hesitation in his voice as he pierced me with his direct gaze. Reaching into his pocket, he passed me the keys to my car. I'd completely forgotten he'd driven me to the hospital in my own car the previous evening.

God... Our arrival to the hospital felt so long ago, when it had been less than twenty-four hours since I'd walked through the doors of the Emergency Room.

"Thanks."

Lifting the keys from his open palm, I listened as he told me where he'd parked the vehicle. Hefting my purse onto my shoulder, I walked around Saffi's bed giving her a kiss.

"I'll be back in a little while, baby girl."

Studiously, I avoided eye contact with Gene as I walked away. I felt his assessing stare as I left the room.

It seemed to take an eternity to make it through the maze of hallways in the hospital to the parking structure before I located my mid-sized SUV. I'd no sooner placed my phone on the charging pad between the seats, when it began to ring.

I saw Gene's name on the console display screen. *Damnit.* I guess I wasn't as circumspect as I thought. I pressed the button on the steering wheel to answer the call. Putting the car in gear, I pulled away from the parking spot.

"Hey Gene. What's up? Did I forget something? Or did you need me to bring you something when I come back?"

I spit the questions in rapid succession hoping to derail what I knew was coming.

"Nah, Step... Don't play me. Where are you really going?"

Ignoring my questions, he left no doubt he didn't believe me when I said I needed to go home for a bit.

"Gene..."

"Don't play me Step. Saffi can't hear me. I stepped out for the nurse to check her bandages and change them. Spill." The hard edge to his voice left no room for argument. Audibly drawing in a deep breath, I released it slowly.

"Fine.... I really *am* going home. I'm just going to make a stop on Crawford first." I confessed a portion of my plan hoping to appease my over-protective cousin.

"Crawford? What's on Crawford?"

"I think Saffi's tablet is there." Closing one eye, I shrank back in my seat when Gene's voice boomed through the speaker.

"WHAT THE FUCK!" In the background, I heard his steps as he presumably moved farther away from the door to Saffi's room. "Are you serious right now? You took your ass out of here going to look for a damn *tablet*. BY. YOURSELF?!"

"Gene, it's not like that. Please just listen, ok? I didn't say anything because I don't expect there to be any problems. I used the *Find my Device* app on my phone to find it. I think they tossed it in a ditch or something, because it's on a stretch of Crawford where there's nothing except empty lots and woods."

Concentrating on driving, I stopped trying to convince Gene he didn't need to freak out. I patiently waited for his response. I'd fudged the truth a little, but I was mostly honest with him. *Mostly.*

I heard his harsh breathing on the other end of the line. He didn't try to talk me out of what I was doing though. We both knew he couldn't talk me out of it; however, there was always the chance he would call someone and they'd show up to watch my back.

I really didn't think it was necessary. I wouldn't deviate so far from my plan I'd confront someone right now. Flossie and Nee-Nee weren't the sharpest pencils in the box. They'd kept the status symbol items tossing the item they deemed worthless.

"If anything, and I mean ANYTHING, looks suspect you don't step foot out of the car. You pick up the phone and you call me. Immediately. Do you hear me?"

I practically heard his teeth grinding through the phone. In my mind's eye, I saw the fiery expression on his face.

"I promise, Cuz. If I see anyone or anything that's not right, I won't put myself in danger. I'll call."

I assured him, relieved he wasn't pressing the issue further. I promised to stay safe and actually go home to rest after my stop on Crawford. I disconnected the call turning the vehicle towards the less than affluent side of the city.

I was hopeful I'd at least be able to get Saffi one of her items back. Not for the materialistic aspect, purely because of the symbolism of the device itself. It was a source of joy for her. I wanted her to have something normal right now.

It didn't take long to reach the section of Crawford Street I was looking for. It was just as I thought. The area was basically an open field on a stretch of road right before an on-ramp to get onto the interstate. Finding a safe place to pull over, I guided my SUV to the side of the road.

There wasn't much traffic to speak of, which was fine with me. Too many people would put me on edge. I switched from the tracking app to the one Alanna put on my phone which I never thought I'd need. It pinged the tablet causing it to emit a series of beeps.

In no time at all, I found the reader in the high grass, completely unscathed. Thankful for Alanna's foresight and the apparent stupidity of Saffi's attackers, I got back into my vehicle and headed home.

~

I entered the house through the door from the garage which opened into the combination mudroom and storage area. Taking my shoes off, I walked in farther. My focus was on getting to my bedroom to change and gather what I needed.

As I was driving home, Nikki called to let me know her sources had come back with information on Flossie and Nee-Nee. I expected her to come by soon. I wanted to be prepared.

Shucking my clothes, I quickly showered. Then, I tossed on a black t-shirt and cargo pants. I grabbed my boots from the closet, but didn't put them on. While I was gathering my supplies, the doorbell rang. I checked the camera feed before I opened the front door to let in my childhood friend Nichelle.

Giving me a quick hug, she launched right into telling me what she'd dug up about Tweedledumb and Tweedledumber.

"Girl! Those grown ass women who attacked Peanut work at the Gold Tip as strippers."

She moved through the foyer, entering the kitchen and walked over to the bar top style island.

"I still don't know how they know Dani, because even when she's working, she doesn't strip. You know she thinks she's too good to be a stripper. She normally works out a temp agency as an office clerk or some shit, right?"

I nodded in agreement. Dani didn't do hard work. No matter what people thought, stripping wasn't easy. It was physically demanding. So, it didn't make Dani's short list of potential jobs.

Reaching into the satchel thrown across her shoulder, Nikki pulled out a laptop. Placing it on the granite counter top, she opened it up.

Sliding her six-foot frame onto a barstool, she turned the laptop so we both could see the screen.

Waking the device with the press of a button, she tapped a few keys, and swiped her finger over the mousepad. Photos populated the display. I leaned closer to get a better look.

Pointing her finger to a spot on the screen, she explained, "This one is Flossie and this one is Nee-Nee. Their real names are Francine and Kanesha."

I took in the women on the screen. They couldn't be more than twenty-five, from the looks of them. Even though they looked young, it was obvious they'd lived hard lives. It was all over their faces. So... these are the people who thought it was okay to attack a child?

"Any idea where they live or hangout?" I asked.

"Nah, according to Junebug, they normally work Saturday nights. So, I know where they will be in..." she checked her watch, "eight hours or so."

"Cool. Did you get a chance to talk to Pootie about borrowing Safari?" I asked her while going to the refrigerator to grab a bottle of water. Holding it up to her, I gestured silently offering her a bottle. She waved me off.

"Yeah. That's how I got here. I took him my car and picked up his before coming over. He made me promise not to hurt his baby."

A smirk tipped up one side of her lips. We both thought the way he loved his car was funny.

"He doesn't have to worry about us hurting his baby. I'll even make sure to get it the deluxe detail when we're done with it."

"The deluxe detail?" Nikki questioned me with raised eyebrows.

"What the hell do you have planned to make a **deluxe** detail necessary? That shit costs two hundred dollars on the low end."

She closed the lid on the laptop giving me her complete attention. "I'm listening."

I stood across the island from her, pulling her into my thoughts. Together, we planned. The logical, law-abiding side of me knew I should contact the authorities. I **should** use the business card I got from Officer Gregory. I **should** give the police the names of Saffi's attackers along with the rest of the information Nikki uncovered.

I knew all of this, nevertheless I didn't do it. Instead, I planned with Nikki. We put together my Kick-Ass kit and stored it in the back of Safari—Pootie's 1996 Impala.

Once we finished prepping, Nikki left and I finally listened to my body and went up to my bedroom for a much-needed nap. I texted Gene to make sure he was still okay staying at the hospital while I rested. After getting confirmation he was fine with the arrangement, I set an alarm. I crashed face first onto my California King platform bed.

Chapter Six

JIAN

I entered the hospital ready to start the second night of my night shift rotation. Surprisingly, I slept during the day, only after I tired myself out with a quick workout. It probably wasn't the best idea to exercise after the meal I'd eaten, but I was too keyed up to sleep when I initially made it home.

My one big splurge when I purchased my Buckhead condo was my home gym. I figured if I was going to spend the kind of cash one had to spend to buy a home in the area, I was damned sure going to outfit it in a way suitable to my lifestyle.

Living in Buckhead put my daily commute to thirty minutes one way, on good traffic days. On bad traffic days, it took so long, I considered relocating, or purchasing a second property closer to the hospital.

My need to tire myself out in order to get some sleep wasn't related to my body's adjustment to working the night shift. I'd long ago developed a routine which allowed me to adapt to those quarterly rotations. No, it wasn't the night shift. I had to wear my body out to force my brain to stop tormenting me with thoughts of Stephanie Barker.

I'd never felt such an instant connection with anyone. If I'm being honest, my attraction to her was distracting, although it appeared to be completely one-sided. Direct hit to my otherwise healthy ego.

I got the impression she wasn't really thinking of me the same way. Given how we met, I really didn't expect her to have me on her mind. Not the way I was thinking of her.

Shaking my head, I mentally chastised myself. Why was this particular woman tying me in knots when I knew next to nothing about her? It wasn't logical, except logic didn't apply to intense attraction.

Greeting the night nurse, I checked through my patients' charts and reviewed the board for surgical assignments. I didn't normally schedule nighttime surgeries, however in emergency situations, just like with Chloe, there was a chance I'd have a surgery scheduled during the night shift.

At the start of my shift, I purposely performed my rounds to make sure she was the last patient I saw. I knew the way I did rounds wasn't a typical surgeon's routine. When I worked nights, I made two rounds checking on my patients following up with anyone who may be experiencing difficulty. I looked in on them to see if there was anything we could do to ease their discomfort. If time allowed, I'd go by the surgical ICU and Cardiac Unit to check on the nurses.

Rapping softly on the door, I entered Chloe's room to see her awake, sitting upright in bed, with her aunt semi-reclined on the small sofa next to the room's lone window.

"Good evening, Little Miss Barker. It's good to see you awake. I'm Dr. Jian Anderson. I'm just following up to see how you're feeling." I moved farther into the room, made eye contact with Stephanie giving her a quick nod.

Chloe's brow wrinkled. I could tell she was struggling with what confused most people when I gave them my name. My Chinese features didn't mesh with my very Anglo sounding last name. I debated on whether to broach the subject myself, but she asked outright.

"Dr. Anderson? I don't understand. How can your name be Anderson? You look Asian-American. I didn't know Asians had last names like Anderson."

"Chloe Sofia!" Her aunt started to chastise her. I held up a hand to stop her before she got started.

"It's okay. She's not the first, and probably won't be the last. I'm not offended." I assured her.

From looking at my features, I was, very obviously, of Asian descent. I appreciated her not assuming my ethnic heritage. It's surprising considering most children, if they even notice, weren't nearly as tactful when they approached the subject.

Her curiosity was completely normal. Her use of the term *'Asian-American'* meant she'd been exposed to other cultures enough to be sensitive to making assumptions.

I'd met adults who assumed every Asian looking person they encountered was Chinese or of Chinese descent. It happened to be true in my case, but they didn't know that from looking at me. Culturally insensitive people called every person, who looked remotely like me, Chinese.

Turning back to Chloe, I pointed to my face answering her question. "I know. I know. This face doesn't scream *'Anderson'*. I was adopted by a couple of really great people when I was a baby.

My birth mother was Chinese. My adoptive parents are Caucasian. Hence the Chinese first name and the not-so-Chinese-sounding last name."

I smiled at her expressive face. I could tell she'd soaked up the information and had follow up questions. But, a quick glance at her aunt seemed to deter her from asking the other queries she diligently tried to suppress.

"Any more questions?" I asked. She opened her mouth, her burning questions threatened to spill forward, but she snapped it closed without uttering a single word.

I smiled leaning against the foot rail. "Anything?" I prodded. "Ok... Going, going, gone. Now, let's get down to business,"

I chuckled shifting the subject to asking her specific questions. Donning gloves, I checked the port and listened to her breathing. Everything looked and sounded good. She was progressing well enough that it made me comfortable scheduling the removal of the port tonight.

Taking off the gloves with a slight pop, I informed them of my plan. I was proud of myself for resisting the ever-persistent urge to be closer to and touch Stephanie. She'd left the little sofa to stand on the other side of the bed. So close, yet so far...

While I was proud of myself for fighting my baser instincts, I was disappointed that I couldn't touch her. I didn't question my pull towards her; I just wasn't prepared for the lightning speed nor the strength of my desire.

Going back to the foot of the bed, I rested a hand on the rail. "Any last questions? Anything about what to expect when we take the port out?"

In my short interaction with an awake Chloe, her inquisitive nature was evident. She had an air of intelligence about her. I made a point to encourage a child's curiosity and learning whenever possible. I had a feeling about Chloe. Behind those big brown eyes, I could almost see the wheels turning in her head.

I didn't have a long wait before the questions began to tumble out. The quality of her questions and her ability to understand the terms I was using was impressive. According to her chart, she was twelve years old; however, her level of understanding and follow up questions were well beyond a normal twelve-year-old's capacity.

When I was sure we'd exhausted all of her questions, I prepared to leave, reminding them once again of what was going to happen next. "Once I have a firm time, the nurse will be back to prep you."

I'd just reached the door when Stephanie seized my attention with a parting remark. For the majority of my visit, she'd remained silent allowing Chloe to ask her questions. It appeared, so long as the pre-teen didn't venture to an area she deemed out of bounds, she didn't feel the need to speak.

"Dr. Anderson, thank you for taking the time to speak with us and explaining everything so we could be at ease. I really appreciate it." I let her slightly scratchy voice roll over me while I worked to maintain my professionalism and focus.

As if her aunt's statement reminded her, Chloe piped up, "Yeah, Dr. J. Thanks for answering all of my questions. You're pretty chill."

It felt like my smile literally stretched from one ear to the other. I'd just earned a nickname. A pretty cool nickname—I'm surprised I'd gone this long without someone slapping the moniker on me.

Leaving on a high note, I exited the room. At the nurse's station, I put in the orders for the bedside removal of the port making sure the appropriate staff was available to assist.

I could've set it up in radiology. The procedure was commonly performed at the patient's bed. Honestly, I kind of liked the idea of Stephanie seeing me at work. However, as lovely as she was, I wouldn't put Chloe at risk simply to impress her—no matter how much the cocky side of me wanted to show her a small part of my capabilities.

With somewhat of a plan in place for the evening, I tried to keep my mind on task. It didn't work, since my thoughts kept going back to Stephanie. The scent of the lightly floral perfume she wore tickled my nose, making me want to search out every spot she'd sprayed the fragrance. Search them out and kiss each and every one.

It wasn't even that she was dressed to get attention. The t-shirt and cargo pants she wore were strictly utilitarian. No frills. It still couldn't hide her generous curves. Those curves were my undoing. They're the reason I had to leave to get my mind back on my responsibilities.

When I returned to the quiet of my office, I sat down to review a few notes and charts. Instead of working, I found myself replaying the conversation with Chloe and Stephanie. Doing so made me think of a time in my life when I was much like Chloe—innocent. The way others viewed me, the juxtaposition between my last name and my obvious Chinese heritage, wasn't even a blip on my radar.

Sixteen years ago

I stood in the foyer of the frat house with Asher at my side. Being a part of the same pledge class, we'd been inseparable since freshman year. Despite him being a jock and me being a very studious pre-med student, we'd bonded with one another in a way we hadn't with the other members of our class. Now, in the first semester of our junior year, there was no one I trusted more.

Frozen in place, we stood just outside of the large common room trying to wrap our minds around the conversation we heard going on through the open doorway.

"I told you man, if it were up to me, I wouldn't have even given him an invitation during rush week," Paul Phillips could be heard clearly speaking through the open space.

Somehow, without knowing how the conversation started, I knew my entire relationship with my frat brother was about to change. Paul had never warmed to me or Ash.

Even though Ash was a star athlete, he was a scholarship student. He didn't come from money like me and many of the other guys in the prestigious fraternity. To Paul, Ash not having family money somehow made him undesirable for membership. I'd spent many nights of our pledge period talking Ash out of kicking Paul's ass.

After the pledge period was over, Paul still made little comments about his financial status designed to get under Ash's skin. At least he did until Ash lifted him up by his neck with one meaty hand and had a 'conversation' with him. Ash let Paul know the fraternal bond wouldn't protect him from the ass whipping he was campaigning so hard to get.

I did nothing to intervene because Paul wasn't my favorite person. Besides, the confrontation was long overdue. Despite his financial situation, Ash had never missed, or been late, on even one payment of the insane fees we were asked to pay monthly in order to be considered members in good standing.

As for why he had an issue with me, I couldn't say. He didn't throw verbal jabs at me; he was just cold and standoffish. If I had to guess, I would say the reason he didn't go further is because I was a legacy. My father was a member of the same fraternity while he attended this university. He remained a large donor following graduation.

So, when I heard Paul through the door saying he didn't want someone in the frat, my mind automatically went with the assumption he was speaking of one of us. I could hear grumbling in the room, but no one actually spoke against Paul's statement.

"I'm with Paul," Dustin Hansen's voice joined the discussion over the mumbles. "It's bad enough we had to rush a Ching Chong. If he didn't have the Anderson name and money behind him, him and his meathead, trailer trash buddy would have both been left out of the pledge class."

Dustin's statement was confirmation they were talking about me. Heat rushed to my face. I felt my skin reddening. Up to this point in my life, I hadn't really experienced overt racism, nonetheless I recognized the hateful term Dustin used.

I looked to my right meeting the eyes of my best friend, who shook his head at me. He held up a hand and mouthed, "Not yet."

I was surprised *he* wanted *me* to wait. I was usually the calm one. Ash was quicker to anger. This was a change. Despite his warning, I took a step forward—only to be stopped by a large hand in the center of my chest.

"Wait," He stated quietly.

"What is it you expect me to do guys?" Carter Jones, our chapter president asked. "It's not like I can kick him out for dating a black girl. That shit wouldn't fly, even in this frat."

Now I understood why Ash wanted me to wait. Through the haze of my anger, I heard Carter's words. The understanding of what was happening fell on me like a ton of bricks.

The frat had a party the night before. I'd brought the girl I was seeing with me. In truth, McKenna Frost was more than the girl I was seeing. At least I hoped she was more than just the girl I was seeing.

She was beautiful, kind and intelligent. She was everything. I was head over heels for her. I was trying to convince her we should date exclusively; especially since we'd already met each other's parents one weekend during a campus visit.

"The hell you can't!" Paul yelled. "It's bad enough we have to deal with him being here and calling him *'brother'*, but he goes and brings a nig—" Paul's words are cut off when his eyes landed on me entering the room.

For all of his bravado while it was just him, and some of the other white members of the frat in the room, he visibly shrank within himself when we walked through the doorway. Part of me wanted him to keep talking; wanted him to continue spewing his venom so I could use my fists to shove the hateful words down his throat. Fortunately for him, he was smart enough to know when to shut up.

Holding his hands up in front of him, Carter stepped between me and Paul, breaking the heated glare I was giving my former *brother*. After hearing what he had to say about me and McKenna, there was no way I could still consider him my brother—if he ever was.

"Now...Anderson, Peterson, let's just calm down. I don't know what you think you heard, but let's just not get ahead of ourselves here." Carter's words reeked of insincerity.

Eyes blazing with hurt and anger, I didn't attempt to hide, I spit out, "What I *think* I heard? I'm not deaf. I know exactly what I heard. I also know what I didn't hear."

Pointing to Paul and Dustin, I continued, "What I heard was these two assholes spewing racist bullshit. You want to know what I didn't hear? I didn't hear you nor anyone else in this room tell them that shit wasn't okay."

If I was holding out hope that Carter or one of the other guys would dispute my statement, for any of them to say they didn't agree with what our so-called brothers had spouted, I would've been sorely disappointed. A deafening silence dropped over the room.

"And for the record," Ash's deep voice cut across the silence. "That shit isn't okay. It's disgusting and ignorant."

I didn't think I needed his assurance; however, I experienced a rush of relief knowing the person I considered my best friend didn't share their beliefs.

It appeared Dustin found the courage Paul lost, because he pulled himself up to his full height like it was supposed to mean something. My guess. He thought he could intimidate me with his size. Yeah, he was a couple of inches taller than me, but shit like height didn't matter in the heat of the moment. I was furious.

Looking at me while speaking to Carter, Dustin puffed out his chest. "Why the fuck are you trying to back away now, Carter? You know we didn't want this slant eye in our brotherhood to begin with. Then he goes and brings a nig—"

I slammed my fist into his face, stopping the rest of his hate vomit. I followed the punch to the face with another to his torso, knocking the breath out of him. After I robbed Dustin of his breath, all hell broke loose in the frat house common room.

Punches were thrown, bodies flew around the room. Furniture was left in useless pieces. Ash and I stood back-to-back like warriors, cutting down the young men who'd once pledged to be our brothers.

When all was said and done, Ash and I stood over the moaning bodies of our so-called brothers. A few scrapes and bruises littered our bodies. Overall, we were virtually unscathed.

Breathing heavily, I turned to look at my best friend. His shirt was pulled from his jeans. It was ripped from the collar mid-way down his chest. I didn't need to look at myself to know my clothing was in similar condition.

"This isn't over," Dustin moaned into the carpet.

"Yes, it is." My voice sorrowful in the aftermath of the melee.

Shooting Carter's semi-conscious form a look of disgust, I told him, "I'm out. I want nothing else to do with this *brotherhood* or any of you ever again."

Reaching into my reserve of control, I resisted the urge to kick Dustin to punctuate my statement. I stumbled a little when Ash smacked me on the back with the catcher's mitt masquerading as his right hand. "Let's go. The air in here stinks."

Present

I blinked hard sitting back in my chair. How long was I lost in my memories? The day I broke ties with my fraternity brothers was the day when I realized what a sheltered life I'd led.

Until I experienced direct, overt, racism from my supposed brothers, I'd lived my life the way my white parents raised me—completely oblivious to racial biases. For people like Paul and Dustin, I wasn't then, nor had I ever been considered one of them—white.

My racial identity always separated us. I didn't see it before that day, because my parents had raised me to believe race wasn't important. For them, a person's character was the most important part of who they were. Their race was incidental.

As it turned out, by trying to create an environment where I never felt ostracized, they'd left me vulnerable to people who didn't feel or believe the same way. I didn't have the tools to navigate overt racism, because I was insulated from it by their wealth and status.

The day I was forced to truly see myself as an Asian man was eye opening. It was tough. But, in actuality, my path to self-discovery really occurred after the incident. It happened when I spoke to McKenna about it.

She pointed out how I never associated with people who looked like me. The majority of the people I spent my time with were white. My experiences were those of a person of privilege because of my white parents. Their affluence kept me protected from most of the ugly parts of being a person of color living in the United States.

McKenna and I didn't make it as a couple, but we remained friendly. Her involvement with the Black Student Alliance led me to seek out a similar group for Asian students on campus.

If not for my abrupt exit from the white fraternity social scene, I wouldn't have sought out such a group. Through the Asian Student Alliance (ASA) I was put on a course to learning more about my heritage.

I really found myself as an individual due to the ASA. I attended meetings and found another organization which held quarterly gatherings allowing adoptees, such as myself, opportunities to meet with other people of the same or similar cultures. In the gatherings we had a chance to learn things we couldn't learn from our non-Asian adoptive parents.

I'd met some really great people through those gatherings, including another close friend, Daisuke Sano. He was there in the capacity as a type of mentor—teaching others about his Japanese heritage. He and I got closer through the ASA and kept in touch after Med school. Those douche-bag frat boys actually did me a favor. I probably would've gone the rest of my college life without truly finding myself if they hadn't revealed their true colors that fateful day.

Scrubbing a hand down my face, I tried to clear my head. I hadn't allowed those memories to occupy my thoughts for such a long while. Checking the time, I buckled down to finish updating my charts. The removal of Chloe's port was the only procedure on my scheduled for the night and I didn't anticipate any issues with it.

Chapter Seven

STEPHANIE

When I woke from my nap, I gathered myself and went back to the hospital. Before I left, I called to check in with Gene. I learned he'd taken a break himself to have a late lunch with his wife Charmaine. In his place, Joy stayed with Saffi. I was grateful beyond words for how those two stepped in to help me.

Nikki had the bag I'd packed earlier, so I carried only my soft-sided sling purse. I'd packed an extra set of clothes in the Kick-Ass kit I'd given her.

My conscience pinged me again. I ignored it. Again. I had no intention of relying on the police. They probably weren't even looking for the people who jumped my baby. Since, I hadn't heard a word from the detectives who were supposed to look into the incident, it was more than a possibility.

At the hospital, I considered my options for when to slip away without arousing suspicion. I needed to give Nikki a timeframe. We'd agreed she would pick me up.

The time passed without much incident until the shift change and Dr. Anderson brought his fine self in to check on Saffi. I'll admit, he was a welcome distraction. I wouldn't tell Joy she was right about the potential spark between us. I wasn't ready to concede to her just yet.

Since the initial stress of Saffi's situation had dissipated, I looked at him to really appreciate him as a man—not just as the surgeon who saved my baby's life.

Some might say he didn't save her life. They might also say her condition wasn't serious, and the medical staff would've found the issue eventually. I chose to believe he saved her life. He had my undying gratitude for his part in keeping her on this side of heaven with me.

When he walked into the room, I was no longer seeing through a veil of anxiety. I was able to sit on the little sofa enjoying the view of excellent man candy. My gaze drifted over his tall, lithe physique. Even in a white coat and scrubs, his lean muscles were obvious. My stare drifted to his hands. They were...Goodness!

I jerked to attention when Saffi's voice penetrated my daydreaming. Did she just ask him how he could have a name like *Anderson* when he looked Asian? I wanted to fall through the damn floor.

"Chloe Sofia!"

Embarrassed, I literally wanted the floor to open up and swallow me whole. Kids were inquisitive. Saffi was so mature about so many things I sometimes forgot she was still very much a child with a child's curiosity about the unknown. She wanted to know, so she shot her shot.

I wondered the same thing myself. Only, as a tactful adult, I figured it wasn't my place to ask. Thankfully, he wasn't offended. After I recovered from utter embarrassment, I listened raptly to his response. Realizing he was more amused than anything else allowed me to relax.

After he left, I didn't get on Saffi again about being nosey and insensitive to other people's cultures. Her questions really weren't disrespectful. They simply caught me off guard.

Dr. Anderson scheduling to remove the port gave me the time I needed to meet Nikki. Certain he'd sedate Saffi again, I figured she'd be asleep following the procedure.

At such a late hour, she should sleep through the rest of the night. Aside from the nurses making their rounds to check on her, no one else would come to her room. I sent Nikki a quick text message receiving an almost immediate response.

~

Hours later, after making sure Saffi was sleeping deeply, I found myself sitting in Pootie's Impala in a darkened corner of a parking lot. Nikki sat in the driver's seat as we waited for Flossie and Nee-Nee to leave the strip club.

Since we'd last spoken, Nikki had found out Dani's so-called boyfriend owned a few of the clubs around the city. Those two tricks rotated between them on various nights. They didn't just work at the Gold Tip. On Saturday, they worked at Club Peek-a-Boo.

According to Nikki's source, they didn't normally stay until closing time. It was a little after midnight; so, we expected them to leave soon. For whatever reason, they were always together—like they were joined at the hip or something.

I checked my app confirming the dots representing Saffi's purse and phone were directly atop the Peek-a-Boo on the map. It was less than an hour, yet it felt like we sat there forever before the two women exited the club.

The light over the exit was bright enough to recognize them from the pictures. They still wore their performance make-up. Although they no longer sported their stripper gear, what they were wearing didn't leave much to the imagination.

A few of the men hanging around outside called out to them. They responded, but didn't stop to engage in conversation. Good. The sooner they left, the sooner we could move on to the next stage of the plan. Giving me my wish, they got into a compact car and drove away.

Nikki pulled out of the lot to follow them, taking care to keep her distance. Since they were dumb enough to still have Saffi's phone and purse, I tracked them using the app. So, we didn't have to keep them in sight.

I couldn't tell where they were heading as we moved away from the congested area around the club. Reaching into the bag between my feet, I pulled out the two pair of gloves and the black ski masks I'd stashed inside. I pulled one mask over my hair passing the other to Nikki.

They made a series of turns before finally coming to a stop. We pulled onto the street in time to see them parked in front of a bungalow style home on a quiet road. This part of the plan was a little shaky. If we wanted to avoid being seen, which we did, approaching them in the open was out.

Stopping a few houses down, Nikki turned off the headlights, but kept the car idling while she pulled the ski mask over the mass of kinky coils she'd tamed into a low bun.

"What do you think?" she asked while we watched the vehicle ahead of us.

"I'm not sure." I responded. "We might have to scrap it if they pick up someone else. If it looks like they're going to split up, we'll take them separately. Hell, divide and conquer might actually be better." I thought of the possibilities while we both kept our eyes on the stationary vehicle.

They were still sitting there. Neither had exited the vehicle. The taillights gleamed brightly onto the otherwise darkened street. Just when we thought we'd have to scrap the plan, the passenger door flew open and a woman exited, slamming the door behind her.

She was part way up the short walkway leading to the front door before I could tell who it was. It was Nee-Nee. She'd turned back toward the street allowing the light of a lone streetlight to illuminate her face.

Making agitated gestures, she yelled at Flossie, who remained inside the car. Between the distance and rolled up windows, I couldn't hear what was being said. It was obvious they were having a disagreement. The argument was possibly the reason Flossie didn't immediately pull off when Nee-Nee got out of the car and walked away.

Lowering my window, I strained to hear what was being said. "Bitch! Your dumb ass don't know nothing. I told you what we need to do, but you still think that mufukka shit don't stank." Flossie yelled through the open car window.

Flinging an arm out in Nee-Nee's direction she continued, "Take yo ass on in the house then. I'm done. I know what the fuck I bring to the table. I ain't gotta keep putting up with this shit."

"Fuck you, Flossie! You think you know everything. Vincente said—"

"Fuck what Vincente said! He's a fucking liar!" Flossie yelled out. The engine of the car revved as she pulled away from the curb.

"What do you want me to do, Step?" Nikki asked, her hand poised to put the car in gear and follow the retreating taillights. Quickly, I checked the tracker observing one of them moving away from the location, while the other was stationary.

"Follow the car." I quickly decided. The house Nee-Nee entered had an open carport. No other vehicles were parked outside and her only apparent mode of transportation had just driven away. She was most likely stationary for the remainder of the night. Flossie was mobile.

Steering the Impala down the quiet street, Nikki asked, "So what do you think they were arguing about?"

"If I had to guess, I'd say Flossie has reached the point where she doesn't want to live the way they're living anymore—whatever that is. Who knows?" I shrugged.

"Since they're separated now, what do you wanna do?" She asked.

My adrenaline had spiked when it looked like we were close to actually putting hands on the duo, and the ski mask was getting hot. Tugging at where it rested on my forehead, I kept watch on the tracker giving Nikki turn instructions while we tossed around potential strategies.

When the dot stopped moving, we were in a different, much less homey, residential area. I looked around at the dilapidated apartment buildings with their pothole littered parking lot. The only similarity to the bungalow was the absence of decent lighting.

Parking several spaces away from the compact, donning our gloves and pulling our masks completely over our faces, we got out of the car. Hurrying along the back side of the other parked cars, we closed in on our target.

Oblivious to her surroundings, Flossie sat in the vehicle with the overhead light on. Nikki and I crouched behind the trunks of the two SUVs Flossie was dumb enough to park the compact car between.

She'd unknowingly given us perfect cover from prying eyes. We didn't fear anyone actually reporting anything they saw in this neighborhood. Finally, she stepped out of the vehicle. Peering at her from my vantage point, I saw her juggling a tote bag. I signaled Nikki to be ready. As soon as she turned and closed the car door, I was on her.

For a person who talked as if they're street tough, Flossie had terrible situational awareness. She had no idea I was there until I grabbed her arm flinging her to her knees. Her cries of protest were cut off when I forced her face into the side of the taller vehicle by pressing my forearm into the back of her neck. The tote fell to the ground and she thrashed her body from side to side trying to wiggle out of my hold. Nikki appeared beside me with a gag and duct tape to prevent any further cries for help.

Moments later, I closed the trunk of the Impala with the now hooded, bound, and gagged Flossie lying inside. Pulling away from the parking lot, we made the turn back towards the bungalow to pick up our other guest.

The drive back to the bungalow was short. Getting Nee-Nee outside was ridiculously easy. Nikki unlocked Flossie's cellphone in a matter of seconds. It was simple enough to find Nee-Nee's number in her call log. We parked on the street behind the bungalow, approaching the house from the unfenced backyard. From our position to the right of the door leading to the carport, we sent Nee-Nee a series of texts drawing her outside.

Even less street savvy than her cohort, Nee-Nee didn't even look in our direction when she opened the door and stepped outside. Once she cleared the stairs, I slammed her to the ground. I quickly duct taped her mouth and put a black bag over her head. Nikki grabbed her arms slapping the zip tie cuffs on her faster than a cowboy roping a calf.

We didn't bother closing the door she'd left ajar before we marched her through the darkened yard. Shoving her into the trunk with her *friend*, we said nothing as we rounded opposite sides of Safari.

Our ability to easily kidnap two adults should've bothered me. It didn't. Not in the slightest. Flossie and Nee-Nee had picked the wrong child to fuck with and they were about to find out.

Once Nikki slid behind the wheel, she turned up the volume of the music. The thumping baseline vibrated through the car, shaking the windows.

Lifting the trunk, I was immediately struck by the scent. One or both of our *guests* had urinated on themselves.

"Shit!" I stepped back holding a hand over my nose to block the pungent odor.

"What is it?" Nikki asked, joining me at the open trunk. As soon as she stood beside me, her hand shot to her face as well. "Damn! Did they piss themselves?" Her hand clamped tightly over her nose and mouth. "Why does it smell so strong? That ain't normal."

Wishing the ski mask included a filter with more layers, I responded. "I don't know, but it's ridiculous. I'm gonna have to pay extra for the cleaning it's going to take for me to stay on your boy's good side after this."

Glad we'd thought to line the trunk with drop cloths and plastic, I looked at the two pitiful figures curled into the space.

Looking at one another, we came to a silent agreement before reaching into the dimly lit interior. Each of us seized a body part—I grabbed the bound hands while Nikki grasped the feet of the body closest to the edge of the cavity.

We made quick work of removing them from the trunk. Forcing them to their knees, we ripped off the bags covering their heads. Eyes wide with fear, they shrieked behind the gags secured with duct tape over their mouths.

I wasn't worried about them telling anyone about this place or how to get here. We'd driven for a little under thirty minutes to reach the deserted location outside of Logan City. There were no houses or businesses for miles and no chance of anyone happening upon us.

None too gently, we ripped the duct tape from their mouths pulling out the gags. Immediately, wails of terror rent the air. I was surprised they had any screams left. They started screaming when the lid of the trunk was closed locking them inside. During the entire drive, they'd remained blindfolded while the bass from the music thumped. But, when the tunes faded between songs, I heard their muffled screams.

I'd asked Nikki to get Pootie's car for a reason. The speakers he'd replaced his back seats with produced sound so thunderous it vibrated through your body—even when it was only at half volume. As we'd driven out of the residential areas, we'd put on ear protection and cranked the volume up to the maximum.

I'd learned the tactic years ago from one of my less law-abiding family members. Until now, I'd had no reason to use it. Depriving a person of sight, locking them in a small space and inundating them with booming sound from which they couldn't escape. It was disorienting not to mention terror inducing.

Watching them silently, we waited patiently as if we had all the time in the world for the bound strippers to get themselves together. After what seemed like forever, but was actually only a few minutes later, the two silenced their screaming.

It was likely their ears continued to ring, and they were, at least partially, in a state of confusion. I didn't care. I wanted them disoriented and uncomfortable. My baby wasn't comfortable. She wouldn't be any time soon. They deserved far worse considering what they'd done.

Pulling an object from my pocket, I flicked my wrist allowing the stacked circlets to separate into their true form. Brass knuckles. Slipping them onto my left hand, I closed my fingers around them while walking to stand in front of Nee-Nee. Nikki followed my lead, standing at my side, directly in front of Flossie.

My voice sounded deeper and unrecognizable thanks to the distorter on the inside of the ski mask, I leaned in until I was right in Nee-Nee's face.

"So, these are the two triflin' tricks who think it's okay to put their hands on little girls and cut them?" The disembodied voice added another layer of fear, stimulating trembling in Nee-Nee's slight frame.

"What?! No! That wasn't me! I didn't cut nobody! I swear!" Nee-Nee cried out, panic coating her voice.

Flossie's head snapped around to Nee-Nee. She barked through clenched teeth, "Shut the fuck up!"

"Shhhh…" I put two gloved fingers to Nee-Nee's mouth closing her lips together.

"Your buddy is right. You should shut up. I don't want to hear your lies and excuses. I know exactly what you did…

I know how you followed a little girl from her mama's house. I know what you said to the little girl. I know you had the nerve to put your stankin' hands on a child who doesn't belong to you."

Pushing her head, forcing it to rock back on her neck, I stopped talking to her and started talking to Nikki.

"Friend?"

"Yeah, Friend?"

"Did I tell you everything these two hoes did?"

"You told me some stuff friend, but I don't know if I heard it all. I mean... Look at them friend. They look like they're scared of their own shadows."

"I didn't tell you all of it?" Feigning surprise, I stood to my full height. While not as impressive as Nikki's six-foot stature, my five-foot, two-inch frame towered over the women on their knees.

"Don't let the snot and tears fool you. These two broke the baby's ribs, beating her black and blue."

"Say what? Come on friend. These two grown ass women," shoving Flossie's head to emphasize her point, "laid hands on a child like that?"

Showing more bravery than her cowering friend, Flossie spoke up, "Listen, I don't know who the fuck you are. Go on and do what the fuck you're gonna do and stop talking shit."

"Shh! Flossie, be quiet!" Nee-Nee rushed to quiet Flossie. Visibly shaking, Nee-Nee snapped her gaze to her friend then quickly looked down at the ground.

Nee-Nee was the weakest link. It was obvious. Catching Nikki's eyes, I tipped my head. Divide and conquer was the unspoken consensus.

Yes, I wanted them to suffer for what they did to Saffi. I also want to know *why* they attacked my baby. To get more information, Nee-Nee needed to be separated from Flossie.

Was it possible they only wanted a phone and the small designer crossbody? There had to be more to the story than theft. I was damn well going to find out. Rounding Nee-Nee's kneeling form until I stood behind her, I grabbed her bound hands jerking her to her feet.

Flossie moved as if to stand, and Nikki pushed her back to her knees with a hand to the shoulder.

"The fuck you think you're going?" She asked her. "No one told you to move."

Walking away from the two, the sound of Nikki's electronically enhanced voice faded. Nee-Nee stumbled and moved like her legs could barely hold her as I pushed her to the front of the car directly in front of the glaring headlights. She reeked of fear. The stench of urine I'd smelled earlier wafted from her body.

Depriving me of the pleasure of beating it out of her, Nee-Nee spilled her guts immediately after I shoved her back to her knees. It was actually kind of pathetic. She wasn't mentally equipped to handle the life she tried to lead.

I've lived through some rough shit, so I had a few rough edges. Nevertheless, I'm not, by any stretch of the imagination, so hardcore to make a person piss themselves with one look. This chick was a blubbering, apologetic, begging mess before I even pressed her.

After she told me everything she knew, despite her apparent cooperation, I still made a show of adjusting the brass knuckles on my left hand. Wide, fearful eyes followed my movements. She should be afraid. I intended to make sure she knew exactly how it felt to be at the mercy of someone stronger and be unable defend yourself.

"Wait!... Please don't! I told you everything I know. I promise. Please don't hurt me!" She begged.

She wouldn't get one ounce of sympathy from me. I stepped back and her shoulders relaxed. I knew she thought her begging had worked. It hadn't. I needed working room.

The first blow snapped her head to the side breaking through the skin of her cheek. Crying out in pain, she crumpled trying to fold her body to protect herself. Her bound hands restricted her ability to ward off the attack. She was as defenseless as Saffi had been.

"Didn't that little girl beg you to stop? Didn't you say she gave you her things? She didn't try to fight back. Yet, you and your so-called friend beat her anyway?" I growled into her face.

"Why the fuck would I show you any mercy when you didn't give her any? What have you done to earn my sympathy?" Raising her head with one hand, I rammed my fist into her face again. I heard the tell-tale sound of her nose breaking. It brought a smile to my face.

Crying out in pain, she crumpled completely to the ground. Remembering Saffi's broken ribs, I delivered a few swift kicks to her sides and midsection. I beat that bitch until *I* got tired. When I'd had enough, I stepped back looking at my handiwork. Breathing heavily, I stood over her still silently raging, but no longer feeling completely unhinged.

After a few minutes, I grabbed a fist full of her disheveled extensions dragging her to her feet. She was unable to fully stand. So, I half tugged, half dragged her behind me. I took her to the rear of the car shoving her into the trunk, her blood and tears adding to the fluids collected on the temporary plastic lining.

Looking over my shoulder, I watched Nikki standing over a prone Flossie rubbing her gloved hands down the sides of her legs.

"Is she out?" I asked. I left the trunk open as I walked towards them. I was unconcerned about Flossie's well-being. I was concerned we might have to lift dead weight to put her back into the rear of the car.

Shaking her head, Nikki responded, "Nah...She likes to fake. She thinks if she's out cold, I might stop kicking her ass." Proving her point, Nikki pulled back one booted foot driving it into Flossie's midsection like she was taking a free kick on the goal in a championship soccer game. She was hyper focused as she put her weight behind the kick.

Air whooshed through Flossie's lips, she curled into a fetal position crying out in a strained whimper, "Mufukka! You just wait! I'm gonna fuck you up! I'm gonna find out who you are and I'm gonna fuck you all the way up!"

Delivering a kick to her back, Nikki taunted her, "You ain't gonna do shit to nobody. You don't know how to fight alone. You jump on little girls and even then, you need help." The sneering tone in her voice clear even through the distorter.

Tapping her shoulder, I jerked my head towards the car. "The other one gave me what we need. Let's go."

I didn't whisper, because I didn't care if Flossie overheard. Causing additional strife between the two of them would just add another layer to their punishment. Mental warfare and not knowing who they could trust was only a sliver of what they deserved.

Chapter Eight

JIAN

I could've left it to a resident, but I planned to do it myself. Unconcerned about appearances, I went to Chloe's room when it was time. Hospitals are a hotbed of gossip, so I was well aware of the buzz surrounding my attention to this patient. No matter what they thought, no one batted an eye when I ordered IV Benadryl for Saffi before we began.

She'd already proven to be sensitive to medication, so the Benadryl should do the trick to mildly sedate her and keep her comfortable. Had this been the dayshift, I might have pressed for a small OR. Typically, the OR doesn't run twenty-four hours. If I'd wanted to use one during the night, it would've taken certain approvals and been more of an expense than such a minor procedure required. It wouldn't take long to complete, even with putting in stitches to secure the port site.

Sweeping my eyes around the room, I checked the setup to verify everything we needed was close at hand. The team had turned the area around Chloe's bed into a sterile area for us to work safely. Once I was satisfied, I turned my attention to Stephanie.

"Are you ok with staying here while we do this?"

Her eyes flicked to the sleeping child before she answered. "If you're sure it will be okay, I'd like to stay. I don't want to do anything to cause issues though."

Heaving an inward sigh of satisfaction at hearing she planned to remain in the room, I explained how it worked again. Gesturing to the rolling station with the implements we needed atop them, I gave another quick description.

"We've created a sterile area around the bed. So long as you stay over here away from the bed, you'll be fine. However, once we've started there can't be anyone in or out of the room until we're done."

"Ok. I can stay here on the sofa. We aren't expecting visitors at this time of night. In and out traffic won't be a problem."

Her face was drawn in concern compelling me to do something to ease her apprehension.

"Don't worry. There's no reason everything shouldn't go well. I'll take care of her. It'll be fine. I promise."

Never make promises. One of the first things we learned as residents was to never make promises. You can't guarantee outcomes. It was a rule I followed religiously. Until now.

Something inside me didn't want her to experience even one moment of anxiety. So, I broke the rule. I promised her everything would be fine.

"Thank you, Dr. Anderson." Her face split into a genuine smile showcasing her full lips and the dimple in her left cheek.

My reward for breaking the unwritten rule was a smile followed by a warm thank you. *I'll take it.* Before I got myself into trouble, I clapped my hands, returning to the bedside to finish putting on my protective gear.

"Great. Well, let's get to it, shall we?"

Once we were properly geared, I didn't waste time. While I was aware of Stephanie's eyes on me, my focus was on completing the task as efficiently as possible. In all honesty, a first-year resident could've been given this assignment. However, I felt duty-bound to do it myself.

After I removed the port, I closed the small opening with stitches before the nurse placed bandages over the wound. While the rest of the team reset the room, removing the items brought in for the procedure, I stepped away from the bed. Taking off my protective gear, I smiled at the still slightly anxious looking Stephanie Barker.

"We're all done. When they've wrapped up over there, you can move closer to check her out for yourself. She should sleep the rest of the night thanks to our friend 'Benny' in her IV."

Normally, I would have left the room as soon as I briefed the family. Considering I'd done very little as I normally would since meeting Stephanie, I rattled on about the procedure assuring her it went perfectly.

As I moved closer to her, I smelled her natural fragrance. I was certain the aroma didn't come from a bottle. The scent was enticing. In addition to the assault on my olfactory senses, her plain black t-shirt tugged across her chest, drawing my gaze to her full breasts.

I pulled myself from the precipice of my licentious thoughts with an internal admonishment to snap out of it. That's when I noticed she still seemed a bit antsy. The procedure was over, there was no reason for her to be fretful about it now.

Was it me? Did I make her uneasy? As much as I wanted to be closer to her, I stood a few feet away—even if I was on the same side of the hospital bed.

Unsure, yet unwilling to let it stand, I placed a hand on her shoulder squeezing gently. My touch appeared to jar her from whatever thoughts swirled in her head.

"Since the port is out, when can I take her home?"

Checking my watch, I noted the time. An hour from midnight. If I started the paperwork, she could take Chloe home before they brought the morning meal at seven a.m. The timing gave us almost eight hours to observe her for complications.

"I'll start the ball rolling. You should be able to take her home in the morning."

Relief flooded her face. "Thank you, doctor."

"You're welcome. If you need anything else, let me know."

The words were out there in the air. I didn't call them back. I'm a surgeon. I didn't do regular wellness checks. I didn't do, *if you need something* requests. I'm a specialist. So, why did I volunteer my services beyond surgery? This damn woman had me and she didn't even know it. *I need to get out of this room.*

Her phone vibrated giving me an excuse to leave without calling further attention to my uncharacteristic offer. Already focused on responding to the message on her phone, she waved smiling slightly as I left the room.

Twenty minutes later, I was at the nurses' station when the door to Chloe's room opened and Stephanie stepped out with her satchel thrown over one shoulder. I thought it a little odd for her to go into the stairwell, but I didn't dwell on it. Everyone needed the occasional break. Chloe was asleep, so it wasn't like the pre-teen would miss her.

A couple of hours before the end of my shift, I was called into an ER consultation. The corridors away from the ER were empty as I made my way back to my office. My mind on a certain woman with a compact curvy body I longed to touch, I wasn't as focused on where I was going.

Lack of attention to my surroundings was how I found myself colliding with the very person consuming my thoughts. It was like my desires manifested themselves into the thing I wanted most. To know the feeling of holding her in my arms again. Because, that's what happened.

I rounded the corner crashing into Stephanie—chest first. She let out a combination yelp and squeak, then grabbed onto my biceps to balance herself. I quickly wrapped my arms around her to aid in her quest to remain upright.

"Oh! So sorry. Didn't see you there." I rushed to apologize, all the while knowing I'd do it again. This time was truly an accident, although the feeling of her plush body pressed against me was an experience I wanted to repeat.

"It's okay. I guess I need to watch where I'm going. Can't go around hospitals bowling over their best surgeons."

Her voice held a breathless quality to it. It made me wonder if being this close together was affecting her the same way it affected me. The darkness in her eyes said it did.

Too soon for my liking, she gave my biceps a slight squeeze patting my arm as she pulled her upper body away and tried to step back, out of my embrace. I didn't like it.

I looked down at her left hand currently tapping my arm in more of a calming stroke than a pat. I noticed a slight reddening just below the second knuckle of each finger. Instinctively, I grabbed both of her hands in my own.

"Are you okay? What happened?" My concerned gaze lifted to see a look of discomfort on her face. "Does it hurt? I can get you something for it."

Tugging her hands away, she clasped them together pulling them to her chest. "I'm fine. It's fine. I just banged them a bit on the car door. No big deal."

"Are you sure? It's no problem. I can help." I dipped my head to recapture her eyes when she turned her face away. Rotating back, a smile wiped the tense look from her face. As disarming as it was, her smile didn't make me believe there was nothing to what I'd seen.

"I'm sure, Doc. I've done far worse. This little bump is nothing."

My brow creased with curiosity. It's not my specialty, however I knew a door bang injury when I saw one. Her hand hadn't been banged in a door. She didn't trust me enough to tell me what really happened. It stung. But...she didn't know me to trust me with personal things.

"If you're sure then, I'll let you be on your way to wherever you were heading before I tried to run you over." Stepping back, I extended my arm in a flourish allowing her to continue down the hall.

A chuckle and another smile were her response as she tossed me a quick goodbye while walking away. We were nowhere near Chloe's room, so I wondered where she was going to or coming from. I wouldn't and couldn't ask her about that either.

I noticed she'd changed clothes though. The clothing was similar, but not identical, to what she was wearing earlier, from the black tee all the way down to the black-on-black chucks on her tiny feet.

An hour later, I discovered myself standing inside Chloe's room as we prepared to release the pre-teen from the hospital. Yet another thing I was doing which I rarely ever did.

"Thank you again, Dr. Anderson." Stephanie stooped beside Chloe's bed helping her put on a pair of sneakers.

"You're quite welcome. We're here to help." Cringing internally, I regretted the corniness of the statement. It was out there now.

Georgina's resident stood silently beside me. She'd already gone over wound care for Chloe's face. She'd also given Stephanie the information she needed to schedule the follow-up appointments with Dr. Maxwell. I thanked the heavens and all its occupants I was in the room to overhear the date and time.

I had no idea how I was going to bridge the gap, but I knew I wanted the chance to see and get to know Stephanie Barker. For now, the only way to do that appeared to be at this hospital.

Groaning, I threw my arm out slapping against the night stand searching blindly for the blaring cellphone. It seemed like I'd just closed my eyes when the thumping music boomed loudly in my ear.

My hand finally locating its target, I swiped the screen without opening my eyes. "Yeah?"

"Wake your ass up."

Hearing Ash's grumbling voice made me pop straight up in bed—now wide awake.

"I'm up. Why are you? Do you have news about the case?"

"Well, aren't you eager? Also, It's after one o'clock in the afternoon. Normal people are awake at this time of day."

Scrubbing my face, I checked the clock. It was one forty-five p.m. Even if it felt like only minutes, I'd been asleep for almost five hours.

"I'm normal. I'm just the kind of normal person who worked a night shift and needed some shut eye."

"Well, you've had enough. I'm doing you a favor. If you'd slept much longer, you'd be up all night. If you are, you won't be worth a shit tomorrow morning when you have to haul your ass back into the hospital."

"Please...I went for days without sleep during my residency."

"Dude, you were in your twenties when you did that shit. You're an old man now."

"Fuck you. Thirty-seven isn't old. If it is, you got there first. You're almost a year older than me."

Whipping the covers off, I climbed out of bed heading to the bathroom. I placed the call on speaker as I went about my routine.

"Whatever. I don't have time to trade old man stories with you. I called to tell you about the assault you asked me to check on for your woman."

"I never said she was my woman."

"You didn't have to say it. You calling me at the butt crack of dawn bribing me with biscuits said it for you. That and the way you looked when you talked about her."

"What? I didn't talk about anyone except to say a little girl had been attacked."

"You don't think you talked about her, but you totally talked about her. Anyway, I didn't call to argue with you about whether or not you had a woman. I called to tell you what I found out when I checked with Johnson."

"Johnson?"

"The detective who caught the case."

"Oh. Okay. What's the latest?"

"The latest is the suspects were delivered to the 302 last night or really early this morning around three a.m."

Pausing in the act of washing my face, I looked down at the phone as if seeing it would make the words I heard sound different. "What do you mean by *delivered*?"

"Exactly what I said. According to Johnson, when he got in this morning, there were two women in custody who'd been found bound and gagged in a compact car illegally parked in front of the precinct."

"Okaaay..."

"Oh, it gets better." Ash sounded almost giddy in his retelling. "There was a note under the wiper blades detailing who the women were and what they'd done. Johnson said whoever left them there beat the ever-loving shit out of them before they dropped them off. Both of them had black eyes with bruises everywhere."

"Damn."

"Damn is right."

"Do they know who did it? Who left them there?"

"Nah. They didn't catch anything on camera because the precinct doesn't have cameras with the right angles to see clearly. It was almost like whoever left them knew about the blind spot. One camera caught an image of two people in dark clothing wearing masks, but it was grainy. There wasn't much to go on other than one was tall and the other was shorter."

"I've never heard of suspects being gift wrapped then dropped off with the cops before."

I went back to cleaning my face while Ash filled me in on the rest. While I listened, my thoughts drifted to seeing Stephanie walking around the hospital around four a.m. wearing dark clothing. Different dark clothing than what I'd seen her wearing earlier in the night.

She couldn't have had anything to do with it, could she? The woman was understandably upset. Enough to seek vengeance? I didn't know her well enough to answer that question. I damn sure wasn't going to suggest it to Ash.

Dismissing the thought, I listened as my friend recounted what he'd learned. One of the women continued to deny the contents of the letter, claiming she was innocent. She wanted a lawyer to press charges against the people she said kidnapped and beat her.

The other woman was cooperating in hopes of gaining leniency. She couldn't give a description of the people who delivered them to the cops. Nor was she able to distinguish the sex of her assailants. The woman did admit to her role in Chloe's attack, but emphatically denied cutting her face.

Making my way to the kitchen, I filled a glass with water thinking of what I wanted for lunch. Since I was awake, my stomach growled demanding to be filled.

"So, what happens now?" I asked Ash.

"They'll both get public defenders, if they don't have attorneys. Then they'll be arraigned. They won't let them go because a couple of the items reported stolen were found in their possession. Based on the value of the items, they're facing grand larceny charges. That's on the low end, because they also found a switchblade in the car which could've been used in the assault. If the young lady identifies them as her attackers, it's a wrap. Not sure what, if anything, will happen to the people who attacked the attackers."

"Well, I guess it's a good thing it's going to be over quickly."

"You could say that."

"I *am* saying it. You didn't see her. If you did, you'd understand. I can't drum up an ounce of sympathy for adults who attack children. The fact neither of them needed surgery says their attackers showed restraint."

"Not surgery, although they had to be stitched and patched up before Johnson saw them. One had a broken nose."

"I'm so sad they had to feel a portion of the pain they inflicted." I deadpanned. They'd get no compassion from me. Not a drop.

"Okay... Well, Johnson was on his way to update the family when he left here, so the mother's probably hearing the news right now."

Learning the little tidbit of information caused my stomach to tighten. I wanted to be there with them. With Stephanie, to offer her support. But, I had no rights to her. It would be way out of bounds. Knowing it wasn't feasible didn't stop me from wanting it though.

"Thanks for calling, man. And for checking up on it to begin with. I owe you one."

"Yep. You do. I gotta get back to work on my own shit now. I'll talk to you later."

"Later."

I swiped the screen ending the call. I placed the phone on the countertop. After I pulled together a sandwich and a salad for lunch, I sat at the small bistro style table my mother had insisted on buying, allowing my thoughts to run rampant.

The way I'd met Stephanie was unconventional, but my attraction to her was undeniable. Now, the question was, what should I do next? I was completely out of practice with pursuing a woman. Especially a woman who affected me the way she did.

Had *anyone* touched me this way before? No. Never. I didn't know where to start. At least I had a date of when I could possibly see her next. At Chloe's follow-up appointment with Georgina. I needed to make the most of it.

Pulling my phone closer, I opened the internet browser and typed in, *Stephanie Barker*. Everything's on the internet. At least I could learn the things she was willing to share with the public.

I stopped short of having Ash run a background check. A little internet sleuthing was expected nowadays. *That's my story. I'm sticking to it.*

Chapter Nine

STEPHANIE

I should take up acting. I stood in my foyer listening to Detective Johnson relay the latest information on Saffi's case. I didn't actually think anyone had been assigned until the lanky middle-aged man, smelling of cigarettes and stale coffee, showed up on my doorstep.

I spoke to him in the foyer, because Saffi was in the other room. I knew she wouldn't want to be trapped in her bedroom, so I'd fixed her a spot on the sectional in the family room. Until and unless it was absolutely necessary, she wouldn't meet the detective.

Not one hint of mine and Nikki's exploits showed on my face when Detective Johnson told me how Flossie and Nee-Nee were found in front of a police precinct. Nikki was the architect of that part of the plan —leaving them in their car in front of the police station. My idea was to dump them on the doorstep.

Her idea was better. Mine would've gotten us caught on camera driving Pootie's baby. Her way, we manipulated the blind spot in their security keeping ourselves in the clear. Even if the police managed to get an image of us, we had no identifying markings showing. We wore the masks covering our face and hair.

"Ms Barker, do you recognize either of these people?" Detective Johnson held out a tablet showing images of Flossie and Nee-Nee which were obviously DMV photos.

"No. Should I?" I raised questioning eyes—my expression devoid of any type of emotion or acknowledgement.

"According to the letter under the wiper blade of the car they were found in, these are the two women who assaulted your daughter."

Wrinkling my forehead, I reached for the tablet taking another look. "Really? I've never seen them before. Did they say why they did it?"

"Unfortunately, their reason was the one thing we can't pin point." He stated solemnly with a head shake. "Although one of the women is cooperating, the most we could get from her was they wanted the phone and purse. They didn't think the little tablet was worth anything. So, they tossed it.

The physical assault seemed a bit extreme to only be about those things. I'm afraid neither of them would own up to anything beyond wanting the stuff."

"That doesn't make any sense. You could buy those things for next to nothing if you know the right people. Why attack Saffi?" I really played up the confused mother bit. The detective had no reason to suspect I was anything but what I told him about myself. I was the parent of a child who was viciously beaten.

"You said the operative phrase—if you know the right people. Maybe they didn't. Them not having a plug seems hard to believe considering how they make their living."

"What kind of work do they do?"

The detective raised his bushy eyebrows. "Oh, I didn't tell you? They're featured strippers at three different Atlanta strip clubs. They perform in different places depending on the night."

Effecting a shocked expression, I kept my act going. "Wow...now I'm really confused. I've always heard strippers made good money. Them committing a robbery doesn't add up."

"Ma'am, we may never know the real reason any of this happened. At least we have one confession. We can use her statement to charge both with felony assault."

"Well, that's good." I rubbed my arms looking around. "What does it mean for Saffi?" My baby was my main concern. Flossie and Nee-Nee could slow roast like pigs on a spit for all I cared.

"You've brought me to the other reason I'm here. I need to show her a photo array to see if she can positively identify them. If she can, I'll take the information to the DA. They may be able to get them to plead guilty based on the evidence. If they do, there won't be a trial—just a sentencing recommendation. She won't have to testify."

"But if they don't plead guilty, there'll be a trial." I finished for him.

A grave nod was his response. I didn't want her to testify. I didn't want Saffi near them again, even if it was in a courtroom.

If it came down to it, I'd encourage her in whatever she wanted to do, but I wouldn't force her. I already knew she'd need therapy behind all of this. If we could take testifying off the table, we'd save her additional trauma.

Leading Detective Johnson into the family room, I interrupted Saffi's viewing of the latest release from the House of Mouse. Introducing the detective, I explained why he was there.

I dreaded the next few minutes because I knew he had to ask for her accounting of events. As much as I didn't want her to keep reliving it, he needed to hear it directly from her. Only Joy and I were privy to her version of the story up to now.

The primary reason the police were involved was due to Miss Myrtle calling 9-1-1 when she saw Saffi crying on the ground in front of her house. The little bit of information the police had to go on was due to her quick thinking.

After Saffi's retelling of events, the detective got right down to business. He showed her photos of ten different women and asked if she recognized any of them. She quickly picked out Flossie and Nee-Nee from the fourth and eighth pictures she was shown.

Detective Johnson asked a few follow up questions, then thanked Saffi for her bravery. He left me in the foyer with his card. He also promised to get back in touch with any new developments. He was confident the evidence and Saffi's identification would be enough to keep the case from going to trial. But, he didn't make any definite promises.

Surprisingly, the rest of the afternoon wasn't ruined by the unexpected visit. Kids were resilient. We spent the rest of the day watching her movies of choice with me providing snacks or support when she needed it. In that time, I'd texted Nikki, Joy, and Gene to bring them up to speed on everything.

Joy and Gene knew nothing other than what I'd told them. Their return texts didn't hint they suspected I was involved in the suspects spontaneously appearing in police custody. Nikki was different.

Not only did she know the whole story of what happened, she knew why Flossie and Nee-Nee went after Saffi in the first place. Just thinking of the driving force behind the attack had me closing my eyes, counting, praying, and meditating to keep myself under control. Dani's boyfriend was the catalyst for all of it.

He was shaping up to be the worst in a long line of shitty men my sister allowed into her life. Sure, he was a business owner. So, he could keep her in the lifestyle she liked. But, our late night 'chat' with the not so dynamic duo revealed he was also a pimp. Vincente Renfroe was a pimp who went after and groomed young girls.

Before I beat Nee-Nee so bad she couldn't speak past the pain, she'd told me how Vincente was playing Dani. He'd originally planned to just have her as one of his side pieces for a while until he'd seen a picture of Saffi.

I didn't even know Dani had a picture of Saffi out where people could see it. Saffi must have given it to her, because I didn't give her shit unless she asked—sometimes, not even then.

Nee-Nee told me Vincente wanted to meet Saffi, so he played up the single mother thing to Dani—who'd apparently informed him she'd sent Saffi to live with me because it was safer. Not the truth, she'd not had custody of the child she'd birthed since the day she brought said child home from the hospital.

Vincente wanted Saffi. On top of everything else, Dani had hooked up with a fucking pedophile. She'd been avoiding my calls, nonetheless we would have it out about this one. Her access to Saffi was completely cut off. Period. She should count herself lucky I hadn't been able to lay eyes or hands on her yet.

I couldn't tell Gene about this until I handled it. I didn't need him flying off beating the shit out of Vincente and ending up in jail. I fully recognized the irony of me trying to protect him when I had done exactly that with Flossie and Nee-Nee.

I looked into Saffi's smiling face as we walked into the suite of offices connected to the hospital. I marveled at how well her wounds were healing. We'd come in for a follow-up appointment with Dr. Maxwell.

The stitches the doctor used had dissolved after a couple of weeks with minimal scarring. What I could see, looked like it faded a little each day. My observation could be wishful thinking on my part, which is why I'd wait to hear the doctor's assessment before I celebrated it as a success.

It wasn't the thought of Saffi having the facial scar which made me so adamant to have a plastic surgeon repair the cuts. It was the potential re-living of the traumatic experience that concerned me. I didn't promote excess focus on physical appearance. Beauty was not a goal to achieve.

It simply existed. It also faded. Being a genuinely good person was the goal in our home. Focus on beauty was Dani's downfall.

I still hadn't gotten my hands on her trifling ass. Every time I went by the house, she wasn't there. I couldn't even say she avoided me because I didn't call her in advance to tell her I was coming. My visits were completely random. It was like she had some kind of radar alerting her to when I planned to show up.

Keeping the thoughts swirling in my head from showing on my face, I checked us in with the receptionist. I appreciated the brevity of the wait before we were led to the exam room. After a quick examination, Dr. Maxwell expressed her pleasure with how Saffi was healing.

"Everything looks really good, young lady."

"Thank you, Dr. Maxwell." Saffi bashfully accepted the praise.

"It appears you followed my instructions to the letter and it's paying off. Keep up the good work." The doctor smiled encouragingly.

I liked her. Besides being highly skilled, she was kind. Kindness was a personality trait harder to come by in certain professions. I found people who had the sort of accolades Dr. Maxwell had behind her name, tended to be arrogant and hard to deal with. She was none of those things.

This was our second appointment with her. Each time she'd been the same. Warm, competent, and kind. I also liked her being a woman of color. My desire was to expose Saffi to all the possibilities for her future. I wanted her to see women of color in different types of high-profile professions and careers. It reinforced the idea that anything was possible. Even for a young black girl.

"Everything looks good, Ms Barker. Do you have any questions?"

"No. Thank you again, Dr. Maxwell. I appreciate you making time to see us today."

"Nonsense. It's why I'm here. Besides, I like to see my handiwork on such a cute little canvas." She said patting the blushing Saffi's shoulder. Standing from the stool, she gathered the electronic tablet she'd brought in with her.

"If there's nothing else, Camille will see you out."

Her assistant Camille appeared at the door as soon as her name was called. While we were walking through to the hall, I caught a glimpse of a familiar profile.

Dr. Anderson. I hadn't seen him since Saffi was released from the hospital. What was he doing here? Curiosity creased my brow as I allowed my eyes to roam over his fit physique. That man knew he was fine! I hadn't seen him since Saffi was released from the hospital.

When Saffi was still in the hospital, a chatty nurse informed me Dr. Anderson was a specialist. He didn't have regular patients. Knowing he didn't have regular patients made me wonder if he'd given Saffi special attention. Who am I to look a gift horse in the mouth? I'd made an appointment with her pediatrician to follow up on her injuries.

Dr. Anderson was at the end of the hall. We were getting closer to where he stood speaking to another doctor. As we drew near, he turned to us.

The smile he gave us seemed to take over his entire face, lifting his cheeks putting a glint in his eyes. *Damn. He needed to tone that shit down.* Can't be inflicting his dazzle on people all willy nilly.

Hoping my expression didn't display the thoughts flying across my brain, I responded with a slight grin. Abandoning the doctor he was speaking with, he took the few steps to meet us in the hallway.

"Ms Barker and Little Miss Barker, nice to see you again." I smiled even wider at him referring to Saffi as 'Little Miss' considering she was much taller than me.

"Hey Dr. J!" Saffi's happy greeting put a different smile on his face. Almost paternal... Mentally shaking away the notion, I redirected my attention to the doctor walking away.

"Hello, Dr. Anderson. Please don't let us interrupt your conversation."

Giving a negligent wave of his hand he captured my eyes with his direct gaze. "You're not interrupting. We were done talking."

"Oh. Okay."

Releasing me from his thrall, he turned his attention to Saffi. "How have you been, Chloe? All healed up and ready for school?"

"Yes, sir. It itches right here where I had the stitches, but I'm okay. Aunt Cee-Cee says I have to wait on playing sports though." Saffi's expression saddened. She aimed her big brown eyes at me in a pitiful puppy dog expression.

"No ma'am. Don't start. You think you have an ally in Dr. Anderson. You might, however I have to do what's best for you. Your body isn't ready for that kind of contact yet."

Dr. Anderson's warm hand landed on my shoulder drawing my attention from Saffi's sad face. Moving closer into my space he recaptured my gaze.

"Far be it for me to interfere, although I might be able to offer some insight." His fingers delivered a gentle squeeze to my shoulder causing butterflies to take flight in my stomach. *Down girl.*

"What sport does she play? Maybe there's a way to find a balance."

Pinning him with a skeptical expression, I pondered how I felt about him inserting himself into the situation. As he waited for my answer, his steady stare didn't falter. His eyes were locked on mine. I wanted to look away, but I was caught. *It was simultaneously unnerving and stimulating.*

"She plays soccer."

"Oh..." Regret covered his face when he looked at Saffi. "Sorry, Little Miss. She's right. Soccer has too much contact. You didn't get many stitches, however you're only four weeks out from your injury. You need a little more time to heal before you attempt something so physical. You could still re-open a wound or hurt your ribs again if you get hit wrong."

Saffi's face dropped when she realized her potential ally betrayed her. Our little group fell into silence.

While he delivered the bad news, his hand drifted lightly down my arm, his fingers grazing over mine. My core fluttered from the light touch. He lingered for the briefest of moments before pushing his hands into the pockets of his jacket. I missed the contact immediately.

I need to get laid. If a slight touch on the shoulder and an even slighter grazing of fingers could elicit such a response, I was overdue for a dick appointment. Not that I had a human I could call to scratch such an itch.

I severed my connection to my last service provider over a year ago. He got the job done. When he started angling for a real relationship, I was done. Negative ghost rider. He had too much going on for me to even consider making us more permanent.

Trying to lift Saffi's spirits after crushing her soccer hopes, Dr. Anderson chatted with her about safer activities. While I appreciated the back-up, I wanted him to take his fine self on away from me. He was too distracting.

"Dr. Anderson. I didn't expect to see you over in the suites. Is there something you needed?" Dr. Maxwell's question cut through our conversation.

"Oh! No thank you, Dr. Maxwell. I was just speaking with Dr. Vail when I ran into the Barkers. I haven't seen them since Chloe was released, so I stopped to check in."

Dr. Anderson's lightly tanned skin reddened a bit in the cheeks as he spoke. *Was he blushing? That's cute.*

Skepticism painting her expression, Dr. Maxwell nodded, then bid us goodbye again before entering a nearby examination room. Her appearance nudged us to move our little gathering to the cashier's window so I could pay the co-pay. Besides, I'd taken the afternoon off, because Saffi and I had a late lunch date with Nikki.

"Well, we have to get going. It was nice to see you again, Dr. Anderson. Thank you for the advice."

I produced what I hoped was a graceful smile. A smile I prayed didn't let on how much his proximity affected me. Not sure it worked, but I tried.

"It was my pleasure, Ms Barker." The smooth tenor of his voice causing an internal shiver down my spine. "You take care. You as well, Little Miss." Giving one last nod, he walked away.

I couldn't tear my eyes away from his retreating back. The long white coat hid everything except his broad shoulders. Despite the obstruction of my view, I watched anyway. The sound of a throat being cleared along with a tug of my sleeve from Saffi brought me out of my stare-fest.

Startled, I jumped slightly redirecting my attention to the current situation. I really liked the efficiency in this place. Camille had already passed the paperwork along and the clerk was ready with the amount owed. So, I handled the bill as soon as I stepped up to the window. We walked out in less than five minutes. That is, after I got myself together and stopped staring at the fine ass cardiothoracic surgeon who just happened to be in the plastic surgeon's suite of offices.

Thirty minutes later, we were parked outside the bougie sandwich shop Saffi liked. Through the shaded windows of the entrance, I observed Nikki standing inside the doors waiting for us. Since it was a regular workday, she was dressed in a slate grey business suit which went great with her dark brown skin. Her hair was slicked back into a ponytail which fell between her shoulder blades. She loved those ponytails when she didn't have her hair in a protective style.

She cut a striking figure in the pantsuit skimming her six-foot curvy frame to perfection. Add in the four-inch heels she was sporting, and every eye in the vicinity was drawn to her.

Nikki was far more than most people expected when they first met her. If they met her as she was now, they would assume she was an executive in finance or some similar industry.

Nope. Nikki worked for an elite security firm. Most of the time, she couldn't tell me what she was doing because I didn't have the security clearance to know such information.

Saffi hopped out of the car, excited to see her favorite Auntie and eat at her favorite restaurant. The replacement backpack purse Gene bought her bounced with each skip-step she took to the door.

Having her adjusting so well, after what happened, brought me peace. Although she'd only had a couple of sessions with the therapist, I felt like it helped. Thankfully, she wasn't having nightmares, but she was more cautious of new people. It wasn't like she super trusting of strangers to begin with.

Entering the restaurant first, Saffi went straight to Nikki, who wrapped her in a warm hug. She asked about her appointment as we were led to our table.

"It went okay. Dr. Maxwell said I was healing really good."

"That's good to hear, Peanut. Keep up the good work." Nikki encouraged Saffi before picking up the menu.

"Thank you, Tee-Tee. I'm really trying, 'cause I wanna start back doing my fun stuff."

Looking over the top of my menu, I stared at Saffi. "Are you saying we don't do fun stuff?"

With more than a little whine in her voice, Saffi dipped her head. "I'm not saying we don't have fun, Aunt Cee-Cee. I just really wanna play soccer."

"Saffi..."

"I know, I know. Dr. J said it has too much contact. I might hurt myself more and I need more time to heal." Dropping her head, she focused intently on her menu even though she probably knew the thing by heart.

"Dr. J?" Nikki pinned me with an assessing stare. "Who is Dr. J?"

"She means Dr. Anderson. The surgeon who fixed her lung."

"Oh..." Nikki looked at me knowingly.

Joy didn't waste time in telling Nikki about her observations of the two of us in Chloe's hospital room. She also took it upon herself to tell Nikki her theory about the potential attraction she'd perceived between me and the doctor.

"So... Peanut, when did you see Dr. Anderson? I didn't know you had an appointment with him too."

Oblivious to the adult undertones, Saffi perked up to tell Nikki all about our chance encounter with the sexy surgeon she'd nicknamed Dr. J. The entire time she spoke, Nikki's eyes were locked on me cataloging my every expression.

Great. Just great. It's not like my friends didn't stay on me enough about taking time for myself. I know how it looked and sounded for us to 'run into' Dr. Anderson during a follow-up visit to the plastic surgeon. Only Saffi hadn't connected the dots.

Heck, I don't know if I was reading it right myself. It really could've just been a coincidence. He was talking to another doctor when we saw him. He could've been consulting with him on a patient. It's possible. *Right?*

Changing the subject to weekend plans, I steered the conversation to safer topics. Saffi was completely unaware, while Nikki threw me a knowing glance. Studiously ignoring the look, I engaged Saffi in a discussion about non-contact activities which would be just as much fun as her beloved soccer.

Chapter Ten

JIAN

Sweeping my eyes around the large ballroom, I was already bored and counting the minutes until I could politely excuse myself to go home. I'd been here over an hour and had yet to lay eyes on my real reason for donning a tux while sipping champagne with the city's elite philanthropists. Stephanie Barker. Figuring she was a no-show, I was ready to call it a night.

With my father being away on business, my mother considered backing out of the event. When I heard Stephanie's name mentioned among the honorees, I planted a seed with my dad, who encouraged my mother to attend without him. In turn, she called me to appear in my father's place. I agreed, never letting on that the whole thing was my idea.

Now, without having glimpsed the lovely Miss Barker, I was ready to hit the door. I resigned myself to an evening of mind-numbing boredom, because I was stuck. Once my mother was in her element at a party, there was no way she'd leave prematurely. So, it was futile to hope for an early exit.

My mind drifted to other ways to reconnect with the woman who'd completely seized my attention and wouldn't let go. It'd been nearly a month since I'd last seen Stephanie. The way my mind constantly turned to her, one would think we'd had an intimate relationship which ended abruptly.

In actuality, I hadn't had more than a few brief conversations with the woman. Inexplicably, I still felt the impact and the loss. Just the memory of the way she felt in my arms, was enough to get me hard. I kicked myself regularly for not coming up with some way to be in her orbit or bring her into mine. Our only connection was through the hospital.

Without coming off like a stalker or an insensitive jerk, my options were limited. I'd gone so far as to book an appointment with a barber at one of her salons. When I showed up for the appointment, I found out she split her time between two locations. It was just my luck I picked a day when she was at the other place.

A flash of crimson interrupted the sea of black and blue formal wear in the room, catching my eye. Turning my gaze fully in the direction of the distraction, I caught a glimpse of a familiar profile before my view was blocked completely. *Was that her?*

My heart rhythm picked up, thumping in my chest. Huffing in irritation, I prepared to move around the obstacle blocking my view when I realized said obstacle was my mother. Wiping the irritation from my face, I focused on her enough to realize she was speaking—introducing me to the person standing at her side.

"Here he is!" She gushed. "Mildred Fontaine, this is my son, *Doctor* Jian Anderson."

Slipping her arm around mine, she tugged me closer to the sixtyish looking woman with a pale complexion. The woman's skin was stretched tightly in an effort to defy her age. The platinum blonde color had been expertly applied to her hair, as was the make-up to her face.

Even with the obvious effort she'd exerted, it was evident. At least it was to me. She wasn't a day under sixty-five. Time spent with Georgina made me capable of spotting surgical enhancements quite easily.

Wearing a smile that didn't quite reach her eyes, Mildred proffered a limp-wristed hand. She extended it as if she expected me to kiss it. *Nega-*

tive. Not happening. I grasped her dangling fingers giving them a quick squeeze.

"A pleasure to meet you, Mrs. Fontaine." I offered, even though our meeting thus far had been less than pleasurable.

"The pleasure is all mine dear." She replied in a delicate southern drawl. "Sarah, you didn't tell me your son was so handsome."

She pressed one hand against her breast in a blatant attempt to draw attention to the barely contained globes stuffed into the black dress. Her dress could've stood being a size larger considering the way it was stretched to capacity.

Completely oblivious to her flirtatious attempts, my mother giggled patting my bicep affectionately. "Of course, he's handsome! He's *my* son."

She said it as if we bore any resemblance to one another, aside from our last names. My distinctly Chinese features didn't resemble her Scandinavian ones with her light grey eyes and chestnut colored hair. We did share tanned skin. Since she spent so much time in the sun working in her garden, the golden hues in her skin slightly matched mine.

My mother launched into her normal dialogue about my accomplishments. She went on about how proud she and my father were of me. Although accustomed to the praise, I was uncomfortable being the topic of conversation. It almost sounded like a sales pitch.

Hell. Who was I kidding? It **was** a sales pitch. She'd been trying to get me married for a while now. I'd bet my company stock Mrs. Fontaine had an eligible daughter, niece, or some other comely single female family member. And no doubt, my mother was angling for an introduction.

There it was again. The flash of crimson appeared in my peripheral vision. Then, a voice I could never forget drifted to my ears. I turned fully to see Stephanie Barker's upturned face beaming while she spoke to Benjamin Waters, a business associate of my father's.

"Well, thank you, Mr. Waters. Nice to see you again as well. Please give my best to your wife. Tell her I'm sorry I missed her during her past few visits to the salon."

Not fully realizing my actions. I zoned out of the conversation between my mother and Mrs. Fontaine leaning my body for a better view of the captivating woman. Gliding my eyes over her form, I admired the way the floor-length crimson dress hugged her curvy frame.

The dress was definitely crimson—not red. Between my fashion-conscious mother and my clothes hound of a best friend, I knew more than I cared to about colors and textures of clothing.

My eyes devoured the vision before me. Embellished with sequin picking up the light in the ballroom, the design of the top of her dress drew attention to the deep vee, exposing the delectable curves of bountiful, mahogany brown breasts. Breasts, Mr. Waters stared at much too long for my liking.

"Isn't that right, dear? Jian? Sweetheart, are you listening?" My mother pulled my attention back to her stopping me from taking the unconscious step toward the old geezer to put a stop to his ogling. I took offense to him staring at *my* paradise so hungrily.

Following my gaze, my mother prompted, "Dear, what has your attention so riveted? Mildred and I were discussing dinner next week. She said her niece would love to meet you."

Her mention of dinner brought me back to the conversation. *What the hell did I miss?* How did we go from introductions to meeting some nameless, faceless relative of the walking mannequin disguised as a human?

"Oh look! It's Benjamin!" Redeeming herself from trying to set me up, my mother refocused her attention to what I considered a much better place. Mildred's expression turned sour when my mother called out to Benjamin.

"Yoo-Hoo! Benjamin!" She waved, grabbed my arm, and Mildred's hand, moving our group closer to where I desperately wanted to be anyway.

"Mildred dear, let me introduce you to one of my husband's former business partners, Benjamin Waters. Benjamin and JT still play golf regularly. Both sit on the Board of this charity."

She gripped my arm as we drew closer to my vision and the ogling geezer. I'd never known my mother to be quite so excited to see Benjamin. Considering I was getting what I wanted, I didn't question it. As we approached, they stopped their conversation to watch us draw near. Completely enthralled, I couldn't stop my eyes from soaking Stephanie up—thirstily drinking in every detail.

I noticed the split in her dress extending from mid-thigh of her left leg to the tips of her toes. With each step she took, the split would display one luscious leg briefly. My mouth watered at the prospect of witnessing a glimpse.

Not stopping until I was almost directly in her space, I noted how much taller she appeared tonight. Her extra height was courtesy of the sparkling peep-toe heels reminiscent of Dorothy's ruby slippers. At her new elevated height, the top of Stephanie's head almost reached my shoulder.

"Hello there, Sarah. It's nice to see you. I didn't think you and John would be here tonight." Benjamin said to my mother as he clasped her hand in greeting.

Withdrawing her hand, my mother looped her arm back into mine, giving my bicep a squeeze.

"Something came up. JT couldn't make it, but he wanted the family to be represented, so I coerced my loving son into being my escort for the evening."

I smiled at her saying she had to coerce me. I'd never tell her about my machinations to get here.

"It was awfully nice of your son to escort you. I was just telling Ms Barker my wife couldn't make it this evening either. I can't pry my daughter away from whatever it is she does on that computer for long enough to hold a decent conversation, let alone coming to a charity event with me." Benjamin chuckled.

Issuing what I was certain was an inauthentic spurt of laughter, my mother took control of the conversation. "Benjamin, have you met Mildred Fontaine? She recently joined my tennis foursome at the club."

While they exchanged pleasantries, I focused my attention on Stephanie. "Hello, Ms Barker. It's very nice to see you again."

My face split into an uncontrollably wide grin. I made no attempt to stop my hand from reaching out to her. Of their own volition, my fingers skimmed the skin from the top of her right shoulder, down her arm to her hand, where they tangled with hers. Inhaling sharply, she lifted startled eyes to mine—confusion clouding her face.

I found her confused expression slightly puzzling. It had been a while since I'd last seen her, however I'm positive I didn't mistake her response to me when I saw her after Chloe's appointment with Georgina. She was affected by me almost as much as I was by her.

"Hello, Dr. Anderson." Her soft response touched my ears as she discretely attempted to detangle her fingers from mine. I couldn't let her go. It was completely irrational, nevertheless I felt if I let her go, she'd run.

That wouldn't do. I couldn't let her go until I had a way to solidify our connection so I could stop resorting to scheduling my hair cuts to coincide with when I thought she'd be at the salon.

Wrapped in a bubble, excluding everyone else, I eased us into conversation. We had limited time before the cocktail hour was over and the dinner portion of the evening began. Once the seated portion of the evening started, she could be who knows where.

"How is Chloe doing?" I asked.

It wasn't idle chit-chat. I actually cared about the kid. But... The question served a dual purpose. I checked on Chloe while also keeping Stephanie talking about a subject I knew she was comfortable discussing.

"She's doing well. Thank you. She had her last visit with Dr. Maxwell who said she healed quite well. It's difficult to look at her face and tell anything ever happened." Her hand relaxed in my grip.

Thankful for the forward progress, I slid closer, dipping my head to hear her better. The action brought us intimately nearer, but she appeared unbothered as she continued to talk.

"I'm so very thankful you and Dr. Maxwell were available that night. The two of you saved my baby. I'll be forever grateful." I felt myself falling into the darkened pool of her eyes.

My mother's voice pierced the cocoon enveloping the two of us. "Jian, sweetheart. Aren't you going to introduce us to the lovely young lady?"

Her nudge to my side garnered a quick glance, before I turned back to Stephanie. The pinch from my mother prompted me to expedite my response.

"Of course. Stephanie Barker, meet my mother, Dr. Sarah Anderson." I grudgingly released Stephanie's fingers to allow her to shake my mom's hand.

Motioning to my mom's new companion, I introduced her as well. My ability to absorb information without giving one hundred percent of my focus aided my recall of the mannequin's name.

"Ms Barker, allow me to also introduce Mrs. Mildred Fontaine." Stephanie extended her hand only to be met with the same limp fingers Mildred presented to me earlier.

Unlike me, Stephanie didn't attempt to grasp the dangling fingers. Instead, she withdrew her hand and uttered a soft, "Pleasure to meet you," in Mildred's general direction.

My mom's eyes danced with glee. "So, you two looked cozy. How do you know one another?"

Knowing my mother as well as I did, I was positive she thought she'd shown a great deal of restraint by waiting a whole five minutes to ask her question.

Stephanie's expectant expression prompted my response. After all, it was *my* mother.

"We met at the hospital last month. She was there visiting someone." I supplied omitting any names.

"Oh... It sounds like there's a story there." My mother enthused with her hands clasped together propping them under her chin with a dreamy grin on her face.

"Not much of one." Stephanie interjected. "Dr. Anderson took really good care of someone I care about deeply. We're all really grateful he was there."

She didn't acknowledge it; however, I saw in her face the second the memory flitted across her mind making her sad for the briefest of instances. Instinctively, I edged closer rubbing her arm gently.

"Barker... I don't believe I've heard of any Barkers in this area. What do you do?" Mildred injected herself into the conversation with an acerbic expression and a borderline snide tone.

I didn't know where she was going with her question, I got bad vibes from Mildred the mannequin.

Before Stephanie could answer, Benjamin volunteered the information. "She works at the salon my wife likes to spend my money in beauti-fying herself every two weeks."

"A salon?" Mildred said slowly, as if the words tasted terrible on her tongue. "As in you're a hairdresser?" Condescension dripped from her voice. Offended on Stephanie's behalf I opened my mouth. Before I could speak, she responded.

"Actually, I'm the owner of the salon along with another separate location. I don't personally see to Mrs. Waters' needs, although she's a valued client. I enjoy speaking with her when she comes in for her appointments."

While Stephanie responded gracefully, it was obvious she'd picked up on the snobbish demeanor Mildred wasn't really trying to hide.

"A salon owner. That sounds interesting!" My mother exclaimed, attempting to salvage the conversation.

Stephanie's appreciative smile was barely in place when an announcement came over the PA system asking everyone to take their seats for the dinner and awards portion of the evening.

Reluctant to allow her to walk away, I asked Benjamin if he would escort my mother to our table—stating a need to speak with Ms Barker for a brief moment in private. Professionally.

If they had a clue about the life of a surgeon, they'd know my excuse didn't hold water. I shamelessly took advantage of their ignorance. I needed to speak to her without the benefit of an audience hanging on our every word.

Bewilderment written across her face, Stephanie allowed me to lead her to the side of the room, away from the people traversing the opening to the larger ballroom where attendants waited to seat them.

"Dr. Anderson—"

"Jian" I interrupted. "Please, call me Jian. Dr. Anderson feels so impersonal."

"Well...I don't really know you in any other way except in your professional capacity as Chloe's physician." She said lowly, glancing around, avoiding my gaze.

"I get it... I'm also trying to change that." I had nothing to lose by being bold. As the saying goes, I had to shoot my shot while I had the chance. Lurking around her place of business like a love-sick teenager wasn't cutting it.

Tipping her head back, skepticism painted her expression. "Excuse me? I don't think I understand."

"Yes, you do. I know you feel it to." Taking both of her hands in mine, I tangled our fingers together. Dipping my head slightly, I captured her eyes. "You've somehow convinced yourself I couldn't be interested in you beyond professional concern for your child. I'd like a chance to prove to you that's not true."

Yeah... It was forward as hell. I didn't care. I'd never forgive myself if I let this woman slip through my fingers without a fight.

"Dr—"

"Jian."

"Jian," she conceded. She held my gaze steadily. Her bewilderment was evident in the slight crinkle of her brow. "I'm not confused because I don't think you could be interested. I'm confused because we've never had a real conversation. Sure, we've spoken about Saffi and around her. You offered me comfort when I needed it. Now, you're acting like we've spent significant time together. It's as if you're ready to take the next step in a natural progression."

"Because I am. Not necessarily the step you're thinking about though." Closing my eyes for a second, I gathered my words carefully.

"What I'm asking for is an opportunity to get to know you away from the hospital. Away from anything related to my role as a doctor. I find you attractive, interesting, and captivating. I wouldn't forgive myself if I didn't at least try..."

"Try what?"

"Try to talk to you and see what it would take for you to agree to be mine."

Her eyes locked on mine. Her probing gaze reached the depths of my soul. Not shrinking away from the probe, I held her stare boldly— blocking out our surroundings.

The heat of our attraction held us immobile. The allure was most definitely mutual. I read it in her eyes. I saw it in the flush beneath her skin creeping up her neck. She may think her darker complexion didn't show her feelings. She was wrong. I saw the change. Her interest was evident to me. I simply needed to get her to trust her feelings.

"Excuse me." One of the event volunteers interrupted our heated stare down. In unison, we broke our gaze turning toward the voice.

"We are ready to begin the program. I was sent to escort Miss Barker to her seat." He seemed like a nice young man, nevertheless when he extended his arm for Stephanie to take, I wanted to break it—and not fix it after.

Stepping up, I grasped Stephanie's hand before she could touch anyone who wasn't me, wrapping her fingers around my bicep. "My apologies. We wouldn't want to hold up the program. By all means, lead the way."

"Um... Yes sir." Recovering quickly, the little welp turned on his heels walking toward the open double doors.

A squeeze from her fingers brought my eyes back to the woman at my side. *Rude!* She mouthed to me. I responded with a slow lopsided grin. No time like the present to teach her I wasn't a man given to letting another man do things I was willing and able to do for her.

Chapter Eleven

STEPHANIE

I walked beside Dr.—no, Jian, in silence after he basically pushed the nice young attendant to the side. The thudding of my heart was so loud, it obscured the sound of the many murmuring voices in the large ballroom. The attendant escorted us to a ten-person table at the front.

Veering away from the traditional dais setting on the stage, the event organizers had placed a single podium at the center with two short sets of stairs leading onto the stage. It was reminiscent of the academy awards on a much smaller scale.

I observed those seated at the table. I noticed Jian's mother, Sarah, was among them. Usually, I sent a hefty donation in lieu of attending these events, so I wasn't surprised I didn't recognize anyone. I only recognized Sarah, because we'd met not fifteen minutes prior.

Purely based on body language, I pinpointed the moment Jian realized we were both assigned to the same table. It's possible the table arrangement was a good thing, but the nervousness settling in my stomach said otherwise. Each seat was occupied with the exception of two conspicuously empty seats conveniently located beside his mother.

With no time for an internal pep talk, I pushed down the nerves.

Jian wasn't off base. I was definitely attracted to him. I felt the draw, even though I tried to ignore it. We didn't move in the same circles. How could anything between us work? Not to mention my life as a single parent.

Pulling myself back into the moment, I nodded politely to the people already seated. Murmuring my thanks to Jian I sat in the chair he pulled out for me.

"Well, hello again, dear! This is a pleasant surprise." Sarah Anderson's eyes, twinkling with mischief, bounced between me and where her son stood behind my seat.

"Yes ma'am." I replied softly. Thankfully, Jian took the chair between me and his mother. Something told me she was a pistol.

Sitting to my left and her right, Jian moved his chair closer to mine draping his arm lightly on the back rest, brushing my upper back in the process. Unable to suppress it, a shiver skipped down my spine.

Momentarily, regret shot through me that the semi-open back of my dress allowed such contact. The stimulation was distracting, especially considering there was nothing we could do about the feelings at the moment.

Looking down at the place setting on the table, I attempted to ignore the assessing grey gaze of Sarah Anderson as her eyes pinged between us—blatantly gauging the situation.

"Stephanie, sweetheart—" Whatever Mrs. Anderson was going to say was cut short when the person, none of us had noticed approach the stage, began to speak.

While Clarice Richards welcomed everyone to the event, I surmised her physical appearance was the very definition of a WASP. Her perfectly coiffed honey blond hair was swept into an elegant chignon. Her flawlessly applied makeup blended well with her lightly tanned skin. The dress draped over her slender frame was cut to accentuate her figure while remaining modest. Of course, it was black. Most people in attendance were either wearing black or dark blue.

My crimson-colored evening gown was a stark departure from the norm. Standing out in the crowd didn't bother me. No matter what I chose to wear, I'd stand out in this group. Atlanta was a Chocolate City.

However, in some charitable spaces, brown faces were still a rarity. That is, brown faces not attached to staff or event workers were rare.

I probably would've worn black as well were it not for Nikki and Joy. They pushed and prodded until I pulled out a gown I'd bought two years ago. I only recently agreed to actually wear said dress in public.

Between the semi open back, the deep vee exposing my cleavage and the high as-hell-split up my left thigh, I had some extremely late buyer's remorse. Did I really want the kind of attention a dress like this would bring on my plus-sized body? Now, seated amongst a sea of black peppered with navy, the point was moot.

From the first minute he'd come close to me tonight, Jian had a hand or some part of his body close to or touching mine in some way. Was it the dress, or was this full-court-press his norm when he was interested?

The questions whirled in my mind. So lost in my thoughts, I detached from the happenings around me. When we'd met at the hospital, I was so focused on Saffi, I really didn't allow myself to think of Jian in any other capacity than as her doctor.

Well... not for long. The man was entirely too fine not to notice—even under those circumstances. I didn't know how to categorize his behavior tonight. My response to him transported me to middle school with my first crush. Butterflies fluttered in my stomach. I wished for something, anything, to settle the feeling.

Giving half an ear to Clarice extolling the virtues of the charity, Hearts and Homes, I perused the printed program they'd left on the table for each of us. Relief relaxed my shoulders when I realized the brevity of the program. I wasn't against networking opportunities, however these events tended to be filled with people who gave to say they'd given—not because they actually cared about the cause.

I'd zoned out so completely, I almost missed the mention of my name. *Why was she calling my name? Was this why Erica was pushing me so hard to attend instead of donating my tickets the way I normally did?*

My eyes flew to the stage meeting a projected image of myself. The head shot from my company website.

"Stephanie Barker has quietly worked with Hearts and Homes for years as one of our most loyal and generous benefactors." Clarice continued.

"Besides her monetary donations, she established an endowment for the children in our program to allow them to attend R.C. Mack Academy, a school for gifted children.

In addition to the endowment, through her company, Barker Properties, LLC she has assisted many of our foster families in starting their own small businesses."

I straightened in my seat, dumbfounded. I didn't crave the spotlight. It wasn't my reason for helping people. I was content working in the background.

My skin warmed under the stares from my table mates, as they listened to Clarice list my personal and business accomplishments along with the ways I contributed to making the charity a success. Then, she said words I wasn't expecting. Had I known any of this was planned, I would've declined. *I've **got** to start actually reading those invitations instead of pushing them off on Erica.*

"And now, without further ado, I present Ms Stephanie Barker, our Person of the Year!" Clarice smiled broadly, clapping her hands, motioning for me to come to the stage.

I felt like I was lifted outside my body. Polite applause broke out. Jian stood, grasped the back of my chair assisting me in standing. In a mental fog, I took comfort in the warmth of his hand on my back as he escorted me up the short flight of stairs.

Glancing up into his face, I quietly thanked him for his support. My decision to attend alone meant, without him, I'd have no support system. I was grateful for his reassuring presence, because I was out of my element. I sincerely enjoyed helping people. I wasn't motivated by accolades and awards.

My face flushed as heat crawled up my neck with each step I took toward the podium where Clarice waited with a crystal-like figurine formed into two hands. It was designed to look as if one hand was pulling while the other reached up.

When I stopped at the lectern, Clarice hugged me, whispering in my ear, "Please don't be angry! We knew if we told you, you wouldn't come. You deserve to be recognized for all that you do."

It was hard to maintain any anger looking into her earnest, sincere face. While physically beautiful, she didn't look like the warmest person. Looks were deceiving. She put her heart into this charity.

She thanked me privately many times before tonight for my contributions. I should've known a day would come when she'd do it publicly. Knowing how much she gave of herself in addition to her level of commitment, extinguished my anger at being put on the spot.

I returned the hug letting her off the hook—slightly. "I'm not angry, but I'll get you for this later." I smiled then stepped in front of the microphone.

"Wow! When I came here tonight, I expected to mingle, have a meal, and listen to all Hearts and Homes has accomplished over the past fiscal year. I thought maybe I'd learn the plans for the upcoming fiscal year. I didn't expect this; however, I'm appreciative."

Raking my eyes around the room, I looked into the many unrecognizable faces before stopping on Jian's handsome visage. Pride filled his expression. *Pride in* **me**?

Understanding halted my words abruptly and emotions crashed in on me. I hadn't seen such blatant pride directed at me since my grandmother passed away. My memories of my father were vague, because he was killed in the first Gulf War when I was still a toddler. Seeing Jian's face stirred something inside me I hadn't felt in a very long time.

Looking down at the statuette cradled in my hands, I spoke again. "Hearts and Homes has been a part of my life since I was a young girl. You see, both of my parents passed away before I was a teenager. My father when I was a toddler then my mother, four short years later. My older sister and I spent almost two years in the foster care system in Savannah before we were fortunate enough to have relatives, my grandparents, become our foster parents before later adopting us as their children."

Pausing, I cleared my throat in an attempt to thwart the tears creeping into my voice. "Hearts and Homes was instrumental in helping us become a family unit as well as finding programs which allowed me to attend R.C. Mack Academy on scholarship.

That opportunity snowballed into me being able to graduate high school early. I went on to earn my associate's, bachelor's and master's degrees before the age of twenty-two. After I became a foster parent myself, I learned more about the much-needed services provided by Hearts and Homes. They offered counseling—individual and family, along with a host of other really great benefits to the families who participated in the program."

As if drawn by a magnet, my eyes are pulled back to Jian's face. I couldn't decipher the element joined with the pride painted across his expression.

"To be recognized by such a great organization, which has done so much good for so many people, long before I began to contribute, is humbling. My sincere thanks."

Gripping the figurine like a lifeline, I nodded curtly to Clarice then walked to the edge of the stage. Before I can set one foot on the descending stair, Jian was there.

Hand outstretched, he once again offered support to navigate my way down. His hand offered support. His eyes promised me so much more. I wasn't sure what to do with the quiver his look elicited in my belly. So, I cast my eyes down, accepted his hand allowing him to escort me back to the table.

The rest of the evening passed in a blur. People offered their congratulations, after which the meal was served. As we ate, other Board members performed the requisite sales pitch to get those in attendance to reach into their pockets a little deeper to support the many great things Hearts and Homes had planned.

The only part of the evening not shrouded in a haze were my interactions with Jian. His nearness and attentiveness to my needs affected me in ways I wasn't prepared for. I wasn't sure I wanted to delve too deeply into the feelings he evoked.

Being one of the honorees squashed my original plan of slipping away inconspicuously. Reaching into the small clutch purse, which was only large enough to hold my cellphone, key fob and a tube of lipstick, I checked the notifications on my phone.

When I planned my attendance, I'd scheduled a car service to pick me up. I cancelled the car when it became obvious I couldn't leave at the time I'd previously intended. I wasn't too worried. Getting a rideshare from this area of the city was easy.

My phone check revealed no missed calls. Saffi was sleeping over at Nikki's. Other than a possible sugar high, I knew she was fine. Knowing she was okay didn't stop me from tapping out a quick text to ask how things were going. Nikki's reply was quick and curt. In no uncertain terms, I was told to mind the business that paid me and leave them alone.

The deep chuckle from my left drew my attention in time to see a smirking Jian who made no attempt to hide he'd read my message.

"Excuse you!" Pressing the sleep button, I slipped my phone back into the small purse.

I gave him my best stink eye. His response was a smile. "Didn't your mother ever teach you it's rude to read someone's text messages?" I hissed.

"Technically... no. By the time cellphones were commonly used, I was well into my teens. Those types of lessons were in the past." The words had no sooner left his mouth, when he jumped in his seat and whisper-screamed, "Ouch!"

Giving his mother a stricken look, he asked, "Mom! Why did you pinch me?"

"I pinched you for being rude **and** for allowing this nice young lady to think I didn't raise a proper gentleman. I shouldn't have to have **specifically** told you not to read someone's text messages. I told you not to read other people's letters without permission.

Text messages are digital letters. You, my brilliant son, are parsing words to suit you and doing it at the expense of my parenting. I won't have it," she said. Then, placing her hand on his trim side, she proceeded to pinch him again.

"Ow! Okay. Okay! I apologize. You did teach me to respect people's privacy." He acquiesced.

"Thank you. Now apologize to her as well." She said, giving him Mom-face to rival all mom faces.

Turning his molten chocolate eyes on me, he actually looked contrite when he apologized. "My sincere apologies. I shouldn't have read your message. It was an accident. When I realized I was intruding, I should have looked away."

The way he tilted his head looking at me through his thick eyelashes, reminded me of a puppy caught in the act of creating havoc. A puppy so adorable you couldn't stay angry.

Jian wasn't a puppy. Not even close. He made it hard to stay angry with him though. Truthfully, I wasn't angry. Mildly annoyed. But not angry.

"Apology accepted." I started to add he should keep his eyes to himself, except the way they lit up when I accepted his apology stole my words. The small change in his expression transformed his face and struck me mute.

～

While it was still technically summer, it was cooler in the evening. When I stepped out into the lobby, I regretted my lack of at least a light wrap. No sooner had I had the thought than I was enveloped in warmth. Jian draped his jacket on my shoulders.

His appearance in the lobby surprised me, because I'd excused myself from he and his mother while they were saying their goodbyes. I didn't expect him to follow me out, let alone meet a need I hadn't expressed aloud.

Looking at him in his crisp white button down and bowtie I appreciated the width of his shoulders and the way his torso formed an almost perfect vee. Not in the over exaggerated way fitness fanatics looked, but a natural taper proportional to the width of his chest and shoulders.

"A-hem."

Throat clearing broke me out of my thoughts. I realized I'd been ogling Jian for who knows how long. Long enough to require someone to 'snap' me out of the stare-fest.

"Oh! Thank you." My eyes flew up to meet his amused orbs. I recovered a bit awkwardly tugging at the lapels of the warm covering. Even with my abundant curves, his jacket was large enough to offer me the necessary coverage to fight off the slight chill.

"Stephanie dear, we thought you'd left without saying goodbye. I told Jian to stop dilly dallying." Mrs. Anderson leaned into my space, speaking conspiratorially. I didn't miss her son's eye roll in response to her little speech.

"No ma'am, I'm still here. I stepped out to order a car to pick me up." I snapped my mouth shut to keep from saying anything else. I'd already said more than I intended.

Something about the woman pulled information from me without my consent. She didn't need to know when or why I cancelled my car service. I surely wasn't about to tell her.

"Sweetheart, you need a ride? Don't call anyone, I'm sure Jian would be happy to take you wherever you need to go. Isn't that right, son?"

"Of course." Although his words were said calmly, his face stretched to reveal the widest smile. His eyes probed mine broadcasting something undiscernible. Or maybe I didn't want to know.

"Oh no. I wouldn't want you going out of your way. I can just get a rideshare."

"Nonsense, dear. I won't hear of you riding with some stranger." She said it as if she'd known me longer than the scant two hours we'd spent together. *She* was a stranger to me.

"My mom's right. It's no problem. I'd be happy to take you home..."

The way he trailed off when he said he'd be happy to take me home sent a shiver down my spine as I tried and failed to ignore the double entendre. Take me home indeed.

In very short order, I found myself ensconced in the front passenger seat of a luxury SUV riding through the city streets. His mother insisted on sitting in the back, since Jian was taking her home first.

Any arguments I had were quickly waved away. Even though my home was not near his place in Buckhead, they insisted it wasn't a problem.

I didn't live near his condo—which his mom volunteered the location of—but I lived in the same direction of his parent's home. They lived in a subdivision not far from mine, but their property was on a lake.

I'd visited the area, then nixed the idea of purchasing a home there. Saffi was still in grade school when I bought my house. Being near a large body of water with a small child, wasn't ideal.

The car ride passed with Mrs. Anderson keeping up a steady stream of conversation. She asked me about everything from my salon to my real estate business, to Saffi. The conversation was so effortless that I found myself, once again, disclosing far more than I intended.

Even with the steady dialogue, I couldn't ignore the undercurrent flowing between myself and Jian. Each time I glanced in his direction, his eyes were waiting. It felt so natural when he intermittently touched my hand as it rested atop the statuette in my lap. I experienced the same feeling when he adjusted his jacket still draped around my shoulders as well.

My libido, which I thought had gone on a permanent hiatus, roared back to life. Heat, which had nothing to do with the buttery leather seats nor the warm dinner jacket, radiated from my center, crept up my neck settling in my cheeks.

Far quicker than I expected, we pulled into the circular driveway in front of a Tudor style mini-mansion. Mrs. Anderson cut off her re-telling of a story from Jian's youth almost mid-sentence. If I'd been paying closer attention, I might've found it comical. As it was, I was happy for the short reprieve to my senses when he got out to walk her to the door.

In almost record time, he escorted her safely inside and was back in the vehicle next to me. Diligently, I tried to ignore the energy flowing between us.

I watched the scenery as we wove our way out of the neighborhood. His warm palm landed on my thigh pulling my attention from the passing landscape.

Stopped at an intersection, he waited until I looked at him. "I was right earlier; I'm not alone in this am I? You feel it too, don't you?" His deep voice was barely above a whisper, but I had no problem hearing him.

My own voice was stuck in my throat, so I nodded mutely. There was no point to denying my feelings. Nervous energy forced me to lick my lips and grip my items resting at the juncture of my thighs.

Jian's eyes locked on with laser focus tracking the movement of my tongue on my lips. Emitting a combination groan and growl, he put the car in park, leaned across the console and closed the gap between us.

"Say yes." It wasn't a request. It was more of a command. The sensual energy between us didn't allow for anything except my full agreement.

"Yes." I responded softly.

His mouth connected with mine in an urgent, demanding kiss. Licking along my lips, he ordered them to open to allow him entry. I acquiesced immediately.

Abandoning the award and clutch, my hands reached for him—one in the soft, short hair at his nape, the other on his chest feeling the thudding rhythm of his heart.

Not to be left out, his digits were busy as well. One reached into the split in my dress, kneading my exposed thigh, while the other anchored itself in my hair creating havoc to my carefully constructed up-do. His fingers fisted in my hair, tugging my head to the angle he desired. Trailing kisses along my exposed neck, he nipped at the sweet spot behind my ear. A gasping moan escaped my lips.

BEEEEP! BEEP! The blaring of a horn penetrated our lustful fog. Breathing heavily, Jian looked into my eyes, his expression promising more. *Later.* Another impatient horn blare prompted him to put the car in gear, taking the right turn as directed by his navigation system.

Chapter Twelve

JIAN

I deserved a fucking medal. Despite my orders from the not-so-silent partner in my pants to hurry the hell up, I obeyed all traffic laws. Well... most traffic laws. Even obeying the rules of the road, I managed a fifteen-minute drive in ten minutes flat.

Cutting five minutes off the travel time may not mean much to most people. But, for me, it was the difference between making love to my woman for the first time in the back seat of my SUV versus stretching her luscious body across a bed when I laid claim to what is most assuredly mine.

Logically, I knew I needed to give her space to catch up to me, but I couldn't. I'd spent far too much time thinking of her. Wanting to be near her—to touch her. My patience hung by the thinnest surgical suture while she entered the code to the front door.

The few seconds it took for her to disable the security system, felt like a lifetime. I waited anxiously as she placed her award and small purse on the side table. As soon as she was free, I was on her again. With their own agenda, my hands reached for her. One grabbed her ample ass while the other threaded into her hair, tugging her head to allow me to recapture her plump lips.

"Bedroom. Now. Or I'll fuck you right here against this wall, leaving a print of your ass on it for everyone to see. Then they'll know you took my dick right here in the foyer."

Kicking my shoes off, I backed her into the wall next to the door. Taking her lips again, I pressed my hips into hers thrusting forward trying to relieve the pressure in my groin as my cock ached to be inside her. I released her lips, tracing the column of her neck with nips and kisses. Damn, she smelled and tasted delicious.

Taking advantage of the high split in her dress, I gripped her ass hoisting her against the wall. Balancing her using the wall and my body, I slipped her feet out of those sexy ruby red heels. All the while, my mouth roved from the pulse point on her neck to her lips then back again.

"Talk to me baby. Are we going to your bedroom, or do you *want* to be fucked against the wall? If that's what you want, I can make it happen."

Moaning, she pushed against my shoulders. I prayed she didn't ask me to stop. I took a step back, going against what my body wanted. To my relief, she grasped my hand leading me to the stairs I'd thus far ignored. My pre-occupation with getting inside her made them irrelevant until now.

Entering the bedroom closely behind her, I swept my gaze around the space. It was feminine without being over the top girlie, not that I gave it much attention. My primary concern was joining with Stephanie in the most intimate of ways. Zeroing in on the bed, I pulled her over to the California King.

Ignoring the short wooden step stool, I turned her to face the bed. If I were more patient, I'd take a moment to admire the cutout in the back of the dress. It exposed a swath of skin at the center extending downwards, almost to the top of her delectable ass.

I lacked the willpower to stop and admire it in the way it deserved. My fingers, nimble from years of working with surgical tools, flew between unclasping the hook at her nape, then pulling down the short zipper.

Once both were released, I quickly moved the material off her shoulders. Sliding it over her hips, allowing the gown to pool at her feet. My eyes swept over every inch of exposed skin thankful the process wasn't hindered by any restrictive undergarments.

"Fuck... Your body is amazing."

Barely contained passion made my voice gruff. Some men had hangups about a woman's size. I'd always gravitated toward generously curved women. I loved their plushness; how they felt against my harder body.

Stephanie's ass, high and round rested atop legs thick enough to support the substantial portion of feminine assets with which she'd been blessed. My mouth watered. I wanted to drop to my knees to kiss the satin covered cheeks, however the jerking of my cock reminded me of more pressing matters. Like getting inside her paradise.

Sliding my fingers into the sides of the silky panties, I pushed them down her legs to the floor. Turning her around, I removed the interesting looking contraption she wore to lift her magnificent breasts. It wasn't a regular bra. I didn't know what it was, but figuring it out wasn't a priority.

She made no objections to the way I took over undressing her. Other than occasional gasps, she silently complied to my every directing touch and nudge. Once I had her fully naked, I couldn't stop my gaze from greedily roaming over every inch of her beautiful body.

"You're so fucking beautiful, Baby." Capturing her lips, I dipped my tongue into her mouth tasting her sweetness. Skimming my hands down her sides, I grabbed two hands full of her superb ass. Bending my knees I lifted her, placing her on the edge of the bed.

Stepping back, I quickly rid myself of my clothes. As much as I wanted to keep touching her, I didn't lay a finger on her again until I was just as naked as she was. Once the barrier of clothing was removed, I used hands and lips to explore my new personal wonderland.

"Lie back, Baby."

I moved her more fully onto the bed, pulling the duvet cover back tossing it to the side. Her beautiful body tempted me. I wanted to spend more time getting to know every inch of her. My dick yelled at me to get him to the promised land between those thick thighs.

Layering kisses from her neck, over her breasts, down to her neatly trimmed pussy, I groaned and tried to slow down—to make sure she was ready so it would be good for her. When her natural scent hit my nose, I couldn't take it anymore.

With one hungry, suckling kiss against her labia I captured her clitoris between my lips. Moaning when her flavor hit my tongue, I closed my eyes to savor it. *Sweet.*

My engorged shaft throbbed, reminding me of our other needs, so I reluctantly released my new treat. I crawled back up her torso, positioning my rock-hard dick against the heat of her opening.

"Wait!" She pressed a hand on my stomach to stop me.

Fuck... Stopping before I entered what I knew would be heaven, I asked, "What's wrong, Sweetheart?"

Looking into her face, I saw the same lust I felt mirrored back to me. So, why had she stopped me?

"Condom," she rasped out.

Double Fuck! How did I forget the damn condoms? Because I was escorting my fucking mother. Who takes condoms with them on a night out with their mom? *Don't answer that. Shit!*

"Do you have any?" Her voice was soft, almost tentative. She squirmed beneath me, rubbing those scrumptious legs along my sides.

"No... Fuck..." My jaw tightened. Dropping my head, I pressed my forehead against hers rubbing back and forth. I couldn't believe we'd gotten this close only to be forced to stop.

Grudgingly, I lifted myself from her flopping onto my back on the other side of the bed. Turning to my side, my gaze roved her body. She didn't cover herself. The turgid peaks of her breasts called to me.

"I don't suppose it would matter if I told you I was clean and I haven't been with anyone in the last year? Or that I've never been with anyone without protection." I threw out hopefully, knowing it almost certainly wouldn't matter.

"No. We can't..." She moaned. It could've been a moan of frustration or pleasure, because I'd begun tracing her tight nipples with my fingertips.

"But..."

"But what, Sweets?" I pinched then gently twisted the bud.

"I think there are...Oh shit...Umm... condoms in the nightstand over there." Her broken, whimpered words, finally registered to my brain.

"You have condoms?" I winced at the sharpness of my tone. It wasn't my intention to sound so harsh. I was borderline ecstatic to hear I wouldn't have to limit myself to pleasing her orally and jacking off in the shower.

When she shrank back, I quickly corrected myself. Placing apologetic kisses on her face, I leveraged myself on my arms above her with my body partially covering hers. "Where are the condoms, Sweetheart?"

Pointing, she indicated which nightstand held my golden ticket. "That one. Top drawer."

Giving no thought to style or form, I lunged for the nightstand ripping open the drawer. Neatly placed in one corner was a stack of condoms in various packaging.

Not caring to consider why they were there, I happily snatched a few. Immediately ripping open a packet, I made short work of rolling it on.

As much as I wanted to, I didn't plunge into her straight away. Instead, I spent some time with my new friends suckling, nibbling and kissing her breasts until she squirmed uncontrollably beneath me. Her hands gripped my hair then skimmed along my shoulders. My fingers slipped between her silky thighs sliding over my treasure feeling her moisture seeping out.

"Damn, Sweets... You're so wet. Are your ready for me? Hmm? Do you want me to stroke this pussy?"

"Mmmm..." She responded in a pleasured moan.

"What is it, Sweets? I can't understand you." I increased the pressure dipping one digit into the heat of her channel. "Tell me what you want. All you have to do is say it and I'll make it happen."

Why the fuck was I teasing her when I was about to burst all over the damn sheets before I could even get inside her? I had no answers. I had nothing except a deep need to know she wanted me as badly as I wanted her.

Sucking, then releasing a nipple, I kissed my way to the dip where her neck met her shoulder. I worried the spot with my tongue—alternating between licks, sucks and kisses. Her eyes slammed shut. Her head tipped backwards as she arched, while her hands returned to my hair, fisted in my short locks. I couldn't tell if she was trying to push me away or pull me closer.

"Please Jian... Don't tease..." The pleading note in her voice broke me.

"I'm not teasing you, Sweets. Look at me."

Lust-filled, dark pools looked up at me through her long thick lashes.

"Do you really want me, Sweetheart? This isn't just about tonight. I've been drawn to you from the moment we met. Tell me, do you feel it too? Is it all one-sided? Am I in it alone?"

I'd already asked her if this was what she wanted, but the desire for validation rode me hard. I needed her to say the words.

Her fingers, that were gripping my hair, traveled down the side of my face.

"I feel it. Even in the midst of stress the first time we met, I still felt it. I didn't know what to do with it then. I do now. I want this. I want you."

Her words released the dam of desire. I pressed my chest to hers as I settled between her gorgeous thighs, rubbing my length along the seam of her plump pussy lips. Without warning, I notched the head of my shaft at her opening and entered her sweet haven. I didn't stop pushing until my balls rested against her—just shy of being sucked into my private paradise.

"Fuck yeah, Sweets..." I groaned into her ear.

We were chest to chest with my face pressed into the side of hers. She shifted, pressing her thighs along my torso with her knees almost in my armpits. The move tipped her hips up allowing me to sink even farther into the depths of the sweetest pussy on earth.

Her sexy whimpers and pants had me too close to the edge quicker than I wanted to be there. Every time she moaned, I felt the contraction of her canal as it pulsed against my dick. It was too much. I grit my teeth as I worked to control the urge to cum. I'm no two-pump chump.

Disentangling myself from the grip she had on my shoulders, I sat up on my knees. With my dick still deep within her, I grabbed the underside of her thighs pressing them to her chest. The position gave me the perfect view of my cock stroking in and out. *Fucking turn on.*

With a dipping twirl of my hips, I pulled out almost completely before sliding back in to the hilt hitting her G-spot on the downstroke, heightening the pleasure for both of us. My Sweets was multi-orgasmic. Even though I felt her quiver and quake beneath me, she continued to urge me to fuck her deeper—to give her all of me.

Breathing in marathon worthy gulps, I wasn't sure how much longer I could hold back. If I was going, I had to take her with me. I pushed her thighs open wider to gain more access.

Laying forward, no longer hovering above her on my knees put us chest to chest once again. I grabbed her hands, entwining our fingers together, pressing them to the bed. The intimacy of the position permitted me to watch her face, cataloging the range of emotions.

The erotic sounds of our bodies moving together rang out into the room. The scent of our lovemaking was almost overwhelming. Pumping my hips faster, I raced toward completion.

Swiveling my hips on my inward thrust to stimulate her clit, I wrung one last orgasm from her sweet body. Roaring with my own release, I collapsed against her, raining soft kisses on her neck, shoulders and the side of her face.

"Damn, Sweets…" I groaned into her ear. I'd come, but my cock was still hard as steel. Reluctantly, I rolled away. Spotting the bathroom, I padded inside to discard the condom.

Done with the condom disposal, I climbed back onto the bed. I knelt beside her grabbing a new condom—rolling it on. Lying on her back, she watched me with hooded eyes. When she realized what I was doing her eyes widened.

"Jian?"

"Yes, Sweetheart"

"You're still hard."

"I know." A knowing smirk tipped my lips upward.

"Didn't you cum?"

"Yes."

"Then why are you still hard?" Confusion marred her smooth brow.

"I'm not done with you. I want more."

"I thought that only happened in romance novels."

Capturing her lips with mine, I cupped her breasts, stimulating her nipples.

"Then I guess this is your real-life romance novel experience. Now, turn over. On your knees." I tapped her outer thigh to get her moving.

Once she complied, I lifted her upper body, pressing my chest to her back. I continued to roam my hands over her, priming her body for round two. Turning her head to the side and tilting her chin, I recaptured her lips, swallowing her delicate whimpers. When the exploration of my fingers confirmed she was ready to take me again, I pushed her shoulders forward until her upper body rested on the bed.

Placing my other hand on her hip, partially gripping her ass, I surged forward without warning, giving her my entire length in one plunge. A muffled gasp escaped her lips as she undulated her hips fucking me back.

"Damn, Sweets, do that again. Show me you want this cock as much as I want your sweet pussy."

Fully in the moment with me, she responded to my encouragement. Even with the limited movement allowable in the position, she fucked me back as eagerly as I fucked her.

I rubbed along her back before grabbing two handfuls of her delicious ass. I was totally gone. This woman was mine. There was no way in hell I would let her get away from me.

Cracking my eyes open, I was temporarily blinded by sunlight streaming through a sliver of an opening between the curtains. It took me a second to get my bearings and realize I wasn't in my own bed. When my actual location filtered into my brain, I stretched out a hand encountering nothing except a cool, empty space.

Turning away from the blinding shaft of light, I wondered when the voluptuous form, which was cuddled into my side when I fell asleep, had disappeared. Where had she gone?

Groggily, I pulled myself to a sitting position heaving my naked body from the bed. I didn't remember when we finally called it a night.

It was after more than a couple of rounds of very intense sex. I frowned at waking alone, because I'd hoped for a morning repeat.

Despite my initial sluggishness, I knew if I'd encountered Stephanie's curves against me this morning, I would've been hard pressed not to start my day deep in her delicious pussy.

Getting myself together, I trudged into the ensuite bathroom where I found fresh towels and a toothbrush, still in the packaging, laid out on the counter between the double sinks. Smiling at her thoughtfulness, I opened the glass shower door turning on the water.

I nixed the idea of going out to my vehicle to retrieve the go-bag I kept there. I always kept a bag in the car, just in case I had to change at the hospital or stay overnight unexpectedly.

Absent the items from my go-bag, I redressed in the clothes I wore the night before—sans underwear. With my jacket in hand, I padded downstairs in my socks listening for sounds to help me locate the woman who dominated my thoughts.

Draping my jacket over the banister, I noticed our shoes haphazardly strewn in front of the door. I lined them up neatly before I followed the sound of music coming from an open doorway.

I walked silently into the kitchen, spotting her standing in front of the farmhouse style sink with a coffee mug in her hand—seemingly transfixed by something outside the window directly above it. Continuing into the room, I didn't stop until I was right behind her. I slid my arms around her waist and nuzzled the crook of her neck. Startling slightly at first, she quickly relaxed her back against my front.

"Good morning, Sweets."

"Good morning."

"Mmm... What are you looking at?"

"Hm? Oh nothing. I was thinking."

"Thinking about...?"

"Nothing specific. Just thinking."

Gently, I took the coffee mug from her hands and placed it to the side. Turning her, I braced my arms on the sink to either side of her, boxing her in.

"Look at me, Sweets." My softly spoken demand brought her eyes from their unfocused stare at the buttons of my shirt, up to my face. "Now. Tell me what you were thinking about."

"I was thinking about—"

Her words are halted when our bubble was breached by the sound of the front door loudly closing and a woman's voice calling out.

"Step! Hey Step! Where you at girl? I brought Peanut home. Heck, by the looks of the fly ass Levante Trofeo parked out front and those big ass shoes by the front door, we might need to turn around and go back to my house."

Looking horrified, Stephanie hastily tried to extricate herself from my embrace. Her actions stung a bit. It almost felt like she was ashamed to be seen with me. *That couldn't be it. Right?*

Despite the sting, I released her. Stepping back, I gave her space. Her beautiful obsidian gaze found mine in an unspoken plea. I had no time to delve into the silent request before we were face to face with the silence stealer.

Chapter Thirteen

STEPHANIE

Before Jian came down, I stood at the sink trying to figure out how to get him the hell out of my house before Nikki brought Saffi home. I didn't do hook ups. I've dated, but Saffi has never seen me with a man.

I didn't like the idea of parading different men in front of her. None of the guys I'd dated had graduated to full-on relationship status. I sure as hell hadn't brought any of them home. *What the hell was I doing?*

When I heard Nikki yell out, I panicked. I froze in Jian's arms for a split second before pushing at his chest to put space between us. She was here and I didn't have a plan. *Shit!*

Nikki rounded the corner into the kitchen then came to an abrupt stop. I knew she was about to say something very Nikki. It was written all over her face.

"Well... Hello... Girl, you should have told me you had company. I would have kept Peanut at my place until you called."

"Umm... It's no problem. Thank you for bringing her home and for letting her stay with you last night. I hope she wasn't any trouble." My hands fiddled with the edge of my robe.

Being in unchartered territory had me floundering. Running

nervous fingers through my messy hair, I took a deep calming breath. I decided to act like it was perfectly normal for there to be a man standing in my kitchen at nine a.m. on a Sunday morning.

I felt Jian stiffen beside me. Despite my effort to distance myself, he was still standing close enough for me to feel his body heat and energy. I tipped my head to the side when I didn't see Saffi standing beside Nikki.

"Where is Saffi?" I asked with a slight frown.

"She went to put her stuff in her room. Stop trying to avoid my questions. You know what? Skip you." Nikki extended a hand to Jian.

"Hello, I'm Nikki, the best friend. And you are?"

"Jian. Nice to meet you." To my horror, the two shook hands then entered into light conversation. Neither was making any move to leave. Nikki normally didn't hang around after a drop off unless we had plans or I had breakfast ready. We didn't have plans. Besides, I hadn't made anything other than coffee.

While they talked, I stood there not sure what to do with myself. I had no clue how to behave. After the handshake, Jian moved right back to my side sliding his arm around me clearly staking his claim.

Even though I knew there was no way Nikki was leaving without getting the tea, I was about to interrupt her conversation with Jian when Saffi came flying around the corner.

"Auntie, I'm hungry. Tee-Tee said she wasn't cooking because you normally cook a big breakfast on Sunday and she—Dr. J?" Saffi stopped complaining about her empty stomach when she spotted Jian beside me with his arm around my waist. Her shock at seeing him there with his arms around me was written all over her face.

"Hello again, Chloe. It's good to see you. How have you been?" Jian replied smoothly, as though it was common for him to stand in our kitchen conversing in his sock feet.

"I'm...fine..." Her forehead crinkled in confusion. "Auntie why is Dr. J here? Dr. J, why do you have your hands on my auntie?

"Well, I'm—"

"You know what?" There was no way I could let Jian finish that sentence. "I didn't make it to the grocery store yesterday, so I don't have everything I need for breakfast this morning."

Total lie. But, I had to say something. I had to get them out of the house. I needed time to get myself together. Also, Jian and I had to talk. I grasped onto the first thing to drop into my head.

"Nikki, would you mind taking Saffi to pick something up? Not fast food though. Maybe the diner Peaches is always talking about. It's not far away. What's the name? Cup and Sup? She says they have a great breakfast menu."

Talking fast, I turned pleading eyes onto Nikki. I attempted to step away from Jian, but the tightening of his fingers let me know it wasn't going to happen. So, any thoughts of getting him to leave in the next few minutes went out the window.

"Uh-huh... Sure... I'll take Peanut out for breakfast. Peanut, go on out to the car, I'll be right there." She stretched out her arm and pressed the key fob, remotely unlocking the doors. However, she made no moves to actually leave herself.

"Give me a call or shoot me a text when you're ready for me to bring her back." She said after a few moments of silent assessment. Thankfully, she didn't add a Nikki-ism before she walked out of the kitchen.

As soon as we heard the front door close, I found myself face to chest with Jian when he abruptly spun around—once again caging me between himself and the countertop. He didn't speak at first.

Silently, he hovered over me, his body coiled with tension. Gathering my courage, I lifted my eyes from watching his chest rise and fall only to be ensnared by his intense gaze.

"Are you ashamed of me? Of what we did together?"

"What?! No! Why would you say that?"

"What am I supposed to think? The moment you heard your friend's voice, you looked terrified. You pushed me away. Then, you acted as if you didn't want me to touch you."

"I'm not ashamed of you."

"Do you regret being with me last night? Is that it?"

"No... I don't regret being with you last night."

"Then what is it? Because, Babe, right now, it seems like both of those things are true from my perspective."

He held nothing back. The hurt was plainly displayed on his face—the look in his dark cognac-colored orbs made my chest tighten, physically constricting at the very thought of bringing him pain.

Searching his eyes, I gathered my thoughts to try to explain the way I felt. Wading through the emotions clogging my throat, stealing my voice, I attempted to explain.

"I'm a single parent."

"I know..."

"Please..." I let the sentence trail off asking him to give me space to finish before chiming in. "I was raised, mostly, with my grandparents until my grandfather passed away. My grandmother never remarried. I never saw her with anyone else, although I'm sure she dated."

I dropped my gaze momentarily, once again focusing on the buttons on his shirt. With two fingers on my chin, he tilted my head bringing my traveling eyes back to his.

"My sister and I had a mix of friends, some had two parent households. Some were single parents. A few of the girls were in homes with single mothers. Things happened to them that shouldn't have happened...

Things were done by their mother's boyfriends. Those were the times when Grandma Vi was vocal about stuff she normally considered 'grown folks business'.

She drilled into us how important it was for a single mother to not bring a bunch of different men around their children—especially their daughters."

Jian's body stiffened under my hands on his chest; his deep inhale indicating his displeasure at the implication of my words. I quickly reassured him I didn't see him as a threat to Saffi.

"I'm not saying you're the kind of man who would harm my little girl."

"What are you saying then?" Tension dripped from every word.

"I'm saying I took those lessons to heart. I started paying attention to those situations growing up. I saw she was right.

Not all of the girls had things happen to them, although the girls who had different men in and out of their mother's lives tended to be the same girls with attachment issues. Guys took advantage of them because they were willing to do whatever it took to get and keep a boyfriend.

The boys who saw the parade of men seemed to not have very much respect for women in general with the exception of their mothers—which is a whole psychology lesson I don't want to go into."

Unconsciously, I rubbed my hands along his chest, smoothing the tension from his body. I didn't realize I was doing it, until his hands landed on mine stopping my movements.

"So... as I was saying, I paid attention. I've never wanted to do anything to warp Saffi's idea of relationships or potentially expose her to a predator. So, I don't have sleepovers. I also don't introduce her to a man unless I feel like he's going to be in my life for a while."

Slipping a hand from beneath his, I slid it upwards tangling my fingers in the hair at the nape of his neck.

"I could never be ashamed of you, but this is unchartered territory for me. I didn't know how to handle it. Put yourself in my shoes.

One moment, you're going about your daily life. You go to work. You come home. In between running your businesses, you take your kid to her appointments and extracurricular activities.

The entire time, you never mention dating or a relationship to your child. Then... Bam! There's a man in your home. In your bed. Standing in your kitchen with his body pressed against yours when your child walks in. How would you react?"

"Well, I wouldn't have a man in my bed. I'm strictly hetero."

"Stop it! I'm serious."

"Ok. Ok. I can see how it could be awkward. But, can you see how it looks to me? One second we're cozy, basking in the morning sun. The next, you're trying to physically distance yourself from me."

"It wasn't just awkward, Jian. I felt like all the talk I did about my sister Danielle not setting a good example for Saffi just went flying out the window. Here I am with a man I never mentioned and it's obvious he'd spent the night. It makes me look and feel like a hypocrite."

Before I recognized what was happening, my legs were wrapped around his waist as he lifted me walking to a clear section of countertop. He placed me where he wanted me nestling himself between my legs. In our new position, I was almost eye-level with him.

"Whoa!" I yelped, grabbing onto his shoulders to keep my balance.

"Easy, Sweets. I've got you. I don't know about you, but my neck was starting to bother me. I thought a change in position might be in order."

"A change which brings us almost eye to eye, placing you closer to me?"

"Win-Win." A negligent shrug and smirk accompanied his reply. Our physical change in position, also brought a change in his demeanor.

"Sweetheart, I know all of this seems sudden to you and you're trying to figure it all out. And, because it doesn't fit in a neat little box, you're struggling to understand how we ended up here.

I'll do my best to give you some space to catch up, just not too much. I can't back up all the way. Not now that I'm finally where I've wanted to be for the past few months."

As he spoke, his fingers drew circles along the sides of my thighs, edging towards my ass before landing there briefly. Then, they moved upwards to continue the circling pattern on my back. His touch was distractingly hypnotic. Not enough for me to miss his words though.

Sure, I had butterflies doing battle in my stomach anytime I was near him. And, I found him insanely attractive. His words tilted my world a bit because he was talking about a whole ass relationship. He was much farther along with his feelings than I was.

I couldn't kid myself, though. This was a relationship. It had to be. It couldn't be a fling. After the fateful night we met, I went about my day-to-day life; however, he'd never been far from my thoughts.

The few times we'd encountered each other after Saffi left the hospital were brief, but filled with unacknowledged sexual tension laced with personal curiosity between the two of us. It was undeniable. I started imagining that I saw him in places where he couldn't have been. I even convinced myself I saw him exiting the barbershop side of the salon a couple of times.

Taking my own fingers on an exploratory journey, I traced the lines of his pecs under the white button down. Concentrating on the task as if it were of the utmost importance, I traced the muscles under the material stretched across them.

"Sweetheart... I know it's not the way you would've wanted it. That being said, I'm not going anywhere. Whether you introduce me as your man today, tomorrow or next week, it wouldn't matter."

"My man? We haven't even been on a proper date!"

"Damn right. I'm your man, and you're my woman. Don't play with me. I meant every word I said to you last night, Sweetheart. This isn't a one-time thing.

There's no going back. We're in this. If dates are what you need to make it real to you, then I'll take you on dates. FYI, I was gonna do that anyway."

As if we weren't already close enough, he dropped his forehead to mine. The way he stared at me made me think he could read my thoughts.

"The one thing I noticed about you from the first moment we met was how great of a mom you are. You do everything within your power to make certain Chloe feels loved, safe and protected.

When I spoke to her, I heard the respect you taught her. I also saw her intelligence, her compassion along with so many other things. I know you're responsible for molding her into such a well-rounded young lady."

His hands cupped my face surrounding it with the warmth emanating from him.

"You're not messing up by letting me in, Sweets. I promise. I'd never do anything to jeopardize what you're trying to instill in her. Ever."

His voice combined with his facial expression—*damn he was entirely too handsome*—were enough to convince me of his sincerity. I responded in a series of slow nods as my fingers applied pressure to his nape to bring his lips closer to mine.

There was nothing to do except move forward. I didn't want to end what we started before we'd really begun. My issue was, I was unsure of how to navigate a morning after situation the likes of which I had zero experience with.

Pressing my lips to his, I shivered slightly at the contact. Memories of the previous night flooded my thoughts causing my insides to flutter and my center to slicken in anticipation.

Although I initiated the kiss, he quickly took over. His tongue swiped at the seal of my lips requesting entry. Granting him access, I sighed at the feelings of arousal his invasion inspired.

While his tongue explored my mouth, nimble fingers tugged at the tie holding my robe together slipping inside once the knot was freed. On a mission, they skimmed my sides on a path directly to my breasts. Inhaling sharply, I unconsciously arched into his touch as his digits plucked at my nipples bringing them to sensitive peaks.

Not satisfied, his roaming hands glided over my curves before landing on the globes of my ass, squeezing. Using his hold on my southern cheeks, he pulled my center closer to where he stood nestled between my legs.

Releasing my lips, he trailed kisses along my jawline before latching onto the special spot just below my ear. *How the hell did he know it was my weakness?*

"How much time do we have?" He murmured into my ear, still gently nibbling and kissing along my neck and shoulders.

"Hmmm...? What?" I responded, unable to focus with the chaos he caused to my senses.

"How long before your friend brings Chloe back home?" He asked, peppering kisses along my shoulder on a path to my lips.

"Ummm... An hour, maybe more. Whenever I call."

"Good to know. I'm thinking we should make the most of our time."

Grasping two hands full of my ass, he pulled me to the edge of the counter lifting me—keeping me close to his body. Instinctively, I tightened my thighs holding on as he began walking. I'm not small. It's been years since someone carried me. In any capacity. So, I was nervous especially when I saw he was moving towards the stairs.

"Jian."

"Yes, Sweets?"

"Can you put me down?"

"Why?"

"I'm too heavy. I don't want you to hurt yourself."

"Who said you were too heavy? I didn't, because that's not what I think."

Jiggling me, he hefted me higher until I had to look down into his face, then he continued, "You're perfect. There is not one thing I would change about you. Not one."

The way he looked at me bordered on harsh in its intensity. Not having the words to respond, I brought our lips back together, translating my feelings through kiss and touch.

The trip to my bedroom was short. Soon we were wrapped up in each other without thought of anyone else. It would be a few hours before he left. When he was gone, I called Nikki to let her know I would stop by her place to get Saffi.

Chapter Fourteen

JIAN

After the first night I spent with Stephanie, we fell into a comfortable routine. It was like we'd been together for years instead of a few months. Wanting to reinforce that my interest in her was more than sexual, I took her on dates—as promised.

I either included Chloe in the activity or pre-arranged for her to be with someone Sweets trusted. Which meant, I'd had more than a few conversations with her closest friends Nikki and Joy.

Sweets was the first woman I'd dated who had a child. Even though the experience was new to me, I enjoyed the times when it was the three of us just as much as I did when it was the two of us alone. Granted, when we were alone the chances of the evening ending in multiple orgasms increased significantly. I absolutely loved giving my sweetheart orgasms.

I was addicted to the way she looked when she reached her peak. I couldn't get enough of seeing it and hearing the way she moaned my name right before she fell over the edge. That shit was so sexy, I got hard just thinking about it.

Today, I had a rare day off. I had some business which could only be handled in person. Thankfully, no surgeries were on my calendar; I felt no guilt at taking the full day off even though the business only took a few hours to complete.

With my afternoon free, I figured it would be nice to have lunch with Sweets to jumpstart our weekend. We planned tonight as my first time sleeping over with Saffi home. I was more than a little eager. I sent Sweets a text when I was leaving my appointment and she was all for a midday break.

Since it was Friday, she was at the salon in the strip mall in Logan City—which was only a twenty-minute drive from her home. I knew the schedule now. I didn't need to orchestrate a chance meeting anymore. We were together.

I still went in for my haircuts, because I liked the way Marshawn took care of my hair. Now, I understood why some men were so loyal to particular barbers. I had yet to be disappointed in his work. I couldn't say the same for the people I'd used in the past.

I called in an order to Sweets' favorite Jamaican restaurant to pick it up. With Friday's being a busy day, I didn't think she'd be able to take a long lunch. So, to maximize our time together, I played delivery boy.

During the three months we'd been seeing each other, I'd learned she owned two strip malls, various pieces of real estate and two salons located within the strip malls. Her many accomplishments at such a young age were impressive.

Thankfully, my original assessment of her age was off. I wasn't bordering on cradle-robbing perv territory. Sweets was thirty-three, which was still young to have achieved so much.

She was talented and savvy. In high school, she'd enrolled in a dual track program earning an associate's degree in Cosmetology while she obtained her high school diploma.

Using her Cosmetology degree, she worked her way through college obtaining a bachelor's in Chemistry before getting her MBA. All by the age of twenty-two. The degrees alone were impressive, but to know she did all of those things while helping her grandmother with Chloe before adopting her niece as her own child, tipped the scales to super shero. My Sweets was a force. I was damned proud to be with her.

Finding a spot in the lot, I looked around at the well-maintained storefronts to locate the entrance to Murphy's Salon and Spa. The business was named in honor of her maternal grandparents. Yet another reason to love her, as if I needed more.

I didn't even stutter step when the thought of being in love with her crossed my mind. It was the first time I'd considered how I felt in those terms There was no point in fighting it. It was inevitable. Sweets was a very easy woman to love.

She also had a close bond with her family—with the exception of her sister, Danielle. From our many talks, I knew her strained relationship with Danielle weighed on her. While she loved her, she couldn't understand Danielle's choices which put them at odds more often than not.

The weight was lifted somewhat because she hadn't seen or heard from Danielle in months. Sweets said it wasn't unusual in their relationship. Although, this time, she felt like Danielle was avoiding her after what happened with Chloe.

Grabbing the handles of the take-out bags, I got out of the vehicle to head inside. Pulling the knit cap farther down on my forehead, I closed my jacket against the wind walking briskly to the glass double doors of the salon entrance.

The doors opened to a reception area comprised of seating to the left and right of the doorway as well as a reception desk where Vanda sat with the phone to her ear.

Trying not to block the entrance, I stepped to the side waiting for her to finish her call. My gaze drifted over the space, looking at the décor and how it distinguished the different areas of the salon. Even though I was now a regular customer to the barbershop side, I still marveled at the set up.

There were two doorways with single glass doors—one on either side of the waiting area. Lettering on the glass designated one as the salon and the other as the barber shop. Directly across from the main entrance, was a heavy painted wooden door leading to the spa service area.

As Vanda finished her call, the door on the salon side opened. Someone I hadn't seen in at least ten years exited, closely followed by my sweetheart. Both women regarded me with wide eyes.

I was positive each woman had completely different reasons for their expressions. I didn't have the luxury of investigating. Semi-frozen, I stood gaping in shock that my past had landed smack in the center of my present.

"Cam? Cameron Anderson?! Oh my goodness, I haven't seen you in years!" McKenna Frost's face transitioned from wide-eyed shock to warm surprise.

An unmistakable look of confusion flit across Stephanie's features when McKenna reached out to touch my arm. Thank God she didn't try to hug me. Things were awkward enough. Still beautiful, her skin practically glowed. While I appreciated her beauty, it didn't hold me captive the way it had in the past.

Of their own volition, my eyes sought Stephanie's as I murmured surprised greetings to McKenna. "Hello, McKenna. Yes, it has been a very long time."

"Well... how have you been? Are you here for the barber or spa services? I'm surprised I haven't run into you before, if you've been coming here as well." McKenna's words flowed together quickly, not really giving me the opportunity to actually answer.

When she paused to breathe, I quickly tried to steer the conversation to a swift end. "I'm well, thank you for asking. I'm not here for the barber or the spa. Not today at least."

I grasped Stephanie's hand, pulling her closer to me. "I have a lunch date with my sweetheart."

I didn't like how stiff her body felt under my touch. Thankfully, Stephanie didn't pull away. "Sweets, McKenna and I attended the same university for undergrad. She handed me my first heartbreak and helped me at the same time."

"You don't say?...*Cam*." Stephanie said quietly, emphasizing the nickname, her expressive eyes pinging between the two of us. The wheels of speculation turned in her head so loudly, I practically heard them spinning.

"Oh, come on, Cam. You know I didn't break your heart. We only went out a couple of times. We were more friends than anything." McKenna produced a glowing smile. Her eyes sparkled happily.

Obviously, she really believed what she said. It wasn't until this moment I knew for sure she had no idea how deeply I cared for her in college.

Looking at Stephanie and I cuddled together, her smile widened more. "You two are so cute together. I'm happy you found one another. I can't think of two people who deserve happiness more."

Unsure how to respond, I murmured a quiet thank you. I didn't press her for information on her current life. I saw the ring on her finger, and assumed she was married. It wouldn't matter if she were single. My Sweets had me so enamored, not even the beautiful McKenna could turn my head.

"I won't hold you two. I have another appointment and need to get going. It was good to see you, Cam. Thank you again Step. I really appreciate you squeezing me in today."

McKenna gave a small wave then went to the cash register set up in the reception area.

Not giving McKenna any more attention, I turned my gaze to meet Stephanie's upturned face. A face devoid of outward expression. No expression meant I had no idea what was going on behind those bottomless obsidian eyes of hers.

Breaking the silence, I asked, "Are you ready for lunch?"

"Sure. Vanda, send any calls to my voicemail." She said smiling at the receptionist. Extending a final goodbye to McKenna, she pushed through the glass door leading to the salon side of the building. I followed quietly.

As we entered the hair salon, my eyes swept the area. I'd never been on this side of the building. There was a mild hum of conversation. Music could be heard over the hidden speaker system. The monitors on the wall didn't display television shows; instead, the screens cycled through descriptions of services and prices.

Along one side of the room, was a wall of waist high mirrors with four salon chairs spaced evenly in front of them. On the other wall, were two pedicure stations. There were also two manicure stations with displays of nail polish lining the area behind them. The back wall consisted of three sinks with a door to the left-hand side leading to what I guessed was storage and possibly Stephanie's office.

While I drank in the atmosphere of the salon with its people, music, and soothing colors, I didn't notice the conversational hum had disappeared until a voice pierced the stillness.

"Hey there Boss Lady! Who is this? You not gonna introduce us? So, you think you can just hustle him back to your office? Rude!" One of the stylist called out.

"Peaches, don't start." Stephanie said to the inquisitive stylist.

"What? I'm just saying. You tried to speed walk this fine man through here, being rude. You didn't even stop to introduce him. Where are your manners, ma'am?"

Stephanie's shoulders lifted and lowered in resignation. She introduced me to the people working at the various stations.

Two of the chairs in front of the mirrors were empty, so the group only included two hair stylists and two manicurists. Each was polite, if not the slightest bit cheeky when they replied to the introductions. No one gave me the impression I was unwelcome.

Once the introductions were done, I was semi-hurried through the doorway at the back of the salon. Despite how amusing I found her reaction, I didn't resist the prodding at my back to get moving. We walked down the short hallway into the office at the end. I looked forward to being alone with Sweets. I hadn't seen her in a few days and I was jonesing something fierce.

Entering the office before her, I heard her close the door shutting us inside. Placing the bag of food on the desk, I turned quickly capturing her in my arms. Maneuvering until I was perched on the edge of the desk with her wedged between my open legs, I waited.

I waited until she finally looked up at me so I could properly gauge what was going on behind those beautiful pools masquerading as her eyes.

"Talk to me, Sweets. I can see and feel the tension in your body. If you don't talk to me, how can I fix it?"

"How do you know it's something you need to fix? It might be something only I can fix. It could also be something where no 'fix' is available."

"Sweets... I feel like you're being contrary for the sake of being contrary to avoid telling me what's going on."

Running my hands along her back, I brought them to a stop at their favorite place to rest—the rounded cheeks of her ample ass. Pulling her closer in the cradle of my legs, I rested my forehead against hers and closed my eyes.

"Talk to me. Don't close me out like this."

"How long were you together? No. That's not important. Me and McKenna aren't close friends, but we are friendly. I don't want this to be awkward. Are you still in love with her? And why does she call you Cam?"

"Ok, so you do have something on your mind. First, McKenna calls me Cam or Cameron, because I used my middle name when we knew each other in college."

Stephanie continued to look at me expectantly when I stopped at only answering one of her questions. "What? What's the face for? I'm not interested in dating McKenna."

"Not what I asked you. Telling me you're not interested in dating McKenna is not a real answer to my question." She pulled back, trying to extricate herself from my embrace. *Nope, Not gonna happen.* I tightened my arms, holding her where I wanted her.

"No, Sweets! No. I'm not in love with McKenna. I probably never was. We were young. She's smart, beautiful, and ambitious. So, I thought we'd make a good match. Ultimately, she didn't agree."

Gathering her close, I continued. "Until I met you, I considered her the one that got away."

Leaning down placing our eyes almost level, I pinned her with my gaze. "Until I met **you**. Now...I see her for who she was. The person who put a crack in my rose-colored glasses, forcing me to take them off.

If I'd never taken off my blinders, I wouldn't have connected with myself. I don't think I'd be a man you'd want in your life."

Shaking her head, she pushed against my chest, once again trying to put physical space between us. I allowed her a few inches, but not complete freedom. Was it a jackass move? Probably. Did I care? No. I couldn't take physical or emotional distance between us.

Realizing I had to tell her in order for her to really understand why I looked at McKenna as the person who helped me find myself, just not as a person for whom I held any romantic love, I braced myself emotionally before speaking again.

Placing my hands on her hips, I set her far enough away for me to relocate to the closest chair. I sat then pulled her into my lap sideways with her legs draped over mine.

Running my hands along her jean-clad legs, I told her about the awful day in college when I realized I'd unknowingly joined an organization filled with racists.

I told her about the fight. I also told her about the weeks following my exit from the fraternity, about how I'd sought out the on-campus student activities group geared toward Asian students. Then, I explained how McKenna's involvement in a similar group for African-American students, and her comments about me never having interactions with people of my own race, led me to even search for such a group.

"So that's what you meant by she helped you find yourself? She made you realize you'd separated yourself from people who look like you?" Stephanie asked quietly. Her head was tucked under my chin while her hand stroked my chest absently.

"Yeah, Sweets. Basically. It was little things she brought to my attention. Looking back, I'd say the biggest motivator was when I stood in the hall and heard guys who had pledged to be my brothers use those disgusting slurs. Hearing those words from their mouths really brought it home for me."

The way she touched my chest had a different effect than the comfort I'm sure she was trying to deliver; so, I placed my hand on hers to stop the gentle caress. As much as I would've enjoyed planting my aching penis inside my happy place, this conversation was important for us to move our relationship forward.

"Until I heard them speak of me with such venom, I'd been living my life thinking I wasn't any different than anyone else, because my parents never treated me as though there was anything different between us.

Essentially, I'd been living like I was white instead of Asian. My parents' wealth and social position insulated me from the ugliness others of my race have to deal with on a daily basis."

I'd stopped her from stroking me, but I unconsciously rubbed her legs causing her to wiggle on my lap. I stilled my hands to calm her movements against my groin, so I could continue.

"When I took my blinders off and really started to pay attention, I saw what McKenna had been trying to tell me. I started working to learn more about my heritage. I also made concerted efforts to connect with other Asian and Chinese-American people."

Using her newly freed hand, Sweets drew imaginary circles on my chest. This time, I didn't try to stop her. I sat quietly, allowing her to touch me. I waited while she ruminated on everything I'd shared with her.

"So... What you're saying is, I have McKenna to thank for you being in my life."

"I wouldn't say that."

"Why not? You said she was the catalyst to you wanting to know more, connect with your heritage and other Asian-Americans."

"True. However, even if I'd never met her, I would have still become a surgeon. My profession is how I met you. How could she get any credit for my medical degree?" I flexed my fingers, pulling her closer to my body, as if she wasn't literally sitting in my lap.

"If you hadn't connected more with who you are, you would have probably already been married to some white woman by the time I met you. I don't date married men, so even if you'd been bold enough to shoot your shot, I would have knocked it down."

I started to refute her statement. I couldn't, because she was right. McKenna was the first person of color I'd ever dated. After her, combined with everything I experienced with my so-called brothers, I'd dated almost exclusively within minority groups—Asian, Latina, and African-American. On rare occasions, I'd dated Caucasian women. It usually fell apart quickly.

Once my eyes were opened to racially motivated slights and microaggressions, I was more keenly aware of being someone's fetish or a dirty-little-secret. Those issues weren't always the reason for the demise of my relationships with Caucasian women. However, it happened more often than I'd like to think about.

Our companionable silence was broken by the grumbling of her stomach.

"What do you say we eat our lunch before your tummy isn't the only loud grumble in the room?"

Gently, I lifted then shifted her from my lap to pull the bags of food closer to the edge of the desk.

Walking to a tall double door cabinet, she pulled out plates, napkins and sturdier utensils than the ones provided with the to-go order. After that, we wasted no time. We dug into the flavorful selection of foods. Soon, the tension dissipated. We simply enjoyed the opportunity to spend time together.

~

Stephanie and I had just finished eating when there were three sharp raps to the door. Before she could call out for the person to enter, the door was flung open.

"Boss Lady! I think you need to come out here in the salon, right now!" Peaches was visibly flustered as she stood in the open doorway wringing her slender hands while shifting from foot to foot.

Standing, Stephanie moved closer to her, "Peaches, what's wrong? What's going on?"

"Sanquisha is out there with some dude talking about they aren't leaving until somebody gives her what she's owed. The clients are getting nervous. I told Vanda to call Herb, but he's all the way at the end of the complex doing something at the clothing store ."

I stood up when Stephanie stood. However, the mention of a potentially threatening individual caused my body to go rigid. Before Stephanie could say anything else, I stepped out into the hallway pointing toward the salon area.

"This way, right?"

"Jian—" Stephanie called my name attempting to stop me. I kept walking. I heard the rapid squeaks and taps of footsteps as the ladies hurried to keep up with my long strides.

Stepping through the open doorway leading into the main area of the salon, I swept the room quickly spotting the large tattooed white man, with buzzed hair, earrings and tattered clothing which vacillated from grunge to wanna-be biker. Definitely a wanna-be, because I knew *real* bad-ass bikers. This guy wasn't one of them.

He wouldn't last five seconds around the guys I knew. Beside him stood a petite, young-looking African-American woman, pretty despite the ugly expression on her heart shaped face.

"Is there a problem here?" I asked directing the question to both of them, while keeping the other people in the salon in my periphery.

"Who the fuck are you?"

The fake-biker spat out. He puffed out his chest and flexed his arms in a pitiful display he probably thought was intimidating.

"It doesn't matter who I am. I asked if there was a problem. You're disturbing these nice people. It's time for you both to leave."

I didn't have to explain a damn thing to either of them, even if I had no real standing to question them other than Stephanie was my woman. I protected mine. There's no way in hell I would allow someone to threaten her or her business in my presence. Not when I could do something about it.

"Like I told that he-she, we ain't going nowhere until that bitch pays Quisha every dime she owes her."

I bristled at the transphobic bullshit. My fingers curled my hands into fists when he referred to Stephanie as a bitch.. I took a step forward —uncaring of the couple of inches and probably forty pounds he had on me.

A soft hand on my forearm stopped me. I looked down into Stephanie's upturned face.

Speaking so quietly I had to lean down to hear her, she pled with me. "Please, let me handle this. If it's too much for me, I'll let you know."

I didn't want to. I really wanted to kick the guy's chest in, but her face pleaded with me. It was her place of business. Her employee.

Against every instinct within me, I yielded. Giving her a stiff nod, I stood up straighter and stepped to her side.

"Sanquisha, would you mind telling me what it is you think I owe you?" She asked calmly as she walked towards one of the salon chairs to reach the counter area behind it.

Until then, I hadn't noticed the base of the chair was nestled closely to some sort of step. Stephanie stepping up to get to the counter brought it to my attention.

Folding her arms across her chest, Sanquisha spoke up, emboldened by her fake biker boyfriend.

"Why you playing crazy, like you didn't know my last check was short a hundred and fifty dollars?"

Keeping my eyes on the couple, I catalogued Stephanie's movements at the counter. She looked at the young woman through the mirror whilst picking up different styling instruments and placing them into open cavities of some type of stand.

I noticed Peaches had quietly moved to the other side of the salon towards the back. She waved her hand signaling to the ladies at the manicure stations to come to her.

I wasn't quite sure about the stand Stephanie was stuffing with tools. I recognized the metal comb and what looked like ancient curlers. The task didn't seem urgent, yet something told me it was purposeful. I was certain the purpose would soon be revealed.

"Check? What checks have you received from this salon? Only employees receive checks. You're not now nor were you ever an employee."

Having filled all of the open cavities in the metal stand, she rotated a black knob all the way to the right. Then, she turned around to face Sanquisha, who's expression remained mutinous except it didn't hold the same level of anger as it had just minutes before.

Bracing her hands on the counter behind her, Stephanie continued. "If I'm not mistaken, and I'm not, I offered you employment, only you wanted to work for yourself. So, you chose to pay a booth rate for the privilege of operating out of my salon."

Twisting, she pulled open a narrow drawer removing a pair of mesh gloves. Thoroughly confused, although still on high alert, I watched and waited. She placed the gloves on her hands, then reached out to grab the handle of one of the metal combs she'd placed in the open cavity.

When she pulled it out, I saw the steam wafting off the now heated metal. That's when I realized the stand was actually a heating station. My skin tingled. The hairs on my arms stood at attention. She'd placed at least six different metal combs and curlers into the heater.

Tapping the surface of the obviously hot metal comb, she appeared to test the heat level before placing it back into the compartment.

"You seem to have selective memory as to what it means to pay a booth rate to operate out of my salon."

"I ain't stupid. I know what a booth rate means, but y'all kept my money until the end of every day. Yesterday RiRi shorted me by a hundred and fifty dollars. I know she did." Sanquisha's voice shook a little at the end as uncertainty crept in when faced with Stephanie's outward calm.

"Oh really? Let's go over a few things, shall we? What was the agreement? You pay the booth rate to operate, correct?"

"Yeah." Sanquisha said petulantly.

"Yes." Stephanie corrected her quietly.

After a brief moment of silence, the younger woman reluctantly corrected herself, "Yes."

This caused the fake biker to speak up. "Why the fuck are you changing what you said for her. She heard you the first time."

The heat in Stephanie's eyes when she swung her gaze to the man was enough to burn him to cinders in seconds. She didn't speak, she just glared at him.

Honestly, if the look were directed at me, I can't say I'd be able to withstand it. Her normally open, kind face was completely devoid of all kindness. She appeared fully capable of meting out extreme bodily harm.

Capturing the younger woman's gaze again, she picked up the thread of conversation as if biker boy had never spoken. "What does booth rate include?"

When Sanquisha remained silent, Stephanie pressed forward. "Hmm? Does booth rate include the use of the salon styling tools?" When Sanquisha didn't answer, she prodded. "Well, does it?" More silence was the younger woman's response.

"ANSWER ME!" Stephanie's voice boomed out into the room causing more than just Sanquisha to visibly jump.

"No, ma'am," was the younger woman's meeker, more subdued, response.

"Ok. Now, answer this question. Does booth rate include the use of *any* salon supplies beyond the chair, sitting hair dryer and the sink?"

"No, ma'am,"

"What did I tell you would happen if you chose not to bring your own tools and supplies in order to service your clients?"

Sanquisha's responded with a jumble of muttered words spoken so quietly she couldn't be heard or understood.

"Speak up! You and this man forced your way into my place of business being loud and disrespectful. Don't clam up now. If you wanna be grown, be grown."

In a more audible voice, Sanquisha finally gathered the courage to speak again. While she spoke, she visibly trembled. "You said if I didn't bring my own stuff I would have to pay extra on my booth rate."

"Yes, I did. Even though I didn't have to explain the reason for the fee, I did. Why did I tell you there would be an extra charge to use salon supplies?"

"You said, if I was using the tools, then your employees wouldn't be able to use them if they needed them. The products used had to be replaced."

"See, I knew you remembered. So, tell me again, why you think Erica didn't give you the total amount of your earnings yesterday when you settled up at the register?"

Mumbling, Sanquisha reverted back to the unintelligible speech. "It's not fair. I already don't have many clients. I didn't use that much stuff."

We hadn't been together long enough for me to know everything about her, yet I read the expression on Stephanie's face clearly. It stated in no uncertain terms she was done with this conversation.

Apparently, Sanquisha read it as well, because she touched the arm of her companion. "Let's just go. I told you she was gonna act like this."

Act like what? From what I saw, the only people being difficult were Sanquisha and the man-boy she brought with her. Stephanie stood silently near her station with one hand resting on the countertop. Silent, but watchful. I divided my attention between watching her and keeping an eye on the not-so-dynamic duo.

Fake-biker-man-boy was loud as he jerked his arm away. "Why the fuck are you backing down? You said she owed you money. We ain't leaving until she pays you every penny. Get the fuck off me. Shut up and let me handle this."

The way he jerked his arm, lifted it in an upward arc in such a way it looked like he was poised to back-hand slap her. Sanquisha lifted both hands to her face, shrinking her body away from him.

Before I could move a muscle, Stephanie was in his space. In each hand she held the smoking metal instruments. She held them like a person trained in martial arts held a knife or short staff. She moved so quickly, it seemed to literally happen in the blink of an eye.

"No!" She yelled out as she stopped less than a foot away from him.

"I can't do anything about what you do at home, but you will NOT put your hands on her in my presence!" Her normally even toned voice hardened in anger.

Taking my cue from her, I placed my body closer, cutting him off from the others in the salon. My hands clenched and unclenched, forming and releasing fists as visions of smashing his face in danced across my mind.

Doing one of the few smart things I'd seen since he walked into the salon, he slowly lowered his arm to his side stepping back from Stephanie. She gave no quarter and moved forward to keep the distance between them the same.

She moved, so I moved. It was obvious she was capable of defending herself. As long as I was here, she wouldn't be doing it alone. The adren-aline coursing through my system made it impossible for me to hang back. The very thought of her *needing* to defend herself, while I was standing right beside her made me grind my teeth angrily.

"What the fuck is wrong with you lady? Get that shit out of my face." The words tumbled out of the fake-biker's mouth in annoyance. They lacked the volume and venom from just moments before when he was speaking to Sanquisha.

Until then, I'd done as Stephanie had asked. I let her handle it. His words were the last straw. I was done with staying silent. "It's time for you to leave," I told him, my jaw clenched tightly.

Part of me was hoping he wouldn't go quietly. I really wanted to at least give him an elbow to his tattooed face. Yeah... He went all out in his attempts to look like a tough guy, with unimaginative tattoos crawling up his neck to this face.

Swinging his gaze to me, he asked, "Man... who the fuck are you supposed to be?"

"The man who's going to teach you the manners and give you the ass whipping you should have gotten as a child, if you don't turn around and get out. Now." The next step I took forward, he stepped back, bumping into Sanquisha, sending her tumbling into the nearby salon chair.

The sudden motion, made the chair spin. She popped back out of it like a Jack-in-the-Box. He never once acknowledged what he'd done to her. His only response was to frown at the contact.

Holding both hands up, in a failed attempt to look conciliatory, he spoke, "Look man. I don't know you and you don't know me. I'm here because my girl said they stole her money. I just want them to make it right. I wasn't even gonna hit her. She acts jumpy all the time. I don't hit her."

"Don't care. Get out."

"Not without Quisha's money."

Without taking my eyes off the man-boy, I spoke to Stephanie. "Sweets?"

"Yes."

"If I heard the conversation correctly, the young lady has already been given her money. Correct?"

"Correct."

"You heard her. You also heard the same conversation I heard. She was paid what she was owed. It's time for you to leave. I won't say it again."

"I don't know who the fuck you think you are. I'm not doing shit until I'm ready." His face twisted in anger; his body projected his intentions before he actually moved.

He lunged toward me, swinging his arm wide. Sidestepping the sloppy punch, I locked my elbow with his, keeping his arm elevated. I landed three punches in quick succession on his side.

The blows took the fight right out of him. Twisting his body, he tried to get away. Using the momentum of his turn, I stepped into it.

Securing his trapped arm at the small of his back, I propelled him towards the glass door to the reception area. As we approached, it swung open. A man in a security uniform walked through.

Quick on his feet, the security guard held the door for me to march the tough guy out through the reception area before unceremoniously dumping him on the sidewalk outside.

Afterwards, I went back inside while the security guard took over the situation. Looking around the reception area, I realized Sweets hadn't followed me out—neither did the young lady at the center of all the conflict. I went back into the salon to see my Sweets in a semi-private conversation with Sanquisha.

I didn't have to hear her to know what was going on. She'd seen what I'd seen. It was obvious Sanquisha was in an abusive relationship. I didn't hold out hope she would accept the help Sweets offered. I knew Stephanie well enough to know she would at least try to help her anyway.

I was back inside for less than a minute, when Sanquisha rushed past me. While Sweets watched in silent concern, Sanquisha quickly exited the salon. Walking past me, into the reception area, Sweets briefly spoke to Vanda. She informed her Sanquisha would no longer operate out of Murphy's salon.

I followed her to the door, halfway listening to what she was saying. I glanced outside to make sure the security guard still had things under control. When Sweets closed the glass door and went back into the salon, I went to her pulling her into my embrace.

Chapter Fifteen

STEPHANIE

Allowing myself a moment, I accepted the comfort Jian offered—grateful he was there to support me. I'd never had this. Blocking out the sounds of people resettling themselves in the salon, I existed in a space where it was just the two of us.

My relationship with Jian wasn't my first. However, only he made me feel this way. The first where I didn't feel like I had to always be in control, yet he followed my lead when the situation called for it.

Even as I stood wrapped in his arms, he gave me what I would've never asked for, but desperately needed. Not saying a word, he was there for me the way I needed him. *Damn I love this man.* When the words floated through my mind, the thought caused me to pop my head up and I pulled out of his comforting hug.

Unwrapping my arms from his waist, I put space between us. Thankfully, he allowed the small separation. Peering into my eyes, he searched my face. He always made me feel like he saw directly into my soul when he focused on me so completely.

"Are you okay?" He inquired softly, keeping our conversation as private as possible in a room with other people.

"Yes, I'm okay now."

Rubbing his pectorals in absent circles, I considered my condition. I really was okay. My adrenaline wasn't spiking. Normally, I'd still be keyed up replaying everything in my head. It was hard to believe not ten minutes prior, I'd seriously wanted to ruin my curlers and hot comb by burning every bit of exposed skin on the fake ass tough guy Sanquisha brought into my salon.

Yet, encircled in Jian's arms, everything was okay. Like... For real. *I'm good.* Vanda interrupted our private moment.

"Boss Lady, we have a problem."

I completely removed myself from the warmth of Jian's embrace to faced my receptionist. "What is it?"

"Sanquisha had clients lined up back-to-back for the afternoon."

"Let me guess. She didn't call them to let them know she wouldn't be here. It was obvious from the way she showed up, she didn't intend to work today."

"No ma'am, she didn't."

"I wonder about her...It's one thing to be mad at *me*, but she's messing with her money. From what I saw, she needs the cash. Calling her clients is a minimum energy task." Shaking my head in disbelief, I pondered the thought process of someone who would cause a scene over money they weren't owed, while not putting in effort to secure money sitting on the table.

"That's not the entire problem though."

"Okay..."

"One of her clients is already here. I told her Sanquisha was no longer working out of this salon. She asked if someone else could squeeze her in."

I didn't steal clients from other stylists; however, I couldn't jeopardize my salon's reputation because of Sanquisha's lack of professionalism.

Reaching for the tablet in Vanda's hand, I swiped to get to the schedules of the stylists working today—including myself. I planned to catch up on some paperwork after Jian left, so I only had one client scheduled. But, I couldn't stay past four p.m., because I liked being home when Saffi made it in from her after school activities.

"Peaches and Rhonda, can you come here for a second?"

"What's up Lady Boss?" Peaches asked, flipping her long ponytail over her slim shoulder.

I never knew which way she would address me from day-to-day. She said she liked to keep me guessing.

"I'm sure you've figured out Sanquisha will not be renting a space here anymore after today."

"Yes ma'am." Rhonda responded politely. She was always so courteous and easy to get along with. I valued her kind nature as much as I did the quality of her work. She was very good at what she did, so her day was usually packed tight with clients.

"After the way she just acted a slap fool, I wouldn't expect anything less. Everybody knows you don't play, Miss Ma'am!" Peaches added with a few snaps to drive her point home.

"So, here's the deal. San didn't contact her clients to cancel or reschedule. She had to know it was possible this mess she pulled would go sideways. Five clients are scheduled, with the first one set for one-thirty. I can't stay past four, so I can probably only handle two or three of them. That's pushing it.

Mrs. Black is already here for her appointment. She's asked if one of us can squeeze her in. If the others follow suit, I may need you two to try to work an additional person into your client list for today."

I hated situations like this. I'd reached the point in my career, where I didn't take on new clients. I rarely worked in the salon during the afternoon. Usually, I reserved time after lunch to handle the business side of things.

Erica had been on my butt to get caught up on my mountain of paperwork. My signature was required on more than a few bank transfers. It wasn't just the salon stuff, I also had to look over any issues with my properties. In addition to salon documents, the proposals for the purchase of new properties were sitting on my desk waiting for me to review and get back with Gene on a direction.

"Vanda, I think I only have one sew in. The rest are just regular shampoo and style appointments. I should be fine to slide someone in." Rhonda supplied. "Miss Stephanie? Do you think we could call over to the college to see if they could send us someone to work the shampoo bowl? It would really help us."

Jian's deep voice cut into the discussion. "If someone shows me what products to use and in what order, I can help with the shampooing."

I hadn't forgotten Jian was there, except I kinda forgot he was there. I was focused on getting a resolution to the situation. Hearing his voice startled me. When he volunteered to stand in as our shampoo person, flutters erupted in my belly. The man was a doctor, a freaking *surgeon*. Yet, he was willing to spend one of his rare afternoons off in my salon being a stand in shampoo person.

"I can't ask you to do that. I'm sure you had other plans for the afternoon. I can call over to one of the schools. I'm sure they have someone who could use the salon hours." I said with as much sincerity as I could muster. I turned to go to my office to make a call to a local beauty school I dealt with.

Enfolding my hand in his, he captured my attention. "My only plans for the afternoon were to be with you. If being with you means I pitch in to help around here, then that's what will happen. Now, who's going to show me where I'm working for the rest of the day?"

His look of determination told me the subject was closed for further discussion, so I zipped my lips and led him over to the shampoo bowls. Just as I finished walking him through the products showing him the best way to shampoo to save him some back pain, Vanda sent the first client into the salon.

My watchful eyes saw the way the elderly woman's gaze raked over Jian's body. A blush crept up her cheeks when she learned he would be running his long fingers through her hair massaging her scalp. Leaving her to her fantasy, I helped Jian get started, then I went to my station to set up for the unexpected afternoon.

Surprisingly, the rest of the day went well, considering how it started. After the initial shock of a man seeing them at less than their best, the ladies were more than happy to have a handsome man shampooing their hair. I never considered myself a jealous woman; however, I had to issue a few gentle reminders to a couple of them regarding the good-looking man at the shampoo bowl. He was not on the salon menu and was very much unavailable.

The only hiccup during the afternoon didn't involve the salon. My cellphone buzzed on the counter behind my station. Normally, I didn't allow employees to have phones in the salon area. They were a distraction. Since, I didn't anticipate actually working on clients, I kept the phone nearby today in case something urgent needed my attention.

Looking at the display, I saw the number for Saffi's school. My heart lodged in my throat. Although her attack was months ago, I still had a bit of anxiety when I received unexpected calls. The school rarely contacted me.

Excusing myself from the client in my chair, I grabbed the phone and tapped the icon to answer. "Hello?"

"Hello, may I speak with Ms Barker?"

"This is she."

"Hello Ms Barker, this is Mrs. Kilgore from the academy. We have a Danielle Barker here. She says she has permission to pick up Chloe after the club meetings are complete."

"Excuse me? Did you say Danielle Barker?"

"Yes, ma'am. She's not on the list, yet she assures me it must be a mistake as she's Chloe's mother. As far as I've ever known, you're Chloe's mother. It states as much in her school records as well. So, I thought it best to call you to clear things up."

"I appreciate your call, Mrs. Kilgore. No. She absolutely does **not** have permission to take Chloe from the grounds of the school. She is not on the list for a reason. She is not to be allowed to even be alone with Chloe."

There was a tension filled pause on the administrator's end of the phone line. In the meantime, I flipped switches shutting down my station. I didn't know what the hell was going on, but I planned to find out—right now.

Finally, Mrs. Kilgore spoke again. "Okay, Ms Barker. As is our policy, we'll respect your wishes as Chloe's parent. Will you be picking her up today, or should we allow her to take the school shuttle to your home?"

Usually, I was thankful the expensive ass school had shuttle services available for the kids. Today, I didn't trust it. "I'll be there shortly to pick her up myself. Thank you for your call. You have a good day."

I heard her response as I pressed the button to end the call. Grateful I'd just finished the last client, I managed to paste a smile on my face while I saw her out.

I barely made it through the door to my office to grab my purse when I felt Jian's hands on my shoulders stopping me in my tracks.

"I see it in your face. I feel it in your shoulders. You're upset. What is it? Tell me."

For the second time in one afternoon, my focus had shifted so drastically I forgot he was there. I mentally kicked myself. *That's not how people in relationships behave woman!* I was so out of practice.

"It was the school. Dani showed up trying to pick up Saffi from her afterschool program. I don't know what the hell is going on. I need to get over there and find out.

I told Mrs. Kilgore, the administrator, not to allow Dani to take Saffi anywhere. But, I need to find out why Dani is suddenly so keen to spend time with Saffi. We haven't seen her in months. Now she pops back up trying to act like a mother. Something's gotta give."

Turning me around to face him, he stilled my attempts to move around the office gathering my things. When I lifted my eyes, his were there waiting for me. His gaze searched mine once again giving me the feeling he could read my thoughts.

"What else?" He asked.

"What do you mean, what else? That's enough for me to be concerned."

"What haven't you told me? Yes, I agree Danielle showing up at Saffi's school is not normal—at least from what I know of your relationship with her. But...that's not enough for this level of concern. What are you not telling me?"

My eyes blazed in response to his probing stare. My frustration was because he was right. He's always right. *Damnit!* Taking a deep breath, I told l him about the events following Saffi's attack.

We hadn't seen or spoken to Dani in months as far as Jian knew. Mainly because I hadn't told him everything.

I told him how Dani started calling to speak to Saffi as if she really cared about her. She didn't start immediately. Her calls started a few weeks ago. I didn't want Saffi talking to her because I still felt like she had a hand in what happened to my baby. My thoughts weren't a secret to Dani. I'd given her a piece of my mind when she first started calling.

The only thing preventing me from hiding her phone calls from Saffi was my promise to not drive a wedge between the two of them. I'd allow Saffi to make up her own mind about her bio-mom. I didn't force Saffi to speak to Dani. I didn't have to. She was a little girl with a desire to be accepted, so she chose to speak with Dani a few times.

"What do you think she wants?"

"I don't know. She gave up her parental rights when I officially adopted Saffi five years ago. I can't figure out her endgame, but I know Dani. She doesn't do anything without there being something in it for her. She has an angle. I just haven't figured out what it is yet."

"Ok. Grab your things. I'll take you."

"You don't have to. I have my car today." Moving away from him, I pulled my purse from the cabinet where I stored it when I was in my office. When I turned back toward the door, he stood in front of me—directly in my space.

"Sweets, somehow you took my statement as a question or suggestion. It was neither. You're concerned, so I'm concerned. I'll take you to get Saffi, then we'll figure out what's going on. Together."

I opened my mouth to speak, only the words got stuck in my throat when he bent down to put himself eye level with me. He always did that when he wanted to be sure I was listening and hearing him.

"You don't have to do this alone. It's one of the perks of being in a real, grown-up relationship. What's important to you, is important to me. Besides, I told Saffi we'd work on her submission for the science fair this weekend since I'm not on call."

Stepping back, he opened the office door. "After you."

Swallowing my objections, I preceded him from the office. Jian secured the door behind us. I stopped briefly to thank my team for their extra effort offering apologies for leaving them early.

I made a mental note to put a little something extra in their next paycheck as a bonus for pitching in. We didn't have to take on Sanquisha's clients. If we hadn't, it was possible the salon's reputation would've suffered. I was appreciative my staff could see the big picture and were willing to help.

～

I breathed a grateful sigh when we made it to the academy in less than fifteen minutes. It was a good thing I worked at the Logan City salon today. If I'd been at the other location, it would've taken at least thirty minutes to reach the school.

Pulling his SUV into the drop off zone in the front of the massive archway at the entrance to the school, Jian put the vehicle in park and hopped out. My emotions rode close to the surface, yet I maintained my calm as I unbuckled my seat belt. I waited, not very patiently, for him to open my door.

With everything I had needing my time and attention, I didn't have it in me to argue with him again about whether or not I was capable of opening my own doors.

Being such a prestigious academy, the façade of the building wasn't tarnished by security turnstiles. However, there was a security officer at a reception desk who called the principal to inform her of my arrival.

When she reached the desk, I asked her if Dani was still on the premises. The principal informed me Dani left with the Latino gentlemen who'd accompanied her shortly after I rejected the request for her to take Saffi from the school.

I guess I'd have to track her down to speak with her after I was done. With her skills at avoiding me, I knew it wouldn't be easy. Enough was enough.

There was no way in hell I wasn't going to find out what bug crawled up her ass to make her show up unannounced to get Saffi. *How the hell did she know this was the day Saffi stayed late anyway?*

"May I speak with you in your office?" I asked, working fiercely to keep my tone even, trying not to display the anxiety coursing through me. As if he read my mind, Jian pressed his hand to my lower back rubbing in slow circles.

"Of course." She responded. "Will the gentleman be joining us?"

She asked, making me realize I'd forgotten to introduce them in my haste to get answers.

"My apologies, Dr. Ogletree, this is Dr. Jian Anderson. I'm comfortable with him joining us for this discussion. It shouldn't take long."

The woman, with creamy russet colored skin and a statuesque build led us down the hallway to the administrative offices. If she was surprised to see me with a man, she gave no indication. The only man she'd ever seen me with or to have any dealings with Saffi was my cousin Gene, who was on the very short list of people approved to pick her up from school.

At this stage, we'd been seeing one another regularly for months. I wasn't adding Jian to the list, but I also wasn't closing him out of the discussion. He was right. He'd stated early on he was fully aware of what he signed up for when he decided to pursue a relationship with a single parent.

He'd told me more than once he was all in. It was time to really let him in—allowing him to do more than to spend time with Saffi and I as a family. Beyond him helping her with homework from her more advanced classes. I couldn't shut him out of this discussion nor relegate him to a role as friend of the family.

Once we were seated in the tufted straight-back chairs in the principal's office, I got right to the point. I asked for a detailed accounting of what occurred when Dani showed up on the campus earlier. Quickly and concisely, she relayed the entire sequence of events.

"So, at no time was Chloe ever made aware of Danielle's presence?" I required clarification to ensure I correctly approached the conversation I intended to have with Saffi later.

"No. Absolutely not." She responded quickly. Leaning forward, she clasped her hands together on the desk. "Ms Barker, may I ask for more context?"

"Context regarding what?"

"This woman told Mrs. Kilgore she was Chloe's mother. Yet we have no record of her anywhere. Chloe has been a student here for two years. There should be something if she was who she claimed to be."

Taking a calming breath. I explained something I'd hope to avoid. However, I knew was necessary.

"Legally, I am Chloe's mother. I adopted her when she was very young. Danielle Barker is my sister and Chloe's birth mother. She signed away her parental rights. She has never been a consistent part of Chloe's life. She is not allowed any unsupervised visits with Chloe. They actually haven't seen each other in months. I'm not sure what possessed her to show up here today. I fully intend to find out though."

"Oh, okay. I don't want to intrude; however, I need to know the status of things so I can keep Chloe safe while she's under our care here on campus."

"Of course. I understand. I'm grateful for all you're doing in that regard. I sincerely appreciate the call to verify before allowing anyone to remove her from campus."

Raising a hand, she replied, "You don't have to thank me for doing my job. Every child here is my responsibility for as long as they're on this campus. Truth be told, if I see them away from this campus, I still feel a responsibility for their well-being."

"Well, I still really appreciate your concern and dedication."

I started to stand, but the hand Jian placed on my leg stopped my movements. He'd remained silent since we entered her office, so I was surprised he had questions.

"Dr. Ogletree, you said Danielle left with a Latino man. Did you happen to get his name?"

"No... I'm sorry I didn't. He never spoke. Ms Barker did all the talking. He stayed near the front entrance the entire time."

"Ok. Thank you."

"Should I be concerned about this gentleman? I already plan to make a note to the staff regarding even allowing Danielle Barker back on the campus. I don't believe he has any ties to a student here. Had he not been with her and she didn't share the same last name, neither of them would have even made it to the reception desk."

I turned a questioning gaze to Jian. I'd been so focused on Dani, I hadn't given a second thought to her not being alone when she showed up.

"Honestly, I'm not sure. It's just something that stuck out to me." Taking my hand in his he stood and pulled me to stand beside him.

"It makes me feel better to know they won't be allowed back on campus. We'd appreciate if your staff could be on alert to any future attempts by *anyone* to gain access to Chloe while she's here at school."

The way he phrased his request wasn't lost on me. He projected us as a family unit. I didn't object. Nor did I try to correct it—I accepted what he'd been clearly stating from the moment we'd gone from acquaintances to a full-on relationship.

He wasn't pushy or overbearing, but he was always upfront and firm. We'd never discussed marriage, much to his mother's dismay. Though, he made no bones about what he considered to be his role in our lives.

It was both comforting and terrifying. There was no mistaking how attached to him Saffi had become. Her affection was even more evident when we exited the principal's office. She walked towards us with her BFF, Elijah, in tow.

"Hey Aunt Cee-Cee! Hey Dr. J!" She exclaimed giving me a quick hug before going through the complicated handshake she and Jian came up with. Excitedly, she launched into her idea for the science experiment he'd promised to help with.

I wasn't unhappy with the way she accepted Jian. I'll admit it stung a little for her to switch so quickly from coming to me about those things. It's not like I don't have a whole ass degree in chemistry. It used to be the two of us pouring through reference books and videos looking for the perfect project for her to submit at the school's annual science fair.

So happy to see Jian, Saffi didn't question why her pick-up service included both of us. She expected me. When I told the school I was coming to get her, they would've told her not to get on the shuttle after her club meeting.

The shuttle was the academy's version of a school bus. It looked more like an airport shuttle bus. Although most students didn't need it, it was available to any student who attended the academy, whether they paid full tuition or were on scholarship like Elijah.

The academy's policy was to inform the child of a pick-up only if the person was on the approved list. Any attempted pick-ups were reported to parents or guardians. The children weren't brought into it. So, unless I told her, she'd never know Dani tried to pick her up.

It was a good policy. Especially in custody situations, it could get ugly if a child was made aware of the person waiting to pick them up. They'd naturally want to leave with the person. When they weren't allowed due to the person not being on the approved list, the melt-downs would be epic. Thankfully, that wasn't our situation. I still wanted to know why the hell Dani tried it though.

Saffi's voice pulled me from my thoughts as we exited the building.

"Auntie? Auntie, did you hear me?"

"I'm sorry. I zoned out. What did you say?"

"I asked if it was still okay for Elijah to come over today? Remember, you said he could. His mom called the school this morning to let them know it was okay for him to leave with you. Is it still okay?"

Without a thought, my eyes sought out Jian's in silent discussion. I *had* completely forgotten about Elijah coming over. I could blame it on all of the excitement of the day, except it wasn't on my mind even before the incident at the salon or Dani's attempt to obfuscate my instructions to the school. Jian met my gaze with a slight shrug which I interpreted to mean it didn't bother him.

With as much enthusiasm as I could muster, I replied. "Of course, it's still okay!"

As the duo practically skipped along in front of us, Jian drifted closer placing a hand at the small of my back. A slight shiver snaked up my spine from the contact. A gasp escaped my slightly parted lips.

Sometimes...Most times...*Shit*...All the time... His touch affected me. The effect depended on the circumstance, whether I received comfort, casual warmth or sexual excitement.

Even though his touch did not appear to have a sensual intent, my body chose its response without my consent. With the slightest pressure from his fingertips, heat radiated from where his hand lay as though he had a direct link to my center.

When we made it to his SUV, the kids clambered into the back seat. As he opened the front passenger door for me, his lips brushed the shell of my ear while he whispered. "Try to fix your face, Sweets. It's going to be at least three hours before I can handle the itch that has you shivering and giving that 'fuck me' face."

My back stiffened ramrod straight. I quickly glanced at the kids to make sure little eyes and ears weren't tuned in to the adults-only channel.

"Pfft! I don't know what you're talking about." My words lacked conviction. Since I couldn't even convince myself, I slid away from him before stepping up into the vehicle.

Leaning over me to fasten my seat belt, he hit me with a knowing look. He bent closer to murmur in my ear again. "Lie to yourself all you want, Sweets. If these kids weren't here, I'd let my fingers do the walking to show you just how wet the pink palace gets from me putting a digit within a foot of actual contact."

He was around the car and in his seat before I recovered enough to respond. At which point, it wasn't possible to continue the conversation. Grudgingly, I admitted it—if only to myself.

He was one hundred percent correct. If we'd been alone, the SUV would be pointed toward the closest secluded area so he could show me the extent of his talented fingers...tongue...hell, his whole body.

Shifting uncomfortably in my seat, I forced myself to look out the window. I turned a listening ear to the chatter, coming from behind me, between Saffi and Elijah to aid in calming my raging libido.

Chapter Sixteen

JIAN

If anyone had told me this time last year I'd look forward to spending a Friday night doing science experiments with two pre-teens while simultaneously trying not to focus on the sensual tension between me and the woman I wanted to fold into every sexual position imaginable, I'd say they'd lost their minds. Yet, that's exactly how I spent the evening —happily.

Elijah's mom, Laura, had to work an extra shift, so he was with us until she picked him up around eleven p.m. By the time Laura showed up, I was ready to pounce on Sweets if she so much as looked at me sideways. Before Laura arrived, the kids were sprawled on bean bag chairs in the family room watching a movie, while Sweets and I lounged on the L-shaped sofa.

Knowing my sexual frustration, she placed her feet in my lap, instead of curling into my side the way she would've if we were alone. While she was opening up to me more, she was still reserved when Saffi was around. From the way she touched me, the way she reacted to my touch, I knew she liked it. Her current actions were the result of her doing the conscientious single mother thing.

She was trying to set an example for her daughter. I respected her decision. Even though Saffi was Sweets' niece by blood, she was officially adopted, so I considered her Sweets' daughter. Even if she didn't call her 'mom'.

Once Elijah left, Saffi went to her room. I grabbed my overnight bag from my trunk. Tonight, was a pivotal point in our relationship, being my first time staying overnight while Saffi was home. Sweets wanted to model a healthy adult life and relationships for Saffi. So, I didn't push for sleepovers. We did things at her pace.

Before joining Stephanie upstairs, I went through the downstairs of the house room-by-room checking things out. I locked up as though it was something I did every night. Honestly, I could see myself living here with them full time. As a family. Surprisingly, the little domestic thought didn't knock me on my ass the way it would've even six months ago.

The amount of time we'd known each other and how long we've been together as an official couple didn't mean anything to me. My instincts virtually screamed **she's The One**. If I've learned one thing in life, it was to trust my instincts. They hadn't steered me wrong yet. Bad things happened every time I've ignored my intuition.

Entering the master suite, I didn't see my Sweets, but I heard running water. After closing the bedroom door, I locked it. My bag was dropped into the overstuffed chair to the right of the entrance. I opened the zipped closure and pulled out a package. My path was clear into the bathroom. Still, I knocked on the frame as I stepped inside.

Sweets stood at the far end of the double-sink vanity in front of what I considered *her* sink. Turning off the faucet, she dried her face as I entered. When she turned back to me after placing her towel on the rack, I almost lost my train of thought. While she fully faced me, I couldn't miss the gap in the satin-like robe she wore.

The opening put more than a sliver of her voluptuous breasts on display. It was like my own private show. My mouth watered in anticipation of having those plump nipples between my lips. Her voice snapped me out of my mini daze. I pulled up short in my unknowing approach, stopping before I crowded her against the wall.

"What's that?" She asked, pointing to the package in my right hand.

Instead of answering, I opened the bundle and placed the contents on the countertop between us. Picking it up, she read the label. The shift in her expression, the widening of her eyes, had me rethinking my approach. *Shit!* Maybe Ash was right. I should've thought of a different way to broach the subject.

Lifting blazing eyes, she asked in a deceptively calm voice, "Why do you have a rapid STI kit? Furthermore, why the hell are you giving it to me?"

"It's not what you think."

"It's not? So, now you read minds?"

Shit. Shit. Double-shit. Things had gone south. Quickly. "No, Sweets. I'm not trying to read your mind. I have a pretty good idea what you're thinking. It's not for you. It's for me—well—us."

"Why do *we* need a rapid STI kit?"

"I want to stop using condoms. When we're together, I want us to *be* together. With nothing between us."

"And you couldn't have a conversation with me? Your bright idea is to show up with an STI kit? Despite not being sexually active for quite some time before we met, I still get checked when I have my annual doctor's visits. If you'd asked, I would've told you."

"I know I could've asked. I believe you when you say you're clean. Like I said, the test is more for me, so when I tell you I'm clean, you can know for sure. You don't have to take my word for it."

Plucking the test kit from her fingers, I placed it onto the vanity. Holding on to her hands, I stepped closer to her.

"Sweets, I apologize. Ok? I fucked this up." Stepping back, I pulled her behind me into the bedroom.

Pushing my bag out of the overstuffed chair, I sat tugging her until she sat in my lap. We'd finally moved past the stage where she didn't want to sit in my lap because she thought she was too heavy. *Complete bullshit.*

I loved every one of her curves and took great pleasure in having her exactly where she was perched. Even though her posture was stiffer than I'd like, at least she didn't object to sitting where I wanted her —for now.

"Sweets, how many times have you heard of people telling their partners they got tested. They tell the other person they're clean only to find out it was a lie?"

I waited a beat for a response, and pressed on. "At our age, we've both heard countless stories of people doing just that. I trust you, but trust is a fragile thing in relationships. The kit was so you could see for yourself and have confidence in me when I tell you my status."

Tilting her chin up, I captured her gaze with my own. "I see too much for me to allow there be even the slightest doubt in your mind that I would do anything to put you at risk."

Instead of pressing further, I sat silently waiting for her response. While I should've expected it, I wasn't ready for her next question.

"Have you considered that even after knowing each other's status, we'll still need to use condoms?"

"Actually, I hadn't."

Angling her head to one side, she threw me a look that gave me pause. "You do know there's more to worry about than contracting an STI, right? I could become the host to a little alien that'll take over my body for almost a year then my life thereafter."

An uncontrollable chuckle rumbled in my chest at her description of a potential pregnancy as being a host to a little alien. My laughter trailed off when she folded her arms over my favorite pillows raising a single eyebrow. *Note to self. Sweets using unique wording doesn't equal making a joke.*

Clearing my throat, I tried a different tactic. At the rate we were going, we may end the night in the same bed, without the giving or receiving of orgasms. Unacceptable.

"I hear you, Baby. Your concerns are valid. I shouldn't have assumed you were already using some form of birth control. Not that growing our family would upset me. However, I'd prefer it happens under planned circumstances."

Skating my fingers along her forearms, I rubbed her skin until her hold relaxed. I slipped both arms around her, pulling her upper body closer. Taking advantage of her tentative mellowing, I nuzzled her neck just below her ear—knowing that kissing her there drove her crazy.

A soft moan escaped her lips. She tipped her head to offer me better access to the sensitive area. Not letting the opportunity go to waste, I placed open mouthed kisses along her neck, gently suckling before drawing deeply. She won't admit it, but she liked when I switched from gentle to rough abruptly.

My efforts were rewarded with a sharp intake of breath. "We aren't done talking," she gasped out. "Don't try to change the subject."

Her upper body jerked slightly with another sharp inhale, when my hand left her side, pulling the robe open and covering her left breast. Initially kneading gently, my hand moved with a mind of its own. The gentle kneading became a firm grasp of the plump globe. Capturing her nipple between two fingers, I squeezed it firmly then twisted. Taking her lips, I swallowed her cries of pleasure—muffling the sounds.

In a quick series of moves, I transported us from the chair to the bed. Tossing back the duvet, I placed her sideways on the bed with her ass almost on the edge. In record time, I rid her of the robe, pressing her knees up spreading them apart.

Staring longingly at my favorite treat, I licked my lips, then positioned myself to pleasure her bud—angling for the release of her sweet nectar. I started calling her 'Sweets' partially because of her inherently sweet nature, but mostly because her essence tasted like the most decadent of delicacies to me.

Ignoring the demanding screams from my aching cock, I dove into the act with a single-minded goal. Make my woman gush for me. I didn't mark time, because time didn't matter.

My hands joined the action as I dipped two fingers into her scorching channel coaxing her clit from its hood. Once my friend made its appearance, I pulled it between my lips lashing it with my tongue, rotating between sucking and flicking the sensitive bundle of nerves.

Using the two fingers I'd slipped into her depths, I first located then stroked against her G-spot. Soon after, she tried to clamp her thighs together. The fingers she'd anchored in my hair gripped my head pressing me closer to her center. Her body didn't fight the pleasure. The jerking of her hips preceded the spasms of her pussy as her orgasm washed over her.

I withdrew my fingers from her clenching walls, replacing them with my mouth to catch every drop of honey flowing from her trembling core. Shouldering my way closer to her center, I pushed her legs up and out so I could get as close as humanly possible to my sweet oasis.

"Oh Jian! Oh damn! Oh shit! You're making me—"

I loved causing her to lose control to the point where she couldn't put her words together. Not willing to let go of my prize, I groaned and growled adding the vibrations to the experience tipping her farther over the edge. Her body seized. Only quick thinking saved me from suffocation when her thick thighs locked tightly around my head.

I took immense pleasure in satisfying her orally. Even as her body randomly shuddered while she came down from her orgasm, I stayed where I was lapping at her folds and flicking her clit. It took her insistently pushing against my shoulders then squirming away, for me to give her a short reprieve.

A reprieve from my oral fixation on her pussy, however I was by no means done driving her over the edge into bliss. Following her as she scooted to the center of the huge bed, I caged her in—planting my hands on either side of her head. Using my hips, I forced her luscious legs apart making room for me.

"You're not slick, Sir. We weren't done talking" her voice barely audible as she attempted to regain some semblance of control. My cock turned granite at her words.

"What did you just say?" I growled. With our noses pressed together, my gaze pierced hers.

"I said, you're not slick."

"That's not all you said." I flexed my hips against the juncture of her thighs.

"Yes it is." She rasped out. Her eyes fluttered at the contact.

"No... You called me something."

Her brow wrinkled as she tried to focus.

"Say it again." I prodded, punctuating my words by grinding my hips against her slick folds.

"Sir?..." She drew the word out in a breathy moan.

"Mmmm.... That's it." Even the uncertain way she uttered the word made my dick jerk. How could such an innocuous word elicit such a primal response?

Tipping her hips, she tried to capture my gliding shaft into her scorching center. "That's it? That's what you like, Sir?"

The sultry way she spoke combined with the motion of her hips was too much.

"Shhh..." Nuzzling the underside of her chin, I seized her lips to silence her, then peppered kisses along her neck making my way to my second—no third—favorite part of her body. Her breasts.

Kisses soon became sucking which led to me grinding against her even harder, running the tip of my dick through her moist folds, before making shallow dips into her wet channel.

"Tell me you want this, Sweets. Tell me you want my dick deep inside you with no barriers between us."

I wasn't playing fair. I knew it and didn't care. It was still possible to introduce protection. I wasn't too far gone to grab a condom. However, even the shallow dips into her pussy felt like heaven. My mind rebelled against the idea of putting anything between us.

Only gasps and moans issued from her lips. Pulling back, I shifted to my knees. Draping her legs over my thighs, I rubbed my hardened shaft against her pearl.

"Talk to me, Sweets. I need to hear the words. Tell me you want this as much as I do." Her non-verbal response was the lifting of her hips as she rubbed herself against the head of my dick.

"Say it!" I ground out. One hand gripped her thigh tightly. My voice was tight with barely restrained emotion. I needed to hear the words. I held on by the thinnest of threads, but I needed the words.

"Please Jian! Please fuck me!" She rasped out in a rushed huff of breath.

"Fuck you how, baby? Raw? With nothing between us?" Total dick move. Didn't care. She writhed beneath me; her hands roamed from her body to mine as if she didn't know where to put them.

"Yes, Sir. Just like this... Give it to me. Don't torture me this way." she pleaded.

Before she completed her request, I plunged into her velvet walls. I tried to control myself, tried not to pound into her like a virgin getting pussy for the first time, only I couldn't hold back. I wasn't a virgin. My senses were overwhelmed, because having sex without a condom was a first for me. I'd never not worn a condom. *Ever.*

No matter the enticement used in the past, I'd never considered **not** strapping up—until Stephanie. My Sweets had me breaking all of my rules.

Fuck the rules. Being inside her bare elicited feelings I didn't expect. Feeling her like this solidified there was no going back.

I couldn't and wouldn't give up this sensation. Addiction is a terrible thing, although it's the best description for the way I felt. I took up a driving rhythm which slid us across the bed. The way her pussy gripped my dick was exquisite. I worked my hips to make sure she received maximum pleasure.

I found it impossible to rein myself in, to slow down. So, I covered her breasts, and neck in sucking kisses. Changing the angle of my thrusts, I targeted the special place inside her while my fingers worried her sensitive clit.

The trembling of her thighs combined with sharp inhales were the only warning I received before her walls began to spasm. She reached her climax with a keening wail.

Holy fuck! The contractions practically sucked the cum right out of my balls. I followed her over the edge, burying my face in the crook of her neck, releasing stream after stream of cum in her tight channel.

The minutes ticked by as I pumped into her until the very last drop of cum left my body. Spent, I lowered her legs and rolled off of her. Maneuvering sluggishly, I snuggled her lush body into my side. *Damn...* We were most definitely doing that again. Tonight. As soon as I caught my breath.

Chapter Seventeen

STEPHANIE

Fresh off Halloween weekend, I sat in my office at the Logan City salon. Neither the documents on my desk, nor my computer screen held my attention. My mind was firmly entrenched in memories as it flung me back into the previous Saturday night.

Saffi spent the weekend with Joy, so the Good Doctor and I were having nothing short of a fuckfest to make up for lost time. He'd just returned from a week-long conference which followed a week with a schedule so packed, we didn't have time for anything more than video chats in the wee hours of the morning.

We'd just finished showering when he led me into the bedroom instructing me to lay on the bed. Grabbing the tub of shea butter moisturizer from the bathroom, he proceeded to massage it in starting with my legs. The whole time his fingers glided over my body, he spoke about how much simply touching my skin turned him on. How the silky smoothness made him want to bend me over the closest surface sinking inside my heated core, not stopping until we both couldn't stand.

"Sweets...You have no idea what you do to me do you? Even after being

inside you most of the day, I still want more." He said as he stroked my calves.

Reaching my feet, he rubbed the moisturizer in using agonizingly erotic circles. I teetered on the edge of orgasm from the brief foot-rub alone.

"Scoot over, Sweets." He tapped my thigh as he issued the command.

Too keyed up to protest, I moved over and he laid down beside me. Grabbing one of the extra pillows, he placed one under his back. The other went under his head and shoulders.

"Come here."

Pulling at my arm, he urged me up. Thinking he wanted me on top, I reached for his thick rod before swinging my leg over his hips to sit on his length.

"Unh-Uh." He shook his head grasping my waist. "Up. I want you on my face."

Frowning at his suggestion, I shook my head. "I don't think me on your face is a good idea."

"Sweets, did what I say sound like a question or a suggestion?" His sharp eyes pierced me with determination.

"No, but I don't think you thought this through."

"I'm a grown ass man, Sweets. I know what I want. What I want is for you to climb your sexy ass up here and put your pussy in my mouth."

"So, you don't care about life anymore? Because, there's a good chance you'll suffocate. Then what will I tell people when they ask what happened to the Good Doctor?"

"Woman...Do you want a spanking? Is that what you're angling for? If I have to tell you one more time to sit your pretty pussy on my face, you're gonna have my handprint on your ass."

His words were swiftly followed by a motivating smack to my butt which got me moving. Crawling up his chest, I positioned myself with a knee on the pillow on either side of his head. Tentatively, I lowered my hips until I felt his warm breath against my folds.

With a grumbling growl, he latched onto my thighs jerking me down until his nose was pressed against my clit while his tongue delved between my folds. All I could do was hold on to the headboard as he ate my pussy like it was the most delicious of delicacies.

It only took one good swipe and suckle of my pearl for me to completely relax on my new throne. Considering his obsession with pleasuring me orally, it's amazing he hadn't put me up here sooner. I relaxed into the sensations of his mouth mating intimately with my lower lips.

Once I got over the fear of suffocating my man, I enjoyed the freedom the position offered. I rolled my hips in time with his ministrations. The way he used his nose to stimulate my clit before sucking it into his mouth almost threw me over the edge into orgasm.

I wouldn't last much longer. The feelings were too new, too overwhelming. He knew I was close. A rumble vibrated against my pussy. I couldn't hold on a second longer. My head fell back on my shoulders, my body seized as I released a scream along with a gush of my essence.

Vaguely, I heard Jian's satisfied moans as he lapped at the reward for his efforts. Once the throws of my orgasm passed, I limply fell to my side on the bed. He never tapped out. Not once. In fact, when I toppled over, he followed me placing soft kisses on my labia and inner thigh. It felt like he was thanking my pretty place for the excellent meal.

"Mmmm... Delicious." He groaned between kisses. "See, Sweets. I told you. Nothing to worry about, I didn't die. You came like you've never come before."

Rising above me on his knees, he swiped two fingers across his nose and lips, then sucked them into his mouth. The entire time, his darkened eyes devoured my body. His expression spoke for him. He wasn't done with me.

My eyes dropped to his straining erection. Slightly angry red in color, just looking at it with its long length and thickness made my core clench in anticipation of being filled. The boneless sensation in my limbs prevented me from reaching for his shaft to test the velvety feel I knew was there. I loved running my hands over his dick, stroking the prominent vein snaking down his shaft.

"Stop looking at my cock like you wanna suck it, Sweets. This isn't for your mouth. He's jealous of my tongue. He wants his turn to be surrounded by your slick heat. To feel your pussy clenching against him, holding him inside."

His voice was uncharacteristically heavy. Filled with desire. My pussy spasmed in eagerness for what he was about to do with the thick rod between his legs.

Crawling over my re-awakening body, he kissed his way from my *stomach over my breast before capturing my lips in a sizzling joining together. I moaned as I tasted myself on his lips. Caught up in the kisses, his initial thrust into my aching channel stole my breath. He filled me so good; I couldn't imagine there was anything more perfect.*

He was made for me, and I was made for him. At least, that's how I felt when we were together. Lost in the sensations, my next orgasm snuck up on me throwing me into the abyss without warning. Fighting against the clenching of my walls, he picked up the pace—pounding into my pussy the way he loved. It was also the gateway to multiple orgasms for me. Fuck, I loved this man!

KNOCK, KNOCK, KNOCK! Sharp raps on the door of my office jerked me out of the memory. Shit! My heart thudded as I nervously smoothed my hair and ran a hand down my chest straightening my shirt. Logically, I knew there was no possible way the person on the other side of the door heard my lascivious thoughts. Still, I guiltily tried to cover them anyway.

"Come in." I called out breathlessly.

"Hey, Miss Stephanie."

"Hey, Rhonda. What's up? You need something?"

"No, Ma'am. Not me. Peaches." Her eyes nervously bounced around the room occasionally landing on mine before quickly looking away.

"Peaches? What's wrong with Peaches?"

"Miss Stephanie, you know I don't like to be in people's business, but she's not herself. She's barely talking. It's her turn to pick the salon music. She keeps playing depressing break-up songs."

Ahh... Now I understood why she looked nervous. Despite working in a place where gossip was considered a staple, Rhonda didn't like talking about other people's personal lives. She'd do it if the person brought up the subject; however, she refused to talk about anyone behind their back. It was a rare personality trait.

"Ok, Rhonda. Thank you for letting me know. I'll be out there in a little bit to see what's going on."

"Miss Stephanie, you know I normally wouldn't say anything. But, I'm worried about her. We aren't as close as the two of you are. So, I thought you should know."

"Thank you, Rhonda. I know you don't like to be in people's business, so I appreciate you bringing this to me. We should all have someone who watches out for us the way you do."

Rhonda's head dipped bashfully as she swiftly left my office mumbling her thanks. I took a few minutes to save and close the files I'd been too distracted to work on. Then, I moved the documents on my desk to a drawer. Giving myself a once over in the mirror hanging on the back of my office door, I walked out.

Before I even made it to the doorway leading into the salon, I heard the depressing strains of Toni Braxton's break-up anthem, *Un-break My Heart*. Good gravy! Were those broken-hearted wails what she's been playing all morning?

I liked a happy work environment, so we generally had music playing to help keep the mood light. Each stylist and nail tech submitted a playlist. We rotated between them allowing everyone a turn. As long as the music was client-friendly, I didn't care what they played.

Since I didn't have any clients today, I'd only walked through the salon giving morning greetings. My first time out of the office was at Rhonda's request. I had no idea Peaches had turned the salon into a 90's break-up sobfest.

The scene which greeted me in the salon was melancholy. I'd cultivated a diverse clientele over the years. The salon environment was usually happy and spirited. The room I entered was shrouded in silence. The nail technicians weren't chattering away with their clients. The patrons in the pedicure chairs had their eyes glued to their cellphone screens.

Peaches had just finished with the client in her chair. Removing the drape from the woman's neck, she thanked her sweetly while walking her to the door. When she returned, I caught her eye and jerked my head toward the door beside the sinks—silently requesting she come with me.

Hanging her head dejectedly, she trudged through the doorway. Before trailing behind her, I set the system to a new playlist. Grateful sighs were heard when the more upbeat music piped in through the audio system.

Reaching my office, I walked in to find Peaches slouching in the leather armchair next to the window. Peaches didn't slouch. She didn't consider it lady-like. Despite what her normal spirited banter implied, she was all about being lady-like. Closing the door, I walked to the nearby sofa and sat in the seat closest to her.

"Do you want to tell me what's going on?" I prodded gently. I was sure she'd figured out Rhonda had spoken to me; so, there was no point in beating around the bush.

"Not really…I mean…I don't know if I should. It's a personal problem. I just need to make a decision. I don't think anyone can help me with doing that."

"Ok. Just so you know. I'm not offering to fix it for you. I'm here to listen. Maybe if you talk about it, you'll be able to see it more clearly. Then, you can make your decision having explored your options. Just a thought."

I shifted on the sofa, resting my back as I waited for her to choose. If she wanted to talk, I'd listen. If she didn't, I'd give her a little talk about trying not to let how she was feeling bleed into her work environment. I'd rather not have the second conversation. Even if it was warranted.

Releasing a heaving sigh, Peaches sat up straight in the chair crossing her legs at the knee.

"You know how long I've been on my transition journey right?"

"Yes."

"Well, I'm finally at the stage where I can have my bottom surgery if I still want it."

"That's great!" I smiled at her encouragingly, before the grin dropped from my lips. "Wait… What do you mean, 'If you want it'? Haven't you worked toward having the surgery all this time? Allowing you to transition to fully live in your truth?"

A single tear slid down her cheek. Swiping at it, she nodded her head as more tears welled in her eyes. "Yes, I've wanted this since I was old enough to understand why boys and girls were *called* boys and girls."

"Okay, so if this is what you've always wanted, what's the problem? What's making you unsure?"

Leaning forward, I stared into her teary eyes. "What turned your definite into an *if*?"

Trembling lips joined the emotional outpouring as the tears she tried to hold in slipped down her face. Moving to the arm of the chair, I pulled her into a hug, stroking her back comfortingly. Whatever happened was tearing her apart inside.

Her words were muffled against my chest, so I pulled back asking her to repeat them.

"If I have the bottom surgery, Clarence said he'd leave me."

"What?!"

Swiping the back of her hand over her eyes, she leaned away from me. Her voice came out a shakily, just above a whisper.

"I told him my therapist and other doctors agreed I was cleared to have my bottom surgery anytime I was ready." Her voice hiccupped.

I passed her the tissue box from the coffee table. Grabbing a few, she dabbed at her eyes mopping the tears from her cheeks. I worked to keep my emotions under control because I was hot as fish grease.

How dare he try to make her choose between fulfilling her destiny and being with him? Closeted, downlow, son of a bitch. I couldn't say anything I was thinking about Clarence to Peaches. She loved that confused fool.

"I thought Clarence knew about your journey."

"He does. We talked about it when we were friends, before we started dating. He knows I've been working on myself and saving to be able to fully become who I feel I am inside."

I rubbed her shoulders while I digested what I heard without flying off the handle about how trifling I thought Clarence was.

"I'm confused then, Peaches. If he always knew about your plans, why is he just now saying your bottom surgery is a deal breaker?"

"He said he likes knowing my penis is there, even if it doesn't always work. He wants to see it and touch it whether it's flaccid or not."

"Does he know you don't want it?"

"He knows."

"Yet, he's still saying if you have your surgery, the two of you are done?"

"That's what he said."

"Peaches, baby...I'm not here to tell you how to live your life. I can't tell you what you should or shouldn't do. It's not my relationship nor my life. But, I have to say, I'm surprised you're even considering not going through with it."

She snapped her head up to look at me. Her tears had tapered off until she was left only with occasional sniffles. Her brow furrowed. "Why? Why are you surprised?"

"I'm surprised because the chick who would consider giving up her dream is not the Peaches I know. It's not the woman who walked boldly into my salon and talked her way into a stylist position when I didn't even have an opening. Such a woman doesn't let someone tell her what she can and cannot do with her own body.

That woman is a force. She would tell anyone within hearing distance to kiss her narrow ass if they even suggested she be anything other than her fabulous self."

"I know... It's just..."

"Just what?"

"He was the only man I'd met who accepted me as I am—a pre-surgery trans woman. He doesn't even refer to me as a trans woman. He calls me his girl, his woman. I don't know if I can find that again.

It can be dangerous out there for a girl like me. Men have been known to beat and even kill us when they find out we aren't 'real women' as if having a crotch pocket determines who's a woman."

Patting her shoulder softly, I assured her. "While I don't know from first-hand experience, I've heard how evil some men are to trans women. I don't want you subjected to those things. It also hurts to see you like this."

Leaving the arm of the chair, I went back to the sofa. "I have one more question for you, Peaches."

Looking at me with dry eyes, she waited. I had every intention of letting the subject rest after one last request. At least for the time being.

"If you decide maintaining your relationship with Clarence is more important than getting your surgery, do you think you could be happy with your choice? Could you be happy tossing aside your years of working on yourself when your goal is within sight?"

My pointed questions brought on the tears again. Vigorously shaking her head, Peaches sobbed, "No, I could never be happy making such a choice. I know it in my heart. That's why this hurts so much!"

I moved back to the arm of the chair and gathered her close. I sat silently while she cried it out with her head in my lap. Giving her the safe space I promised her she'd have with me, no matter what. When her sobs quieted and her sniffles subsided, I lifted her head peering into her eyes.

"All done?" I asked, softly.

"I think so."

"Good. You can use my bathroom to get yourself together, if you want."

Standing, she walked to the door of my executive bathroom, smoothing her hands across her trim hips.

"Thank you, Boss Lady. You know I can't go back out there looking less than my magnificent self. You know my motto."

"Stunt on them hoes. All day. Every day." I supplied.

"You know that's right!"

She gave a sassy flip to her hair, then entered the bathroom already digging into the pockets of her apron for the make-up she kept there. Her logic behind keeping make-up in her apron was a girl never knew when she'd need to fix her face, so she had to stay ready.

When she finished repairing her make-up, we walked back out into the salon area. We were just in time to hear one of my favorite songs drop into the playlist rotation—*Do My Thang* by Estelle featuring Janelle Monae. Turning up the volume, I initiated a dance session to get everyone, mainly Peaches, up and moving.

It was a great song to drive home my point. You can't live your life for others. You had to do your own thing. If they didn't like it, tough. Smiling brightly, Peaches bent her knees to bump her slim hipbone against my much more padded hip.

When she bounced off stumbling, giggles erupted from everyone. My gaze wandered the room until Rhonda caught my eye, giving me a huge smile and a thumbs up.

Crisis averted. At least temporarily. Peaches still had a heartache ridden choice ahead of her. For now, she was reminded of who she was, basking in the glow of being her marvelous self.

Twirling around, laughing and dancing, I missed the opening of the glass door separating the salon from the reception area. Mid twirl, my eyes landed on Jian framed in the doorway.

"Oh!" I squeaked in surprise. Hustling over to the control panel, I tapped the screen to lower the volume.

Jian stood next to his best friend Asher, whose tall, muscular frame and sandy blonde hair had the other women in the salon openly gawking. When he ran his fingers through his hair showing off the undercut beneath the shoulder-length locks, I swore I heard someone actually swoon.

"You don't have to stop dancing on our account. Please continue." Jian chuckled; his lips stretched into a huge grin.

Laughing nervously, I ignored his suggestion shooing everyone back to work as I approached the two male distractions.

"Hey you." I smiled when I stopped in front of them.

"Don't hey me. You know how to greet me, Sweets." Linking his fingers with mine, he pulled me forward until I was within kissing range. Placing a soft peck on my lips, he pulled back looking into my flushed face.

"That'll do for now."

"Do you two need a room?" Ash's Alabama southern drawl cut into the imaginary bubble Jian placed around us.

Jian lifted his head with an annoyed expression. "You know what, man?"

"Chicken got a butt."

Uncontrollable giggles burst from me at Ash's silly, quick, comeback.

"Don't start you two." I tried to look stern when I issued my warning. I'm positive it didn't work, because they immediately launched into their usual banter, taking good natured jabs at one another.

"If I may." I injected into their bromance. "Did you stop by just to show off your haircuts, or was there a reason for this visit?" I asked, looking at the two of them expectantly.

Giving Ash a half-hearted shove, Jian looked at his friend. "See man, you got us off track being silly."

"Whatever." Ash crossed his arms over his massive chest like he gave zero fucks what Jian had to say.

Chapter Eighteen

JIAN

I'd introduced Ash to the barbershop at Murphy's and he was a new convert. He'd dropped his barber. Now he exclusively used Cliff, the second-best barber at Murphy's. My barber, Marshawn, was the best—in my opinion. My only purpose for dropping into the salon was to see Sweets.

I also wanted to remind her about our promise to have a few of our friends over at her place tonight for dinner and drinks. We'd been integrating our friend groups little by little. The gathering would be the first time there were more than four of us at a time.

Sweets was very organized, but she carried a lot. So, I also wanted to assure her I could take on some responsibilities as well. I reminded her we're a team. I was capable of more than standing around looking pretty.

With my assignment in hand, Ash and I left in our separate vehicles. He finally had a break from his task force; so, he'd join us for dinner. Saffi was staying over with Gene and his wife for the night. That was one less worry. I'd grown as protective of her as I would be if I'd contributed the DNA needed to create her.

Even though the case of her attack had been mostly resolved, I'd asked Ash to look into Dani's boyfriend, Vincente. When Sweets finally came clean with me about Dani trying to worm her way back into Saffi's life, she also told me the guy's name. Figuring he was the person with Dani when she tried to get Saffi from school, I had Ash run him.

On the surface, he seemed like a regular business man. However, when Ash dug deeper, he found the guy had connections to some pretty shady individuals. He didn't have a record himself. The same couldn't be said for his associates. They had RAP sheets a mile long.

I didn't feel good about him. It wasn't anything I knew for certain —just a feeling in my gut. The guy was bad news. I'd never met him. What I heard didn't discourage my immediate dislike of him.

There was nothing I could or would do about him being in Danielle's life. She was an adult. Saffi was a different story. When it came to her, I was #TeamSweets. I felt the same way Sweets did about Danielle seeing Saffi as long as Vincente or any man like him was in the picture.

I left the salon to perform the final errands required before our dinner party. *Our dinner party.* The words sounded so domestic. My lips stretched into a broad grin instead of a grimace at the thought of being domestic with my Sweets. I didn't question my reaction; I went with it.

I'd met a fantastic woman and we were moving steadily toward building a future together. She had her own things going. Still, she was supportive of my sometimes-hectic work schedule. It took a while, but I think she finally trusted in us enough to allow me to support her as well.

I knew relying on others was hard for her because she'd been the leader and caretaker for a long time. It felt foreign to her for someone to take care of her. My heart expanded with pride at earning the responsibility of caring for my Sweets—in any way she required.

Ash walked around the living room peering at the framed photos on the walls. He was the first to arrive for the dinner party. Sweets was still upstairs getting dressed, so I was entertaining my friend. I stood at the bar pouring the bourbon he'd requested when he made it to the photos on the mantle.

Picking up one of them, he walked to me pointing at the image in his hand. "Who's this?"

Peering at the photo, I saw my Sweets along with Saffi and Nikki. Based on the way they were dressed along with the background, I'd guess it was a vacation memory. Certain he recognized Stephanie and Saffi, I figured the target of his question was Nikki. I smirked in understanding. I should've fucked with him, yet I managed to restrain myself.

"Sweets' friend Nichelle, or Nikki as she likes to be called. Why?" I asked even though I already knew the answer.

"Don't play crazy with me, Jay."

"Don't get any ideas about Nikki. I won't have you messing up my good thing with Sweets by fucking over her friend."

Even as I said it, I knew it went in one ear and out the other. Ash loved a woman with height in addition to curves. They were his kryptonite. While he preferred to date taller women, he'd date a short woman. Throw in the curves Nikki sported and he'd be a-goner.

"Why would you say that? You know I'm not a player."

"I also know you don't keep anyone around too long."

"Yeah, not having long relationships doesn't mean it's my fault they hit the door. Ever stopped to think it could be them?"

"Look Ash, you're my friend. I know you're a good person, but what I have with Sweets is special. If you don't think you could be serious, stay away from her friend.

They're closer than family. If Nikki gets hurt, my Sweets will be hurt. If my Sweets gets hurt, you'll have to deal with me."

"Jay, you may be a hot shit surgeon, however you know if you weren't my friend, I could snap you like a toothpick right?"

"You could try... Keep in mind that I know at least seven quick ways to incapacitate you without breaking a sweat...It's a part of the fancy learning package us hot shit surgeons get in medical school."

Taking the drink from the bar, Ash scoffed before placing the picture back in its place on the mantle. We were saved from further discussion by the ringing of the doorbell. Sweets and I met at the bottom of the stairs—both on the way to answer the door.

"You look beautiful, Sweets." I slipped an arm around her waist, pulling her body to mine, pressing a kiss to her forehead.

The form-fitting black dress made my fingers itch to touch her everywhere the curve-hugging fabric lay on her frame. Stopping at her knees, the dress accentuated her generous breast and her rounded hips.

The way it conformed to her ass was enough to make me reconsider having guests over. I felt a twinge of regret at it being too late to back out. There were people literally standing on the doorstep. Moving to the door together, I checked the camera display before opening the door to admit my Med school friend, Daisuke and his new wife Kari.

"Good evening! We're glad you could make it. Please come in."

Sweets was all smiles as she welcomed my friend and his wife into our home. Although, I technically didn't live here, the house had grown to feel more like home than my condo. Especially once I discovered the workout room in the basement.

When I met Daisuke's wife for the first time, I knew Sweets and I were destined to meet. The two women were members of the same sorority. Kari was one of the few clients Sweets still saw regularly. They'd known each other for years.

If I hadn't met her the night Chloe was attacked, I'm positive I would've had the opportunity through Daisuke and Kari. Had I known about the connection, I could have used it when I was trying to find ways to get into Stephanie's orbit during those stress filled early days. I kicked myself for missing their wedding, thereby missing my chance to link with Sweets in a social setting.

After going through the routine of removing their coats, they exchanged their outdoor shoes for indoor footwear. We all entered the family room where Ash had moved on from his photo browsing to sitting in one of the oversized chairs staring into the fire.

The evening progressed and the remaining guests arrived. All except one. After he'd asked about her, I didn't tell Ash Nikki was coming to dinner. It was good I hadn't gotten his hopes up, because Nikki texted Sweets about a work emergency. She never made it to dinner. Joy brought her current partner with her. He seemed like a decent guy, but if you asked me, they had no spark. Their lackluster relationship wasn't any of my business though.

Everyone seemed to get along. We talked over dinner, laughed and played a few rounds of a meme-based card game which turned out to be hilarious. Around midnight, we closed the door on the last of our guests. Prior preparation meant there wasn't much clean-up before we went upstairs for the night.

Sweets was uncharacteristically chatty as she disrobed and started the shower. We were both long overdue for a night out or in with friends. Most of our activities of late had been just the two of us or centered around Saffi's extra-curriculars. Neither of which bothered me, it was simply nice to hang out with other adults.

Sweets continued her one-sided conversation. I watched her while mimicking her movements, removing the cable-knit sweater and slacks I'd chosen to wear. As she scooped her hair pinning it up, I grabbed our clothes and took them to the closet. I dropped hers into the hamper. Mine went into the laundry sack I kept in my overnight bag.

One day, I wouldn't have to separate our things this way. When we were finally together as a family, it wouldn't be necessary. Until then, I'd continue to not assume she was cool with me adding my laundry in with her own.

When I made it back into the bathroom, she was already in the shower. I stood there for a moment drinking her in. The water cascaded over her body, sliding down the curves I loved to trace with my fingers and tongue.

Licking my lips at the thought of tasting her, I joined her in the glass enclosure. She must have expected me because the water wasn't the usual boiling hot temperature she preferred. No matter how many times she said she wasn't, I insisted she was trying to burn her skin off with the scalding hot shower water.

Without the barrier of guests, I was free to touch her any way I liked. I took advantage of the opportunity, gliding my fingertips across her shoulders. The water added to the silky texture of her skin, and my shaft thickened in anticipation.

Following the path of the water, I skimmed my digits down her arms before slipping my hands around to cup her full breast. The weight of them in my hands sent a possessive charge through me. I whipped her around so I could feast on the generous globes.

She offered no resistance to the forceful side of my nature. Sighing and moaning my name, she slipped her hands into the hair at my nape tugging when I captured a puckered peak between my teeth.

I worried the nub with my tongue before closing my eyes and suckling deeply. An image flashed across my closed eyes of Sweets cradling our child to this same breast nursing our offspring.

Growling at the thought of planting my seed in her womb, I backed her into the tiled wall, dropped to my knees, flung one thick thigh over my shoulder and dove face first into her dripping core. She was so hot and ready for me she came almost immediately.

It wasn't enough. I needed her to be as crazy for me as I was for her. Determined to send her into orgasmic bliss again, I plunged my tongue into her spasming channel while rubbing the plump bundle of nerves with my thumb. Time was of no consequence as I tipped Sweets from one release to the next making her legs tremble as she weakly held on to my head with one hand while the other grasped the metal bar attached to the shower wall.

Licking my lips to capture every bit of her sweet cream, I stood and pulled her to the built-in bench at the center of the enclosure. Sitting, I nudged her between my open legs taking her lips in a searing kiss. I loved how she didn't shy away from kissing me after I'd pleasured her sweet pussy with my tongue.

The kiss energized her. Her hands latched onto my shoulders. She shoved me back against the wall. Dropping to her knees, she engulfed my aching cock into the warm cavern of her mouth. I nearly came on contact. When she licked up the side of my shaft and lapped at the precum leaking from the head of my dick, I lost it.

"Damnit, Sweets! Get your ass up here."

My voice was so thick, I almost didn't recognize it. Grabbing her under the arms, I jerked her up. I went to lift her leg to straddle my hips, but she pulled away.

Swatting my hands aside, she turned her back to me. Reaching around, she clasped my throbbing length in her delicate hand. Lining her sweet pussy up with my dick, she descended, immersing me inside her wet, hot canal.

"Fuuuuck!"

"Mmmm... You like that, daddy? That's what you want, right? You want to be all up in this good pussy while you have a front row seat to watch this ass bounce. Don't you?"

When the fuck did she decide to start calling me daddy? It's a first, yet it was a turn on I didn't expect. I always thought it was weird when I heard a woman calling her man, daddy. But, coming from Sweets' lips, the word took my dick from hard to granite inside her tight sheath. The response was almost as quick as when she called me 'Sir'.

She was right, I did like watching her ass bounce while she took me deep inside her delicious core. The visual stimulation combined with the feel of being inside her was level twenty on a ten-point scale. Unable to control them, my hands latched on to her hips as she twirled them on my cock stimulating herself while giving me immense pleasure.

I assisted her glide up, before slamming her down on my waiting cock. Smacking one ass cheek, then the other, I marveled at the way it jiggled, bouncing from the strike. I was mesmerized by the up-down motion. The sight alone was enough to drive a man to the brink, then her walls clamped down on my length as she found her release once again.

Crying out, her hands landed on my forearms and squeezed. Following her over the edge, cum was wrung from my shaft by the pulsations of her undulating center.

"Aaah! Fuck, Sweets!"

Breathing heavily, I cradled her in my arms as we sat together out of the direct spray of the water, still connected. My cock jerked sporadically inside her trembling core. We both needed time to recover.

After a few more minutes, I helped Sweets stand. We moved back beneath the shower spray to actually bathe our bodies. The water was barely warm, so we rushed through the task while we still had *some* hot water.

Helping Sweets dry off and moisturize after bathing was a pleasure I never denied myself when I had the opportunity. Even if doing so usually put us in the position of needing to shower all over again. Our chemistry was so all-consuming even mundane tasks could lead to the uncontrollable urge for us to join together.

So far, Sweets had never turned me away. For that matter, I'd never turned her away. We were equally insatiable when it came to each other. We were so good together, it was a little scary.

As I rubbed the moisturizer she liked on her back and shoulders, I couldn't resist dropping a kiss between her shoulder blades. Not straying from our normal pattern, one kiss led to others culminating in me putting my Sweets on her side. I inserted one of my thighs between her thick legs lifting the one on top enough to give me access to her pink palace.

Surging into her to the hilt, I held still for a beat. The gasp she uttered when I entered her sheath told me she needed a minute to adjust. When she started slowly gliding herself along my turgid length, I knew she was ready for me. Wasting no time, I initiated a driving rhythm which had us both crying out our release. Me with my face pressed into the crook of her neck while my cock jerked inside of her.

This time, after we cleaned up, we climbed under the covers and drifted off into dreamland. I had my Sweets gathered to my side with one of her silky thighs draped across mine. I held her to me with one hand possessively cupping a plush ass cheek.

Chapter Nineteen

STEPHANIE

It was hard to believe the holidays were already so close upon us. The Christmas decorations went up before Halloween was over. Those of us who celebrated Thanksgiving were preparing for the holiday. I wasn't so much interested in the manufactured image of the day; I just liked the opportunity to get together with family.

Saffi and I only had each other for immediate family; however, we had extended family in the area. We typically spent either Thanksgiving or Christmas at Aunt Helen's—Gene's mother. It made me feel close to Grandma Vi when I was around Aunt Helen. Out of Grandma Vi's four children, Aunt Helen looked the most like her.

Her home became the family hub after Grandma passed. It remained the place everyone flocked during holiday breaks. Going to my aunt's specifically on holidays was a good way for me to stay connected to my family. It also gave Saffi an opportunity to bond with her cousins.

She didn't have the same exposure to relatives her age that we did growing up in Grandma's house. With the family being so spread out, the only time she saw them were at major holiday gatherings. It was the reason I didn't like to miss those gatherings.

This Thanksgiving would be one of the few times I deviated from our routine. Jian's parents had invited us to their house for Thanksgiving dinner. They ate later in the day than my family, so I could try to make both. The idea was squashed almost as soon as I thought about it. I had no desire to stress myself out with the logistics of pulling off such a feat. Aunt Helen was disappointed we wouldn't make it. I assured her we would still be over for our traditional Christmas Eve dinner.

"Oh shoot!"

Checking my watch, I noticed I almost missed the time I said I'd be ready for Joy to pick me up. Me, her and Nikki were driving to a nearby outlet mall. Scrambling, I finished getting dressed. I'd just made it to the bottom of the stairs when my phone pinged with a message from Nikki telling me they were outside.

This was one of the rare occasions the three of us were together. I was close to both women. They weren't as tight with each other as they were with me. It wasn't that they disliked one another; they just hadn't bonded as tightly to each other as they had with me. However, Nikki made it known *she* was my best friend. The spot was filled. Anyone else could be my close friend, but the position of Bestie was filled by Nichelle Reed. Period.

Slipping on my sneakers at the door, I set the alarm and walked out to meet my friends. With only a few weeks to go until the holiday, shopping centers were notoriously crowded. So, we'd picked mid-morning of a weekday to try to avoid some of the crowd.

"I still don't know why you insist on doing in-person shopping, Joy." Nikki said as I settled into the back seat.

I agreed with her. I did ninety percent of my shopping online. I didn't set foot into a retail outlet unless myself or Saffi absolutely had to try on the item before purchasing. I was never much of a shopper anyway. My fashion updates usually came from Nikki.

"Y'all know I don't get out much. If you work it right, physically shopping can be considered going out."

Rolling my eyes, I inserted my two cents. "If you say so."

"What do you mean you don't get out much? I thought you were dating old boy from the Earth Sciences Department." Nikki brought up the subject I'd been avoiding.

I didn't like Earth Sciences guy. I didn't even bother to learn his name because I knew the moment she brought him up his days were numbered.

"Oh, that guy. We're done." Joy responded dryly.

I didn't know when it was officially over, she never said. I didn't ask. She didn't have to tell me. Whenever she stopped talking about a guy, he was on the way out or already gone. When she was ready, she'd tell me what happened. Until then, I'd follow her lead and act like he didn't exist.

"Damn... You can't even call him by name? The dick must have been straight trash." Nikki's laughter followed her declaration.

"Let's just say, I recited my dissertation the last time we were together. Needing to cite my sources sealed it for me." Joy said.

"Shit! That's worse than trash dick! If you were even thinking of your dissertation, his dick was worse than trash. Trash is too good." Nikki's comment made me giggle. It wasn't just what she said, her delivery made it hilarious.

"Since he's an Earth Sciences guy we can call it toxic refuse." I suggested.

Nikki turned in her seat to look at me. "I like it. It sounds fancy. We can say T.R. for short."

She lifted her hand over the seat for a high-five which I immediately supplied through my giggles. Pushing Joy's shoulder, Nikki prodded her to respond.

Try as she might, Joy couldn't hold back her own giggles. Waving her right hand at Nikki she tried to sound stern.

"Stop it! I need to concentrate on the road. You're gonna have me swerving all over the place fooling with you."

"I'm just saying..." Nikki trailed off.

Joy was a college professor. Her life was filled with tests, papers and faculty obligations. She was a junior professor. I suspected it wouldn't be much longer before she was offered tenure. She didn't have classes on Wednesdays. Since she also had no meetings today, the timing was perfect for a day out with the girls. We spent the rest of the thirty-minute drive chatting about life in general.

Turning the car into the first available parking space she found at the outdoor outlet mall, Joy put the car in park. After we'd sufficiently bundled ourselves to combat the wind, we got out of the car. Although I dreaded in-person shopping, I did relish the opportunity to spend time with Joy and Nikki.

If you looked up the definition of shop 'til you dropped in the encyclopedia, I think Joy's face would be the picture beside the description. We made two trips to drop bags in the trunk before I finally convinced her we'd done enough damage. I had a child who would be home from school soon.

At least she'd let us stop in the food court for a quick lunch before dragging us off to the far end of the mall, so we could work our way back to where we were parked. Did I use my child as an excuse to bail early? I most certainly did. Did I feel any guilt about it? I did not. Zero guilt so long as it got me away from the now crowded mall.

Dropping me off at home, Joy and Nikki left. Nikki had a dinner meeting. Joy said she wanted to go over the papers her TA was supposed to grade for her. Looking at the time, I knew I only had an hour before Saffi would be home; so, I hustled inside to put the bags away.

I'd actually found some things Saffi wanted for Christmas that I hadn't seen online. I also bought a few things for Jian. Although we hadn't discussed Christmas presents beyond what Saffi wanted, there was no way I would allow the holiday to pass without getting him something as well.

Securing the packages in the closet island, I deemed them sufficiently hidden until it was time to wrap them. Even though I wasn't a clothes and shoe hound, the closet design was something I didn't compromise on when I was outfitting the house to suit our lifestyle.

The closet itself was the size of a small bedroom. The set up was the organized person's dream. The ivory-colored cabinetry, cubby holes and hanging sections were eye catching. The part I liked most was the closet island. It contained drawers and cabinet spaces on three sides.

On one of the long sides, there was an opening where a tufted stool was stored when not in use. I used the stool when I was getting dressed or doing my make-up. Not one to splurge often, I'd tuned out my internal spendthrift when it came to my closet space. Turning off the light, I left the closet and went downstairs to start dinner.

I've never desired to be a housewife. However, growing up with Grandma Vi, I was accustomed to home cooked meals. Usually, I meal prepped on the weekend because I wasn't fond of cooking daily. Advance planning allowed me to have a hot meal ready for Saffi when she got in from her after school activities.

I was pulling the bubbling pan of Chicken Tetrazzini from the oven when I realized, it was well after five p.m. and Saffi still wasn't home. Retrieving my phone from the counter, I checked the activity schedule. Had I forgotten a meeting or something?

I didn't see anything after four p.m. on the schedule. So, I scrolled through my notifications again. I didn't see any messages or reminders pertaining to activities that would last past five. My stomach clenched in dread. Taking a deep breath, I reassured myself everything was fine.

Tapping the call icon on the phone I called Saffi's mobile number. Nothing. The phone went straight to voicemail. Not getting an answer didn't necessarily mean anything. Students weren't allowed to have their devices on during the school day, so she normally turned her phone off. She could have forgotten to turn it back on.

It was possible, but unlikely. Saffi had turned into a typical teenager once she officially reached the teenage milestone of thirteen years of age last month. For the most part, she abided by the 'no active devices' rule during school. However, as soon as the dismissal bell rang, she religiously turned the phone on and began texting.

So, there was no way she didn't have her phone turned on. Something was wrong. I felt it in my gut. As the churning increased, I pulled up the applications I used to monitor her online activities.

Like any concerned parent, I watched her behaviors on her electronic devices, only not to the level where I read every one of her text messages. I'd need to stop working at fifteen minutes to three daily to keep up with her texting alone. To make up for it, I did random checks of texts, emails and the one social media account she was allowed to have.

There were no new messages in the text log. Not one message since ten p.m. the night before. That alone was strange. Kids had long ago stopped actually talking on the phone. Text was life. For there to be zero messages was a huge red flag. Now I was beyond concerned.

Sinking into a chair at the kitchen table, I opened the locator app. Desperately, I searched my memory to recall what she was wearing when I dropped her at school. Calling up the mental image, I saw her in her pink bubble coat, jeans, red sweater and those atrocious fur-lined boots she wanted to wear with everything.

Unsteady fingers on shaking hands tapped the screen filtering the options to include only the things I knew she would keep with her at all times—her phone, electronic tablet, the earrings Jian gave her for her birthday, the locket from Grandma Vi and those ugly ass boots.

Initially, Jian gave me a hard time about putting trackers in the earrings. Honestly, I wouldn't have even told him about the trackers if he hadn't caught me installing them the day after he'd given them to her.

She cherished those earrings as much as the locket from Grandma Vi. Although she was barely older than a toddler when Grandma passed, Saffi had vivid memories of her. She would sometimes bring up things I'd forgotten about my grandmother.

With the filtering set, I turned on the feature to display all of the selected devices at once. I had to turn the phone sideways to view the entire map along with the side panel which gave the exact coordinates and street names.

Saffi wasn't at school. My heart jumped into my throat with the discovery. The pounding in my ears was so loud, I had to close my eyes for a moment. I went through deep breathing exercises to get myself under control. Once I felt capable of focusing, I opened my eyes. I looked at the list of items and the corresponding dots on the interactive map.

Saffi's electronic devices were at Grandma Vi's house. *What the fuck?* Dani! What in the hell had she done now? Concentrating fully on the location of the electronics, I didn't check for the location of the jewelry. The dots were stacked on top of each other; it was hard to distinguish one from the other. I should have looked more closely. I'd regret it later.

Pulling up Dani's number in my contacts, I called her. The phone rang multiple times before rolling over to voicemail. *Shit!*

Dashing up the stairs at break-neck speed, I grabbed my purse, my gun and the spare keys to Grandma Vi's house. Pushing the cordless earphones into my ear, I called Gene as I rushed about the room.

"Hello?" Gene's deep voice answered on the first ring.

"Gene! Where are you?"

"I'm leaving the property on Wilford, what's up?"

"Saffi didn't come home from school. I checked the trackers. Some of her stuff shows it's at Grandma Vi's house. Can you meet me over there? I don't know what the hell is going on with Dani. I'm sick of her shit. There's no way Saffi went over there on her own. I know Dani lured her somehow. I know it!"

"Hold up, Step. What? Lady Bug wouldn't just go somewhere and not tell you. It's not like her."

"She's changed a lot in the last month. Something about turning thirteen. It's like a switch flipped inside her when she got the word *teen* in her age."

Trotting down the stairs, I walk through the kitchen to the mudroom where I slipped on the first pair of shoes belonging to me.

"Aiight, look. I'm getting in my truck right now. I'll be there in twenty minutes tops. Do. Not. Go in without me."

"Uh-huh. I'll see you there." I mumbled as I exited the mudroom, stepping out into the garage.

"Step! I'm serious. I can tell you're on edge right now. I'm not worried about you hurting Saffi. Dani is another ball game. You don't need to end up in jail for putting your sister in the hospital. Wait for me."

"Uh-huh." I muttered as I buckled my seat belt and pressed the button to raise the garage door.

"I'm serious, Step. I'm on my way. We should get there at the same time. If I'm not there when you arrive, wait for me."

"Why do you keep saying that? I hear you!"

"You hear me, but you aren't listening. I need to hear the words. Tell me you'll wait for me. Tell me you won't go in the house without me with you."

Mutinous silence was all I had for him. I didn't want to lie. Gene was the brother I never had. Growing up, he was at Grandma Vi's so much, it was like he lived there. He constantly played mediator to me and Dani. Many times, he saved Dani from an ass whooping once I stopped allowing her to bully me.

"Stephanie!"

I jumped at Gene's voice booming through the speakers. The call had automatically switched to the car's Bluetooth when I started it up, so his voice resounded loudly in the interior of the SUV.

"Fine! I won't go in without you. Happy?"

"No, I'm not happy. I wish none of this shit was happening. At least I can try to keep you out of jail. That's no place you ever want to be."

"I hear you, Cuz. I promise I'll wait for you. I gotta focus on the road. I'll see you there."

Taking the turn leading from my subdivision, I pressed the gas pedal to the floor and prayed. I prayed I didn't get stopped for speeding. I prayed for Saffi's safety. I prayed I could restrain myself from beating my sister to a pulp for scaring me like this.

No matter how much Saffi changed or pushed limits, totally cutting off communication wasn't like her. She knew if she didn't answer the phone when I called or reply to my texts in a timely manner, she'd lose her electronic privileges. It was an established rule which had been proven effective when she lost her phone and internet access for two weeks. I'd never had a problem with her after that.

Cursing, sometimes under my breath and sometimes out loud, at every red light or any driver who slowed my progress, I made it to the house in just under twenty minutes. Turning the vehicle off, I attempted to wait patiently for my cousin to arrive.

I promised I'd wait, but as the seconds ticked by, it grew harder and harder. It was dark out. I saw the lights on inside the house. Dani didn't have a car. So, seeing the empty carport didn't cause suspicion. I looked at my watch.

Twenty minutes. It had been exactly twenty minutes. Gene wasn't here yet. Done waiting, I murmured a quick apology, stuffed my phone and keys into my back pockets, hopped out of the car speed walking up the sidewalk to the front door. Not bothering with the doorbell, I banged on the door.

"Dani! Dani, open this damn door. Where is my baby?" I probably looked and sounded unhinged. Because I was. I didn't care what anyone thought of me. Every fiber of my being was screaming at me to get to Saffi right now. Dani didn't open the door. Pressing my ear to the wood surface, I heard very faint thumping noises.

"Danielle Anise Barker! I hear you in there. Open this damn door and give me my baby!" I banged on the door again. Again, nothing from inside.

Finally remembering the spare keys, I pulled them from my pocket. I unlocked the door and swung it open so hard it struck the wall behind it then rebounded off. Crossing the threshold, the stillness of the house caught me off guard.

Considering the way I burst through the door, I fully expected Dani to come down the hallway cursing me out. I heard neither Dani cursing, nor Saffi's quick footsteps running to assure me she was ok. What I did hear was the faint thumping sound again. Slowly swiveling my head, I stepped forward trying to pinpoint the origin of the sound.

"Ah!" I screamed out when two strong hands grabbed my shoulders.

"That's what your ass gets. I told you to wait for me."

Shrugging from beneath his hands and swatting them away, I turned to look at Gene. "I did wait. You were late."

"Two minutes. It took me two minutes longer than I said to get here. You couldn't wait two minutes?"

"No! Something's wrong, Gene. I feel it. Listen." I held a hand up to stop him from talking. "Do you hear that? The thumping sound?"

"Yeah..." Twisting his head from side to side he listened as well. "It's coming from upstairs."

By silent consensus, we agreed to stop talking and not call out to Dani or Saffi. Peeking into the living room then kitchen as we passed the doors, we checked for anything suspicious. Everything looked normal. There were some knick-knacks strewn about and some dishes in the sink, otherwise, there were no signs anything out of the ordinary was going on.

We didn't go into the formal dining room nor laundry room at the back of the house. For Dani, those places might as well not exist. She never used the dining room. Whenever she used the laundry room, she closed the door to keep the noise down. The door was wide open. A quick glance inside as we climbed the stairs, confirmed it was empty as well.

Leading the way, Gene's footsteps were muted by the carpet on the stairs. As we approached the unknown, I regretted leaving my gun in the car. *What's the point of having it, if I was just going to leave it there?* I asked myself the question, even though I knew why I'd left it. I didn't want to run the risk emotions would get so high I'd actually use it. I'd like to think I'd never shoot my own blood, except I never said never when it came to Saffi.

The upstairs had three bedrooms and two bathrooms. One bedroom was on one side along with the bathroom. The second bedroom was on the other side of the stairs. The largest bedroom was located at the end of the hall and contained the second bathroom. When I'd moved out of the house, I'd left Saffi's old bed. It was one of the old twin beds, I'd slept in growing up. That bed was still in the spare room on the right.

The bedding was mussed like someone had recently slept there. We poked our heads inside the room, but didn't see anyone or anything to match the thumping sound. The sound had stopped; so, we couldn't follow the noise to find it. The silence prompted us to search each room individually—including the hallway bathroom.

Reaching the room at the end of the hall, Gene tentatively pushed the door open. When the door fully opened, he sprang through it so quickly, it startled me. I hung back for a second until I realized what had him moving so swiftly. Dani was lying on the floor beside her bed. Blood pooled around her, soaking the carpet.

"Call 9-1-1!" Gene shouted as he crouched next to her.

I already had one hand in my pocket, reaching for my phone, when he called out to me. I pressed the phone to my ear and walked closer to them. *Come on, come on, come on!* I chanted in my head as I waited for the call to connect.

"Is she still alive?" I asked Gene, choking back tears. Although Dani wasn't the best sister in the world, she was the one I had. Seeing her like this, battered and bloody, brought tears to my eyes. It wasn't her condition which had me on the verge of completely falling apart.

Other than Dani, no one else was in the house. So, where was Saffi?

Thinking of her had my heart racing out of control. Tears tumbling down my face unchecked. *My baby was officially missing!*

"9-1-1. What's your emergency?" The monotone voice of the operator finally flowed through the phone.

"My sister, she's been hurt and my daughter is missing! We need an ambulance and the police!" I could hear myself yelling, only I couldn't control the volume of my voice. My normally calm demeanor was non-existent in the face of Saffi's disappearance.

"Ma'am, I need you to slow down and give me more information. Okay, can you do what I'm asking?"

"Yes, I can. But, I need them to hurry."

"Yes ma'am they will. First, what is the address for the emergency?"

"Rogers Lane, Two Five Six Five Rogers Lane."

"Okay. That's good. So, you need an ambulance and police at Two Five Six Five Rogers Lane. Is this in the Atlanta area, ma'am?"

"Yes!" Impatient with the process, I started pacing from the bed to the door.

"Ok ma'am. You said your sister was injured? Can you tell me about her injuries?"

"Gene, she's asking about Dani's injuries."

Looking at Gene, I put the phone on speaker and placed it on the floor. Kneeling on the other side of Dani, I looked into her abnormally pale face. Even though her eyes fluttered, they didn't open.

Gene was speaking to the operator telling her what he could see. He was trained in first aid, so he didn't try to move Dani. Instead, he'd lifted her shirt to look at her stomach, where most of the blood seemed to come from. She'd been stabbed. Several times.

Gene had snatched off his shirt immediately to press the material into the wounds, trying to stop the stem of blood. While Gene was talking to the operator, I leaned closer to Dani's face.

"Dani!" I whisper-screamed at my semi-conscious sibling.

"Dani! Where's Saffi?" Her eyes fluttered. I shook her shoulder to force her to open them. Gene quickly pushed my hands away.

"Stephanie! Stop it! I know we need to find Saffi, but if you can't help with Dani, you need to get out of the way."

Contrite eyes met his over my sister's prone frame. I'd lost control. The little I'd gained at his words was barely in place.

Pointing toward the door to the ensuite, he gritted out, "Go to the bathroom and get me some towels. I need more than my shirt to try to stop this bleeding."

The entire time, he was talking to the operator telling her what he saw. She offered suggestions to help us keep Dani alive until the ambulance arrived. I rushed to the bathroom grabbing a stack of towels from the linen closet.

I was starting to give up on Dani ever waking up when I looked down into her face and saw her hazel-brown eyes staring back at me.

"Ste-phan-ie…" Her voice came out in a pained whisper.

"Dani! Oh my God! Dani, who did this? Where's Saffi?" Completely blocking out Gene and the operator, I leaned closer to Dani's face to capture every word.

"Talk to me, Dani! Tell me who did this."

"So…sor-ry…sis…didn't know." Her words came out in halting breaths.

"It's okay. It's okay. Just tell me what happened. Tell me where my baby is."

I'd say anything to get Saffi back. So, if I needed to let Dani think all was well between us, I'd do it. Stroking the hair out of her face, I spoke to her softly, coaxing her to tell me what I needed to hear.

"Tell me, Dani. Tell me who did this? Did they take Saffi?"

"Y-ess…"

"Who, Dani? Who took her?"

"Stephanie!" Gene shouted. "The ambulance is outside, go open the door!"

"Give me a second!" I knew if I left, I wouldn't get the answers I needed. Dani knew who had my baby. She may even know where they were taking her.

"Stephanie!"

"I said give me a second, damnit!" I snapped at Gene and leaned over Dani's face whispering to her, my voice shaking with fear.

"Tell me Dani, who did this? Who has my baby?"

"Vin-cen-te…" Dani released the name in a slow, faltering breath.

"Stephanie! Now!" Gene yelled. I jumped up from the floor and rushed down the stairs to open the door to the paramedics.

Once I opened the door, I showed them where to go. They quickly got her onto the gurney and into the ambulance. Gene didn't trust me to ride along, so I followed behind them in my vehicle. Finding Saffi was my first priority. The answers I needed were in the ambulance with Dani. There was no choice except to follow the answers.

On the way, I tried to call Jian, but I didn't get an answer. I left a voicemail and hung up. My next call was to Nikki who said she'd call Joy then meet me at Talbot Memorial Hospital.

Chapter Twenty

SAFFI

"Where's Dani?" I asked Vincente, her boyfriend, when he got into the car.

It felt weird to call my birth mother by her first name. It felt even weirder to call her *Mama*. That's not who she'd been to me. I barely knew her. Not because I didn't want to. Since she wasn't around much, there weren't many chances for us to really know each other. When I did see her, it was never for very long.

"She said she didn't feel like eating anything. She has a stomachache. She asked me if I could go on and take you home instead of going to dinner like we planned."

"Oh..." I shrank into a corner of the back seat of the luxury car.

I'd never been in a car with a driver before. It felt odd being driven around by a stranger. I stared at the back of the guy's head for a minute before turning to look out of the window—watching Grandma's house get smaller and smaller.

I fiddled with the straps of my backpack. Vincente made me nervous. Something about the way he looked at me made my skin crawl.

Thinking of being alone with him, for as long as it took to get me home, put a knot in my stomach.

I needed to call Aunt Cee-Cee, but I was scared. Not of her hurting me, scared of what she'd say when she found out I didn't stay after school today for my club meetings like I told her. I lied to her. I also lied to the shuttle driver to get him to drop me off at Grandma's house instead of at home.

I dreaded calling her, although I knew I had to. The moment this fancy car pulled into our driveway, she'd have questions. I had to tell her I wouldn't be on the shuttle; someone was bringing me home. Reaching into the front pocket of my backpack, I felt around for my phone.

It wasn't there. Shifting in the seat, I felt my back pockets. No phone. I knew I had it when I made it to Grandma's house because I remember playing a game on it while I waited for Dani to finish getting dressed. Unzipping the bigger pockets of my backpack, I pulled out my notebooks searching for the phone.

It wasn't there. It had to be at Grandma's. We had to go back. I needed my phone. We weren't too far away.

"What's wrong, Little One? You look upset. Did you lose something?" Vincente asked.

"My phone. I can't find it." I kept my face turned away to hide my expression. The way he called me *little one* made me feel icky.

"Can we go back? I need my phone."

I finally looked at him to ask the question. When he started shaking his head no, I rushed to tell him why we had to go back.

"Please can we go back for my phone? I had to work really hard for it and Aunt Cee-Cee will be mad if I lose it. Please?"

My eyes filled with tears of frustration as I begged him to take me back to Grandma's. Why wouldn't he take me? I didn't understand.

"Sorry, Little One. Maybe Danielle can bring it to you later. Look at the traffic. It would take Julio forever to fight his way over to try to turn around to go back for your phone. You'll be alright without it for one night. You kids are on your phones too much anyway."

"I don't understand. Why can't we go back? Maybe if we go back we can stop and get Dani something for her stomach."

My mind overloaded thinking of how to convince him we had to turn around. I was already in enough trouble. I didn't want to add to it. Aunt Cee-Cee was right. Whenever you tried to hide things the truth always came out. She was going to find out everything I'd been keeping from her when I got home. From being driven by a strange man to not having my phone, it was gonna be bad...

I knew she didn't want me around Dani, but when Dani started texting me, I couldn't help myself. I had to talk to her. She was my birth mother. How could I turn my back on a chance to spend time with her? Today wasn't the first time I'd slipped away to see her. It was just the first time I'd gone back to Grandma's house since Flossie and Nee-Nee jumped me.

The other times I saw Dani, I slipped away from campus to meet her, then slipped back in time to catch the shuttle home. It was always after school let out, when I was supposed to be in a club meeting. I told the teacher I couldn't stay for the meeting. I never told Aunt Cee-Cee I wasn't going to every meeting.

Instead of answering me, Vincente looked out of the window on his side of the car. *Maybe he was thinking about it?* I stayed quiet. I didn't want to whine and cry to get my way. Against my will, my eyes filled with tears. I couldn't hold back the whimpering noises. *This was so bad!*

Swiping at the tears on my face, I turned to look out the car window on my side. Familiar scenery flew by along with other vehicles on the highway. Vincente's driver was flying, as Tee-Tee Nikki would say.

Staring out of the window, I watched as we drove right past the exit ramp to take me home. I leaned forward and tapped the back of the front passenger seat.

"Excuse me. I think you just passed my exit."

"Sit back, Little One. Julio knows exactly where he's going."

"But, this isn't the way to my house." I said, still leaning forward to grasp the back of the seat.

"I said sit back!" Vincente's face was red. He looked so angry.

I jumped and scrambled back into my corner—my eyes wide with fear. I was past being uncomfortable around him. He frightened me. My throat nearly sealed itself shut from the tears clogging it.

"You aren't taking me home, are you?"

"No. I'm not."

Saying the words aloud, and hearing him confirm it, took the whole situation from uncomfortable to terrifying. I'm for real being kidnapped. *Oh my God! What do I do?*

I was too terrified to even think straight, let alone fight them. Besides, who could help me? The windows were tinted so dark, no one would be able to see me if I tried to signal for help.

I don't even know what signal to use. Aunt Cee-Cee and Uncle Gene talked to me all the time about being safe, but we didn't talk about what to do if I ended up inside a moving car with strange men taking me to an unknown location. The main thing they did was teach me ways to avoid this very situation.

If I'd been alone and not at Grandma's with someone I knew, I never would have gotten into this car. I'm sitting here now because I trusted Dani. She said she wanted to see me. She said we were going to go out to dinner, like a real family.

I didn't think of Vincente as anything close to family. However, Dani was my birth mother. I was desperate for her attention—any way I could get it. I trusted her, and she tricked me. She still didn't want me. She only pretended to want me. For him. *Why?* Why would she do something like that?

I'm a kid. It didn't mean I was stupid. I knew about men like Vincente. I've never met one until now. Still, I knew about them. After what happened with Flossie and Nee-Nee, Auntie said it was time for me to learn certain things. So, we had a more grown-up talk about men who liked little girls.

She said the best way to keep me safe was for me to know about men like him. Men who preferred little girls over grown women. I was so scared I couldn't stop trembling. All I could do was curl into a ball and pray somehow, someway, someone would save me.

As the car sped along, I looked at the sun setting in the sky and thought about my real mother. Aunt Cee-Cee was the only real mother I've ever had. What would she do when she found out what happened? Would she be angry or sad? Would she come looking for me? Would Dr. J? Or Uncle Gene? Or *anyone*?

It was fully dark by the time the driver drove the car into the garage of a huge house. From what I saw, it looked like a mansion. There weren't any lights on the dark road leading to the house, so I couldn't tell where we were.

I wanna go home...

Chapter Twenty-One

JIAN

"Ok. I think we've got it." I said to Pearson as I looked into the chest cavity of the fifty-two-year-old man suffering from a congenital heart defect.

Pearson had become a regular in my OR following the night he assisted me with Saffi's procedure. As I'd thought, he was sharp and capable. We'd worked on this patient over the past three hours. It was touch and go considering the man's other underlying conditions, but he was now stable.

"Alright, Pearson. Give me a recap. Let's see what you learned today."

Pearson started from the first cut, recounting the procedure. He rattled off the reasons for each incision—each stitch. While he was talking, we went through the protocols and began closing the patient's chest cavity.

"Dr. Anderson?"

Turning to the large monitor, I saw a nurse on the screen. All of the major operating rooms had cameras and monitors so students could view on-going surgeries. They were allowed to ask questions when permitted.

"Yes?"

"I'm sorry to interrupt. There's an emergency. I was asked to inform you you're needed downstairs." The young man shifted nervously in front of the camera.

"Did they give any more details beyond saying it's an emergency? This patient and his family would say what I'm doing right now is an emergent issue."

"No, sir. They didn't. I was just told to get you right away. They said not to take no for an answer."

Who in this hospital would have the nerve to pull me from an ongoing surgery? As if he knew I was on the verge of telling them they'd have to wait, he blurted out.

"They told me not to say anything until I got you out of the OR, but you've got to come now. It's about Stephanie Barker, Dr. Anderson. She needs you."

"You should have fucking led with that!" I growled at him as I stepped away from the instruments. Barking out orders to Pearson and the others to finish closing the patient, I rushed from the room ripping the protective coverings off me as I walked.

As I exited the operating suites, the nurse met me—apologizing profusely. I didn't want his damn apologies. I wanted to know what was so dire Sweets needed them to pull me out of surgery.

She never even called me while I was working, so I knew it was something bad. My brain fed me one horrifying scenario after another. Waving a hand to cut him off, I demanded more details.

"Tell me everything you know. Right now."

Jumping slightly at my terseness, he answered. "I really don't know much, Dr. Anderson. Dr. Maxwell and the Chief sent me to get you. They said tell you it was an emergency. I was instructed not to tell you about Ms Barker until you left the OR."

"I'm out of the OR and all you can tell me is it involves Stephanie? Do you at least know where she is?"

"Yes, doctor. She's downstairs in the Chief's office."

I moved toward the elevators then stopped, turning back to the nurse. My eyes locked onto his. "For future reference, if you're ever asked to pull me from an OR, I don't give a damn who told you what. You tell me exactly what's going on from the moment you open your mouth. Do I make myself clear?"

Nodding mutely, the nurse gulped and clasped his hands together in front of him. "Yes, doctor."

As much as I wanted to rip him a new one for feeding me partial information, I couldn't waste time on him. I had to get to my Sweets. The elevator wasn't moving fast enough, so I dashed down the hall to take the stairs.

I made it to Chief Warren's office in record time. Breathing heavily and sweating, I stormed past his administrative assistant. I pushed open the door to his office. Inside, I saw Sweets. Staring silently into space. She looked broken. My heart stopped for an instant before starting up again thudding loudly in my ears.

Georgina was beside Sweets on the sofa, with an arm around her shoulders speaking to her softly. Chief Warren was at his desk and Gene sat dejectedly in a chair to Sweets' left.

Striding over, I skirted the coffee table dropping to my knees in front of Stephanie.

"Sweets, what's wrong?" Putting my face directly in front of hers, trapping her eyes with mine, I prodded her. "Talk to me, sweetheart."

It literally tore me up inside when her eyes welled with tears. Seeing the tears kicked my protective reflexes up even higher. It was imperative she tell me what happened. I needed to know if I was consoling her or kicking someone's ass. No one hurt my Sweets. No one.

Her tear-filled voice cracked when she spoke. "It's Sa-Sa-Saffi!" She wailed. "Saffi's missing! She's been kidnapped! We-we-we can't find herrrr!"

Falling into my arms, she sobbed into my chest. Scooping her into my lap, I sat on the floor holding her, my heart thumping out of control. *Saffi had been kidnapped?* When? How? I needed answers. I had to get Sweets calm enough to talk to me.

It's almost like seeing me triggered something inside her. She released all the emotions she'd held back. Cradling her in my arms, I looked to Gene and Georgina.

"Can one of you tell me more? How do we know Saffi was kidnapped? When did this happen?"

Scrubbing a hand down his face, Gene answered my questions.

"We know she was kidnapped because Dani told us." Raising a hand, he stopped my next words. "Yes, we're sure Dani told the truth."

"How? I want to talk to her." I don't know if I could make her talk any more than they could. I was willing to try anything. Sweets' pain was palpable. I had to make it stop. If it meant using my position to get into her sister's room to interrogate her, I'd do it.

"You can't talk to Dani. She died almost an hour ago." Gene's voice cracked with emotion delivering the information.

"What?" My mind spun out of control trying to absorb the bits and pieces of information which weren't fitting into the puzzle.

"Doc... Just listen before you ask any more questions. Ok?"

Squeezing Sweets to me tightly, I kissed the top of her head comfortingly before looking back to her cousin and nodding.

"When Saffi didn't come home at her regular time, Step got worried. First, she called Saffi. When the call went straight to voicemail, she pulled up the tracking info.

It showed Saffi at Grandma Vi's old house, so she called Dani. When Dani didn't answer the phone, Step called me. I met her at the house. When we got there, Dani was the only one there.

She'd been stabbed multiple times in her chest and stomach. She was barely alive. We called 9-1-1 asking them to send help. Before the paramedics came, Dani told us Vincente had taken Lady Bug.

We don't know more, because we didn't get a chance to talk to her again. She died and was revived in transit, but she didn't survive the surgery. We have no idea when he took Lady Bug or where. We just know he has her."

Dropping his head, the big man cried softly into his hands. *This can't be happening.* Not to Saffi. Not to the teen who loved science, math, reading and superhero movies. Not her.

No matter how much I told myself it couldn't be real, it was real. Sitting in the Chief's office, we were losing time. I dreaded doing it, nevertheless I nudged Sweets until I got her to stand. We needed to get to my office, so I could get my things and call Ash. I wanted to know which cops were assigned to look into this. I also wanted to know why the hell they weren't here right now.

Gene stood to leave with us, while Georgina and Chief Warren walked us to the door.

"Jian, please let me know if there's anything Ralph and I can do." Georgina squeezed my arm while she patted Stephanie's shoulder. "Seriously, whatever we can do to help, we'll do."

"Thanks, Georgina. We appreciate it."

I didn't doubt if there was something she and her husband could do to help, they would do their best. Although she dispensed some good-natured ribbing at the beginning of our relationship, she took to Stephanie quickly.

Chief Warren walked us to the outer office. "Don't worry about anything happening here, Dr. Anderson. I'll handle it. You take care of your family. That's all you need to focus on."

"Thank you, Chief."

Stephanie and I weren't married, but she and Saffi were my family. It hadn't even been a year, yet I'm not sure who I'd be without the two of them in my life. We had to find Saffi. *We had to.*

Inside my office, I sat Sweets on the small sofa. I quickly grabbed my cell from the desk drawer. I noticed the missed calls before clearing the screen and to call Ash. The phone rang several times before rolling to voicemail. Cursing, I ended the call. Immediately, I called back. Looking at my watch, I saw it was close to nine p.m.

What the hell was he doing? Why didn't he pick up? I started to give up and leave a voicemail when he answered. His Alabama drawl even thicker than usual with sleep.

"Hullo?"

"Asher, I need your help."

He cleared his throat, then I heard rustling in the background. "What's wrong? You **never** call me Asher. This has to be big."

"Saffi's been kidnapped."

"What?! Start from the beginning." All traces of sleep were gone from his voice. I heard the thumping sounds I associated with him moving about. I knew he was either putting on clothes or getting himself together.

Putting the call on speaker, I let him know Sweets and Gene were with me in my office. Although he'd never met Gene, he knew who he was. I only knew what Gene had relayed to me, so I needed them to give Ash the information first hand.

After they told him all the details leading up to where we were, I asked him, "Can you find out who's supposed to be working on this? I don't like how it's been more than two hours since they reported it and no one has called or come to the hospital or anything."

"Man...They probably won't send anyone until tomorrow if then." Gene interjected. I looked at him in shock.

"Why do you say they won't send anyone until tomorrow?"

"Because, the ambulance got to the house before the patrol car. We talked to two patrol officers while Dani was in surgery. They didn't seem too bothered.

They made out like Lady Bug probably went home or ran away when she witnessed the attack. Since we couldn't give them a description of the guy or the car he was driving and all we had was Dani's word, they claimed there wasn't much they could do other than put out an Amber Alert."

"What the FUCK?!" Ash's voice boomed through the speaker. "Please tell me you got their fucking names." He gritted out.

"We did, but it won't matter. *We* love Lady Bug. *We* care what happens to her. To them, she's just another teenaged black girl who didn't come home from school."

"We'll see about that shit." Ash growled. "Give me their names. I'm going to make some calls. Jay, where are y'all going when you leave the hospital?"

"I'm taking Sweets home. We'll come up with a game plan there." I told him, slipping my jacket onto my shoulders.

"Ok. I'll meet you there." The declaration was followed by the beeps indicating the call had ended.

I coaxed Sweets from the sofa. She hadn't said more than a few words since she told me Saffi had been kidnapped. I was worried about her. Where were her friends? As much as they loved Saffi, it's hard to believe they weren't with Sweets at a time like this.

"Where are Nikki and Joy, Sweets? Do they know?"

Slowly, she lifted her head, her tortured eyes finding mine. "Joy is at my house, just in case Saffi comes home. Nikki is at her office."

"Ok. That's good." I was so relieved she responded. I was starting to think she'd retreated completely inside herself. "Is Nikki coming to the house later then?"

"Maybe. She said she could help me better from her office. She has access to more there. She doesn't think the cops are going to help either. She's working her contacts."

Sweets hadn't told me much about what Nikki did for a living, only divulging Nikki worked in private security. Hearing her say Nikki was working her contacts, had me wondering if there was more to it than what I'd been told. I didn't doubt it and didn't have time to dwell on it. Any help we could get finding Saffi was appreciated.

When we made it to the bank of elevators, we parted ways with Gene. I took Sweets with me. He took her car keys to follow us in her vehicle.

Sweets seemed to come to life as I drove out of the parking deck. She didn't want to go home yet. She wanted to go back to her Grandmother's house. When she reminded me that the tracking signals for Saffi's devices pointed to the house, she said she hadn't seen them when they were there earlier. She wanted to go back to look around.

Unsure if it was the best thing we could do, but knowing we had to do something, I adjusted my route. At least she was talking again. As hard as this was for me, it had to be even worse for her.

We placed a quick call to Gene to tell him the change in plans. Since his truck was still parked there, he said he'd stop at home to get his wife, Charmaine, so she could drive it to Sweets' house. It was the general consensus for everyone to gather there until we heard news or found Saffi.

We rolled to a stop on the street in front of the craftsman style house. Sweets hopped out of her seat before I'd put the vehicle in park. Cursing under my breath, I hurriedly switched off the ignition, bounded out and jogged to catch up with her. I reached her as she put the key into the lock of the front door.

It was nothing like the movies where there was crime scene tape advising people to keep out. There also wasn't a patrol car outside to secure the scene until either detectives or forensics went over it. They really were treating Dani's stabbing and Saffi's abduction as if they didn't matter.

As if a woman being stabbed in her own home nor the missing teenaged girl were of no consequence. My ability to remain calm and controlled was sorely being tested. I had to keep it together though. For Sweets. We couldn't both fall apart or go into rages. One of us had to keep a clear head.

Pulling out her phone, Sweets pulled up the tracking app she used. I didn't know if I'd ever get used to the idea of putting trackers on our kids. Despite my ambivalence, I hoped something, anything, came up on the screen.

Her thumbs flew across the display as she made selections and adjusted filters. Once she finished, she walked around the room holding the phone out like a metal detector. When it actually started emitting electronic beeps, my eyes widened in shock. *What the hell was Sweets into?* That's not tech regular, every day citizens have.

Waving the phone in front of her, she followed the beeps as they increased in volume and frequency until they led her to the sofa table along the wall beside the stairs. There, inside the left-hand drawer, were Saffi's cell phone along with her electronic tablet.

"Saffi never goes anywhere without her phone and tablet. She wouldn't have just left them here." She said as she removed the items from the drawer to inspect them.

Gene arrived shortly after the discovery of the devices, his wife at his side. Charmaine rushed to Stephanie. The two hugged while I filled Gene in on what we'd found. I wondered if Vincente had spent any significant time with Dani at the house. Maybe he'd left something we could use to locate him, since the other trackers were still offline.

"Hey Sweets, Gene, do either of you know if Vincente was here a lot?"

Lifting her shoulders and shaking her head, Stephanie answered, "I wouldn't know. I told you Dani's been avoiding me. Even if she wasn't, she didn't talk to me about her boyfriends. Gene, Charmaine, have you heard anything about him hanging here a lot?"

"Whenever I came to check on the property, she wasn't here, so I've never seen the dude." Gene responded.

Charmaine said she didn't know either. Dejected, my shoulders slumped. It was a thought. We still looked around the house, despite us having very little expectation we'd find anything usable.

When Sweets placed her foot on the step to ascend the stairs, I didn't need the head tilt from Gene to nudge me to follow her. I remembered what was up there—the room where Dani's life drained away.

Following behind her, I accompanied her upstairs to continue searching for anything which might help us find Saffi. Going straight to the room at the end of the hall, she stuttered to a stop at the doorway. She stood transfixed in the entrance. Standing behind her, I looked over her head into the room.

Inside, a four-poster bed took up a large portion of the available space. A tall chest of drawers was on the opposite wall next to a walk-in closet. The hard wood floor was partially covered by a large multi-colored area rug. There on the rug, looking like Rorschach inkblot, was the dried pool of Danielle's blood. It had already turned to the brownish coloring one expected after some time had passed.

Wrapping an arm around her waist, I whispered in Sweets' ear. "Are you okay? Do you want me to do this for you?"

With a quick shake of her head, she squared her shoulders before she stepped inside the room. "No. I've got it."

Skirting the stained rug, she went directly to the closet. She began pushing around clothing and pulling lids off shoe boxes. Not having any idea what we were looking for, I scanned the room searching for anything that looked out of place. Directly across from the bed was a small vanity with an oval shaped mirror attached to the wall above it.

I can't say what drove me to the vanity; I was just compelled to move closer to the piece of furniture covered with various containers of cosmetic products. As I drew nearer to it, amongst the bottles and compacts was an envelope. Somewhat covered by a small clutch purse, I made out part of something scrawled across the outside in a block script.

Moving the little purse aside, I discovered the writing wasn't just any writing. It was Stephanie's name.

"Sweets!" I called out to her.

"Yes?" Came her muffled reply from the recesses of the closet.

Picking up the envelope, I took it to her. "Look at this." I held the envelope aloft so she could see her name.

"Where'd you find this?" She asked, taking it from my hand.

Nodding in the general direction of the vanity, I told her. "I found it over there underneath a little purse."

Turning it over in her hands a few times, she walked out of the closet lifting the flap to reveal the folded pages inside. All movement stopped. The air was heavy with anticipation as she read the words printed on the lined pages.

I didn't attempt to read what was there. Besides the fact the words weren't intended for me, I was too busy watching Sweets—reading her facial expressions. They ranged from confusion to annoyance before transforming to down-right fury.

"That BITCH! She'd better be glad her ass is dead. If she wasn't dead I'd kill her!" Releasing a string of threats laced with curse words, she lamented all the ways she'd harm her sister if she were still alive. She threw the pages and envelope to the floor. Her body shook with fury to the point I worried about her bursting a blood vessel.

As unlikely as the scenario was, for a few short minutes it was my reality. Picking the letter up, I refolded it, placed it back into the envelope and tucked it into my back pocket.

Placing my hands on her shoulders, I rubbed them trying to sooth whatever sent her into such a rage. Again, I chose not to read the letter. I was confident she would tell me if the sheets contained information to help us find Saffi. Probing her eyes, I tried to pull her back to me.

"Sweets...Sweets...Come on, Baby. Look at me."

Angry tears ran in rivulets down her flushed faced. Behind me, I heard Gene and Charmaine enter the room.

"Hey, we heard y'all all the way downstairs. Well, we heard Step. What's going on?" Gene asked as he too skirted the blood-stained carpet on his path to stand beside us.

"I found a letter Danielle left for Stephanie."

"Oh? What did it say?"

"I don't know. We were just getting to the contents of the letter when you came in." *At least I hoped we were.*

Shrugging off my hands, Sweets strode to the open door. She spoke through clenched teeth. "I've gotta get the fuck out of this room before I rip all this shit up."

Gene reached out to her. I put out a hand to stop him. "Give her a minute. She'll tell us. Just give her a minute."

Trailing her out of the room, we all stopped and stood in the door of the small room at the top of the stairs. The one which held a twin bed with mussed sheets.

Sweets sat at the foot of the bed absently straightening the bed coverings. "This used to be Saffi's room. It was mine before it was hers. The mattress is different, but we both slept on this little twin bed at different times in our lives."

Being in the room seemed to calm her. Allowing her some time to gather herself, I entered and sat in the chair in front of the little classroom style desk. Gene and Charmaine stepped away from the door. I was certain they were still nearby.

After a few silent minutes, I asked her. "Sweets...Did Danielle say anything in the letter which might help us find Saffi?"

She turned her sad, dark eyes to me. "Dani wrote a lot of stuff on that paper. Most of it was a listing of her petty grievances. The rest sounded like some sort of fairy tale she'd dreamed up.

I honestly don't know if it was true to even say if any of it is relevant. She mentioned Vincente and their plans. It sounded so far-fetched I just don't know."

She stood from the bed looking around the room without focusing on anything in particular. I stood and reached for her hand. Tangling our fingers together, I tugged her gently—urging her to follow me. We'd done everything we could do here. It was time to go.

Chapter Twenty-Two

STEPHANIE

My gaze was glued to the darkness of the night sky during the drive home. A million thoughts raced through my mind. At the base of them was the absolute terror we may lose Saffi forever. Thinking of her loss, in particular, had me in a choke hold. *What if we didn't find her?*

All of the precautions I took. All of the ways I tried to protect her, to keep her safe. They amounted to nothing in the face of the harsh reality she was taken. There was a chance I may never see her again. A strangled sob burst through my lips. I clamped my hands over my mouth to muffle the sound.

Jian's warm hand landed on my thigh, rubbing and squeezing as he tried to comfort me.

"I know, Sweets. I know... It's okay to be upset, Baby. You don't have to hide it. I'm here. We'll get through this together. I promise. We won't stop until we have Saffi back home with us."

Lowering my hands, I dropped them to the one he placed on my thigh. He immediately turned his hand palm up tangling our fingers together. *God, I love this man.*

Turning my gaze to his face, I found his eyes waiting for mine. The determination in his expression projected his clear belief in his words. He had no doubt we would find her. His confidence helped me maintain hope.

Joy was waiting for us when we made it home. She'd been there for hours. When we entered the kitchen through the mudroom off the garage, she was standing at the island with a coffee mug in her hand and an expectant look on her face. I wished we had something good to tell her, but we didn't.

Searching my face, her own drooped in sadness. "No news, huh?"

Shaking my head, no, I felt a fresh wave of tears attempting to overwhelm me again.

"Ohhh, honey... Come here..." Putting her cup on the counter she rushed to me and wrapped me in her arms. My emotions were swinging from one extreme to another on a fast-moving pendulum. I was either enraged or totally despondent.

Where was my middle ground? Where is the calm I prided myself in? My normal ability to marshal my emotions had deserted me. I felt like a walking, talking, bag of emotional turmoil.

The pinging of Jian's phone pierced the quiet. I pulled away from Joy. Maybe it was Ash. Normally, I didn't move when his phone dinged with messages or calls. This wasn't a normal time. I watched him read the message searching his face for any clue it was about Saffi.

He read the text and tucked the phone back into his pocket. "That was Ash, he'll be here in five minutes."

My shoulders dropped at the brief message. "Oh. Ok."

Wrapping an arm around my shoulders, Joy led me to the family room. "Come on, Step. Why don't you sit down? I'll fix you a cup of coffee."

Mutely, I followed her lead and curled into the corner of the L-shaped sofa with my legs tucked beneath me. I didn't realize Gene and Charmaine were in the house until Joy offered them something to drink as well. Jian posted himself at the window waiting for his friend.

While he waited for Ash, I pulled out my phone to text Nikki. My logical mind knew if she had anything to tell me, she'd call. But the emotional beast riding me was hungry to hear something, anything, which put me one step closer to having Saffi home safe.

Nikki replied, telling me she was still working her contacts. She'd run a background check on Vincente and was going through the information. She also had a couple of guys visiting his businesses seeing what they could come up with. I don't know how many favors she had to call in to do all of those things. Whatever she did, she had my endless gratitude.

Joy was back with steaming mugs of coffee when Jian opened the door to a grim-faced Ash. Dipping his head to avoid knocking his manbun on the top of the doorframe, he entered the family room.

Coming straight to me, he sat on the chaise lounge part of the sofa. Jian, sat next to me and grabbed my free hand. His fingers tangled with mine as we listened to Ash.

"I'm so sorry this is happening, Stephanie. There's an Amber Alert out for Saffi. I ripped those patrolmen a new one. They're on my shit list. The Sergeant is getting detectives on it, except I'm not waiting for them."

Tapping the file in his hand against his leg a few times, he flipped it open. "This is everything I was able to dig up on Vincente Renfroe."

"Wait!" I stopped him, putting the mug on a side table and picking up my phone. "I think we should call Nikki; she's been digging into him as well."

"Nikki? Your friend Nikki?" He asked, his face scrunched in confusion.

"Right, the one who works in private security. You've met her before." I explained as I tapped the screen putting the phone on speaker. I lay it on the chaise lounge between me and Ash.

"Not officially, but if she has access to more information, I'm all for it."

Nikki picked up on the third ring. "Hey, Step. What's up?" As close as it was to midnight, her voice held no trace of tiredness.

"Hey, Nik. I've got you on speaker. Ash just got here. He has a file with some information he dug up on Vincente." Ash may not know Nikki, however I'd told her all about Ash after I met him.

"I thought we should call you since you've been looking into his background as well."

"Oh, Ok. Cool. I'm listening."

Laying the file next to the phone on the cushion, Ash rattled off the information he'd acquired. We all listened as he told us about the various legal and shady—but not illegal—businesses Vincente had his hands in. While it was eye-opening, I didn't see how it would help us find Saffi. I said as much after Nikki confirmed she'd uncovered much of the same information in addition to the names of associates Ash didn't have.

Those people's activities were definitely illegal. They also weren't the kind of people who allowed anyone into their circle who wasn't just as dirty as they were. Ash confirmed one of the task forces he worked with had been trying to infiltrate the organization for years.

"How does any of this help us find Saffi?" I asked in frustration. "All it does is make me even more worried about where she is and what she could possibly be going through. It's been hours. For all we know, he could have taken her out of state. Didn't you say these guys have access to private jets?"

Rubbing my shoulders, Jian tried to keep me from going over the edge into full on hysteria. "Shh, Sweets. We can't think like that. Those guys may have significant reach. We don't know if Vincente has those same connections. We have to keep hope."

"He's right, Step. We have to consider the circumstances; we can't assume the worse. All we can do is find out his connections and look for ways to ferret out where he might have taken her." Nikki's voice was calm, only I was sure she was irritated at not having more to go on by now.

"Speaking of connections," Jian spoke up. "Did you tell Nikki about the letter from Danielle?"

"Letter, what letter?" Nikki asked before I could answer.

"When we went to Grandma's looking for clues, Jian found a letter Dani wrote to me. It was a bunch of petty bullshit and gibberish. It's just more of Dani blaming everyone else for how her life turned out. The difference was, she blamed me this time."

"Stephanie, there's no such thing as a small or insignificant clue in times like these." Nikki said grimly. "The fact that she wrote a letter says there was some kind of plan in play. I want to hear it. If you don't want to read it, go to your office, scan it then email it to me."

When she called me Stephanie, I knew I'd lost this round. She rarely called me by my whole name. It was Step, Lil Bit or Short Stack, not Stephanie. Maybe they were right. Maybe my initial anger at Dani blinded me.

Pulling the envelope from his back pocket, Jian passed it to me. I unfolded the lined sheets of paper and spread them in my lap. Clearing my throat, I read the letter aloud.

Stephanie,

By the time you read this, I'll be gone. I'm taking Chloe with me. I'm her mother, even if you don't like to admit it. You and Grandma took her from me. You poisoned her against me, but I'm taking her back. I know you think I don't know how to do anything. You think I can't be a good mother. You're wrong. All of you are wrong. Y'all tried to make it seem like you were better than me. Even Mama and Daddy did it. From the day they brought you home from the hospital, they acted like you were the best thing to ever happen to them. You don't remember Daddy, but I do. I remember how we were as a family before you came along. Daddy and Mommy were fun. They loved **me** *and played with* **me**. *They told* **me** *I was special. That all stopped when you were born. I hated you for taking my daddy from me long before the army sent him to die in Iraq. Taking my daddy wasn't enough for you though, you had to take Andres too. I knew he wanted you when he started coming back around. You were in college and thought you were too good for a low-ranking soldier in the army. No matter what I did, even getting pregnant with his baby, he still wanted you. He was always asking how you were doing in school. He said he didn't think of you the way boys thought of girls they liked, but I knew better. When he wouldn't marry me and take me out of Grandma's house, I didn't need him or his crying ass baby. It's the reason I left for those six months.*

Now I have a new man. A good one this time. He has money. He has power and he **wants me***! I know you think I don't know how to pick a man, but you're wrong. I picked a good one this time. He wants a family and everything. He even bought a big house in the country for us to live in. I've seen it. It's a big beautiful mansion with acres and acres of land around it. He wants me to bring Chloe home with us so we can be a real family. He even wants us to have more kids together. We've already started trying. He doesn't have to know I got fixed years ago. By the time he* *figures out we won't ever have kids together, I'll have him so much in love with me, he won't care.*

Anyway, don't come looking for us. You'll never find us. Vincente has powerful friends. He has ways of keeping us from being traced. My advice to you is for you to get your own life. Have your own family. Stop trying to steal what's mine. Since you're dating a fancy doctor, maybe he'll put a baby in you to replace Chloe. You have everything. You don't need to keep my child away from me and steal my happily ever after with Vincente.

Have a good life. Leave us alone!

Danielle

I finished the letter and tossed it onto the floor. It incensed me as much the second time I read it as it did the first time. How could she think I would just have another child and forget all about Saffi? Who does that shit? Just replace one child with another like you're picking out a new dress? *Evil bitch!*

Deafening silence shrouded the room as everyone digested the contents of the letter. By the looks on their faces, they had similar questions to the ones floating in my head. Nikki broke the silence with a question for Ash.

"Mr. Detective, can you run back the list of investments and properties you found for Vincente?"

"Are you thinking what I'm thinking?" He asked as he riffled through the pages.

Sitting up straight, I picked up on their urgency. "What? What are you two thinking?"

"I'm thinking, the part of Dani's letter that mentioned the house in the country might be worth looking into. It might not be a fairy tale. The place may really exist. If it's isolated enough, it would be the perfect place to hold someone you didn't want found." Nikki said.

I heard her fingernails tapping away at her keyboard. As Ash called off the addresses of the properties, we heard Nikki keying the information into her system.

"Step, we need to switch this call to the computer. Go to your office or grab your laptop. We need to connect it to the TV. I want the detective to see what I'm looking at."

"Let me grab it. Give me five minutes." My office was too small for all the bodies in the room to fit and still see the information on the computer clearly. So, the family room was the best option.

Clicking off the call, I hopped up from the sofa. My energy renewed with the possibility of a real lead which might help us bring my baby home. Almost sprinting down the hall, I went to my office and grabbed my laptop from the docking station.

By the time I made it back to the family room, someone had already turned on the big screen television mounted on the wall. Waking the computer, I started up the video chat selecting the share option to display the images from Nikki on the bigger screen. All attention in the room was on the TV as Nikki cycled through photos of properties.

"Stop!" Ash called out to her when she moved from an antebellum style home to a beachfront condo. "Go back to that one. Do you have an area map? One covering about, let's say, a one-hundred-and-fifty-mile radius with the center of Atlanta as the starting point?"

"Hold on." Nikki replied.

More clicks with a few movements of the mouse and a topical image of the area was on one side of the screen while the photo of the property was on the other.

"Now, let's see. Can you show the physical location of the property on the map?" He asked as he stood and walked closer to the screen.

We all watched as the map transformed zooming until one of those little red identifier balloons hovered over a spot densely populated with the green tops associated with wooded areas. In the center of the wooded area was an expanse of flat lighter green land. Just off the highway running parallel to the woods, we saw one road leading into the woodlands ending at the massive structure.

Even looking at the satellite image, the house looked huge. It could very well be the mansion Dani described in her letter. A sliver of hope crept its way into my heart.

"Any way we can get more up to date images on what's happening at this place?" Ash asked.

"Detective, I'm good, but I don't have that kind of info at my finger-tips. I'll have to call in some favors to get my hands on recent satellite images." Nikki's voice had an edge of mirth to it, only I knew she wasn't making light of the situation.

People routinely expected her to work miracles, because she regularly worked miracles. Ash seemed to know it instinctively.

"I don't have those kinds of connects either, although I may know a guy. It's late; however, I think he'll answer my call." Ash dug into his pocket and pulled out his cellphone.

"You do what you can. I'll see what I can come up with on my end. I'll call if I have something. Y'all call me if you come up with anything."

"Ok." I said since Ash had already walked into the hall to make his call. "Nik? Thank you so much for everything you're doing." I said to my friend, tears clogging my voice as I tried to express my gratitude.

Suddenly the image on the screen was replaced by Nikki's face. Her piercing gaze was leveled at the camera. "You know I'd do anything for Peanut. You don't have to thank me for using everything I have available to me to help out. I know you would do the same and more if the situation were reversed."

"I know. I'm grateful anyway."

"Mhmm. Let me see what I can do about getting eyes on this place. We need to know sooner rather than later if we should focus our attention elsewhere."

"Right."

"I'll hit you back when I know more."

"Ok. Bye." I pressed the icon to disconnect the call. Nikki's image disappeared from the monitor and the big screen TV.

Jian's hand landed on my shoulder. He pulled me into his side. How did he know I needed him to hold me? My emotions were all over the place. I wanted to be hopeful about what Nikki and Ash might find. But, underneath, I was worried we were going down the wrong path. I was afraid Saffi was getting farther and farther away while we were spending time on something which might not pan out.

"This is a good thing, Sweets. I can feel it. What Ash and Nikki said makes sense. I believe we'll have her home with us very soon. We won't stop looking until we do." He declared with a kiss to my forehead as he held me to his chest.

"I hope you're right." I muttered.

As Jian held me in his arms, I looked at the people gathered around the room. Some family, some friends. All of them loved Saffi. They were here to help and support anyway they could. Distantly, I heard Ash's voice as he spoke to his contact.

Even though he was Jian's best friend, I'd only met him a few times. His work schedule was really hectic. Yet, he'd dropped everything to come help us. Knowing we had people in our lives who cared about what we cared about, filled my heart to the brim. The tears, previously hovering on the periphery since the start of this ordeal, trickled down my face before being lovingly swiped away by Jian as he murmured encouragement.

Joy picked up the remote and changed the TV channel to the local news station before quickly switching it off when the Amber Alert ribbon displaying Saffi's name scrolled across the bottom of the screen. Gene and Charmaine had their heads tipped together, not talking, simply offering one another comfort. The room dropped back into silence.

The quiet was broken by the ringing of Jian's cellphone. My heart lurched inside me as my mind immediately went to him being called in for an emergency surgery despite the Chief assuring him no one would disturb him during this time.

Pulling away, he slid the phone from his pocket and held it up to his face. I released the breath I didn't know I was holding when I glimpsed his mother's face on the screen with Mom displayed across the top.

"Hey, Mom." Jian answered. I heard his mother's urgent voice begin speaking. I couldn't make out the exact words, because they were muffled and she was talking a mile a minute.

"Yes, ma'am. I'm sorry I didn't call earlier..." He sat up and scrubbed a hand down his face. "I know. I've been focused on Stephanie. Yes, ma'am. Yes. I understand...I know...Yes, I called Ash. He's here trying to help. No, the other police haven't been very helpful. He's doing what he can."

Ash walked back into the room. The two locked eyes. Strolling back to his original seat, Ash sat at the end of the chaise lounge, scooped up his folder and closed it.

"Ma'am? I don't know, Mom. What did Dad say? Ok..." Holding his phone out, he offered it to Ash. "Here, my mom wants to speak to you."

You'd think Jian had offered him a dirt covered sandwich. Ash rapidly shook his head and held up his hands. Stretching over me, Jian dropped the phone in Ash's lap. "Here's Ash, Mom." He called out.

Mouthing threats to Jian, Ash scooped up the device putting it to his ear. "Hello, Mrs. A... Yes, ma'am. I did talk to them and the Sergeant. Mrs. A... I don't have enough pull to do more than what I've already done there. I have some feelers out to some people I've worked with in the past."

Nodding like she could actually see him, he listened for a few minutes before he spoke again.

"I don't know if a call to the Mayor will help or not. If they show up now, they might get in our way. I wouldn't mind if she lit into their ass about their lack of response to the situation though. It's ridiculous how slow they've been."

My eyes were glued to him, wishing I could hear both sides of the conversation while using context clues to fill in the blanks.

"Yes, ma'am. I will. I'll make sure he does as well. I understand. Do you want to talk to him? Oh. Ok. Goodnight." Heaving a sigh, Ash passed the phone back to Jian.

"A little warning next time." He grumped.

"You got as much warning as I got. She called me and got into my ass about not calling her as soon as I heard. I could barely get a word in edgewise." Jian tucked his phone into his pocket then placed his arm back around my shoulder snuggling me into his side.

Joy, looking for a way to be useful, stood. She asked if anyone wanted anything to drink. Charmaine's eyes were starting to droop, but she shook her head no. Gene declined as well. I hadn't even finished the first cup of coffee she'd given me. So, I didn't want anymore, neither did Jian. For a medical professional, he rarely drank the stuff. Ash accepted. Joy disappeared into the kitchen to put on a fresh pot.

"Were you able to get in touch with anyone?" Jian asked Ash.

"Yeah... about that." Ash's face broke into an uncomfortable grimace.

Chapter Twenty-Three

JIAN

When Ash's face morphed with a constipated look, I knew whatever he said next might not be what I wanted to hear. Something told me whatever caused the expression, might be an emotional land mine for me, Sweets or both of us.

"So, do you remember the time I was assigned to assist with a Secret Service detail? It's been a while." He started.

"Yeah... almost ten years ago not long after you joined the force." I had vague memories of it. I wondered what this had to do with Saffi.

"Well, I kept in touch with one of the guys. He's been local for the last four years. I don't have the contacts to get satellite images. He's still with the Secret Service, so I thought he might have an in with one of the other agencies."

"Ok.... Having agency contacts sounds like good news, but your face says otherwise." I prodded him to get to the point.

"It is good news. He's going to reach out to some people. While we were talking, we started working on a skeleton plan just in case this is the place. We agreed we should start pulling a team together."

"I'm still waiting on the part that has you looking constipated. Why are you so uncomfortable?" I prompted.

"He wants to bring his Section Chief in on it. Apparently, the guy is a tactical and incursion expert."

"Okay..."

"His boss is your ex-girlfriend's husband."

I frowned at him. "What? Who?"

I racked my brain trying to figure out what ex-girlfriend was married to law enforcement. I tried to remember which break-up was so messy I would have a problem with their husband helping us rescue Saffi. Sweets stiffened beside me. Without conscious thought, I rubbed her arm in reassurance.

"McKenna. Her husband, Driscoll Kelly, is my buddy Kenneth's boss."

"Listen, man. I appreciate you trying to make sure there's no awkwardness. You have nothing to worry about. First of all, I dated McKenna more than fifteen years ago. She's not even on my radar.

Besides, this isn't about me. It's about Saffi. I don't care who he is. If he can help us bring her home, he's welcome here. Right, Sweets?"

I looked to Stephanie whose expression echoed my words. Looking at Ash, she added her thoughts. "Although I've only interacted with him a few times, I don't see why it would be a problem. I've met Driscoll. He and McKenna are good people."

There was no need for further discussion. Bringing our little girl home was the top priority. Anything else was negligible.

With a curt nod, Ash continued. "Good to hear because I already told Kenneth to reach out as soon as we get the confirmation we need from the satellite images."

I wasn't angry at all he'd already gotten the ball rolling. He had first-hand knowledge of how into McKenna I was back then. He knew how hard I took it when she broke things off. That was then.

Now, I had Sweets. What I felt for McKenna all those years ago was hollow in comparison to my feelings about my Sweets. Within minutes of meeting her, my heart knew what it took my mind a little while to admit. She was my future; nothing before her mattered.

Once things were settled about McKenna's husband, Ash laid out his tentative plan. With the various task forces and undercover assignments he'd been a part of over his career, Ash had met people he trusted who he was confident would agree to help.

I'd never been more grateful he'd chosen to join the force after he retired from the NFL. While he gave us a little background and the credentials of the people he wanted to bring on board, I was already counting myself in the group.

I knew he wouldn't like it. I knew Sweets wouldn't like it. But it didn't matter. Nothing would stop me. My gut told me the satellite images would just be the start. When vehicles rolled out to find Saffi and bring her home, I fully intended on being in one of them.

The soothing press of Sweets body increased against my side. I looked down to see she was struggling to stay awake. Knowing she'd put up a fight about lying down didn't stop me from suggesting it.

Rubbing along her arm, I spoke softly into her ear. "Sweets, why don't you go lie down for a bit? You need some rest."

Jerking until she was sitting straight up, she shook her head vigorously. "No. I'm fine. I don't want to sleep. I'm good. I need to stay awake. What if Nikki calls back with information? I can't. I have to be ready."

Holding her by her shoulders, I captured her eyes with mine. Even as she fought against it, the fatigue was obvious. "Sweets...I'm not saying go sleep for eight hours. I'm saying take a short nap. Give your body the break it needs. I promise, if a phone call comes in or anyone comes by with information, I'll wake you."

"No!" Pulling away, she lurched to her feet and started pacing. "I'll just drink some more coffee and...and..." Her eyes scanned the room until they landed on the laptop she'd placed on the coffee table.

"I need to check the tracking app again. Maybe the earrings and locket are back online." A stricken expression painted her face. "I haven't checked in over an hour! What if they came online? What if I missed it!" Rushing to the laptop she opened the lid, swiped shaking fingers across the mouse pad to wake it. She tapped nervously on the device until it complied with her request.

"Sweets..." I tried reaching her.

"No! I need to check." The hard set of her jaw let me know it was a lost cause to try to stop her, so I backed off.

While she pulled up the desktop version of the tracking app with one hand, she fumbled with her cellphone with the other. Unlocking it and setting it beside the laptop.

I didn't hold out hope the trackers had miraculously come back online. Still, I didn't try to stop her from checking. My heart hurt for her when the screen didn't show a signal for the jewelry Saffi wore daily.

Sweets slumped forward. She covered her face with her hands. Stress and heartache came off her in gut-wrenching waves. Slipping one arm under her legs, I braced her back with the other sliding her backwards onto the sofa.

Enfolding her in my arms, I gave her the only support I could. With every fiber of my being, I wished I could do more. But, I couldn't. My inability to do anything to ease her pain was almost unbearable.

She didn't struggle against me, which I took as a good sign. Shaky breathing alerted me to her fresh tears. I tightened my arms around her, rubbing her back. Once again, the room fell into silence.

The only noise interrupting the stillness was the sound of Ash tapping away at the keyboard of his own laptop. He must have retrieved it from his car during one of the times he left the room making phone calls.

Uncounted minutes went by as I held Sweets in my arms listening to her soft breathing. She fought it, but her body finally gave out. She slept fitfully against my chest. I dared not move a muscle, worried the slightest motion could wake her.

She'd been running off of pure adrenaline. According to the clock on the mantle, it was three a.m. Her normal day started at five-thirty a.m. She'd been going for almost twenty-four hours with more than half of the time being spent in emotional turmoil.

Her pain and discomfort made my blood boil. I longed for the chance to meet Vincente Renfroe face-to-face. I had detailed plans for how he would suffer for the pain he'd put my Sweets through. I wouldn't even allow myself to think about Saffi being hurt, or else I would completely lose my shit. Just thinking of it had my jaw clenched so tightly, my teeth ached.

The notification chirps from Stephanie's cellphone rang out into the room at the same time Ash's phone let out the first strains of his custom ringtone. Jerking awake, Sweets reached out blindly for her device as Ash stood and placed his phone to his ear.

I passed Sweets her phone. She swiped the screen while she answered in one motion.

"Hello?!" After a brief moment of listening, she nodded as she swung her legs from the sofa flipping her laptop open again. Gene, Charmaine and Joy all sat up rubbing their eyes groggily. In less than a minute Sweets re-established the connection to the TV.

"Ok, Nik. I'm ready."

Dropping the phone, she selected the icon to connect the incoming video call. We were once again privy to the information from Nikki's system. Although it was a video call, we didn't actually see Nikki's face since she was sharing her desktop.

Ash didn't leave the room to take his call. Instead, he put the call on speaker quickly introducing us to Kenneth Holmes. It turned out both Kenneth and Nikki had new info about the house where Saffi was potentially being held. Nikki shared her desktop for us to see everything as we discussed it.

"Ok, I'll start with the bad news first."

My stomach dropped at Nikki's words before I reminded myself her mention of bad news meant there was also good news. I reached for Stephanie's hand tangling our fingers together—giving her digits a supportive squeeze.

"It took a little bit to get to a satellite in position to show us anything. When we did, it didn't give us much. Given the time of day, we really didn't have high expectations. Nevertheless, we held out hope." She displayed the images on the screen. The video showed nothing more than an outline of the structure with easily identifiable edges of the surrounding woods.

"As you can see, there's very little movement outside other than what looks like a couple of guards on the perimeter. There's some type of shielding on the structure making it damn near impossible to get any idea of what's happening inside from above. We'd have to get closer with a drone and some infrared. That's the bad news."

Before she moved on, Kenneth chimed in with agreement—stating his agency contact found much of the same. He agreed to keep an eye on the area for as long as possible.

"It's still early morning. The sun will be up soon, so we should be able to see more going on then." He said.

"I'm thinking the same." Nikki said. "Now, to the good news."

I brought Sweets' hand to my lips, giving an encouraging kiss to the back of it. There *was* good news. We needed some good news.

"You remember I had a couple of guys going to his businesses to see what they could dig up? I got a call from one of them. What he reported has me one hundred percent sure the plantation house is where we'll find Peanut. I'm thinking we'll find Vincente as well."

I felt the hopeful anticipation vibrating through Sweets' body. I didn't blame her, I wanted Nikki to speed up this little exposition.

"According to my guy, Vincente takes all of his *special* girls to that house."

Sweets emitted a choked gasp. Her free hand flew to her mouth. Apparently, it was loud enough for Nikki to hear. She rushed the rest of her statement to stop Sweets from completely falling apart.

"Wait! Wait! Wait! Before you jump to conclusions. Him taking her there specifically is actually a good thing."

"How could it be a good thing, Nik? She's been kidnapped by a potential sex trafficker. I can't see anything about this as being a good thing."

"Wait, Step. Just listen, ok? When he takes girls, and they are usually girls not women, to the plantation house, it's to isolate them for his grooming process. He considers himself one of the good pimps because he never hits them in the beginning. He'll try to buy her affection. He'll attempt ingratiate himself to her by pampering her.

He won't hurt her. At least not yet. He likes to trick them into thinking it's their idea to come to him. We know Saffi. It won't be easy for him to win her over."

I didn't like it, yet I understood what Nikki was saying. For now, we had time to get to Saffi before she came to physical harm. She'd no doubt have emotional trauma from all of this. But, if Vincente held true to form, he wouldn't touch her physically any time soon.

Smoothing her hair from her face, I cupped Sweets' jaw. I felt her elevated pulse beneath my fingers. She was still thinking the worst.

"Sweets. Look at me." Dark, tortured eyes met mine. "I know it doesn't seem like it, but this is a good thing." Pushing the hair back from her forehead, I pressed a kiss to her skin.

"Breathe, Baby. Breathe. We're getting closer." Inhaling, Sweets released a shuddering breath. We stayed locked together for a few moments—breathing in and out together. The exercise was good for me as well. I needed the reminder to keep me from succumbing to the desire to get in my car and drive out there with nothing except the fire inside me.

Finally, she nodded. We turned back to the monitor. "So, what do we do now? If we're sure she's there, what do we do? Tell the police? Go out there ourselves?" She asked.

As if she plucked the thought from my head, Nikki responded. "We definitely shouldn't go out there half-cocked without a plan. I think she's safe as long as he feels safe. Which means, we have to play this close to the vest. No cops."

Ash cleared his throat at the proclamation causing Nikki to amend her statement.

"No additional cops."

Kenneth started coughing then.

"Ok, fine... None of those dipshits from the city police who haven't even bothered to show up to even get Step's statement or at least pretend they're looking for Peanut."

"If it makes you feel better, I'm keeping the group small. Everyone knows and agrees this is strictly off the books." Ash supplied.

"What group do you have? Are they the same people you were talking about earlier?" Gene asked.

For the most part he'd been silent since we'd come back to the house—only speaking when someone spoke to him directly. However, his question was valid. Ash may know and trust these people, but we didn't know them. I trusted Ash with my life. Still, I wanted to actually meet the people who claimed they were willing to take such risks to help us.

"Yes. When I talked to Kenneth the first time, we came up with a short list of people. I reached out and he did as well. They are just waiting for our call back. They'll be ready."

"I want one of my guys in on it. I'd come myself, but I run comms better than they do. I can be more useful here."

"Who are you thinking of sending?" Sweets asked Nikki.

"Dilsher. You've met him before. So has Peanut. I want her to see a familiar face."

"She'll see a familiar face." I said, finally re-entering the conversation. "I'll be there."

"What?! Hell no!" Ash objected.

"Jian, I don't think that's a good idea." Sweets regarded me with wide, pleading eyes.

"Sweets...I'm not backing down on this. I'm going. I'm going to bring our little girl home."

Ash huffed. "Think about what you're saying, man. We have no idea what kind of people are holding her. They'll most definitely be armed. You aren't a cop. You have no training for a situation like this. You're a fucking surgeon, for crying out loud."

"I know who I am. I know what I do, but this is **my** family." I gritted out.

My expression dared him to challenge me on my assessment. In my mind and heart, Sweets was my life partner. The legal joining together was just a formality.

"If he's going, I'm going." Gene spoke up. Ash threw his hands up, surrendering control.

I didn't object. It was a good idea. If it came down to splitting up to search, there should be more than one familiar face and voice so Saffi would know she was safe.

When Sweets opened her mouth, I stopped the words before they formed. "Don't even think about it. I need to know you're safe. Besides, you'll need to be here in case the detectives assigned to the case actually show up."

When she went to speak again, I pressed my lips to hers—silencing her with the kiss. "Please...Let us handle this." I husked out, pressing my forehead to hers.

Eventually, she nodded in silent agreement. Gene moved to the armchair closer to our little group while Joy and Charmaine went to the kitchen stating the need for nourishment to fuel the planning session.

Once it was established Gene and I would join the rescue effort, Nikki started to run down the logistics of any helpful gear and tech she could access. Kenneth let us know he and Driscoll would arrive within the hour, before hanging up.

When Kenneth ended the call, Ash fired off a series of text messages. He received confirmation the other members of our hastily assembled team would also arrive by six a.m. Nikki ended the video chat with the promise to call back and send Dilsher to the house.

True to his word, Kenneth showed up approximately an hour later with a large dark-haired man in tow. Driscoll Kelly. McKenna's husband was a big guy, not quite as large as Ash, still an impressive size if intimidation was the goal. Shaking his hand when he was introduced, I thanked him for his willingness to assist us.

"We really appreciate this." I told him. The stoic expression on his face never cracked as he assured me he was more than happy to help. They followed me into the family room where Gene and I had set up a table in anticipation of the larger group.

"You're more than welcome. When Kenneth called, there was no way I could say no. I've been in similar situations as an agent. I know how critical the first twenty-four hours are."

Sweets entered the room with her hands wrapped around another coffee mug. "Hey, Driscoll. Do you want some coffee? We just made a fresh pot."

Driscoll's stoic expression finally broke when he gave Sweets a sympathetic smile while declining her beverage offer.

"No, thank you. Maybe later."

"Ok. Well, Joy and Charmaine just finished cooking breakfast, so if you change your mind and you want coffee or a bite to eat, just let us know."

"Thank you again." He dipped his head in response. Before we could get settled, the doorbell rang again. I went to answer it while Sweets got set up for Nikki to video conference with us once the group was assembled.

I opened the door to find two people I didn't know on the doorstep.

Before I could ask who they were, Ash walked up behind me and greeted them.

"Morgan, Josephs, thanks for coming. This is the friend I told you about. Jian, this is Audrey Morgan and Ryan Josephs. We've worked together in the past. They agreed to lend us a hand."

I stepped back to allow them inside, shaking their hands as they entered. Morgan was a medium height African-American woman who looked to be in her mid-thirties. Josephs was a thickly built Caucasian man about the same height as me who appeared to be in his early forties.

Ash waved a hand in their general direction. "Follow me. I'll introduce you to everyone else. We're still waiting on one more person, then we'll be ready to start."

We didn't have a long wait before the person Nikki sent arrived. Dilsher Khatri entered politely nodding to everyone present. The blood red turban on his head stood out starkly against his lightly tanned skin.

With everyone assembled, we did a quick recap of what we knew about the area from the satellite images. Nikki shared the most recent images. Dilsher provided more background on Vincente.

"Do we have a floor plan of this house?" Driscoll asked.

"Give me a sec." Nikki replied. Her desktop transitioned from showing only the satellite picture to a side-by-side with what looked like architectural schematics.

Once the internal layout of the house was up, Driscoll took over the planning. It became even more apparent why he was here. The way he explained the details and possible incursion scenarios was impressive.

It was around nine a.m. We were finalizing the plan when the doorbell rang. We weren't expecting anyone else, so I stopped Sweets before she went to open it.

"Check the cameras first, Sweets." I looked at the feed with her. There were two men who had to be cops standing on her porch. Taking a quick scan of the room, I knew some swift adjustments were in order before we could allow them inside.

No doubt they'd seen the cars in the driveway, but they didn't need to see the laptops and schematics. They might be lazy as hell. It didn't mean they were stupid. I quickly relayed the information. The group immediately started removing all evidence of our strategy session.

Chapter Twenty-Four

STEPHANIE

My heart lurched a little when I saw the detectives on my porch, then I quickly switched to anger. If they'd done their damn jobs, we wouldn't have our own task force assembled in my living room. We wouldn't be planning ways to infiltrate the domain of a human trafficker if they'd treated Saffi's disappearance with even an ounce of urgency.

While the group moved around resetting the family room, Jian and I went to the front door. He was so amazing. He hadn't left my side from the moment he found out.

My emotional well filled knowing he didn't just talk a good game, he backed it up. His hand rested at the small of my back as we opened the door together.

The short, balding detective looked at us then down at the notepad in his hand. "Hello. We're looking for Stephanie Barker."

Folding my arms across my middle, I gave him a blank expression. "I'm Stephanie Barker."

I didn't have it in me to make them feel comfortable. I was highly pissed it had taken them more than twelve hours to respond to a missing person report for my minor child. I was furious. I didn't care if they knew it.

Raking my gaze over the two, I took in their differences. Where one was short, balding with a paunch and rumpled clothing. The other was slightly taller, whipcord thin, with a full head of shaggy hair wearing a Sherlock Holmes style trench coat.

The shorter detective spoke for the two of them. "Miss Barker, I'm Detective Clayton and this is Detective Burger. We're here to discuss the report you filed regarding Chloe Barker. Can we come inside?"

I stood staring at them so long, Jian nudged me to get me to answer. I seriously wanted to slam the door in their faces, but I knew that wasn't smart. If it turned out we were wrong about Saffi being at the house in the country, we needed them to continue to search for her. If they ever even started.

Opening the glass storm door, I stepped back to allow them inside. Still standing in the foyer, I introduced Jian.

"This is Dr. Jian Anderson."

"Her fiancé." Jian added as he shook their hands. It took everything in me not to give him side eye. *When did we get engaged?*

Keeping my surprise well hidden, I leaned into his side when he slid his arm around my shoulders. As angry as I was at the situation, I had to know if they'd looked into Saffi's disappearance at all.

"Do you have any information on Chloe? Any leads?" I asked Detective Clayton since he seemed to be the spokesman for the two.

He shook his head. "No, ma'am. We checked the tip line before we came out here. There was nothing related to Chloe in the call log. We were hoping to ask you some questions."

"Now you want to ask questions..." I sucked my teeth. Logically, I knew they weren't personally responsible for the slow response, I just couldn't seem to rein in my anger.

Trench coat spoke up after my remark. "Miss Barker, please accept our apology. We just got the assignment when we came on shift this morning. We came right over after we did some preliminary checks and reviewed the report from the patrolmen."

"Interesting. We were assured detectives had been assigned to the case *last night*. Weren't we?" I asked looking up at Jian.

"Yes. Yes, we were." He stated giving the men a hard assessing gaze.

Both detectives looked shocked at that bit of information. "Ma'am. Would you mind telling us who told you detectives were assigned last night?" Detective Burger's bushy brows drew together in a frown.

"Maybe we should sit to have this discussion. Like I said, we'd like to ask you some questions if we may." Detective Clayton spoke up cutting off any response to Detective Burger's question.

I didn't trust my voice, so I turned leading them into the family room. Not for a second did I think Ash lied to me about the detectives being assigned last night. These guys though. These guys, I didn't trust.

I could have taken them to the kitchen to avoid the crowded family room, but I wanted to see their faces when they saw Ash. I wanted to know if they'd stick to their story about when they were assigned to the case.

When we walked into the family room, all evidence of our planning session had disappeared. Only the extra chairs remained. All except two were occupied with Driscoll, Audrey, Ryan, Kenneth and Dilsher. Gene and Charmaine sat on the short sofa while Joy was on one end of the L-shaped lounger.

At the sight of the detectives, Ash popped up from the recliner—rising to his full height. Looking very Thor-like, he scowled at our most recent guests.

"Oh! Peterson. I didn't expect to see you here." Detective Clayton squeaked out.

"I can tell." Ash said.

It was obvious he wasn't a fan. His entire demeanor screamed his dislike from the hard set of his jaw to the tension in his broad shoulders. Ash had to be close to seven feet tall. Normally, I didn't notice it. Now... Now, he seemed to grow in the presence of these men for whom he held a clear dislike.

The other detective's eyes rounded in surprise. I wasn't sure if it was from seeing Ash or the other people in the room. I didn't ask. Instead, I tested them to see if they would stick with the story they gave us in the foyer.

"Detectives, it appears you already know Detective Peterson. Ash, Detectives Clayton and Burger were just telling us how they were assigned to Chloe's case at the start of the shift. They rushed right over after they'd reviewed the patrolmen's report and checked the call log."

"Bullshit." Ash spat out before Clayton or Burger could respond.

"Well... Miss Barker, I may have misspoken." Burger stuttered, trying to recover. *I knew his ass was lying.*

"What I meant was we started working on it first thing this morning when we got to the precinct." His face reddened in embarrassment.

"So, you're telling me you were alerted to the situation of my ***minor*** child being missing. You decided to wait until nine a.m. the next morning to start trying to find her? Am I hearing you correctly?" My voice was calm, but inside my anger was churning.

I knew why they weren't in any rush to find my baby. It made me even angrier. Little black and brown girls didn't get the same kind of attention when they went missing. Especially if they're teenagers. It's always assumed they just ran off. It was infuriating and heartbreaking all at once.

"No, ma'am. That's not what I'm saying..." Burger stumbled over his words. Nervously, he put his hands in the pockets of his trench coat before pulling them out again.

"Maybe you should just ask your questions." Jian suggested.

Driscoll rose and grabbed the backs of the two empty seats. Lifting one in each hand, he placed them with the backs to the fireplace. Wordlessly, with a wave of his hand, he encouraged the detectives to sit. His posture was similar to the one Ash displayed. He didn't care for the detectives either. If his carriage didn't tell the story, the scowl on his face did.

The way he arranged the seats was lost on no one. They were positioned in front of us like the detectives were the ones being interrogated. They sat, shifting nervously in the seats rocking from one butt cheek to the other as though they were seated on an uneven surface.

I didn't spare them one iota of sympathy for their discomfort. Any shame they felt was well deserved. They might be following the lead of their management, nevertheless they knew how critical time was when it came to missing children.

Thinking of how time wasn't on our side was the only thing which moved me to get this show on the road. As much satisfaction as it gave me to watch them squirm, they were here. I wouldn't be the one to stand in the way of any effort to find Saffi—no matter how small.

Joy moved to the opposite corner of the sofa allowing Jian and I to sit on the short side. By the time we were seated, Detective Clayton collected himself. He pulled his little notebook out again. Clearing his throat, he asked some of the same perfunctory questions the patrolmen asked the night before at the hospital.

In my peripheral vision, I saw Gene shift angrily in his seat and Charmaine patted his thigh. With each question they asked, I felt Jian's tension incrementally increase. Between me and Gene, we'd told him everything that happened right up until he walked into the Chief's office. So, he knew the questions were repetitious.

"Are you fucking serious right now?" Ash barked out. I guessed he'd had enough. "Are you seriously sitting here asking the same questions as a responding officer with nothing new to add?"

"Peterson, you know the routine. We have to ask. Sometimes details come to people after the fact." Clayton said.

"Yeah, I know the routine. I also know you're fucking detectives. You should have dug deeper before you set foot in this house. The report from the responding officers had the name of a suspect. Did you even look into the suspect? His associates? Anything?"

"Well...We plan to look into it." Burger answered.

"You plan to?" Driscoll's deep voice cut in from the other side of Ash. "What are you, fresh out of the Academy? You coming here like this is not only a waste of time, it's disrespectful to my friends."

"And who are you?" Burger found a small well of bravery. As Grandma Vi would say, he tried to 'bow up' at Driscoll.

Driscoll stood, pulled a bi-fold wallet from his pocket. He flipped it open to show his badge. "Very Special Agent Driscoll Kelly. United States Secret Service."

Wide eyes went from the badge to Driscoll's scowling face. Their Adam's apples bobbed furiously as they swallowed trying to come up with the right words. They probably felt like they were on the same level with Ash, they were slowly coming to the realization they'd fucked up.

The lIttle girl they were supposed to be looking for came from a family with connections. So wrapped up in my grief and angst before, I didn't realize it until I allowed myself to think of the people gathered in my home. I considered the lengths they were willing to go to in order to find Saffi. For us.

At this point, Ash and Driscoll were standing over the detectives firing questions at them. Asking them about the investigative steps they should have taken by now. They asked how they planned to make up for their late start in the search. There wasn't a fire in the fireplace. You couldn't tell it from the way Clayton and Burger were sweating.

Jian's cellphone rang. He fished it from his pocket. The moment he answered it, the person on the other end started speaking. This time, I made out every word even though he didn't put the call on speaker.

"Son, how are things going? Do the police have any leads? Tips?" His father asked anxiously.

"No, Dad. The detectives just arrived not too long ago."

"What do you mean they just arrived? I talked to the Mayor and the Chief *last night*. Both apologized for the lack of response. They assured me detectives would get right on it. You mean to tell me they just got there?!" His father's anger vibrated through the phone line.

"I don't know what to tell you, Dad. They got here around nine a.m. They've been asking questions."

Jian didn't try to hide the conversation or leave the room, so everyone was privy to his end of the call—including Clayton and Burger. The two exchanged guilty expressions before quickly looking away from one another.

I heard Jian's dad instruct him to keep his phone close by, then he disconnected the call. Something told me this day was about to get a lot worse for the two detectives. From what I'd learned of them so far, it couldn't happen to better guys.

No more than five minutes later, Detective Clayton's cellphone buzzed in his pocket. He patted it with one hand, but didn't pull it out. It stopped buzzing, then immediately started again.

"Don't mind us." Ash said.

"Yeah, it could be important..." Driscoll added. The two had developed a sort of tag team style of speaking to the detectives. I'd hate to be on the receiving end of an interrogation with either of them.

Hesitantly, Clayton pulled the phone from his jacket pocket and looked at the screen. Leaning over, Driscoll read the display.

"Oh yeah. You definitely want to answer your phone. The Police Commissioner doesn't like to be kept waiting." If I wasn't mistaken, he looked forward to the ass chewing the detectives had coming.

Swiping a shaking finger across the screen, the detective answered the call.

"Hello?" He croaked out. His Adam's apple bobbing uncontrollably.

While I couldn't make out the Commissioner's words, the nervous bobbing of Clayton's head and Adam's apple clued me in to the context of the conversation. The call didn't last long. The detective spent the majority of it gulping, bobbing his head and mumbling "yes sir" at random intervals.

When the call ended, he hung his head heaved a deep sigh and slid the phone back into the inner pocket of his jacket. When he looked back up, he glanced at his partner before turning his gaze to me.

"Miss Barker, please accept my sincere apologies. My partner and I haven't been as responsive to this case as we should. There's no excuse for it."

"Damn right there isn't." Ash chimed in.

He didn't actually touch either of them, although his bearing didn't rule out the physical option. Not for the first time, I wondered what was at the root of his zeal. He and Jian had been friends for at least twenty years, but he was going hard for us. He didn't give a shit about the blue line.

Even if Ash hadn't said anything, I didn't plan to verbally respond to Clayton's apology. While it sounded more sincere than Burger's earlier attempt, I wasn't inclined to believe he meant it. He was only sorry the Commissioner handed him his ass for not doing his job correctly.

The generic ringtone of Jian's phone saved me from enduring another minute of their fallacies. The frown on his face made me sit up a little straighter.

"What? Who is it?" I asked

"I don't recognize the number." He replied. Considering the situation, not answering wasn't an option. So, he swiped to connect.

"Hello?"

Faintly I heard a woman speaking. It didn't sound like his mother. The voice was so low, I couldn't make out much.

"Thank you, ma'am. We appreciate it." He looked at me with an unreadable expression.

Nodding his head, he continued. "Yes. Yes, they're right here... Sure. I can do that."

Taking the device from his ear, he placed it on the coffee table in front of us and pressed the speaker icon. "The Mayor would like a word with you detectives."

Various shades of **oh fuck** sailed across the two men's faces. Not only had the Police Commissioner called to personally get into their asses, now the Mayor of the city was on the phone. It was never a good thing when people in high places knew your name because of what you did wrong and not something you did right.

"Detectives?" The single spoken word from the Mayor carried a slight edge. The authority in it was enough to make both men sit up straighter in their chairs.

I'm certain astonishment covered my own face. From our brief interactions, I knew Jian's parents moved in very different circles from me. But this...I didn't expect them to go all in this way. They got a Police Chief out of bed the night before. Now, they had the Police Commissioner **and** the Mayor calling personally. It was surreal.

The detectives stumbled over themselves acknowledging the Mayor. Were it not for the seriousness of the situation, it might have been comical.

"Gentlemen, I'm highly disappointed in the response to the report the Barker family filed for their missing child. Their **child**...A child, who at this moment is probably terrified and just wants to come home. Do you understand?"

A low chorus of 'yes ma'ams' came from the detectives. Their eyes were glued to the phone as if they could actually see the Mayor's disappointed face.

"No. I don't think you do. If you understood, you would have given this case your full attention when the Chief called you last night. I know the Chief called you, because I heard him place the call with my own ears. If you respected the criticality or actually treated it like a kidnapping and not a run-a-way, Chloe could possibly be at home with her family right now instead of God knows where."

"Ma'am, with all due respect. We got on it first thing at the start of our shift this morning." Burger had the nerve to interject.

"Let me ask you a question, Detective. If Chloe was a little blue-eyed, blond haired white girl, would you have gotten on the case first thing the next morning? Or would you have dragged your ass out of bed last night and started doing your damn job? Don't answer that, because I already know you would be on your sixth cup of coffee trying to stay alert to make the mid-morning news to update the community on the missing child's status."

She released a frustrated breath. "It's hard enough to get people of color to trust law enforcement, then you go and do something like this. You know as well as I do little black girls are going missing around this city at alarming rates. They aren't *all* running away.

It's been discovered time and time again they're victims of human trafficking. Yet you get handed a case with a clear suspect, a crime scene along with a cooperating family and you're dragging your feet. It's unacceptable.

You have blackened the eye of the Department and this city for the last time. Leave Ms Barker's home. Report back to your precinct immediately. Your Sergeant will let you know if you still have jobs."

She waited a beat for their response before continuing. "Ms Barker?"

"Yes?"

"From myself and the city, I extend my deepest apologies for how this has been handled. Rest assured two competent Detectives have been dispatched. They are on their way to your home right now. They should be there within the hour."

I was so taken aback I could only eke out a polite thank you in response.

"You're more than welcome. Please save this number. It's my

personal line. If you have any more issues, don't hesitate to give me a call."

"Thank you, Madam Mayor. You have no idea how much this means to us."

"It's the least I can do. This city has a long way to go with how we respond when children of color go missing. Especially our young black girls. We both know how vulnerable our girls are."

She gave us the names of the Detectives newly assigned to Saffi's case before she politely ended the call. Clayton and Burger still sat in the folding chairs in front of the fireplace, only now they looked genuinely contrite. Too little too late in my opinion.

Once again, they apologized for their part in the delay on the case. This time, I actually believed them. Ash volunteered to show them to the door and followed them from the room. When he didn't return quickly, I didn't give much brain power to figuring out what he may be saying or doing.

Instead, I snatched up my phone to call Nikki. I filled her in on what just happened. Ash came back into the room after he'd confirmed the Detectives had left my property. Dilsher went out to his vehicle returning with two duffle bags filled with gear courtesy of Nikki and their agency.

This time, instead of setting up in the family room, we moved to the rarely used formal dining room to allow him to spread everything out on the long table. It also allowed us to not worry about relocating everything if and when the other Detectives arrived.

With Nikki on speakerphone, they went through the items Dilsher brought with him. Occasionally Kenneth chimed in displaying his knowledge of the various gadgets and protective gear. By the time the new Detectives arrived, we were all seated in the kitchen. Amid firm encouragement from Jian, I managed to eat a few bites of the breakfast sandwich Charmaine slid in front of me.

The new Detectives, Cutler and Robbins gave off much better vibes than the other two. Ash and Driscoll must have thought so as well; they didn't growl at them once. In the short time they'd been assigned, the Detectives had already assembled a team. They asked me for permission to search Dani's house. As her closest relative and the owner of the property, I readily gave my permission.

No matter how much they impressed me with their enthusiasm, I didn't tell them about the letter from Dani, nor did I mention the house in the country. If they were any good at their jobs, they would uncover the house in due time. I couldn't place my faith in them, because they were still a part of the Department which severely dropped the ball.

I did tell them about the tracking devices. I provided the information when I recounted how I discovered Dani. I explained the devices were how I was certain Saffi had been kidnapped. Their questions and responses were far more intuitive than the other Detectives. They asked to see Saffi's electronics. I retrieved them.

I wanted to hold back about the earrings and necklace, but I eventually told them about those as well. They were still offline. I'd set up a notification on the application to alert me if they came back online—even for a brief moment. But, it hadn't happened so far.

Gene and Charmaine volunteered to go with the Detectives to the house. That way, Gene could make sure the property was being respected. He would also be there to answer any questions the Detectives had. Other than myself, he was the only person who knew everything. He was there from the first moment we realized Saffi had been kidnapped.

Considering his tenuous relationship with the police, I was surprised. However, I appreciated he and Charmaine for agreeing to go in my stead. Promising to return once the police were done at the house, they left immediately after the Detectives.

Earlier, during planning, the team determined it was best to wait until dark before approaching the house. It gave them the best opportunity to get close undetected. It also gave Nikki and Kenneth's contact an opportunity to get better surveillance information. Darkness was five hours away, so the group split up—agreeing to come back together at six p.m.

A few hours later, I lay semi-reclined on the chaise lounge section of the sofa with Jian's chest beneath my cheek. The rhythmic thuds of his heart beating in my ear comforted me as I counted down the minutes until we could bring Saffi home. The hours ahead of me felt like days. I was too keyed up to sleep, even though I knew I needed the rest.

I tried focusing on Nikki's words from earlier. I prayed Vincente kept to his pattern. I prayed he wouldn't hurt Saffi. My fingers gripped the front of Jian's shirt as I considered what could go wrong with the rescue. I was terrified of the possibility of not only losing Saffi but him as well.

"Sweets..." Jian rubbed soothing circles on my back. "I can feel you worrying. Try to think positive. Ok? We have some of the best people possible on our side. We're gonna get this right. We'll get Saffi back unharmed, then we'll all return safely. You have to believe the best." Delivering a kiss to my forehead, he squeezed me closer to his chest.

For the first time in years, I put my faith in someone other than myself. I resolved to trust him and believe everything he told me would come to pass.

Chapter Twenty-Five

JIAN

In the wee hours of the morning, several hours after I held Sweets in my arms assuring her everything would be okay, I stood beside Ash in the deep cover of woods approximately four hundred yards from the house in which we believed Vincente held Saffi. I prayed to every deity I knew that I hadn't lied to her when I promised we'd get Saffi out and return safely.

Ash was right—in part. I didn't have the right experience to be here. It didn't matter. I'd be damned if I stayed on the sidelines. No, I didn't go to the Police Academy. Nor did I receive tactical training. However, I was raised in an affluent southern family. Firearms including firearm training was standard operating procedure. So, I was licensed to carry. I had my Smith and Wesson strapped to my right thigh.

In addition to firearms training, I studied a few types of martial arts and self-defense techniques. I'd done so for years. I was never picked on about my race as a child; however, until I hit a growth spurt at fourteen, I was small for my age.

Small boys are a bully's favorite target. My parents made sure I had the tools to stand up to them physically, if necessary. So, I was as skilled with the knife strapped to my other thigh as I was with the gun. Those skills could come in handy should I need them tonight.

Between Nikki, Dilsher, and Kenneth, we each had earpieces, and protective clothing along with hand-held devices roughly the size of Saffi's e-reader. Kenneth had shown up with a drone equipped with infrared viewing capability. He set the devices up to receive the images from the drone in real time, while Nikki had someone in her office controlling the drone remotely.

"From my eye in the sky, I see everyone is in position." Nikki's voice came through the earpiece lodged in my left ear. We'd broken up into four two-person teams around the perimeter of the property. Ash and I were together on the east side.

Audrey was paired with Ryan on the north side of the property. Gene and Dilsher were on the west side. Kenneth and Driscoll were to the south at the back of the house. As the most experienced with this type of thing, they'd enter first through the most vulnerable location— the sliding glass door leading to the pool.

After Nikki's announcement, I looked at the viewscreen on my device reviewing the image from the drone feed. The surveillance during the day paid off. We had a pretty accurate count of the number of people inside the house. If our information was correct, there should be less than ten people inside—including Saffi.

The surveillance confirmed they were using a signal blocker. That's probably why the trackers in Saffi's jewelry showed as offline. We also had images of Vincente from earlier in the day. He came out several times; each time he was near the in-ground pool on the back of the house talking on his cell phone. We only had video. No audio. So, we didn't know who he'd spoken with.

Kenneth's first assignment was to locate the signal blocking device and disable it. Otherwise, we'd lose contact with one another once we went inside. Being out of communication wasn't a deal breaker, but having access to everyone definitely helped. Knocking out the signal blocker would also allow us to pick up the locations of the people inside the house.

I glanced down at my watch then back up at the house. It was almost go-time. Lights illuminated portions of the property, although there were still large areas in the shadows. We'd use their poor security measures to our advantage. Each team knew to stick to the shadows as much as possible.

The meager security on the outside told us Vincente was more concerned about keeping the people inside from getting out than he was about keeping people on the outside from getting in. In his arrogance, he left himself open to our incursion. I'd take every advantage we could get.

Watching the drone feed, Ash and I observed Driscoll and Kenneth moving toward the glass door. We inched closer to the edge of the woods. As soon as they gave the signal, we'd sprint the remaining distance to get to the entry points. Our goal was to take Vincente's crew by surprise. We wanted to minimize the possibility of Saffi being used as a shield or hurt by Vincente once he realized he was cornered.

My adrenaline shot up as I mentally ran the scenario. I had to block thoughts of Stephanie from my mind. My heart hurt when I pictured the look on her face while I drove away. I wanted to wipe that anxious look from her face permanently.

Re-focusing on the drone feed, I watched as Driscoll and Kenneth entered the house. Minutes later, Kenneth's voice was in our ears.

"Move now! The security feed is looped. We have maybe five minutes, tops before they realize it and come outside to check."

A series of replies came from the rest of the team. I wasn't sure how those approaching from the sides were getting in. Ash and I sprinted to the front door at top speed. I was faster, but his longer legs allowed him to stay close behind me.

"Pick the lock or kick it in?" I asked him when we reached the doorstep.

"The fuck do I look like? A master thief? I don't carry a lock pick. Move, I'll put my shoulder into it." Shaking his head, Ash pushed past me to the door.

I assumed the law enforcement guys had a plan for how to get inside. So, I didn't commit every detail to memory. Putting a hand out, he seemed to test the wood before he grasped the curved, brass door handle. Tightening his fingers around it, he leaned away before throwing his weight into the door. The wood splintered then cracked.

His hand on the handle kept the door from flying open banging into the wall. Still, our entry was far from quiet.

Entering quickly, we drew our guns as we scanned the entryway, prepared for whomever came to investigate the noise. The outer door opened into a large foyer with two openings on either side. The glow of a TV filtered into the hallway from one doorway, while the other room was pitch black. The volume of the television must have masked our entrance, because no one appeared on either threshold.

Ash swiftly swept the darkened room before coming out giving me a negative shake of his head. I followed his lead as he lifted the night vision goggles and approached the room from which the sounds of an action show could be heard. While he moved into the room, I gave another quick sweep of the hallway before following him inside.

There on the sofa, stretched out snoring, was a man in joggers and a t-shirt. My adrenaline spiked again. *It couldn't be this easy, could it?* Could we have happened upon a sleeping Vincente Renfroe?

The man didn't so much as twitch while we walked over and stood above him. Peering into his face, disappointment washed over me. The sleeping face wasn't Vincente's. It was an older Caucasian man who looked nothing like Saffi's kidnapper.

Pulling zip-tie cuffs from one of his many pockets, Ash flipped the man over. He had him cuffed hand and foot before the guy even awakened. He came to with a start. I clamped a gloved hand over his mouth before he could call out for help.

My other hand held the long-bladed hunting knife with the black grip. Pressing the sharpened edge to his throat, I watched as understanding of his situation filtered into his brain. His eyes bugged in their sockets. Tears gathered in the corners.

Faced with his own mortality, he succumbed to his emotions. How could a person who lived the kind of life he lived working for Vincente be so quick to crumble? I had no intentions of killing him. He didn't need to know my plans though.

"I'm going to lift my hand. If you try to yell out for help or draw attention to us in any way, I'll make it the last thing you ever do. Do you understand?" I pressed the blade firmly, nicking him slightly to emphasize my point.

Tears streamed unchecked from the corners of his eyes as he nodded vigorously in agreement. I lifted the hand covering his mouth allowing him the freedom to respond to questions.

"Where is the girl?" I growled.

"Wa-Wa which one?" He stumbled out.

My eyes locked with Ash's. Saffi wasn't the only victim that scumbag was holding here. There wasn't any need to discuss it, we wouldn't leave any innocents behind. But, Saffi came first.

"The one who got here yesterday."

"Oh, the little cutie with the nice rack?"

I had to move the knife from his neck to keep myself from slitting his throat. *No cutting the throat, but punching was allowed.* I hit him across the face with the hilt of the weapon. The renewed tears and blood dripping didn't stir any sympathy for his plight. He was just as sick as the fucker who kidnapped Saffi.

"I'll give you another chance to answer my question. Where is the girl your boss brought here yesterday?"

He rolled his tongue around in his mouth before turning his head to the side and spitting. A bloody tooth landed on the carpet at my feet.

"You knocked out my fucking tooth." He moaned.

"A lost tooth will be the least of your worries if you don't start talking." Ash grumbled.

He was standing next to me with his gun aimed at the bound man. I drew my knife-hand back prepared to strike again. Our blubbering captive started spilling his guts.

"She's downstairs in the basement."

"Why?"

"Boss man has a suite of rooms set up down there with all kinds of shit females like."

In my ear piece I heard the others as they checked in while searching. Ash relayed our status. Morgan and Josephs were heading our way. Once we got the info about Saffi, we'd find out about the other girls. Our plan just got way more fluid.

By the time we learned of the basement suites, they were standing in the room beside us. We quickly extracted the details of the other girls being held. We learned there were only three men on the premises, including himself and Renfroe.

Apparently, the boss man didn't like a lot of other men around his underaged harem. The more I learned, the more I wanted to sever Renfroe's tether to this life. Disgusting piece of human waste.

Once we obtained everything we could from our prisoner, Morgan produced a roll of tape she used to cover his mouth. We left him trussed up in the far corner of the room. If one of his accomplices should happen by the room, they wouldn't see him.

Morgan and Josephs spoke with the rest of the crew. The new plan was quickly developed. Dilsher and Gene would join us in the basement. I wanted Saffi to see more than one familiar face when we found her.

Driscoll and Kenneth confirmed they'd taken care of the other guard, so Renfroe was the last of the kidnappers. The info from the blubbering idiot confirmed Renfroe preferred grooming the girls over using force. Plying them with gifts until they came to him willingly, or so they would think. The mere thought of it enraged me. He'd better pray I didn't get a minute alone with him.

Ash and I moved through the kitchen as silently as possible. Gene and Dilsher met us on the other side of the room at the door leading down to the basement. We all wore balaclavas, so Gene's face was obscured from view. But his eyes... they blazed with anger. Seeing the fire there caused me to wonder what they learned on their sweep of the west side of the mansion.

With one hand on the doorknob, Ash gave us one last assessing look before he pushed the door open. He started down the stairs. As we followed, I noticed the transition from the upstairs. The furnishings on the main floor were muted in color. They leaned toward comfortable sofas with companion recliners. Descending the staircase, my gaze landed on more brightly colored decor.

At the foot of the stairs was a large space resembling a luxury spa. The walls and furniture were varying shades of pink, green and gold. A flat screen television took up most of one wall. Plush gaming chairs were placed at optimal angles in front of it.

To either side of the large room were hallways. Not knowing which led where, we'd have to split up. Gene and Dilsher took the hallway on the left while Ash and I went to the right. Shining a light down the darkened passage, I hoped we'd find Saffi unhurt. I also desperately wanted to find Renfroe before anyone else did. He needed to suffer by my hand for the trauma and destruction he'd wrought.

For each room we entered, my hope would spike only to be dashed when we found neither Saffi nor Renfroe inside. Finally, we reached the last door. If she wasn't inside, we'd back track to join Gene and Dilsher in the other hallway.

Ash twisted the knob. It didn't turn. This was it. I knew it in my gut. Renfroe wouldn't lock himself in a room, but he'd lock Saffi in—especially if she wasn't cooperating with his plan. Ash leaned away preparing to force it open when I stopped him.

This situation was frightening enough. Whether she was sleeping or awake, I didn't want to add to her terror by crashing through a doorway. Not even to save her. Pressing my ear to the door, I knocked softly.

"Go away! I don't want your things. I want to go home!" Saffi's voice, thick with tears, reached my ears.

Beneath the tears was a strong resolve which filled me with pride. She'd been fighting back the only way she could, by denying Renfroe the opportunity to buy his way into her good graces. Clearing the emotions from my throat, I breathed a sigh of relief.

"Saffi, Sweetie. It's me. Dr. J. I'm here to take you home."

"Dr. J?" The sliver of hope threaded into her voice almost broke me, yet I held it together.

"Yes, Sweetie. It's really me." With my ear still pressed to the door, I heard noises as she scrambled closer. When she spoke again, I could tell she was much nearer.

"You came to take me home?"

"Yes, Sweetie." At the confirmation, soft crying noises filtered through the barrier.

"Saffi, I need you to back away from the door. It's locked. We don't have a key. So, we have to knock it down."

She continued to cry softly but didn't respond. "Saffi, can you back away from the door, Sweetie? I promise we aren't leaving you. We don't want you to get hurt when it swings open."

Crashing noises sounded from the other end of the hall temporarily drawing our attention away. We stayed frozen for a beat—watching the darkened hallway seeing if anyone came our way. There was no one. Tension kept my shoulders tight. As much as I wanted to get my hands on Vincente Renfroe, Saffi came first.

"Saffi? Answer me, Sweetie."

"I'm here." Her response was muffled behind the door and possibly her hands.

"Ok. I need you to back away from the door. Can you do that for me?"

"Back away?"

"Yeah, back all the way to the other wall if you can. Let me know when you're there, ok?"

"Okay."

I kept my ear to the door listening intently for any indication she was doing as I asked.

"I'm here."

Hearing she was out of harm's way, I stepped back. Not waiting for Ash, I kicked directly beside the knob splintering the wood sending the door slamming into the opposite wall. I immediately scanned the well-lit room finding Saffi standing beside a canopy bed with her back pressed against the floral wallpaper.

When I stepped over the threshold and ripped the balaclava from my head, she flew across the room launching herself into my arms. Relief flooded my senses. Tears pricked my eyes joining her waterfall of emotion.

"Sh... It's going to be ok. We're gonna get you home now."

Incoherent words obscured by sobs were muffled against my chest. I allowed her time to feel her emotions while Ash swept the room and relayed our good news to the rest of the team.

The whoop of joy blasting into my earpiece came from Gene. I didn't fault him for a second. I'd known Saffi less than a year. I already loved her like my own child. He'd been a constant in her life from the day she was born. He'd earned his joyful celebration.

Pulling away I checked Saffi's face and extremities looking for any signs she'd been hurt or physically mistreated. I was certain Sweets would do a more thorough check later. Protectiveness drove me to assure myself she was clear of any cuts, bruises or other forms of injury.

"Did he hurt you?" I peered into her eyes watching for any indication she'd been harmed beyond the trauma of being kidnapped. My relief at finally seeing her again was overshadowed by anger at the possibility she'd been abused by that sick fucker.

"He didn't hit me or anything; he just locked me in this room. He kept trying to give me things. He brought me food, but I didn't want his stuff. I just wanted to go home. Can I go home now?"

"Yeah, Sweetie... You can go home now. Your aunt is going to be so happy to see you."

I'd meant to reassure her by mentioning Stephanie, except it seemed to have the opposite effect. She stiffened. Her eyes welled with fresh tears—and they weren't happy tears.

"Hey... What are the tears about? Your aunt has been worried about you. She'll be overjoyed to have you home. Why are you crying?"

"She's not mad at me?"

"Why would she be mad at you, Baby Girl?"

"Because...I lied. If I hadn't lied and gone to Dani's behind her back none of this would've happened. It's all my fault." Her last words came out in a wail as she succumbed to tears once again.

Ash and I turned at the sound of hurried footsteps approaching. Gene stood framed in the doorway. He'd also removed his face covering. The earpiece dangled on the cord around his neck. The look of joy on his face quickly morphed when he saw Saffi crying.

"Lady Bug?" Stepping closer, he spoke softly. "Lady Bug, are you hurt? Did he touch you?" He asked in a tortured whisper. I understood the dread in those words. It was one of our fears when we learned she'd been taken and by whom.

Releasing her hold, Saffi transferred her koala-like clasp from me to Gene. Hugging her, while patting her back he gave me a questioning glance over her head. I quickly filled him in on her current distress. Understanding coated his expression. He began quietly speaking to her, reassuring her no one was angry with her.

While I watched Gene comfort Saffi, I listened to the conversation going on with the rest of the team. The crash I'd heard earlier was

Dilsher and Gene breaking into the last room on the other end of the hall looking for Renfroe. They didn't find him, but we knew he was on the premises. Nikki was using the drone to scan for him.

I wanted Saffi out of here. We needed to put her in a car to get her home to Sweets. I needed her as far away from that filth as possible. I didn't want her to have to see him another day in her life. Besides, when we found him, and we would find him, I didn't want her to see the depth of my anger. She should never be exposed to my fury. Ever.

We came to the consensus Gene and Dilsher would take Saffi home. Morgan and Josephs would stay with the other girls while the rest of us searched the property for Renfroe. Since his earpiece was out, I informed Gene of the plan just as Dilsher appeared in the open doorway.

Delivering pats to Saffi's back, Gene encouraged her to go with him as he moved toward the hallway with the rest of us trailing behind them. We reached the outside of the house just as the first rays of sunlight spilled over the tops of the trees in the distance.

Before letting them walk away, we swept the outside to be certain Renfroe hadn't somehow made it out. Nikki and her drone pilot watched the area while we were inside. They were certain he hadn't escaped. Both vehicles were still parked out front.

"Ok, so I'm going to take Lady Bug home." Gene stood with an arm draped across Saffi's shoulder as she clung to his side.

"Correct. Tell Stephanie I'll be there soon."

Saffi's head popped up when she realized I wouldn't be leaving with them.

"Dr. J? You're not coming home with us?" Confusion clouded her expression.

"Not yet. I'll be there soon though. I promise."

"Why can't you come now?"

"I need to stay. I have to help out here. I promise I'll be there soon."

Pulling away from Gene, she grasped my arm. "He's a really bad man, Dr. J. You should come with us. We can all go home where it's safe."

Smoothing the springy coils of hair from her face, I peered into her eyes.

"Saffi, have I ever lied to you?"

"No…"

"So, believe me when I tell you I'll be home with you and Auntie soon."

"But he might hurt you!"

"He won't hurt me."

"Promise?"

"I promise."

Dilsher opened the door of the dark sedan and looked inside. "This one has keys." His deep voice held a calming note.

Pressing a kiss to her forehead, I transferred Saffi to Gene. I watched as he put her into the back seat and climbed in beside her. As they drove away, I experience a small measure of relief. I wouldn't—couldn't be fully satisfied until Vincente Renfroe no longer took up space on this side of the dirt.

Chapter Twenty-Six

STEPHANIE

I'd never experienced fear and anxiety the way I did when I watched Jian drive away into the pitch blackness a couple of hours after midnight. The pounding of my heart was so loud in my ears I couldn't hear anything else.

I didn't like this at all. This feeling of helplessness. I've always been a doer. The waiting game had my nerves fried. Joy and Charmaine attempted to comfort me. While I appreciated their compassion, it wasn't helpful. I needed to **do** something. The way I had when Saffi was attacked. When Nikki and I hunted those heifahs down beating their asses for touching her.

Keeping it real, had Jian not been so forceful in his insistence, I would've had my ass in one of those cars going to get my baby. Regardless. I grudgingly admitted he was right when the Detectives called wanting to video chat and update me about their investigation. They'd been to the house, collected evidence. They also went door to door talking to the neighbors.

I already knew the last bit courtesy of Miss Myrtle. She called earlier to tell me about it as soon as they left her doorstep. She also gave me an earful for not keeping in touch. She'd contacted me after the Amber Alert went out asking if there was anything she could do.

She spent most of her days watching the happenings on her street. All she saw the day Saffi was taken was a vehicle with dark tinted windows. Miss Myrtle couldn't make out who was inside. Still, she told the Detectives everything she knew.

I didn't get the necessity of video chatting or the call at such a late hour, but they were under pressure from the Commissioner and the Mayor to stay on top of things. It's not like I could sleep anyway.

Thankfully, Nikki knew I'd be on edge; so, she swore to call me from a separate line allowing me to listen in. I told Joy and Charmaine I was going to my room to try to rest. I really just wanted to be alone. I knew they didn't have the stomach for even listening in on this kind of thing.

Joy's life was neat, orderly, not even peripherally adjacent to the kinds of rough things Nikki and I'd seen. Charmaine also led a sheltered existence. How she ended up with Gene was still a mystery to me.

After about an hour of waiting, long after I got off the chat with the Detectives, Nikki finally called. In my haste to answer, I fumbled the phone and it slipped through my fingers before skittering across the floor. I scrambled from the plush chair in my bedroom to my hands and knees trying to catch it to silence the ringtone.

"Hello?!" Breathing heavily, I sat on the carpet with the device pressed to my ear.

"Step? Girl, you alright?"

"Yeah.... I dropped the phone. I was trying to hurry up and answer just in case Joy or Charmaine came up. I told them I was going to lay down."

"Uh-huh..."

"Please don't start, Nik." I really didn't want to listen to her talk about me coddling people, telling me I didn't give them a chance to show me what they could handle. I disagreed. I just understood who I was dealing with, so I kept some things to myself.

"I didn't say anything."

"You didn't have to. I heard it in your tone."

"Uh-huh. Anyway... I'm going to put you on speaker so you can hear. I'm going to mute you because I can't have you interrupting our flow."

"But—"

"No buts, Step. This is our thing. Let us work. I can't have you causing a distraction."

Closing my eyes, I took a deep breath. She was right. I knew it in my heart of hearts. Still, it stung a little. I was capable of keeping my cool under pressure. I'd proven that more than once. However, in this case... she was right.

I only had audio; they'd have visual images I wasn't privy to. I'd want every detail. So, I'd ask questions. It would be distracting. I stood from the floor and re-took my seat in the chair. Placing the phone on the table, I put my earphones in to keep the call hands-free.

My knee bounced nervously as I listened. Hearing Jian's voice over the comms restarted the pounding rhythm of my heartbeat. If I couldn't be there, he definitely shouldn't. No amount of talking would change his mind. I recalled the set of his jaw when he declared his intentions. I knew then, talking him out of it wouldn't happen.

Although I really, really, wanted to see what they were seeing, Nikki had enough on her plate without trying to broadcast another signal just for me. I'd have to be content with listening. My heart leapt into my throat when Driscoll gave the all clear for them to enter the house.

They had a good plan. I knew it. Knowing it didn't prevent my nervousness. I listened intently as the team members periodically checked in. When Kenneth reported there were other girls in the house, my hand flew to my mouth to catch the gasp. *What kind of monster had Dani invited into our lives?* More girls being held captive, sounded like only the tip of the iceberg.

It seemed like an eternity before I heard the news which filled me to bursting with joy. They'd found Saffi. She was with Jian and Gene. She was safe. Tears streamed in unchecked rivulets down my face. *They found her!* Jumping from the chair, I ran to the door, flinging it open.

"Joy! Charmaine! They found her! They found Saffi!"

The gratefulness pulsing through my body wouldn't let me sit back down as I continued to listen. Joy and Charmaine raced into the room. Snatching the earphones from my ear, I put the phone on speaker.

"They found her! They found Saffi. She's safe!" Smiling through tears, I happily returned their hugs parroting their prayerful words of thanks.

Nikki interrupted our praise session to let me know Gene and Dilsher were on their way to bring Saffi home. Swiping at the wetness on my face, my brow wrinkled in confusion.

"Gene and Dilsher are bringing Saffi? What about Jian? Where is he?"

"Jian's staying behind."

Taking the phone off speaker, I pressed it to my ear. "Why? Why is he staying behind? They have Saffi. There's no reason for him to still be there."

"Step..."

"No. You get on that comm link and you tell him I said bring his ass home. He has no reason to still be there."

"Step... They didn't find Vincente in the house."

"I don't care. There are six well-trained people who can keep searching. He needs to come home. Tell him."

"Step..."

"Tell him damnit! I can't get Saffi back just to lose him. This isn't a trade! He needs to bring his ass home!"

"I'll try. I can tell you now, I don't think he's going to listen. Your man has a protective streak the size of the Pacific."

Charmaine and Joy stood next to me stroking my arms. Their attempts at comfort weren't working. Why was he doing this? He's a fucking doctor not a mercenary!

The minutes crawled by as I listened to Nikki talking to Jian. For some reason, she didn't allow me to hear both sides of the conversation. In the end, she came back to me with what she predicted. He was staying. She could only secure a promise he wouldn't go off alone. Ash would stay with him.

Having Ash with him was better than nothing. It didn't stop my gut from churning, but it was something. I'd gone from almost paralyzing worry over my child to nearly crippling concern about my man. If Dani were alive, I'd choke her.

I had the thought then immediately felt guilty for thinking it. My sister had suffered on her floor before succumbing to her injuries. Here I was contemplating resurrecting her just to take out my anger on her. Was the situation partially her fault? Yes. Shit. More than partially, nonetheless I was raised better.

Shaking the morbid thoughts from my head, I went to Saffi's room. I began preparing for her arrival by laying out pajamas and straightening the room. I never cleaned her room anymore; the task kept my hands busy. Even if they didn't obey traffic laws, it would take them an hour to make it here from Vincente's house of horrors.

Joy and Charmaine gave me space citing the need to prepare breakfast. They were certain Saffi, Gene and Dilsher would be hungry. I didn't comment on their desire to constantly feed people. Maybe it's how they coped.

I wouldn't knock it. My elation at knowing Saffi would be home soon, warred with my concern for Jian still being firmly in the lion's den. I loved him so much. *Why hadn't I told him?* Why did it take him risking his life for me to realize just how much I cared for him? Those questions rolled around in my head heightening my anxiety.

I had confidence in Jian. He could handle himself, except the things I'd heard about people like Vincente made me question Jian's decision.

People involved in human trafficking were ruthless, heartless people. Jian wasn't that kind of man. He saved lives for a living. He repaired hearts and restored lung function. He didn't stop the operation of those organs.

While I was setting Saffi's room to order, the strains of a hip hop tune sang out. It was Gene's ringtone. Snatching the device from my pocket, I quickly swiped the screen to answer.

"Hello?!"

"Hey Step. Sorry it took so long; I just got my phone back. We had to leave them behind in the other cars."

"Gene, don't apologize it's fine. I know you. I know you would have called sooner if you could."

"Still, I know you wanna talk to our girl."

I heard slight fumbling, then the voice I feared I'd never hear again floated into my ear. "Hey Auntie! I'm so sorry! Please don't be mad!"

Hearing the distress in her voice was heartbreaking. What had I done to her for her first worry to be if I was angry? I'd tried to provide her with a nurturing supportive environment. Had I failed?

"Saffi, baby. I'm not mad at you. Okay? I'm just glad you're safe. Your safety is what matters."

"Auntie, I lied to you. I lied to the school. If I hadn't lied, none of this would have happened."

"Baby, listen to me. This isn't your fault. You didn't put yourself in this position. I don't want you blaming yourself. You hear me?"

"But Auntie—"

"It's not your fault. You hear me?"

"Yes ma'am."

"I love you so much, little girl."

"I love you too, Auntie."

Swiping at the tears streaming down my cheeks, I asked her to give Gene the phone. I didn't ask him for details. I'd get those later. I had questions I wouldn't ask Saffi. She was fragile enough and already blaming herself.

"Yeah, Cuz."

"How does she look? Cuts, bruises? Did he put hands on her?"

"None that I saw. Doc said the same"

"Thank God."

Relief flooded my senses with his words. Knowing Jian also checked her over was comforting as well. Having Saffi sitting right next to him, Gene's answers were clipped and concise. I understood. Although she was getting older, the need to protect her any way we could was strong.

"How much longer until you make it here?"

"Looks like...another thirty-five to forty minutes."

"Okay. We'll be waiting. Gene?

"Yeah, Cuz?"

"Thank you so much for bringing my baby home."

"You never have to thank me for stepping up. I'd do it all again without a thought. We're family. I gotchu."

"Still... I appreciate it more than you know."

"Mhm. I'll see you soon."

"See you soon."

Disconnecting the call, I went downstairs. The smell of sizzling bacon met me midway down the staircase. My stomach grumbled in response, reminding me I hadn't eaten much of anything since learning Saffi was taken. With part of my stress relieved, my body was reasserting itself.

While my mind was still pre-occupied with thoughts of Jian, a small part of me had come back when I heard Saffi's voice. That's when it became real. She was safe. She was actually on her way home to me. If only my good doctor was sharing the ride. My desire to have them both here in my arms had me unconsciously hugging myself as I descended the stairs.

Joy and Charmaine's expressions of delight were contagious as we stood in the kitchen embracing once I told them I'd spoken to Saffi on the phone. We were so consumed with our celebration, Joy almost burned the home fries she was making.

Breaking away from the group hug, I took up post at the window in the foyer watching the street attentively. I alternated between checking the time and looking at the empty road. Each time I heard the rumble of a car engine, I perked up only to realize it was a neighbor leaving or returning.

When the dark colored sedan pulled into my driveway, my heart stopped. I didn't recognize the vehicle. I held my breath in anticipation. The back door on the passenger side opened. I glimpsed the top of Saffi's curly afro.

Flinging open the front door, I nearly tore the glass barrier off the hinges as I sprinted barefoot from the house. Engulfing her in my embrace, I thanked every deity I could think of for bringing my baby back to me. Collapsing into me, Saffi released a torrent of tears amid broken expressions of love and apology.

Stroking her hair, I rubbed soothing circles on her back. I allowed her to feel her feelings—to express them however she needed. I wouldn't rush her to compose herself. We both needed time. I don't know how long we stood there in the curved driveway with the morning sun beaming down on us.

Eventually, we pulled apart and went into the house. I had questions, but they'd have to wait. First, we'd get her cleaned up so she could feel more like normal. Then, we'd talk. I walked the sniffling Saffi into the house where she went through another round of tearful reconciliations with Joy and Charmaine.

I knew what I should do. I should call the Detectives. I should call everyone involved to let them know she'd been found, yet I didn't. Instead, I took Saffi upstairs. Gently probing, I confirmed Vincente hadn't touched her sexually. I didn't understand his sick game. However, I was eternally grateful sexual assault wasn't on the list of things she'd need to discuss with her therapist at her next appointment.

An appointment I'd schedule for her as soon as possible. I also made a mental note to see if her therapist could squeeze in some family counseling sessions for us. An environment where she felt comfortable expressing herself was necessary. It would take a while for her to stop blaming herself for being kidnapped.

Should she have told me about the contact with Dani? Of course, she should have. But, I didn't fault her for doing what any child who wants their parent's love would do. She was vulnerable and Dani knew it. Vincente duped Dani who in turn duped Saffi. The blame rested firmly in the laps of the adults in this situation.

As far as I was concerned, this was a lesson learned for Saffi. The hard way. What came after this would be the rebuilding of trust. The trust between the two of us, but most importantly her ability to trust herself. Both would take time.

Opting for a bath instead of her customary shower, Saffi sat in the bubble filled tub letting the water sift between her fingers. I sat in a chair I'd pulled into the bathroom at her request. Memories of kneeling next to the tub bathing her as a toddler flit across my mind. This wasn't the same, except when I looked at her, I saw her little toddler face as it morphed displaying a range of emotions.

"Auntie?"

"Yes, Baby."

"Where's Dani? Why did she let him take me?"

All the air whooshed from the room at her question. I'd hoped we could wait. I was still so angry with Dani; I wasn't sure I could properly convey her death to Saffi without coloring the information with my resentment. Taking a deep breath, I pushed down my hurt and disappointment in my sibling.

"Who told you Dani let him take you?"

"No one. We were supposed to go out to eat. When it was time to go, Vincente came out to the car."

"What did he say when she didn't come out?"

"He said she didn't feel well. He said that he was gonna bring me home. Only he didn't."

She went silent, frown lines marred her brow. She stared at the bubbles covering her extremities. I knew the look. It was her thinking face. She wore the expression anytime she tried to puzzle anything out. Knowing she'd need a few minutes to filter through her thoughts, I sat back in the chair and waited. After a few minutes of contemplation, her eyes found mine again.

"Dani didn't set me up? She didn't give me to him?"

"No, Baby! Never think such a thing. She didn't give you to him. Why would you think she'd given you to him?"

"She gave me to you..."

"Aw, Baby..."

Unmindful of getting wet, I dropped to my knees beside the tub and pulled her into a hug. Hearing her beliefs vocalized tore at my heart. No child should have to go through life thinking their parent would just arbitrarily give them away.

Pulling back, I captured her face in my hands. I held her gaze. "Saffi, I don't know all of Dani's thoughts and actions, but I do know this. She didn't give you to that man. She had no idea he planned to kidnap you."

"She didn't?"

"No. She didn't."

"Then where is she? Why isn't she here? Auntie Joy and Auntie Charmaine are here. Did you tell her she couldn't come? Are you mad at her for what her boyfriend did?"

I'd promised myself and Saffi a long time ago I'd never lie to her. My memories of my mother were littered with her lies as the drugs took over her life a little more each day. Before we were removed from the home, Dani and I couldn't trust anything she said. We only believed what we could see.

Because of my self-induced pact, I searched for the words to respond to Saffi truthfully. Even now, I was trying to protect her from Dani's ugliness.

I opened my mouth, then snapped it closed. I had to stop this. I had to stop trying to shield her so much she wasn't prepared for life to switch up. Inhaling, I sent up a short prayer to guide my words.

"No. I didn't tell her she couldn't come. Yes, I'm very angry with her. But, I didn't tell her to stay away. She can't come, Sweetie." Knowing how deeply my next words would her hurt made them stick in my throat.

"Why can't she come? Does she not want to come? Did you call her? Did you tell her Uncle Gene was bringing me home?"

Taking a shaky breath, I smoothed her mass of springy coils from her face.

"She can't come because she died, Baby."

"Died?...How?...When?" Her eyes filled with unshed tears.

"She was attacked the day Vincente took you. We tried to help her. We got her to the hospital, only she didn't survive the surgery."

"But why? Who attacked her?"

Her tears flowed freely now. I wished I could save her from this pain. I knew I couldn't. It didn't stop me from wanting it. Badly.

"We don't know for sure. We think it was Vincente."

Rounded, tear-filled eyes searched my face for any sign of deception. Although I'd never lied to her, I could see her probing for the holes in my statement. She wouldn't find any.

Everyone who met Saffi marveled at her intelligence. Her only real blind spot was with Dani. Her desire for love and acceptance from my selfish sibling kept her oblivious to Dani's true nature.

"She's dead? Like Grandma Vi?"

"Yes, Baby."

"He killed her so he could take me?" It was a question, yet her tone suggested she didn't require confirmation. I answered anyway.

"We believe so."

The wails I anticipated never materialized. She did cry—just very softly. Hugging her knees to her chest, she placed her forehead to them releasing her emotions silently. Placing a comforting hand on her back, I closed my eyes and grieved with her.

No matter how angry I was with Dani, she was my sister. I didn't celebrate her painful demise. I'd probably need my own therapy sessions to deal with the relief I felt that she would no longer be around to spread her special brand of selfish chaos.

When she started shivering from the cold water, I encouraged Saffi to quickly finish her bath. Robotically going through the motions, she complied. Afterwards, I got her into the pajamas I'd laid out, then tucked her into bed.

Her grumbling stomach was the only noise in the room. Slipping my phone from my pocket, I sent a quick text to Joy asking her to fix a small plate and bring it up. Just this once, we'd bend the 'no eating in your room' rule. Just this once.

Chapter Twenty-Seven

JIAN

As I watched Gene and Dilsher drive away with Saffi, I heard Nikki's voice in my ear. She let us know she'd told Sweets about us finding Saffi. I appreciated her keeping my woman in the loop. She'd been completely despondent when we left earlier. She deserved to know what was going on as soon as possible.

"Jian?"

"Yes, Nikki."

"I've switched us to a private channel."

"Okay... Why?"

"Stephanie lost her shit when I told her you were staying behind. She wants you to come home."

"I will. Just not right now."

"Listen, I know you've gotten attached to Peanut, but you're stressing my girl out."

"Attached? You think I'm simply attached? I'm not. I love that kid as if Stephanie and I created her together. I'm far more than attached."

"Oh... Well damn. What you just said is even more reason for you to leave with Gene to get back to Step."

"I can't. Gene and Dilsher are already gone. I'm not leaving this place until I'm certain that piece of shit, Renfroe, isn't able to come after Saffi or any other little girl ever again."

"What are you saying?"

"Do I need to spell it out for you?" I gave her a few moments to let my words sink in. I knew what I was saying. I didn't care if she'd eventually figure it out. I had every intention of watching Vincente Renfroe take his last breath.

After an extended period of silence, her voice reached me again. "Ok. I hear you. I'll let her know you won't be alone. Ash will stay with you."

I'd said nothing of the sort, but if it's what Sweets needed to hear to ease her mind, I wouldn't object. Nikki put us back in the general comm loop effectively ending the private conversation.

With great effort, I pushed thoughts of Sweets from the forefront of my mind. I refocused on what was happening around me. The team, minus Morgan was discussing the plan for searching the property again for Renfroe. We'd already searched every room. There were no out buildings close by he could have gone to without being picked up by the drone.

"Nikki?" Kenneth's face lit up with an apparent epiphany.

"Yes?"

"Have you tried the deep structure penetration feature on the drone?"

"The what?"

"The drone has built-in infrared; it also has the capability to look for more than just heat signatures. You should be able to switch to a structural view. It might look freaky at first. Give it a second. Eventually, it should look like an aerial view of building plans."

He pulled a small tablet from the pocket of his tactical pants and started swiping at the screen. After a few minutes, he guided Nikki through the keystrokes needed to yield the images he mentioned. Once she had them, she transferred them to his tablet.

We all gathered around the small screen. Overhead, I heard the hum of the drone as it moved above and around the massive house. With each pass, the screen morphed. Kenneth was right, it did look a little freaky.

As the drone moved, the framework of the house was displayed in sections on the screen. We saw the large room where Morgan was waiting with the other teens Renfroe was holding hostage. Positioning the drone at different angles even revealed the basement level.

"Wait. Go back." Driscoll said suddenly.

"Which way?" Nikki asked.

"The basement."

"What is it?" I asked. "What did you see that we didn't?"

Hovering a finger over the screen in Kenneth's hand, Driscoll responded. "It's not what I see, it's what I don't see."

"Okay..."

"McKenna and I are building a house. I've been up to my eyeballs in construction plans. These drone images are basically like those plans. I see the plumbing and electrical on every floor except the basement."

"Fuck!" Kenneth exclaimed. "You're right. There should be something beneath the concrete floor of the basement, but absolutely nothing is showing up."

My eyes caught Driscoll's and we said together, "Panic Room."

"If your observation is correct, it's more than a Panic Room. There's an entire shielded level below the basement." Nikki interjected. "Apparently, Renfroe is more paranoid than we thought."

"Looks like it." Kenneth said.

"Okay. Since we know where he's probably hiding, how do we get to him?" I asked.

From my inspection of the images on the tiny screen, the obscured area ran the entire length and width of the mansion. There was also no clear entry point. We'd have to go back inside to look for a hidden door —searching room by room.

Our crew size was reduced to five with Gene and Dilsher gone to take Saffi home and Morgan closed off with Renfroe's other victims. To speed up the search, we'd have to somewhat break up the teams. We'd have to go into each room alone. We agreed to contact the rest of the group if we found an entrance.

I caught Ash's gaze as we all walked back into the house making a beeline for the basement. Immediately upon entering the basement, we split up. Josephs stayed in the center while the rest of us went in pairs down the hallways flanking the large room.

Separating from Ash, I entered the first room. Uncaring about stealth, I flicked on the light switch. I started to my left searching the room meticulously for any sign of a hidden opening. Pulling out my flashlight, I turned over the bed to search underneath. I tore up the closet, pushing aside every other piece of furniture. Nothing. Dejected and getting angrier by the second, I left the room.

I repeated the process in the next room then the next before ending at one of the rooms adjacent to the one where Saffi was held. No one had sent up a proverbial flare, so I held out hope I'd be the one to find Renfroe. My internal struggle regarding my intentions when I found him was brief.

I'd never taken a life. My entire career was spent abiding by a code of ethics. To do no harm. A code which motivated me to do everything within my power to save lives. This was different. I'd never had a child before now. I'd never had my family, people I loved, threatened this way. It flipped a switch inside me. I had no desire to fight the darkness building.

Knowing he hadn't physically touched her didn't matter. He wanted to touch her. The sick fuck had stolen her to further his goal of defiling Saffi. He couldn't be allowed to draw breath another day. I gave not a thought to consequences. Damn the consequences.

The last room was bigger than the others. I hadn't noticed the difference before. It wasn't a full suite like the one in which Saffi was held. There was a huge bed made from dark wood with a tall headboard against the wall. The room had a decidedly masculine feel from the dark woods, bed coverings and leather furniture pieces.

An old-fashioned roll-top desk sat against one wall between two sets of curtains draped to look like they covered windows. *Odd*. This was a basement. Even if there were windows, they'd be higher on the wall. They'd also be much narrower than the curtains implied.

That's it. One of those drapes concealed the entry to Renfroe's hidey hole. I just knew it. Inspecting them closely, I noticed an odd protrusion in the curtains on the left. Advancing closer, I swiped the heavy fabric to the side to discover the square outline of a safe with the door slightly ajar.

Opening it the remainder of the way, I shined my flashlight inside. Two four-inch stacks of cash were at the very back. Reaching inside, I pulled them forward for inspection. They were neatly banded one-hundred-dollar bills. Given the height of each stack, it amounted to thousands of dollars. Sweeping the interior once more, I looked for anything else in the space. There was nothing. Only the stacks of cash.

Partially closing the safe, I examined the desk before moving to the other set of curtains. When I saw the outline of the door, my hand lifted to tap the earpiece, but I stopped midway. I couldn't involve the others. Not yet. Of the group, Ash was the only one I was certain wouldn't slap cuffs on me for what I was thinking of doing to the filth hiding behind the door.

I couldn't risk their interference. I'd deal with the fallout later. There was a door without a door knob. I searched around, pressing different locations on the barrier. Nothing worked. Seeing as it was obscured from the drone scans, it was definitely heavily reinforced, so kicking it in wasn't an option.

Stepping from behind the curtain, I scanned the room. I experienced a brief moment of regret for not spending more time with my mom watching those old murder mysteries she liked. There were always hidden passages and books on shelves which pulled out triggering doors to open or wall panels to slide sideways. That's what made me think there had to be some external trigger to open the damned door.

The thought of it requiring an electronic signal flit across my mind, but I quickly dismissed it. He was using signal dampeners. He'd have to turn those off like we did in order to use such a device. My gaze traveled the room, landing on various items before coming back to the desk.

I had nothing to lose, so I started opening drawers on the desk stopping each time to listen for any sign of the passage opening. I lifted the roll top to find leatherbound books with an ancient quill with an inkwell built into the desk. Next to the inkwell was an antique music box—the kind with a ballerina on top. It was out of place, especially in what was clearly a bedroom intended for a male inhabitant.

Instinct drove me to turn the key protruding from the front. No music issued from the box as the ballerina spun in her little circle, only a light whooshing sound came from behind the curtain. My eyes darted to the coverings as they swayed gently.

I definitely should've contacted the others then, but I didn't. Instead, I went to the door leading to the hallway and closed it. Then I switched off the overhead lights. I put the night vision goggles back over my eyes. Slipping behind the curtain, I started down the spiraling staircase—carefully picking my way with silent steps.

In my ear, I heard the others checking in. I listened to the voices. However, I didn't add my own. Eventually, they'd come looking for me. I only closed the door to the hallway; I left the passage open when I entered. They'd find me soon enough. I hoped for enough of a head start to accomplish my goal before they could.

At the bottom of the stairs, I stopped. *Fuck!* Before me was a tunnel which branched off into three directions. That fucker could be anywhere by now. It had been more than half an hour since we'd begun this second round of searching. I stood at the apex listening to the sound of my own breathing. Closing my eyes, I attempted to focus.

In my mind's eye I thought of the tunnels like veins in the body. Recalling the landscape outside, I designated the road leading away from the property as the Superior Vena Cava. All other veins branched from it in some way, if he made it to the road he could go anywhere. The other tunnels would most likely lead to other properties.

Orienting myself belowground, without a compass took a few minutes, but I finally decided which passageway was the best choice. If he was smart, he'd have some method of transportation stashed, the same way we did. So, he'd head for the road. Taking the safety off my gun, I moved down the darkened center passage.

When I started down the tunnel, the chatter in my ear stopped. I guessed whatever they'd used to obscure the passageway also knocked out my comms. Not for one second did I consider turning back. At first, my stride was tentative. As the idea of Renfroe escaping became more pervasive, I quickened my pace.

I could only hope our sudden arrival kept him from gearing up. If he didn't have night vision eyewear, he wouldn't be able to move as swiftly as I did. I was counting on him not having time to gather everything he needed. The cash left behind gave me confidence in my theory.

Seconds melded into minutes while I moved from a swift walk to a jogging pace, not all out running due to the unevenness of the ground. I no longer tried to move quietly. Speed took precedence over stealth. I'm not sure how long I followed the path. I began to think I'd made the wrong choice.

That was until I heard a male voice cursing loudly in Spanish. Adrenaline pulsed through my system as I slowed to a walk. The abrupt appearance of light almost blinded me until I removed the night vision goggles clamping them to my waistband.

Although I'd never actually heard Vincente Renfroe speak, I knew it was him. As I approached, I listened to him curse the obstruction blocking him from exiting the tunnel. While not completely fluent in the dialect he spoke, I understood enough to know he couldn't get his door to freedom open. *Too bad for him.*

The passage spilled out into an oval-shaped cavern lit with wall sconces semi-coated with dust. It had the look of a storm shelter. Protection from a storm may have very well been the original intent. It would offer its current occupant no protection from the storm raging inside me.

Directly in the center of the space was a wooden ladder. Standing on the ladder, banging on the hatch above his head, was Vincente Renfroe.

"You have to regularly operate those doors to keep them functional. You never know when you might need it."

My voice startled him so badly, he grabbed onto the ladder hugging it tightly to keep from falling off.

"Who the fuck are you?" The accent from his earlier tirade against the door disappeared when he switched from Spanish to English.

"Who I am doesn't matter. Get down. You won't be leaving that way."

Leveling the weapon at him I cocked the hammer to let him know I'd have no problem shooting him to get what I wanted. I wouldn't shoot him though. Not yet. He needed to suffer first. My dark thoughts were contrary to my normal self, but I went with them anyway.

The appearance of the firearm turned him into a different person.

Backing slowly down the steps, he reached the bottom. He almost tripped on the duffle bag he'd left there. Stumbling, then righting himself, he put his hands in the air.

"Señor, please. There's no need for the gun. This is all a misunderstanding." He said smoothly. His accent miraculously reappeared and all signs of aggression were gone—except for the glint of malice in his eyes. In the place of aggression was a confident, conciliatory demeanor.

"What exactly have I misunderstood?" Knowing what came out of his mouth would be a lie, I asked anyway.

"I'm a businessman. I provide services to those who request them."

"Services? What service are you providing with teenage girls?" My eyes narrowed in suspicion.

Leaning his head slightly to one side, he waved one hand negligibly. "Whatever service my clients request. They have varying and exotic tastes."

The tenor of his voice combined with the way he spoke implied he had no shame in the destruction he wrought in the lives of those teens. He exuded a confidence announcing his belief he would escape this situation with no consequences.

"You and your clients are sick freaks."

"You judge me based on some puritanical standard I don't subscribe to. I understand. It's not the first time someone has met me and rushed to judgement. A man of my race experiences it regularly."

"What I think of you has jack shit to do with race. It has everything to do with what you've done."

He gazed at me assessingly. Undoubtedly looking for a way to slither out of this situation. "What do you know of what I've done?"

"Enough." The words pushed between my clenched teeth.

"Listen... I'm sure there's a way we can come to an agreement." Dipping his head toward the duffle, he continued. "The bag right there has at least a million dollars inside. It's yours. All you have to do is turn around and tell the rest of your little cop friends you couldn't find me."

My chuckle at his offer held no mirth. Of course, he'd think he could buy his way out of the situation. Considering the extent of his criminal activities, he probably had dozens of law enforcement personnel on his payroll.

"One. I'm not a cop. Two. I don't need your money. A million is chump change to me. Besides, there's no amount of money you can offer me which will result in you walking away with no consequences."

"Nooo... Señor. Everyone has a price."

"In your world. Not in mine."

Silence reigned while I waited for my words to penetrate. His brow furrowed causing his dark eyes to look almost black in their slightly sunken sockets. Lowering his hands, he squared his shoulders and cleared the negotiator façade from his face.

"If you can't be bought, then we're back to my original question. Who the fuck are you?"

"The father of the teenager you thought you could take and no one would come looking. That's who I am." I ripped the balaclava from my head showing him my face.

Sinister laughter bubbled in his throat. "You're someone's angry daddy? You? You're lying. I don't have any Chinese chicks right now. Not even half-Chinese. Try again."

"You find my anger funny? Go ahead. Chuckle it up. I guess even you deserve a little laughter before you breathe your last breath."

Either my words or my tone triggered something in his memory because recognition sprang into his eyes.

"Wait... I know you, or at least I know your voice. It was you earlier. You stole my new piece of slash."

Hearing him speak of Saffi so vulgarly, I closed the distance between us in a flash. I smacked him across his filthy mouth with the butt of the gun. The blow threw him off balance and he stumbled backwards over the duffle bag landing on his ass.

Holding his jaw with four fingers, he ran his thumb over his now split lip which was rapidly swelling. Ominous laughter rose from his chest when he saw the blood on his digit.

"Don't like that huh? When I call your little princess anything other than 'princess'."

Spitting blood to the floor, he pushed up until he was again standing. He was closer to the wall putting more than an armlength of space between us. I watched him as he shifted sideways, inching toward the tunnel I'd just exited.

"Yeah... I know you now. You're her precious Dr. J. The one she went on about in all her text messages."

I couldn't conceal my look of surprise hearing him speak of Saffi's text messages.

"Didn't know about the texts, huh? I'm not surprised. I had the messages scrubbed from the system. Couldn't leave a trail back to me even if the messages went to Dimwit Dani's phone and not mine."

My finger twitched on the barrel of the gun now dangling at my side. Swiping at his lip he shot me a pitying expression.

"Did you know her dumbass of a mother gave her to me? Huh?" He revealed blood-stained teeth as he gave me a sadistic grin. "That's right, stupid bitch put her daughter right in my hands."

Shaking my head, I refuted his statement. Stephanie, and no one else, was Saffi's mother.

"You can lie to yourself all you want. Don't bother lying to me. First of all, Danielle may have given birth to Chloe, but she's not her mother. Never was. I know for a fact Chloe's **real** mother would **never** give her to you."

"You don't have to believe me. I know the truth. **Danielle** was all too happy to unload the little piece for the right price. Like I said, everyone has a price.

Only, I decided, I didn't wanna pay. I gave the bitch what she deserved. A slow, painful death. What kind of mother brings a man around her young daughter without knowing him?"

I had no intention of answering his question. He didn't need my input since he answered himself. "The kind who shouldn't be a mother. Trash."

He spat the last words into the dirt packed floor along with the blood pooling in his mouth. I must have knocked a tooth loose. His potential pain brought me a small measure of enjoyment.

"If Danielle was trash, why did you waste time trying to con her?"

At his look of confusion, I continued. "You said Danielle gave Saffi to you. While I can believe Danielle knew you were a pervert, she also fell into the fantasy you painted for her. Your little fairy tale is how we found you, you know."

A frown marred his expression. "I'm sure you wondered who sold you out. You've operated a long time without so much as a speeding ticket on your record, yet your little hideaway gets raided. You're forced to use your escape tunnel to try to get away."

"There's no way that bitch sold me out. I put enough holes in her to make sure she bled out before anyone found her."

Tsking, I shook my head. "Well, you didn't do a good job. You should have gone for an artery instead of the veins. She was found alive. She lived long enough to point the finger at you."

"You're lying! She's dead!" Anger contorted his face.

"Nope. No need to lie. You're right about one thing. She is dead. *Now*. But, she lived long enough to implicate you in her murder. The real damage? You did the real damage to yourself, Mr. Sauvé. You sold yourself out."

"What?"

"It's true. You were so busy conning Danielle you not only claimed you would move her to a big house, you showed her the house. She described it perfectly in the letter she left her family. The one she wrote so they wouldn't come looking for her and Saffi after you whisked them away from the big bad city life. She described the house so well we located it based solely on her description."

"Stupid Puta!" Redness creeped up his neck until it engulfed his face. "I knew I should have just killed her ass and took the girl the first time she brought her to me. If I hadn't had a buyer for both of them, I would have."

Pacing along the wall, he cursed Dani and himself for his predicament. I watched as he tried to surreptitiously move closer to the tunnel with his pacing.

"Dumb bitch. She fucked everything up. First, she tried to grow a conscious at the last minute. She thought she could go back on our deal. Thought I would just take her and not the piece I really wanted. *As if*. She wasn't worth a tenth of what I could get for an untouched piece of ass."

Listening to his tirade, hearing him refer to my little girl as '*a piece*', set flames licking through my veins. He was a monster wearing human skin. He didn't view Saffi, or any of them as people. They were commodities to him. To use as he saw fit.

Unable to control myself, I lifted the gun and pressed the trigger. Shock colored his expression as he grabbed his leg, blood seeping through his fingers.

"Son of a bitch! You shot me!" He yowled. His former bravado was gone. It was replaced by a pained posture. The glare he leveled at me spoke of his desire to end my existence.

"Stop whining. What do they say in the movies? It's just a flesh wound. Trust me. If I'd wanted you to be dead in seconds, I'd have shot you three inches to the left."

Crouched as he was over his injured leg, I didn't detect his movements until it was too late. Yanking a small blade from a hidden sheath, he threw it at me. Quickly shifting to the side, I tried to avoid it. I registered the pain as the knife flew past me, tearing through my shirt slicing the outside of my forearm. My fingers loosened, then the gun fell to the dirt packed ground.

When I stooped to pick it up another blade flew past my face so closely I felt the disturbance of the air. Instead of trying to get to my gun, I kicked it away. I drew my own blade from the sheath strapped to my left leg. I didn't give the shallow cut on my arm another thought.

Keeping my focus on my nemesis, I dodged the projectiles he tossed at me until he was left with two longer blades. He held one in each hand. Instead of throwing them at me, he took up a defensive stance with the blades held out in front of him. He favored his uninjured leg as he shifted, once again trying to skirt the wall to get to the tunnel.

"Not so cocky now, are you? You've felt the sting of my blade. I won't be dying here tonight. You will." He taunted.

I didn't reply. The time for talking was over. With laser focus, I watched him and waited. I had a few inches on him in height. Plus, my reach was longer. Mentally, I choreographed my next moves.

Adjusting to keep myself between him and the exit, I altered my grip on the handle of the hunting knife in anticipation of giving Renfroe a taste of his own medicine. He enjoyed using knives on others. We'd see how he liked being on the receiving end of the tempered steel.

Lunging slightly, I lured him into taking a swipe at me. Spinning, I ducked under his arm stabbing deep enough to reach the radial artery in his left forearm. Grabbing the spot, he jumped away still gripping the knife in his right hand as he tried to stem the flow of blood.

The mistake most people made was going for the veins. Veins collapse. Arteries pump until there's nothing left to give. Through the veil of anger, I zeroed in on my targets and used the hunting knife to mete out punishment.

In overwhelming pain with his mobility limited by his injury, Vincente's defensive swings were wide. Taking advantage of his wild flailing, I delivered another stabbing slice to the inside of his upper arm striking the brachial artery. Ignoring his pain-filled moans, I danced away from his attempts to strike back at me.

Harsh breathing filled the space as he struggled through each inhale and exhale. Watching the blood drip from his wounds, I wished for my scalpel. With it, I could've been much more precise, but the hunting knife did the job well enough. I repeated the process on his other arm, striking at the brachial and radial arteries in that limb as well.

Within a few scant minutes, he was too weak to fight back. He dropped to the floor. I'd purposely stayed away from the subclavian and carotid arteries. Couldn't have him bleeding out too quickly. Gasping for breath on the hard dirt floor, Vincente faced his mortality by lashing out at me one last time.

"You think you ended this by killing me?" A type of coughing laughter passed through his lips. "I'm one of many. Like the Greek monster. Cut off the head, three more take its place. You might think you've saved those bitches. Jokes on you. They'll be back under someone else's thumb in a week's time."

It's possible he was right. It was also possible he'd issued an idle threat. Either way, I was done listening. Dropping to one knee, I grabbed the leg I'd shot earlier. Holding it down, I cut through his pants to expose the wound. Giving zero fucks about his screams of pain and the weak flopping of his arms, I used the hunting knife to dig out the bullet I'd put in his leg.

When I was done, I picked up one of his discarded blades. Rolling it through my fingers, I inspected the quality. The hilt was almost longer than the blade, but it would do the job. It was time to end this. Using his own weapon, I plunged it into his femoral artery, then twisted before pulling it out. As I stood and backed away, the fog of anger lifted enough for me to hear my name being yelled. Looking over my shoulder, I saw Ash flanked by Driscoll and Kenneth.

It was Ash who'd drawn me out of the fugue. I shook my head as if it could knock the remaining rage from my mind. When I was calmer, I began putting myself back together.

Robotically, I slipped my knife back in its sheath, and placed the bullet into my pocket. Locating my gun, I picked it up placing it back into the holster. Standing mutely before my friend, I waited for what would come next.

Chapter Twenty-Eight

STEPHANIE

Joy brought up a breakfast sandwich for Saffi in lieu of the big breakfast they'd cooked. Charmaine and Gene stayed downstairs. According to Joy, Dilsher declined breakfast. He left in the car they'd used to bring Saffi home. His own vehicle was still parked at the edge of my circular drive, so he'd be back at some point.

As Saffi sat with her back resting on pillows propped against her headboard, I continued my inspection of her condition. Dark circles gave her eyes a sunken look. She took big chomping bites out of the sandwich. When Joy saw how she was tearing through it, she went back down to get her another.

"Slow down, Saffi. Chew your food. I don't want you to choke."

Swallowing, she dragged the back of her hand across her lips. I passed her the napkin, Joy brought with the sandwich, to use instead. Gulping down almost half the glass of orange juice, she smiled ruefully.

"Sorry Auntie. I'm just so hungry! I haven't eaten since lunch at school two days ago."

"Two days?"

"Yes ma'am. Vincente—" She halted as if she abhorred even speaking his name. "He had them bring me food, but I wouldn't eat it."

"Why not?"

"I was scared he might try to put drugs in it or something."

That's my girl. At least something I'd said to her sank in. In all the ways I tried to preserve her childhood, I was equally as diligent in talking to her about drugs. Being the child of a drug addict made me hyper-aware to the point I tended to overcompensate.

Hearing her explanation, I didn't say a word when Joy arrived with a second sandwich. Saffi scarfed it down almost as quickly as she did the first. After she finished eating, she slid down in the bed. I climbed in beside her as I had every time she'd had a nightmare as a small child.

Only this time, her nightmare didn't happen while she slept. It was real... Very real. Even without being physically assaulted, she'd experienced something horrific. It was imperative she felt safe to wipe away the anxiety. Joy climbed in on the other side of the Queen-Sized bed and we enclosed her between us.

Slowly, she began to open up about the events leading to the kidnapping. Dipping into my well of self-control, I managed to listen without interrupting. Despite the flashes of hurt and anger I experienced as she spoke, I didn't press her or admonish her in any way. Blaming her wouldn't help anything.

When she told me how she came to be in a car alone with Vincente, she didn't attempt to downplay her fear. Listening to her, I got the feeling she didn't have the words to effectively express herself. Her re-telling of that portion of the story was relegated to repeating the conversation she had with him. Then, she moved on to how she'd spent the previous thirty-six hours.

She described the house and how the basement was set up. From her description, it sounded like every little girl's dream—with the exception of the no-cellphone, no-social media rule. When I thought about it, I amended my previous assessment.

The place was more so what an adult male thought little girls wanted. Cutting a teenager off from social media was a sure-fire way to start a revolt in a household. Especially if the teen was accustomed to the privilege as Saffi was—even though I'd limited her access with parental controls.

"He kept trying to give me gifts too."

Her voice was slightly muffled as she snuggled closer to me. She'd moved on to talking about Vincente's attempts at grooming.

"Gifts? Like what?" I asked.

"First, it was outfits. Then he tried to replace the tablet Miss Alanna gave me with a new iPad. But, I remembered what you told me."

"What did I tell you?"

"Don't take things from men. Especially men who aren't family."

Yet another lesson far too many young black girls were taught early in life. The sexualization of little black girls made it so I started talking to Saffi long before her body began blossoming. It was one part of her childhood I couldn't preserve. Part of her innocence was stripped away far earlier than I wanted.

The way Jian slipped into our lives so seamlessly was a testament to his innate goodness. We both sensed it. He'd never given me reason to think his attention to her was lascivious in any form. Far from it. When I watched the two of them together, I saw how she could bloom as an individual under his guidance.

I couldn't dwell on thoughts of him too long otherwise I'd lose the battle to keep the tension from my body. Worry over him staying behind to search for Vincente still lurked near the surface of my mind.

"When I wouldn't eat and wouldn't take his stuff, he locked me in a room by myself." Saffi dropped into silence for a few moments.

"Saffi baby, were you locked away alone for a long time?"

I felt her shoulders lift under my fingers as she shrugged. "I don't know how long. There wasn't a clock or windows. I didn't have my phone." Springing up, her dark eyes widened with panic. "Auntie! Did you find my phone? I know I had it that day."

"Yes. We found your phone and your tablet at Grandma's house."

"Where is it? Can I have it?"

Unsure if her question was related to normal teenage desire to keep their device attached to their fingers, I asked. "Why do you need it?"

"I have to call Elijah. Let him know I'm at home." Capturing her lower lip with her teeth, she dipped her head and looked up at me.

"Does he know what happened? If he doesn't, he'll worry I'm sick since I didn't come to school yesterday or today."

"I spoke to Elijah's mother. He knows. We can message them in a bit. We'll set up a call or a visit okay? First, you need to get some rest. It looks like you haven't slept at all."

The mere suggestion of being fatigued had her lowering herself back to the bed snuggling close to me again. She and Elijah had been thick as thieves since they were placed in the same class two years ago. Of course, she'd want to talk to her best friend. It would happen, just not right now.

Exhaustion combined with the warmth of her human cocoon pulled her into the sleep she'd denied herself while being held captive. We lay there with her until I was certain I could move without waking her, then we slipped from the bed. Tucking the covers in around her, I backed away and stood at the door of the bedroom watching her.

Joy wrapped an arm around my shoulder. She somehow managed to steer me out of the room. I needed to assure myself Saffi was real. She was home. She was safe. Grateful tears filled my eyes. Now, if I could just get my man home safely...

Reluctantly, I left the hallway outside of Saffi's room and headed downstairs with Joy. Having relocated to the family room, Gene and Charmaine were seated side-by-side on the chaise lounge end of the L-shaped sofa. As soon as I entered the room, he stood.

"How is she? She didn't say much on the ride here."

"Much better than I thought. Sad, tired, emotionally hurt, yet overall ok. As much as one can be under the circumstances."

Placing a hand on my shoulder, he scrutinized my expression. "How about you? How are you?"

"I'm ok."

"Cuz..."

Patting the hand on my shoulder, I assured him. "Really. I'm ok." The twist of his lips told me he wasn't buying it, so I relented. "I'm better. I'm still worried about Jian though. I'm beyond grateful to have Saffi home healthy and safe, but until he's home too, I won't be fully ok. I can't be. I still don't understand why he couldn't come with you and Saffi."

"I do." Gene's quick reply surprised me.

"You do?" Confusion marred my brow.

"Yeah. I do. That man loves the hell out of you and Lady Bug."

"His love for her is even more reason for him to come home—not go chasing after a hardened criminal."

"Nah... It's why he had to stay. Dude has to pay for kidnapping Lady Bug. I hope he gets everything coming to him." Reading the disbelief on my face, he continued.

"Look, Step. A man, especially a man who has the means and the skills, is going to protect his family. Jian isn't coming home until he can look you in the eyes and tell you he personally eliminated the threat. He has to be certain you don't have to worry about ole boy making another play for Lady Bug."

"But he—"

"We know what he is. What you need to understand is *who* he is. If you don't, y'all ain't gone make it."

"And I suppose you know who he is?" Folding my arms across my chest, I watched him.

"Yeah... I do. It's not for me to tell you. This is a discussion you should have with him. Not me." Speaking his piece, he dropped his hand from my shoulder, went back to the couch and sat beside his wife.

Joy wandered off while I went to the plush chair adjacent to the window. Pulling my phone from my pocket, I placed it on the arm of the chair. Once again, I considered calling the Detectives, except I held back. Until Jian was home and I knew the rest of the story, I wouldn't involve the cops. Despite the more competent Detectives being assigned to the case, I still didn't trust them. Besides, how would I explain what happened without implicating the people who put themselves at risk to help us?

The only sound in the room was the low hum of the television. I didn't look to see the show, my eyes alternated between watching the street and looking at the face of my phone.

The sound of a car door closing jerked me from my dozing state. Sleep had grabbed hold of me without my consent. The distinctive noise snapped me awake. Groggily, I peered through the glass to see the black-on-black SUV in my driveway.

When Jian came into my field of view, I scrambled from the chair, flung the door open and raced to his waiting arms. Gathering me close, he said nothing as I vacillated between dispensing grateful kisses to fussing at him for making me worry. He accepted the chastising along with the kisses without complaint.

Once I regained some semblance of composure, he squatted, placed his hands on the backs of my thighs telling me what he wanted with one word.

"Up." Reflexively, I wrapped my legs around his trim waist as he lifted me from the ground. It was his turn to chastise me.

"Why are you outside with no shoes on your feet, Sweets?" His chocolate eyes trapped me under their scrutiny.

Ruefully dipping my head, I responded. "I guess I got a little excited and forgot my shoes."

"A little?" A smile split his face as he started walking, carrying me into the house.

As he stepped over the threshold, Gene, Charmaine and Joy converged on us in the hallway with expectant looks. Placing me on my feet, he tucked me into this right side. There was no resistance from me as I wrapped an arm around his waist in response. I needed to touch him. I required tactile proof he'd returned to me safely.

Ash's deep voice broke the brief silence. "Do I smell bacon?" Rubbing a hand on his belly, he inhaled deeply licking his lips. "Oh yeah... that's bacon, biscuits, and on my granny's soul, I smell home-made gravy."

His thick southern Alabama accent drew out each word. The broad grin gave his otherwise stern looking face a child-like appearance. His declaration was quickly followed by the loud grumbling from his empty stomach. It sounded like a wounded wildebeest.

Who started first? I couldn't say. What began with a tittering laugh soon escalated into guffaws which had us each making shushing noises at each other to try to stem the tide. Stumbling into one another, we eventually made it into the kitchen.

Although Gene had already eaten, he still sat in the seat opposite Ash and accepted the plate Charmaine put in front of him. When I took a step towards the stove, I was quickly turned around by two pairs of hands.

"No ma'am." Joy said.

"Right. You sit right on down. You need to eat too." Charmaine said drawing Jian's piercing gaze to my face. *Shit.* Why did she have to call me out?

"Sweets? You still haven't eaten?" While he spoke softly, his voice was laced with steel. He wasn't happy with what he heard.

"No... But, I'm going to." Trying desperately to ignore the stares from our small audience, I responded to his unspoken request to come to his side.

With our height difference, I wasn't much taller than his seated form. Strong fingers bit into my waist when he pulled me closer, wrapping his other hand around the side of my face.

"Sweets, don't lie to me."

"I'm not lying. I was going to fix your plate, then mine before they turned me around like this isn't *my* kitchen."

Shaking his head, he tsked at me. "Don't try to shift the focus, Sweets. You know you should have eaten something by now."

"I know..." Feeling like a scolded child, I slid into the chair he pulled out next to his at the head of the table. I said not a word when Charmaine placed a plate in front of me. Joy set plates in front of Jian and Ash.

The delicious scents assailed my senses. My long-lost appetite reared its head with a rumble almost as loud as the one from Ash setting off the fit of giggles in the foyer. Picking up my fork, I dug into the sumptuous feast of southern delights.

Jian didn't even reach for his fork until he'd seen me take more than a few bites. Then, and only then, did he touch anything on his own plate. For a while, the clanking of utensils hitting plates accompanied by Ash's low grunts of appreciation were the only noises from the table.

"Where is everyone else?" Joy asked.

Once I saw Jian step out of the vehicle, I was solely focused on him. I hadn't given the others a thought. A pang of regret passed through me when I considered they'd put themselves at great risk to for us and I'd been able to put them from my mind so easily.

"They stayed behind." Ash lifted his eyes from his plate, then quickly went back to inhaling his food. His behavior piqued my interest.

"Why did they stay behind?"

In response to my question, Jian's and Ash's faces contorted into expressions tantamount to having flashing neon guilty signs above their heads. Their gazes locked. A silent conversation between the two ensued. Not even the clinking of utensils on plates broke the quietness. Finally, Jian turned to me.

"Sweets...We went there to find Saffi and bring her home. When we got there, we learned she wasn't the only teenager he held captive there."

Simultaneous gasps combined with shocked exclamations issued from Charmaine and Joy. I'd heard it over the coms when they'd found other girls, but I hadn't mentioned it to them . Their questioning eyes turned to Gene only to be met with a contrite bow of his head. We knew Vincente was into trafficking, but it was still startling to hear that he'd kept more girls at the plantation house. The words in my throat almost choked me.

"How many?"

"Six."

"Were they—"

"Don't, Sweets. We aren't sure about them. I actually never saw them. Audrey was with them once they were found."

I didn't finish my sentence after he cut me off. I stopped talking while my mind continued sifting through what I'd heard. My brain burned to know more about the teens. Even though I was certain very little good could come from me knowing their exact circumstances, part of me still wanted to know.

"So, they're seeing to those girls and it requires all four of them?" I probed.

Ash picked up the conversation before Jian could answer. "The original plan was to find Saffi and bring her home. Afterwards, we were going to call in a tip to have the place raided. Finding the other girls changed the plan.

Driscoll and Kenneth have connections I don't, so they're getting the ball rolling on services to help them. Since the girls didn't need to be with yet another group of strange men, Audrey stayed behind. It just made sense for Ryan to stay as well."

"Ok. That does make sense. So, what do *we* need to do? We have Saffi home safe. I didn't call the Detectives because the rest of you weren't back. Do we need to call them? Since the Commissioner and Mayor got involved, do we need to tell them she's home? I'm grateful to have her back. Now we have to call off the search. How do we cancel it without getting you all in trouble?"

"Don't worry about it." Ash stated calmly.

"Don't worry about it? We have to tell them something. It's wrong to let them keep searching when we know she's safe."

"It's taken care of. You don't have to call them to tell them anything. The search has been called off officially. The next time you hear from them, it will be them apologizing again for the delay in getting started. They'll state their pleasure at hearing Saffi is home safe. They won't ask you how she got here. She won't have to talk to Detectives about what happened."

A frown creased my brow. "What? How are any of those things even possible?"

Dropping his fork, Ash pushed his plate away. "It's possible because I called Cutler and Robbins. I made a deal with them."

"What kind of deal?"

"The kind where they get to take the credit for rescuing those girls and taking down one arm of a human trafficking ring involving under-aged girls. Credit which is contingent on them agreeing to leave Saffi's name out of any of the proceedings and convincing the Commissioner to go along with it."

"How are they going to do that?"

Shrugging, Ash shook his head. "Don't know. Don't care. It's totally on them. If they want the accolades and attention, they have to figure out how to persuade him it's best not to include her."

"How do you know they won't turn on you? What's stopping them from telling your superiors you went off script and gathered a team of vigilantes?"

"One word. Ambition. Once you see the news reports you'll understand. This is a career making bust. They know it. Robbins has his eyes on being Chief. A bust like this pushes him closer to his goal years sooner than he planned."

My palms splayed flat on the table on either side of my plate; I sat all the way back in my seat. Giving each of the three men at the table equal scrutiny, I tried to reconcile what Ash said with the logical next steps I'd thought we'd be required to take. My relief at knowing I didn't have to fabricate a story was dampened by the feeling there was something else they weren't telling me.

When my mind landed on the source of my unease, I settled my gaze once more on Jian.

"What about Vincente? He kidnapped Saffi. How will he be punished without her testifying?"

"We don't have to worry about him or his punishment." Came Jian's stoic response.

"What does that mean?"

"It means, he is no longer a concern." Pushing his plate away, he lifted my hand and laced his fingers with mine. "He'll never hurt Saffi or anyone else again."

Swallowing the words on the tip of my tongue, I stared into his eyes and understood. While my mind burned to know more, I wouldn't press him. Not now. Not in front of the others.

Done with the late breakfast, we all stood from the table clearing our empty dishes. My entire body felt lighter with the weight from the past two days lifted from my shoulders.

A pulsing musical baseline drew my attention to the cellphone I'd left on the chair arm when I saw Jian through the window. The song was Nikki's custom ringtone. Rushing to the device, I scooped it up simultaneously swiping the screen.

I hadn't spoken to her since hearing Jian was staying behind. She checked in on Saffi, asking me about her condition physically and emotionally. After I'd answered to her satisfaction, she ushered me off the phone with a promise to come by later. I made her swear to go home and rest first. She'd been hard at work going on forty hours straight.

Reluctantly agreeing, she hung up the phone. No sooner had I pressed the icon to end the call, than the screen lit up again with an incoming call. It was the Mayor. I turned from the window, searching for Jian. Reading my unspoken request, he cut off his conversation with Ash and Gene.

Holding the phone for him to see, I answered, putting it on speaker. The low murmur of conversation stopped as the others listened in on the call.

"Hello?"

"Hello, Ms Barker, this is Mayor Topp. I just heard from the Commissioner. He said your little girl has been found."

"Yes ma'am. She has. She's here now. Thank you so much for your help getting her home to us."

"You're very welcome. I don't want to take up too much of your time, because I'm sure you want to get back to her. I just wanted to once again apologize for the slow response of our Police Department.

I'm very pleased Chloe was found safe. I assure you I'm going to personally stay on the Commissioner about cases like hers. We have to root out Officers and Detectives who think they get to decide who's important enough for them to exert effort. They're all important."

"I agree. They are. They all deserve to have someone searching for them."

"Rest assured that message has been sent loud and clear." After a brief moment of silence, she continued. "As I stated earlier, I don't want to take too much of your time. Please extend my best to Mr. and Mrs. Anderson as well as Dr. Anderson. And, you take care as well."

"I will. Thank you, ma'am."

Following the exchange of pleasantries, we disconnected the call. My face was a mask of disbelief. The conversation went exactly as Ash predicted. She hadn't asked me one question. Not one.

"Told ya." Ash's bright blue eyes sparkled with mischief.

Apparently, he couldn't resist reminding me of his foresight as he stood in the foyer preparing to go home. No longer being under overwhelming stress, I managed to drum up a smile to his light teasing.

Before leaving, he said the others would come by at some point to pick up their vehicles, but most likely wouldn't come inside. It was fine with me if they didn't come inside. I was beginning to drag. Joy, Gene and Charmaine opted for the guest rooms to crash. I trudged up the stairs with Jian at my back.

Chapter Twenty-Nine

JIAN

As I walked up the stairs watching the sway of my Sweets' hips, I mulled over the events of the past couple of days. Not for the first time, I marveled at how much my life had changed over the past year.

As we drew closer to Saffi's bedroom, we slowed to a stop outside the closed door. Making as little noise as possible, Sweets turned the knob. She pushed the door open wide enough for both of us to see inside. Saffi lay under the covers with only the top of her bonnet covered head visible above the comforter. Instrumental music played at a low volume courtesy of the speaker on her bed-side table.

Knowing she was safely tucked in, allowed me to relax. When I sent her away with Gene earlier, I still worried about her mental state after seeing she was physically okay. With one arm wrapped around Sweets I guided her from the doorway as I pulled the door closed behind us.

Entering our bedroom, I twisted the lock closing us inside securely. At the click of the lock, Sweets looked over her shoulder giving me a questioning look.

"An early warning system." I said softly, advancing on where she stood in the middle of the room.

"Mhmm."

Tracing my fingers along her arm, I stopped at her fingertips. Lacing our fingers together, I tugged, pulling her into the bathroom with me.

"I need a shower." I said by way of explanation.

"And I have to be with you because...?" She quirked one eyebrow and one side of her lush lips tipped upwards.

"Because, I also need you with me."

Dropping a quick kiss to her lips, I tugged at my shirt pulling it over my head. I'd removed all the tactical gear on the drive back, so I only had on the long-sleeved black t-shirt with the coordinating cargo pants. I'd left the heavy boots on the shoe stand beside the front door.

Tossing the shirt aside, I reached for the button on my trousers. Sweets' stopped the motion with a firm grip on my right wrist.

"What's this? Are you hurt?" The line between her eyebrows returned as she glared at the bandage on my forearm.

"It's nothing, Sweets. Just a little scratch."

Hard obsidian eyes met mine. "Scratches don't require bandages like this. Try again."

Inhaling deeply, I released the breath in a huff. I knew I'd have to tell her something. Deciding how much to say was my problem. I didn't regret ending Vincente's life. He'd earned a one-way ticket to hell long before he made the mistake of kidnapping Saffi.

The darkness I'd experienced and the actions I took were so far outside my normal personality, even *I* found them disconcerting. How would she react to knowing the things I'd done in the name of protecting my family? I loved her so much; I was unsure how I'd respond to her pulling way after hearing the details.

Her gaze was unwavering as she waited for me to explain the binding on my forearm. Drawing her over to the tufted bench beside the garden tub, I sat pulling her into my lap facing me with her legs straddling my hips. My mind drifted back to the tunnel. I told her about finding the hidden entrance and tracking Renfroe to the storm shelter-like room at the end.

I didn't tell her the things he said about Danielle verbatim. I didn't feel it was necessary to repeat his crass words. Despite the burning questions I saw behind her eyes, she listened without interrupting. Her hands rested on my shoulders while mine rubbed along her legging covered thighs.

Pulling my injured forearm in front of her, she stroked the bandage. "What happened to you not going off alone?" She asked.

"It couldn't be avoided. We split up to make the search go faster." I wouldn't throw Nikki under the bus by telling Sweets I never said any such thing.

Her assessing gaze telegraphed her disbelief in my stance that it was unavoidable; however, she let it slide.

Easing back into my retelling of events, I finally made it to the point where Renfroe threw the first blade, inflicting my only visible injury from our interaction. Anger flared in her eyes when I spoke of the way he rapid fired the knives he pulled from various pockets and sheaths.

Any thought of her directing her ire at me was squelched when she hissed out curse words calling him every vile term she could come up with. Unburdening myself in a way I hadn't with the guys when they discovered me severing Renfroe's femoral artery, I not only told Sweets what happened, I told her about the all-consuming rage which drove me while I exacted cut after cut to his body.

I finished by telling her how I hadn't heard Ash yelling my name until after I'd dug the bullet from Renfroe's wound with my hunting knife and plunged his blade into his leg. The silence was heavy between us while I waited for her response to my revelation. Not wanting to see the disappointment, I looked over her shoulder avoiding her face.

"Jian, you could have been killed."

"I wasn't."

"No. You weren't. It doesn't change the fact you could have been." Soft hands landed on either side of my face as she tilted my head until we were eye to eye. "Why, Baby? Why would you chase him down alone? I don't understand. What drove you to do such a thing?"

"Do you know what an involuntary response is?" I asked her.

"I think so..." Confusion marred her expression. My question probably seemed completely off topic, but it wasn't.

"An involuntary response is something our body does, something our brain makes us do, without us consciously participating." Rubbing my hands up her back, I slipped my fingers into the curls at the nape of her neck.

"I love you, Sweets. For me, loving you is an involuntary response. I didn't *choose* to love you. I've never forced myself to feel the things I feel when I'm near you. Loving you is as natural to me as breathing.

I couldn't make myself stop any more than I could stop the next beat of my heart. It's because of my love for you that I couldn't let him draw another breath. I *had* to protect my family. I couldn't pass it off to someone else. *I* had to do it."

The seconds ticked by as she stared into my eyes. We didn't speak aloud. Still, so much was said in the silence of the moment. I watched as my words took hold and filled her with emotion.

"I love you." Her voice, thick with feelings, washed over me speaking the words I longed to hear.

"Sweets, you have no idea how much it means to hear those words from you." Capturing her lips, I tried to convey how I felt with my touch. "I love you, Sweets."

Kissing and touching quickly escalated. Transporting us from the bench to the shower was accomplished in a blur of activity. Not denying my Sweets the release she deserved, I quickly relieved her of her clothing before attacking what was left of mine.

Reaching inside the mostly glass enclosure, I turned the knobs releasing the spray. Water poured from multiple showerheads heating quickly. While not as hot as she preferred, it was hot enough to rapidly fill the space with steam.

Making short work of the basic bathing tasks, I speedily washed away any remaining grime from my early morning activities before snagging Sweets around the waist and pulling her naked body to mine. Licking her plush lips, I requested entry to taste the sweetness of her mouth.

Groaning at the sensation elicited by the tangling of our tongues, I glided my hands over her wet skin tracing my way up her torso before engulfing her breast. So abundant, they overflowed my hands. I relished in the throaty moans she uttered when I tweaked the turgid peaks. *That shit turned me on.*

My length hardened. As it hung stiffly between my thighs, precum leaked from the sensitive tip. I needed to be inside her, only not yet. She wasn't quite ready to take me. Guiding her backwards, I pressed her shoulders until she sat on the bench.

Finally releasing her from our heated kiss, I gently pushed her thighs apart making room for me to sink to my knees between them. Kissing down the side of her face, I stopped to worry the spot just beneath her chin. I knew it drove her wild. Familiar with her sounds of arousal, I listened for the hitch in her breathing.

When I slid a finger between her petals and into her sheath, I heard it. The sound combined with the slickness I encountered let me know she was ripe for the taking. Only...since I'd felt the slippery cream with my fingers, I wanted to taste its sweetness on my tongue. Her corresponding moans were all the encouragement I needed.

Unwilling to deny either of us, I slipped my arms under her thighs, grabbed a lush ass cheek in each hand, then tilted her hips to present her honeyed center for my feast. And feast I did.

Enjoying the pureness of her essence was as pleasurable for me as it was for her. The way she rocked her hips and latched onto my hair urged me to bring her to the precipice. It demanded I send her flying over the edge into her release.

"Ahh! Oh Jian! Oh Baby! What are you doing to me? I can't. I can't." Words tumbled from her lips in breathy bursts as she shook from her orgasm while I lapped at her folds relishing in the decadent spoils of my victory. And it was a victory, even if the match was far from finished.

Levering myself from between her thick thighs, I kissed my way back to her upper lips swallowing the last of her incoherent phrases, letting her taste herself on my tongue.

"I need to be inside you, Sweets." I groaned.

"Yes. Please." Her soft hands roamed my back, her nails digging into my skin when she grabbed on, pulling me closer.

I didn't tease her the way I normally would by gliding my shaft between her folds toying with her clit. No time for teasing this round. Notching my throbbing cock at her entrance, I sank into her silken walls.

"Fuuuuck...."

The way her channel gripped my shaft had me on the verge of

spilling after just one stroke. Dropping my head forward, I rained kisses on her breast before latching onto one of the stiffened peaks. The action caused her channel to tighten on my already aching length pulling another tortured moan from my throat.

Jerking, I lost control of my hips. They started a forceful rhythm plunging into her depths, swiveling, retreating and repeating the process until we both crashed into a wall of bliss. Breathing heavily, I nestled my face into the crook of her neck. Lazily, she stroked my back with one hand while the fingers of the other sank into my hair scratching my scalp lightly with her nails.

It felt so good, I was tempted to stay locked inside her. However, once the haze of lust lifted, the tiled floor bit into my knees. Pulling my semi-flaccid cock out of her warm cavern, I stood, tugged her up from the bench, and guided us both back under the spray of water for a quick clean up. Not that it mattered. If I had my way, we'd come together at least twice more before the day was done.

Lack of adequate rest over the past two days combined with our other activities caused the two of us to sleep for hours, only waking in the early evening due to the grumbling of our stomachs. Even then, we stayed in bed a bit longer talking as she lay with one generous thigh draped over mine. When the growling noises overtook the conversation, we finally left our cocoon and ventured out.

Hand-in-hand we walked down the hall stopping at Saffi's now open doorway. A quick look inside showed nothing but rumpled bed coverings on the bed. No Saffi. My fingers tightened on Sweets' when I felt her tension at discovering the empty bed.

"Relax, Sweets. She's probably downstairs." Wrapping her in my embrace, I rubbed her back in comforting circles.

"I know, but..." Her sentence trailed off and she laid her head on my chest.

"I know, Sweets. It'll take time to not feel panic anytime you don't know exactly where she is—even when we're in the same house. Everything's really raw right now. I understand."

While I didn't say it, I felt the same fleeting alarm when I saw the empty bed. It took a second before I reminded myself it was perfectly normal for her to leave her room. It didn't mean she'd left the house. The likelihood of her seeking a meal was far greater than the more sinister alternative.

"Come on. Let's go downstairs."

As we drew closer to the bottom of the stairs, voices filtered up. Saffi's higher pitched voice was among them. Lifting Stephanie's hand, I pressed a reassuring kiss to the back. Her shoulders relaxed and her steps quickened. Rounding the corner of the open doorway, we entered the kitchen to a heart-warming scene.

Saffi, along with our remaining houseguests, sat at the kitchen table. Gene sat on one side of the table while Saffi and the ladies sat on the other. Saffi's face split into a smile at something Gene said just as we crossed the threshold. When she saw us, her smile shone even brighter.

"Hey Auntie! Hey Dr. J!" She chirped before taking a big bite of the overstuffed taco in her hand.

"Tee-Tee ordered tacos!" She said around a mouth full of the crunchy meat-filled shell.

"Don't talk with your mouth full." Sweets admonished.

Greeting everyone, we helped ourselves to the small buffet of Mexican food in foil containers on the stove. I spied the name Taco Locos on the aluminum covering on the containers. Charmaine and Joy had been cooking machines the past couple of days, but it looked like even they took breaks. Either way, I appreciated the already prepared meal.

Sitting around the table, talking and laughing, things almost felt normal. I mostly listened as everyone else talked, only occasionally interjecting or responding to direct questions. Being together this way filled my heart with such warmth.

It made me realize what I'd missed as an only child in a household without much in the way of extended family. I had very few memories of meals around the dinner table. I wanted this. Every day.

Not necessarily with the others, but I wanted to come home each day to my Sweets and Saffi. I wanted to sit around the dinner table discussing our days or whatever was on our minds. I wanted to watch

Sweets' belly grow when we added to our family—maybe give Saffi a younger brother or sister.

Listening to the chatter around the table, I allowed my mind to drift to the future I envisioned. In those brief moments, it was hard to tell just twenty-four hours prior, we'd been in the grips of a horrific ordeal.

After we finished our meal, Gene and the ladies said their goodbyes before leaving us to our own devices. Although they didn't say it aloud, I figured they'd stayed around so Saffi wasn't alone while Sweets and I were sleeping. I'm sure there would be days in the future where she would be left to her own devices while we slept, only not today.

Since the three of us had slept through a large part of the day, we were wide awake—even after our large meal. So, we opted to watch a movie in the family room. All traces of our previous planning sessions had been removed. Sweets and I settled on the L-shaped sofa while Saffi dragged her beanbag chair with a blanket into prime position in front of the large flat-screen television.

Searching for something light-hearted and kid friendly, we settled on a teen movie from the house of mouse. Positive I would have to suffer in silence, I draped an arm around her shoulder snuggling Sweets' blanket covered body into my side. I couldn't have been more wrong.

As I watched the story of the teen girl coming of age, navigating the perilous pubescent social structure, and learning to love herself in spite of what the world told her, I was completely caught up. Although the movie had comedic mishaps sprinkled in, the underlying message was thought provoking. The parallels between the character's life and my own, trying to straddle two worlds, gave me pause.

Is that what our children would go through being bi-racial? Is it what Saffi experienced? While she never knew her birth father, his Latino genes were prominent in her features. Did she feel as lost as the teen in the movie? Did she feel disconnected from her heritage the way I did as a young man? We'd never discussed it. But, the movie elicited the questions rolling around in my head.

Unlike the teen, my identity crisis happened when I was much older. The impact was just as significant. It was compounded by the resurgence of my feelings of abandonment. I'd always known I was adopted. Before I was old enough to understand the difference in our races, I understood I was adopted.

My mother always told me I was the child of her heart—if not of her womb. Despite my parents' unconditional love, I still had to work through the sense of loss at never knowing my birth parents. I didn't even know my birth father's name, but I knew my biological mother died not long after giving birth to me.

She had no choice in leaving me behind. He did. He chose not to acknowledge his child. When I went in search of my heritage in my early twenties, I battled the resentment I held against my bio-dad for not being the one to teach me the cultural things I learned from kind strangers.

As with all entertainment geared toward children, the main character reached a happy, peaceful resolution to her dilemma. The ending credits rolled as a pop star sang about loving all the parts of yourself because they're all beautiful. The room lapsed into silence until it was broken by Saffi's voice.

"Auntie?"

Stephanie stirred against me and sat up straight. "Yes?"

"Why didn't Dani want me? Why didn't she want to be my mommy?"

"Oh... Sweetie... I wish I could tell you what you need to know. Unfortunately, it's a question only Dani could have answered. Come here, sweetheart."

Tossing off the blanket, she held out her arms inviting Saffi to sit in the space she created on the sofa. I moved over to make room for her between us.

"I tell you what I do know. I know whatever Dani thought or felt had nothing to do with you. You're amazing. You've been amazing from the first day I saw you." Cupping Saffi's face, she swiped at the lone tear trickling down her cheek, then gathered Saffi to her bosom.

"If I'm so amazing, why did she leave me? Most of the time, at least until she met... *him*... she acted like she didn't even want to know me."

My eyes clashed with Stephanie's over Saffi's head. We held another wordless conversation. She had to tell her the truth about her mother. She couldn't continue to shield her from the uncomfortable facts.

"Saffi, sweetheart. I'm sure you noticed Dani was selfish. I'm not saying that to make her look bad or make you feel better. I'm saying it so you understand there was nothing you could have done or said to change things between the two of you.

Dani had beliefs which unfortunately led her to do things without thought of how they affected other people."

Pulling back, she captured Saffi's eyes with her own watery gaze. "Sweetheart, what Dani did or didn't do isn't on you. You had no control over her choices. For your sake, I wish things were different. Do you understand?"

"I think so..." The sadness in her eyes tore at my heart. Her face pinched. We watched as she wrestled with her thoughts before gathering her courage to say what else was on her mind.

Observing the two of them in such emotional turmoil wasn't easy. Sweets because she wanted to spare Saffi pain from all things, and Saffi because she was coming to terms with some hard truths.

"Saffi, do you remember the first time we met? You asked me about my last name." I drew her attention to me with the question.

"Yessir."

"So, you know I'm adopted. What you don't know is my birth mother hand-picked my parents to be my parents." At her wide-eyed expression I continued.

"My mom was her college professor. My bio-mom told her she knew my mom would love me and care for me as if I were her own. And, she has. I couldn't ask for a more loving and supportive mother. Even with all the love I received from my adoptive parents, I still felt like something was missing. Do you know what I mean?"

She nodded in understanding. We had that in common. "My bio-mom had no choice in leaving me, but my bio-dad...He did. He decided not to know me, not to give me his name or acknowledge my existence in any way.

Almost like Danielle did. She missed out on being your mother. It's not your fault. Nothing she did is your fault. She made her choice. The same way your aunt chose to step into the role. She chose to be the mother you needed.

Just like me, you were blessed to be the child of your aunt's heart. I'd bet everything I own she wouldn't change her role in your life for the world."

Cloudy eyes turned from my face to look at Sweets' tear-streaked expression. Answering the unspoken question, Sweets cupped Saffi's face and placed a kiss on her forehead.

"He's absolutely right, Sweetie. You are the child of my heart. I wouldn't change not one millisecond I've spent being your mother. You are my greatest joy. Never forget that."

With those words, Saffi fell into Stephanie's arms. With one hand patting Saffi's back, Sweets stretched out an arm to include me in the moment. Pressing a kiss to the top of Saffi's head, I joined in the emotional hug.

Working through her issues would take a while and definitely some time with a therapist, although we'd crossed a significant milestone. Holding my woman and the child of my heart in my arms felt so natural, so right. I hadn't a clue what the future held for us. Whatever it was, I had no doubt we could face it together.

Epilogue

STEPHANIE

Pressing my shoulders into the buttery leather seat, I sat on the passenger side of Jian's SUV. Outside the window, large suburban homes with immaculately manicured lawns zipped by. One of the perks of living in the south was being able to keep a relatively green lawn even in the winter.

Many of the homes were already decorated for Christmas, while others sported fall themes in honor of the season if not the Thanksgiving holiday. In the back seat, Saffi commented about any decorations she found exceptionally interesting. But, mostly she enjoyed the view.

Looking at her and listening to her, you'd never know she'd gone through the things she had in the last few weeks. It could be because once we'd informed family and friends of her safe return, I immediately made contact with her therapist to book twice weekly sessions for her. She'd experienced nightmares the first week, but they'd tapered off.

One of the things her therapist suggested was allowing her an opportunity to speak to Dani to have closure. A feat which wouldn't be possible in the physical sense. Aunt Helen had arranged a graveside service for Dani the week after she died. Saffi didn't want to attend. I didn't force her.

A few days after her therapist's suggestion, she asked to go to the gravesite. Jian and I waited in the car as she stood above the little placard in the mound of fresh dirt marking Dani's grave.

When she climbed into the back seat of the vehicle, evidence of the tears she'd shed was still on her face. However, she seemed more at peace. We don't know what she said at the little pile of dirt. That's okay. It's what she needed.

Neither of us brought up the trip during our family therapy session other than to say it occurred. Despite his busy schedule, Jian was present at every family session. His inclusion was a natural progression. He was such an integral part of our lives. When I couldn't break away from work, he took Saffi to her individual sessions.

In the days following her safe return, he'd essentially moved in with us. My initial reservations to dating were squashed when I reflected on the way he put his whole heart into our relationship. In every way but one, he was the father Saffi had never known. He was the man I hadn't dreamed of asking for. Seeing his protectiveness and the way he encouraged her made it impossible for me to see him as anything other than amazing.

Amazing, sexy, intelligent, loving, and intuitive. He was almost too good to be true. Almost. We had our tiffs which reminded me he was very much a human being and not a perfect male android. We'd had one such disagreement this morning when he brought up the subject of me having my IUD removed.

"Sweets, you know I love you."

Jian scooted in behind where I sat on the edge of the bed. His long legs snaked around mine as he wrapped his arms around my waist. His bare chest warmed my back while his fingers splayed across my abdomen as if there were already life growing beneath his hands.

"And I love you." I said, stroking his forearm absently.

"So, what's the problem?" His breath tickled my ear as he spoke with his chin on my shoulder.

"We haven't even been together a year. What's the rush?"

"I don't see it as rushing. We love each other. We're committed to each

other. Besides, even if you remove the IUD today, it could take months before we're actually able to get pregnant."

Shifting so I could see his face, I gave him side eye. "We? We won't be gaining a possible forty pounds and pushing a watermelon though a cranberry sized hole."

"Come on, Sweets, you know what I mean...No I won't go through the physical changes, although I'll be there with you through all of it. I'll arrange my schedule to cut my time in the OR to make sure I'm there for every appointment. Anything I can do with you, you won't have to do alone."

Punctuating his statement with a kiss, he almost had me. Almost. Just as he went to deepen the kiss, Saffi knocked at the door.

"Auntie, Dr. J! Breakfast is ready. I made pancakes!"

She exclaimed happily. I heard the light thumping of her footsteps as she walked away from the door. Disentangling myself from Jian's arms and legs, I stood from the bed.

Frowning, he growled making a grab to pull me back. Hopping just out of his reach, I held up a hand of warning.

"Ah-ah-aah... **Our** child has cooked breakfast for us this holiday morning. You wouldn't want to disappoint her by letting it get cold would you?"

Standing, he advanced on me, backing me into the bathroom. "Five more minutes, and I know I would have convinced you."

"We'll never know, now will we?" I teased as I carefully backed onto the tiled floor.

"Give me three minutes." The glint in his eyes challenged me to give him a chance to prove himself.

"No, Sir. We don't have time for your antics." I turned away walking into my closet.

Another rumbling growl issued from his throat. Strong hands stopped me in my tracks as he pressed his body to mine allowing me to feel his hardening length. "You know how I get when you call me that."

"Call you what?"

"Don't play with me woman."

"I have no idea what you mean, **Sir**. I was just saying—" The rest of my sentence was swallowed by his kiss.

The sound of my pretty lace-trimmed black negligée being ripped reached my ears just as his lips left mine and latched onto my now exposed breast. The power of his suckling tug on my nipple nearly caused me to orgasm on the spot.

Somehow, I found the strength to pull away. "No...We can't. Saffi's waiting. We need to get dressed and go down for breakfast."

"Grrr...You're interrupting my breakfast."

"Come on, Baby. She worked hard on it. We can't keep her waiting."

"She's blocking."

Side-stepping his attempt to pull me back into his embrace, I removed the tattered remains of the sexy nightgown.

"That's what happens when you have kids. You can't get it in when-ever and wherever you want. Are you sure you want a baby right now? They'd definitely require more attention"

Leaning over, I opened the bottom drawer of the closet butler. Just as my fingertips touched a pair of leggings, I felt Jian's hands on my upturned ass.

"You tell me we don't have time, then tempt me like this? You don't play fair, Sweets."

Looking over my shoulder, I pinned him with a smoldering gaze. "Who's playing?"

"We're here." Jian's voice snapped me out of the memory pulling me back to the present.

Giving myself a mental shake, I focused on my surroundings. We exited the car with Saffi ooo-ing and aah-ing over the house being so close to a lake. I was happy to hear Jian tell her it was too cold to go out on the boat, shutting down any ideas she had about asking his dad to take her out on the water. He didn't lie. Right as he spoke the words, the wind whipped through my hair reminding me of my forgotten skull cap.

Re-wrapping my scarf so it covered my head, I followed Jian to the trunk to retrieve our contribution to the meal. In the week leading up to the holiday, the guest list had grown from just us and his parents to include a few friends who didn't have family gatherings of their own to attend. So, I'd made a few extra sides along with a banana pudding.

According to Saffi, a holiday wasn't a holiday without my banana pudding.

Serving dishes in hand, we were greeted at the door by Jian's father, JT. With a face splitting smile, he ushered us inside pointing Jian and I toward the kitchen with Mrs. Anderson while he snagged Saffi by the elbow. Her eyes lit up when he told her about the interactive gaming system he'd had installed in the den.

Normally, Saffi wasn't a gamer, but she loved the build-your-own-story style of games. The one Mr. Anderson described had an additional virtual reality feature which made the player feel like they were inside the world they were building, as it was being built.

"That sounds awesome, Mr. A!"

"What did I tell you last time? Stop it with the Mr. A stuff. We're practically family. You can call me Grandpa, Papa, Pops... Take your pick. Anything except Pappaw." He grinned broadly.

"Ok..."

Saffi looked to me for guidance. I purposely looked away to allow her to decide for herself.

"Ok, Pappaw." She said, smiling mischievously.

"I set myself up, didn't I?"

Holding her thumb and pointer finger slightly parted in front of her face she teased. "Just a little bit."

Shaking my head, I followed Jian to the kitchen while Saffi and her Pappaw went off to the den to play games. I didn't have to worry about her at their home. The Andersons were good people. This wasn't Saffi's first time meeting them, nor the second. Following the incident, they called so often to check on her I invited them over for dinner. The rest, as they say, was history.

They saw the way Jian was integrated into our lives and happily stepped into the role of grandparents to Saffi. She soaked up the attention. They seemed over the moon about the addition to their family.

I'd bet dollars to donuts they'd converted one of the guest rooms into a room for her should she ever stay the night. It's not like his mom was subtle when she interrogated Saffi about the things she liked and her favorite colors.

We entered the kitchen to find Jian's mother standing next to the stove holding a turkey baster in one hand with a potholder in the other. Standing completely still, she stared at the clock on the stove so intently, she didn't hear us. She wasn't dressed or coiffed to her usual put together standard. Her hair was in a messy bun, she was dressed in leggings and an oversized flannel shirt.

It wasn't until Jian reached around to kiss her on the cheek that she realized she was no longer alone. Startled, she jumped slightly at his greeting, then breathed a sigh of relief.

"Oh! You're early! I'm so happy to see you both though. You're just in time." Passing the baster and oven mitt to Jian, she quickly removed the apron from around her neck.

"The timer is already set. When it goes off, baste the turkey then reset the timer for another thirty minutes. I need to go change and do something with my hair. I'm so behind. The other guests will be here any minute. Thank you so much, Sweetheart."

Patting his shoulder, she kissed his cheek, then did the same to me before rushing from the kitchen muttering about not having enough hours in the day and how she should have started cooking the day before. I'm positive she wished she'd opted to have the meal catered instead of tackling it herself.

Staring after his mother with a stunned expression, Jian turned to me with the items holding them out to me. Putting up my hands, I backed away.

"No, Sir. She gave those to you. It's your assignment."

Dipping his head, he narrowed his eyes. "What did I tell you about that word?"

Wagging my finger, I backed up a few more steps and bumped into the island. His arms immediately caged me in. He captured my lips in a kiss full of promise.

Beep! Beep! Beep!

The timer went off saving me from potentially being ravished in middle of his parent's kitchen. *Did I really want to be saved though?* Yes. Yes, I did. Mostly. Ok... Not really, but we were at his parent's house. We had to control ourselves until we made it home.

Grumbling under his breath, he picked up the tools his mother gave him and completed his assignment. While he worked on the turkey, I located empty chafing dishes, then transferred the hot side items I'd brought into them to keep the food warm.

By the time we were done, the doorbell rang starting an every-fifteen-minute trend of guests showing up. I invited Nikki since she was alone for the holiday. This year, it fell on her parent's anniversary. They always went away to celebrate.

She would've spent the day with us at Aunt Helen's had we gone there, so it seemed logical to invite her to the Anderson's. They'd apparently expanded the guest list to include a couple of JT's single friends and one of Sarah's graduate students.

The grad student, Emily, brought her pre-teen daughter with her. So, Saffi wasn't the only child present. After hearing about the VR game, the little girl immediately hustled off to the den to join in the story-building fun.

I stood next to the fireplace talking to Nikki when the doorbell rang again. Jian left the room to answer it and returned with Ash in tow.

"Good googly moogly!" Nikki said in an awed whisper. "Who the hell is that?"

Nudging me in the side, her eyes never left Ash's large frame as he stood just inside the entry to the room wearing dark slacks with a royal blue sweater which made his eyes seem even bluer.

"What? Oh. You mean Ash. You're acting like you've never seen him before."

"Because, I *haven't* seen him before. I've heard his voice, but I didn't know the voice was attached to all that super-sized fineness. Your ass has been holding out on me."

Stuck between amusement and being offended, I looked up at her as she composed herself enough to quit staring.

"I have *not*. Do you mean to tell me through all those video chats we had when the mess was going on with Saffi, you didn't see him not once?"

"No! You were the main one in front of the computer, remember? Besides, part of the time I had other stuff covering the screen. So, I wasn't even looking at the chat window."

"Ouch!" I squawked when she delivered a pinch to my arm. "Why did you pinch me?"

"Shh! Stop being so loud!" She hissed, looking around the room smiling to cover up her abuse of my bicep.

"That was for hiding the potential good-good from me. You know big and thick is my thing. The only ones I ever meet who fit the bill are athletes. You can't trust their asses as far as you can throw them."

"I thought you weren't looking for a relationship." I smirked at her.

"Who said anything about a relationship just now?" She countered.

"You just said I was holding out on potential good-good. What *are* you doing?" I asked looking at the way she flexed and released her fingers. Her head tipped slightly to the side as she resumed her Ash stare-fest.

"Looking for hand-holds."

"What?" Her response made zero sense.

Rolling her eyes, she turned her gaze toward me. "Do you expect me to climb a mountain without planning out the best places to put my hands? Think, Step." She tapped me on the forehead and grinned cockily.

All of the bravado faded away when she turned to continue her eye-fuck on Ash only to find him staring directly at her. The heat level of his gaze made me feel like I was intruding on a very private moment. He and Jian made their way across the room with Ash mumbling greetings to the others without ever taking his eyes off Nikki.

When they reached us, Jian and I exchanged knowing glances. Pressing a wine glass into my hand, he dropped a kiss on my cheek.

"Is this what it looks like?" He whispered in my ear. My only response was a shrug as I maintained focus on the developing situation.

"Stephanie, aren't you going to introduce me to your friend?" Ash practically purred, his lips curved upward in a smile revealing the dimple in his right cheek.

Complying with his not-so-subtle request, I gestured between the two. "Of course. Asher Peterson, meet Nichelle Reed."

"Hello, Nichelle. Nice to finally meet you."

"Same..." The hand Nikki extended was immediately engulfed in Ash's much larger one. Watching the exchange once again made me feel like an interloper on their private moment. However, since they insisted on eye-fucking right in front of me I watched. Avidly.

"Oh good, Asher's here!" Sarah's voice garnered everyone's attention snapping Ash and Nikki out of their non-verbal conversation.

I could never tell if Sarah was completely oblivious or extremely cunning with the way she interacted with people. She swept into our little group gushing about how good it was to see everyone. She chattered away as if she had no clue she'd interrupted anything. Declaring the end of cocktail hour, she sent JT to get the girls from the den while she ushered the rest of us through the arched doorway on the other side of the sitting room.

When we moved toward the dining room, Ash fell into step beside Nikki and Sarah took the opportunity to tell them what a striking couple they made. I pressed my face into Jian's arm to suppress the giggles bubbling from my throat.

Sarah was completely without shame. From what Jian told me, she treated Ash as if he were her son as well. She said it was the least she could do since he wasn't able to see his own mother often and he was such a good friend to Jian. It's possible that was true. Who really knew what went on in her head?

Sitting around the table, enjoying the traditional Thanksgiving meal, listening to the various conversations seemed so natural. I didn't feel the least bit out of place. Any past relationships or situationships I'd had never made it to meet-the-family stage. So, my only experience with large family gatherings involved blood relatives.

Even Saffi had slid into the setting with ease. She sat on my left chatting with Emily's daughter, Mia. Intermittently, Jian would place a hand on my thigh and squeeze until he had my attention. I'd smile; then he'd go back to eating or talking after I acknowledged the touch.

I may have seemed detached. Nothing was further from the truth. I was actually reveling in the warmth, and togetherness I felt from the people around the table. Combined with the ever-present sensation of love Jian projected, I was practically giddy. The ability to let go and just *be* was foreign to me, but I settled into it, appreciating the gift.

The conversation hit a lull; so, I heard Saffi's voice clearly when she said, "I don't know. I have to ask my mom and dad."

I froze. The food on my fork hovered in mid-air because I'd halted in the act of feeding myself. Tears pricked my eyes. I blinked to hold them back. Gently lowering the fork, I placed the utensil back on the plate and put my hand in my lap.

My fingers were immediately entangled with Jian's as he flipped his hand over on my thigh squeezing my digits reassuringly. The touch was enough to confirm I wasn't dreaming. This was real life. I'd considered myself Saffi's mother from the beginning. However, I'd never pressed her to call me mom. Not once.

I looked up at Jian. He winked at me and tipped his head to the left. Following his gaze, I turned to find Saffi staring at me. Her eyes sought my approval, not just for the request from Mia. Her dark eyes, so similar to my own, were asking if it was okay for her to call me her mom.

"Ask your mom and dad what, Sweetie?" Her shoulders relaxed at my confirmation of our status as her parents.

"Mia asked if I can come to her skate party on Saturday. Can I? I've done all my homework. I promise to finish my chores tomorrow."

Saffi rarely asked to go places. So, of course I was going to say yes. Before I did, I pulled Jian into the discussion. After all, she'd said mom *and* dad. It was only fair to ask him directly.

"What do you think, Dad? If she finishes her chores, can she go to Mia's skate party?"

Kissing the back of my hand, Jian cleared his throat before he answered. "If she finishes her chores and it's ok with Mia's mom to add another person so close to the date, I don't see why not. A skate party sounds like fun."

"It's fine with me." Emily chimed in. "We have space for fifteen and Mia didn't max out her invites."

The girls erupted into excited giggles, immediately returning to their private conversation. It appeared they'd completely tuned the adults out. That is until Jian asked Emily the specifics about the time and location of the party.

Giving him the information, she added. "If you need to drop her off a little early, I'll be there at three p.m. setting up. I'm sure Mia would love the company while we wait for the others."

"Oh, we won't be dropping her off." Jian slipped an arm around my shoulders. "Stephanie and I are due for a date, so we'll probably stick around."

I'm not sure what Saffi expected when she asked. I'm positive it wasn't for us to invite ourselves to the skating rink during her new friend's skate party. The sharp inhale followed by the crestfallen expression said it all. Spying the look on her face, Jian said something about it before I could speak.

"Don't worry, Saffi. We're not crashing the party. We're going to do our own thing while you do yours. It just so happens, we'll be in the same building while we do it."

While she didn't appear completely despondent, her expression didn't brighten with his reassurance. I couldn't say I blamed her. I would've been mortified if Grandma Vi had stayed with me at a party after I reached the age of twelve. Saffi was thirteen.

When the tell-tale line materialized between her eyebrows, I interjected to head off whatever she was thinking. "Those are the terms. If you go, we go. We won't hover or embarrass you, but we aren't just dropping you off."

"But—"

"You heard your mother." Jian cut across Saffi's objection with a stern expression on his face. *It was kind of hot.* Not the look, the way he had my back. I could get used to that.

Clamping her mouth shut, Saffi conceded her small victory of being allowed to attend and turned back to Mia. Not even pretending they weren't listening to the entire exchange, the adult conversations started again once it was clear our family discussion was over.

Reaching for my fork, I tried feeding myself once more. While I savored the succulent bite of roasted turkey, my gaze swept the other occupants of the table before being caught by Sarah's. Her fingers gripped the cloth napkin, pressing it to her chest. Her eyes glistened with unshed tears.

Mouthing the words, "Thank you," she dabbed the corners of her eyes before pasting a smile on her face. Returning the sentiment with a nod, I resumed my meal struggling to swallow past the lump in my throat. I didn't need more words to get her meaning.

One fateful evening, I received the call telling me Saffi was hurt and in the hospital. During what I thought was one of the worst nights of my life, I'd met a wonderful man. A man, who from the start, made taking care of me and Saffi his number one priority.

Our entire world changed that night. Before I really even knew him, in his embrace, he gave me a safe place to just *be*. I couldn't imagine how my life would look if they'd taken Saffi to a different hospital or he'd not been on night shift.

Jian's hand landed on my thigh and squeezed bringing me back into the moment. When I turned his way, he met my gaze with a sexy half smile tipping his lips up on the right side. *Damn I loved this man.* Beneath the tablecloth, his fingertips drew circles on my thigh.

The noise created by the numerous conversations around the table allowed the words he whispered in my ear to go unheard by anyone aside from the two of us. My face heated as he went into detail about his plans for me when we made it home.

Crossing my legs, I attempted to hide my arousal at his lascivious murmurs. Pulling away, his expression telegraphed his promise to back up every single word. I had no doubt he would. My core clenched in anticipation. Hell, if he was half as creative in his deeds as he was in his words, chances were excellent he'd get everything he asked for—including another child.

Who was I kidding? I was definitely giving this man a baby. My annual appointment with the OBGYN was already scheduled. I'd let him work on his *arguments* a bit more before I told him though.

In all seriousness, we loved each other and had plenty of room to expand that love to include another child. Besides, Saffi could use a sibling or two. In the meantime, Jian and I would have copious amounts of fun trying.

The End

Resources

If you suspect someone may be a victim of human trafficking, there are resources available to you.

- Call the toll-free (24/7) National Human Trafficking Resource Center at 1-888-3737-888 (1-888-373-7888).
- Text HELP or INFO to BeFree (233733).
- Submit a tip online at http://www.traffickingresourcecenter.org/

To report sexually exploited or abused minors

- If a child is in urgent need of assistance, contact law enforcement or child protective services to report abuse, neglect, or exploitation of a child. Contact the Child help National Child Abuse Hotline to speak to professional crisis counselors who can connect a caller with a local number to report abuse: 1-800-4-A-CHILD (1-800-422-4453).
- Call the National Center for Missing and Exploited Children's (NCMEC) hotline at 1-800-THE-LOST (1-800-843-5678).

- Report incidents at http://www.cybertipline.org.

To learn about services for victims

- U.S. Department of Health and Human Services, Administration for Children and Families Services: http://www.acf.hhs.gov/programs/orr/resource/services-available-to-victims-of-human-trafficking
- U.S. Department of Homeland Security, Blue Campaign, Victim Assistance Resources: http://www.dhs.gov/blue-campaign/victim-centered-approach
- U.S. Department of Justice, Office for Victims of Crime, Funded Service Providers List: http://www.ojp.usdoj.gov/ovc/grants/traffickingmatrix.html

To learn about state and local resources

- The National Human Trafficking Resource Center provides an interactive map, which includes in-depth local information and resources.

Milton Keynes UK
Ingram Content Group UK Ltd.
UKHW021839240823
427419UK00016B/475